GRAY MATTER

TOP
20

GRAY MATTER

NICK PIROG

DECIQUIN

Published by Deciquin Books

Cover designed by Nick Venables

CHAPTER 1

THE PHONE RANG. It rang again. It rang a third time. The answering machine kicked in halfway into the fourth ring.

Click.

"Hello, caller. I'm going to be gone for the next couple weeks. I've set out to find the guy who coined the phrase 'It is better to have loved and lost than never to have loved at all' and blow his brains all over the sidewalk. You can leave a message if you want, but odds are I'm either in jail or dead. Happy Holidays. Live long and prosper. Jesus loves you. The pen is mightier than the sword. Vote yes on 3B. Always compare to the placebo. Seat belts save lives. Freedom."

Beep.

A voice gave an exasperated sigh, then started. "Nice message, Thomas. Very eloquent. I would tell you that you're an idiot, but you already know that. I know you're home. In fact, I know you're lying on the couch with your blue comforter. There's probably a jar of peanut butter, the jelly, a loaf of two-week-old bread, and about ten juice boxes sitting on the coffee table."

I lolled my head to the left and peeked at the glass coffee table. Skippy Extra Creamy. Welch's raspberry preserves. Sara Lee Golden Honey Wheat. And six boxes of Tree Top apple juice.

I guess Lacy knew me pretty well.

"Do me a favor and get off your pathetic ass and pick up the phone." She was silent for a second then started back in. "Fine. If you want to self-destruct, isolate yourself from the world, then that's your problem. Have fun."

I will. Thank you.

"Just remember there are those of us who still love you. Even when you're acting like a huge baby."

Ouch.

"Well, I just wanted to call and wish you a happy Thanksgiving. Sorry I couldn't be there for you. I hope you find your way to some pumpkin pie."

A Pumpkin Spice latte from Starbucks would suffice. I hoped they delivered.

"I know I've said it a hundred times already, Thomas, but she doesn't deserve you. You're too good for her. It's been almost six weeks. It's time to get on with your life."

Wrong. I didn't deserve *her*. She was too good *for me*. It'd only been *41 days*. And it was time *to wallow*.

"Bye. I love you."

I hit my head backwards on the pillow three times, then threw off the comforter. I snagged the remote from under the couch and blindly turned on the television. The parade filled the screen and I mentally gagged. This had the potential to be the most depressing day in the history of time.

On-screen, a giant Snoopy floated by. Followed by a giant Charlie Brown. I waited for Woodstock, but he never came. An overly joyous woman commented on the procession, each affected syllable steaming the cold New York air as it left her mouth.

I pulled on my bear paw slippers and padded to the window.

If it was cold in New York then it was *freezing* in Maine. The sky was a dark gray and the earth looked frozen, the dew brittle, tundra-like, the land preparing itself for the long onslaught of winter. The first big snowstorm of the year was expected to start in the late afternoon, early evening. Then everything would be white for the next five months. At least until late April. Old Man Winter wasn't very friendly in the Northeast. In fact, he was one mean old sumbitch.

I made my way to the sliding glass door and peered out on the bay. By bay, I refer to the Penobscot. The last body of water before the Pond, silent *e*'s, and bad teeth.

Anyhow, it was early, around 8:00 a.m., but even so there were a couple brave souls in their sailboats getting one last ride in before the snow began to fall. The water was three shades darker than the sky and lapped idly against the rocky shore. Just off-center was the Surry Woods Lighthouse. The old, tattered lighthouse's light was still visible, a reflective coin on the drab horizon.

Sort of made you want to catch the red-eye to the Bahamas.

On that note, I went into the kitchen, cranked the heat to Bahamian, and opened the freezer. There were five boxes of waffles: Regular, Buttermilk, Cinnamon Toast, Blueberry, and Strawberry. I know, I have a problem. *Hi, my name is Thomas and I'm addicted to waffles. Hey, leggo my Eggo.*

As my waffles toasted, I started a cup of water heating in the microwave. I opened the front door and scampered the ten steps to the paper. It was already half drizzling, half snowing, and I had a feeling the storm was six hours ahead of schedule.

I sat down to the waffles and a cup of steaming apple cider and read the paper. You can tell a lot about a person by the way they read the paper. I was a comics, sports, weather, front page, Dow Jones, Jumble kind of guy. Alex had been a front-to-back kind of gal. Maybe that's why it hadn't worked out.

I retired back to the couch and turned on football. Detroit and Minnesota. One of them was winning. I was looking forward to John Madden's Turkey Leg awards, but it turns out he wasn't doing the game this year. Shucks.

I picked up a different remote and hit the stereo. Some stupid

Shania Twain song was playing (you know the one, "The One I Want for Life"), and I couldn't move. I couldn't even think. I almost—I stress *almost*—started crying. And I'm fairly certain if there had been a gun in the house, I would have shot myself through the heart. I turned the stereo off.

So there I was, about an hour into my thirty-third Thanksgiving and it had already proven to be the worst yet. Well, the first one after my parents' death was awful, but this one was giving it a run for its money.

I packed a bag, turned the heat off, hit all the lights, and recorded a new phone message. When I pulled the front door open, I was hit by a wall of cold. It was officially snowing now, and everything that wasn't made of concrete was white. I took two steps, then froze. I pressed my ear to the door. The phone rang three more times before the answering machine picked up.

"If this is Lacy, I'll call you in a couple days. If this isn't Lacy, stick the phone in your mouth and swallow it."

"Hi Thomas. It's me. Listen—"

It was Alex.

I panicked. I couldn't find my keys. Then I couldn't find the *right* key. By the time I got the door open, Alex was long gone.

I made my way to the answering machine and peered down at the blinking red light. Time for a real gut check. I took a deep breath, picked up the machine, and threw it against the wall. I'd clean it up when I got back. If I *ever* got back.

Two hours later, I was at 37,000 feet.

Headed for Seattle.

CHAPTER 2

THE CROSS-COUNTRY JOURNEY from Bangor International to Chicago O'Hare and on to SeaTac took about seven and change. But I gained three hours during the flight, so when I landed the local time was just after 3:00 in the afternoon.

The weather was typical Seattle November: overcast, gloomy, with a light drizzle. No blizzard in these parts. Old Man Winter in the Northwest had Alzheimer's. He got lost a lot. Mostly in Canada.

I hailed a taxi for the eighteen-mile trip north to Magnolia. A bit of Magnolia lore here: in 1856, Captain George Davidson of the US Coast Survey named the southern bluff overlooking Puget Sound for the magnolia trees growing along it. Had he been a better botanist, he would have clearly recognized the red-barked trees as madrones. The madrone is a shiny, dark green-leafed evergreen species that thrives on west-facing bluffs. The trees, which can reach heights of ninety feet, usually have a twisted, windblown shape. Anyhow, the surrounding community preferred the name Magnolia to Madrone and decided to keep Magnolia to identify the affluent, well-ordered, waterfront properties.

My parents' house—I still had a problem calling it "my house"—was built on the westernmost bluff overlooking Puget Sound. It was too steep to build anywhere near the house so there wasn't anything within a quarter mile in either direction. The main concern was landslides, the wet soil building up over time, the vegetation slowly losing its tenacity in the soft earth. It was a miracle the house hadn't slipped into the Sound years ago as many of its brethren had.

The house was built in 1964. It was a monolith then, a work of art. But then, so once was the Coliseum. When my parents bought it, they began a slow overhaul, gutting it from the inside out. There had been plans for a total facelift, a new kitchen, hardwood floors, upgraded plumbing. But my parents never got around to it. Then it was too late.

The cabbie pulled up alongside the expansive wrought iron fence surrounding the large estate. He wished me a happy Thanksgiving, and I tipped him an extra twenty. When I said I'd packed a bag, I failed to mention I'd packed only a small carry-on of the essentials: contact solution, shampoo, conditioner, mouthwash, and a couple other things, all of which had been red-flagged at airport security because some science wizard had decided three ounces was the magic number. Apparently, three ounces of acid, anthrax, or whatever these zealots make in their caves wasn't going to harm anyone. But four ounces...

So basically, I had the clothes on my back—my favorite pair of jeans and a black T-shirt over a long-sleeve thermal—a rarely-used cell phone, and my wallet.

I pushed through the rusted gate and ambled up the long drive. The once neatly-manicured yard was overgrown with weeds and other debris. Dark vegetation sprung from every crack and fissure of the dilapidated drive. As for the house, the wet Pacific climate and harsh ocean air hadn't been kind in my absence. The five thousand-square-foot Victorian was a combination of rust and sodium-lime deposits. Brown meets green. Almost as if some pesky kids had unloaded on the house with a barrage of aged avocados. Thick foliage had attacked the house from every angle, crawling up, around, and through the gray brick.

Vines spider-webbed across the front door like organic crime scene tape. I cut these away with my keys. The door had warped to the frame so I had to literally kick it in. It gave on the second try, and a wave of musty air washed over me.

I took a step inside the foyer and stopped. I hadn't touched anything in the wake of my parents' deaths. I'd just left. Fled. Denial isn't just a river in Egypt where people wash their clothes, get sick from drinking the water, get bitten by snakes, get eaten by hippos, contract malaria, West Nile, or worse.

There was a small table to my immediate left. A pink vase was at its center, the remnants of a paper-thin stem silently listing over the porcelain edge. I ran my finger over the table, the years of dust coloring my finger a thick black.

I left the front door open and entered a small hallway. I took two steps, my shoes sinking into the inch-long shag. Lowering down to my haunches, I dug my fingers into the long green tendrils. The carpet was reminiscent of the second cut at Augusta, and when I was young, my father and I would take turns setting up golf holes throughout the house. We'd grab our nine irons, a putter, and a couple of those white plastic golf balls and proceed to drive my mom about insane. I stood up, the popping of my knees masking my deep exhale.

Walking forward, I traced my fingers against the eggshell brown walls which had been an eggshell white last I remembered. I came to a set of two doors: one leading to the basement, the other to a bathroom. I poked my head into the bathroom and flipped the light. The two seventy-watt bulbs were clouded with dust and barely illuminated the small room. Evidently, someone— or some financial entity—was keeping up on the bills. The floral wallpaper had begun to peel in many places, its glue well into its late thirties. I heard a soft noise and peered down at the small sink. Water slowly beaded around the head of the faucet before giving way to a single tear.

I shook my head. Those tears could have filled a swimming pool over the course of the last eight years.

I turned the faucet on. After five seconds, a loud rattle shook the foundation of the large house. The pipes screamed and the house shuddered. I held on to the door frame.

It would be slightly ironic if I'd left for eight years, come back for less than an hour, and the house slid into Puget Sound. Or would that just be a terrible coincidence? Or just unfortunate?

The rattling slowly began to subside, and after what seemed like a full minute, water spurted from the faucet. It was brown. I turned the water off.

I spent the next half hour reacquainting myself with the old house. Pick your cliché. *I took a ride down memory lane. Home is where you hang your hat. Absence makes the heart grow fonder. You can't put toothpaste back in the tube. Even a blind squirrel finds an acorn every once in a while. Too many chiefs and not enough Indians.*

Okay, so maybe those last few weren't exactly relevant, but you get my drift.

I made my way into the kitchen. There were a couple cardboard boxes strewn about the linoleum. A roll of packaging tape and a black Sharpie rested on the island centering the small kitchen. Just above the stove was a round clock. I'd bought it for my parents for Christmas three years before they'd died. It was from Brookstone. Kinetic. The hour hand was halfway between the four and the five. Let's see here, plane landed at just after three, half hour drive, hour or so poking around. Yep, I'd say that was the best thirty bucks I ever spent.

I pulled open the refrigerator, picked up the milk, and read the expiration date: 13APR02. It was green and it said, "Where ya been, Thomas?"

I'm lying, of course. The fridge was empty.

I rummaged through the cabinets. There was a lot of canned

stuff, lots of nonperishables, and lots of other things you see in those Thanksgiving donation barrels. I picked up a can of beets and pondered the irony of the situation.

Anyhow, I pulled my cell phone from my pocket and turned it on. There were only a handful of people—and by handful, I mean less than five—who had my cell phone number. I believe the last call I'd made was to my dean at the university telling him I wouldn't be returning to work the following semester. That call had been sometime in early June. In the months since, I'd had all of five missed calls and three voice mails. I scrolled through the five calls. They were all from Alex. Two calls were in October, two in early November, and the last just hours earlier. Being that I was once a detective—albeit a second-rate one—I deduced the messages were also from Alex.

Still got it.

As for Alex, I wasn't sure if I wanted to hear what she had to say. As much as I loved her—and I still did—I could never take a girl back who'd dumped me. It's a pride thing. But maybe that isn't why she'd called. Maybe she wanted her *Fried Green Tomatoes* DVD back.

I picked up the black marker off the center island and wrote on my palm, "She dumped you for a fucking stockbroker." Underneath this I scribbled "toothpaste" and "contact solution."

I located one of the old phone books and, after a couple unsuccessful attempts, found a pizza joint still in service. I inquired if I was the only person to order a pizza on Thanksgiving. The guy informed me that there were a couple others.

At five the pizza came. I grabbed a slice and headed out to the narrow balcony off the kitchen. The sky was a deep gray from which a light drizzle steadily dripped. The sun was preparing for its descent in my right viewfinder, undressing layers of pinks and oranges behind the clouds' satin curtain. A distant island was thinly traced into the horizon on the far left, and I remember my father telling me it was Japan. I'm still not sure if it was or wasn't.

Straight down from the balcony was a thicket of tall, windswept madrones, then black rock, then rippling Sound. It was all very melancholy if you ask me.

I rested my elbows on the railing, ate pizza, and watched the sun lower its landing gear. There was a port a half mile south and I watched as a colossal freighter made its lackluster final stretch. It rode high on the black water, inching across the gray horizon. The ship had traveled thousands of miles and here I was witnessing its last steps. Such is life. I spent the next couple minutes thinking deep philosophical thoughts brought on by a stupid boat, the SS *Aristotle*. I thought about where the SS *Prescott* was in its voyage. And what freight it would carry. How it got here and where it was going. I thought about Alex. Was she cargo? Or was she one of these rogue waves I kept hearing about?

A vibration in my pocket startled me out of my rumination. Staring at the screen, I fought the urge to flip the phone open. It pulsed four times then relaxed, then pulsed again two minutes later notifying me I had a new message. Must be some message. But then again, Alex *loved* Kathy Bates.

I stared at the phone for a solid minute, then reared back and hucked it at the setting sun. For a brief moment I thought it would reach the rippling black water. But it lost velocity, splattering against the rocky shore, its ashes quickly swept away by the incoming tide.

Bye, Alex.

I rubbed my right shoulder and peered over the edge of the balcony then I leaned down and squinted hard. Something was floating in the water. It would hit the black rocks then be sucked back into the channel with each ebb and flow. The white water receded into the black rocks, and I was granted a quick glimpse of arms and long black hair.

It was a woman.

CHAPTER 3

I SHOULD MENTION that in another life I'd been a homicide detective. So I'd seen my fair share of dead bodies. In fact, I'd seen most people's fair shares of dead bodies. For the last four years of my career I'd been a Special Contract Agent to the FBI's Violent Crime Unit. In a nutshell, I outsourced my skills, instincts, cleverness, and good looks to the Federal Bureau of Investigation. Half the time I was working hand-in-hand with the FBI—Fruitdicks, Backstabbers, and Impersonators—the other half I was getting yelled at by them.

Then I went and got killed. But, as you can see, I'm not dead, thanks to some stubborn doctors, a couple of electricity-charged paddles, and eight pints of somebody else's blood.

I bought a quiet house in Maine—wheelchair accessible, of course—and opted for early retirement. I kept myself peripherally related to the world of law enforcement by teaching an intro-level criminology class at the local university. But I'd lost my passion for this as well. I'd lived my life by the age-old axiom: "Those who can, do. Those who can't, teach." But all I wanted *to do* was sit on my couch. Without the job, I wasn't really sure who I was. I was defined by *the job*. I think this may have contributed to Alex leaving me for a day trader, but then again, I might just be Monday morning relationshipping.

But now, here I was, and the last thing I wanted to see was exactly what was staring me in the face this very second. A dead woman washed up on a piece of remote coastline that just happened to make up my backyard.

For Pete's sake.

There were two routes to the water. Route A was a straight shot down four hundred vertical feet. If you did it right, you could get to the water in about five minutes, but one missed step and you were shark bait. Route B had you walking a half mile south to a scenic overlook. One of those places where they have binocular posts bolted to the ground. Most afternoons a decent crowd of tourists could be seen patiently awaiting their turn to drop fifty cents into one of the binoculars for their chance to catch a glimpse of a whale tail or a bald eagle through the foggy lenses. Enough people had made the trek from the viewing platform to the rocks below that a trail had formed, which eventually led to the crescent-shaped cove directly beneath my house.

I decided on route A. I braced myself against two trees and started down. If I could go back and do it all over again, I would have done a few things differently. One, I wouldn't have turned off that football game. Two, I'd have thrown a sinker instead of a fastball. And three, I would have taken route B.

As I continued down the treacherous path to the water, I contemplated a couple possible scenarios. People died on the water frequently. In the two years I lived in Maine, there were nine separate occurrences when someone died in the water. Or at the hands of it. Things were a bit different here on the Sound where there weren't quite as many recreational boaters. The main concern here was fishing boats and ferries, with your occasional scuba diver. Now the Sound isn't exactly the Bering Sea, but it is *connected* to the Bering Sea, and the water temperature was still in the mid-forties. This means if you did happen to fall off a boat—or were pushed for that matter—you had about seven minutes to get your ass out of the water. So logic told us the woman died by accident or in some other benign fashion. But, logic is overrated.

Granted, I'd only seen the body for a split second, and I was gazing down from 400 vertical feet above, and the sun was setting in my eyes, and my contact prescription was three years old, and I'd once mistaken a 300-pound elk for a mailbox. But my instincts told me this was no accident.

This conjecture was based solely on the fact that the woman appeared to be naked. In the summer months on the Penobscot, it was swim trunks, a polo, and docksides for the men. Women were a bit more loosely clad: a skirt and a blouse with the optional bikini underneath, maybe even a thin sweater or jacket. But this was Puget Sound in November. If it wasn't raining, then it was cold, the average high for the month around fifty. Typically, the attire for both men and women was a windbreaker, jeans, boots, and gloves, with optional thermal underwear.

But then again, maybe this woman was a light dresser. Maybe she was menopausal and she'd just had a hot flash. Maybe she'd ripped her clothes off as she thrashed about in the cold water. Or maybe she'd been going at it with Él Capîtan and slipped and fell off the edge. Who knows?

Anyhow, the trees gave way to the black rock and I slowly began lowering myself down the steep bluff. It was far from a sheer drop-off, the grade about the same as the steps in a football stadium. Except instead of steps there was jagged quartzite, and instead of falling into the arms of a drunken fan, you fell into the teeth of an angry shark.

As I mentioned before, the area directly behind my house was shaped like a crescent. It was a stretch of rock separated by two bluffs which my mother had referred to as Prescott Cove. I should also point out that whereas along other parts of the shore the water lapped nonchalantly against the banks, the water in Prescott Cove was white and angry. Which, if you'd known my father, might have been another reason it got its name.

I stopped to get my bearings at a relatively flat section of rock twenty vertical feet above the crashing surf. It was high tide and the small, powerful waves came in six-second intervals. The waves would sweep in high on the faces of the opposing bluffs a milky white, two separate forces destined for a head-on collision. And then they would become one, sending a violent surge of white water high into the air. Droplets of spray found me, as well as the stark revelation that my present undertaking was a bad, bad, bad idea.

The sun was sucking in its final breaths before plunging its head beneath the cold water, and I figured I had less than two minutes before I was engulfed in darkness.

After two more explosions of water on rock, I still hadn't seen any sign of the woman. There was a strong possibility her body had been carried by the undertow and sucked from the cove whereby it would become someone else's problem.

And good riddance, as they say.

I decided to give it one more wave before hightailing it up the rock while I could still find my hand in front of me. Then I saw her, her body twisting and rolling in the white water just off the rock bank. I nearly made a dash for it. I caught myself, and seconds later the cove erupted. The blast would have sent me reeling into the icy water.

At this point, it dawned on me it was going to be impossible to extract the woman from the freezing water without getting soaked myself. I removed my wallet and wedged it between two rocks.

Got to keep those Benjamins dry.

The water calmed, but the woman had disappeared. A moment

later, her body popped up, rolling against the rocks. This was my first good look at the body. Or what was left of it.

Her right arm was missing at the shoulder. Both legs had been stripped down to the bone. Huge chunks of flesh had been ripped from her torso. The remaining flesh was a chalky purple, and the exposed bone was stained a deep red. It was evident the body had been attacked by something. Mauled. I'd said sharks earlier, but a more likely scenario was killer whales. They were abundant in these waters and, although it was rare, they did attack humans. But the odds were this woman was dead hours, or even days, before the feast.

I jumped down the last couple feet and huddled behind a large boulder. The blast came, showering me in salt water. I wiped my eyes and waited for the woman to resurface. She popped up and I took the four strides to the edge of the churning Sound. I could hear the next wave making its approach, but I was at the point of no return. I lowered myself onto the rock and wrenched my arm under the woman's remaining arm.

The body rose with the incoming wave, and I pulled the woman up and out of the water. The blast came, spraying the two of us in a couple thousand gallons of sea water. Freezing would be an understatement. It was a biting cold, one that clawed at your very insides.

I coughed a couple dozen times before pushing myself off the rock. I then dragged what was left of the woman to a haven behind a large boulder.

My chest was heaving as I turned and looked out on the dark water. The sun was gone, a faint reddish glow all that remained.

I turned my attention to the body. The woman was even worse off than at first glance. Maybe a third of her body remained, reduced to mere bones and torn flesh. Half her torso was eaten down to the ribs, and her entrails spilled out through her lower abdomen. Her head and neck had, for the most part, been spared. I brushed the woman's dark hair from her face.

If I had my doubts that this woman had been killed by Shamu and friends, now I was positive she hadn't. I'd only heard of a handful of killer whale attacks, and I'd never heard of a killer whale carrying a gun.

There, just above the woman's left eye, was the distinct finger-print of a bullet. A small, black hole.

CHAPTER 4

I CONSIDERED DRAPING the corpse over my shoulder, but the thought was fleeting. The chances of going up the way I'd come down were slim, so I reluctantly started down the path of route B. I found the trail and slowly began picking my way through the rocks.

As if the traverse weren't hard enough in the pitch dark, ten minutes into my hike it started raining. Which quickly turned to hail. Awesome. Twenty minutes and 2,548 little hail daggers later, I pulled myself under the railing to the viewing platform. This particular scenic overlook was fairly popular, and there was a small covered veranda illuminated by a handful of dimly lit bulbs. Informative posters clinging to the walls displayed what exactly people were paying fifty cents to look at. Another wall housed dozens of pamphlets promoting different ferries, tours, whale watching excursions, and various other ways for tourists to waste their money. Attached to the veranda was a public restroom as well as a pay phone.

I picked up the phone and dialed 911.

I was asked if it was an emergency and I decided it wasn't, seeing as how the lady had probably already been digested by whatever had eaten her, and I was put on hold. I perused a pamphlet on the San Juan Islands as I waited. Apparently, it had never been a better time to visit the San Juans. I flipped over the pamphlet and read the copyright: 1992.

The woman came back on the line and after a short conversation told me, and I quote, "Being that it's Thanksgiving and all, it will be about an hour before we can get anybody out there." I told her I didn't think the dead lady with the bullet hole in her forehead cared what day it was and hung up.

I trekked the half mile back to my place.

I pulled off my soaked garments, tossed them on the floor, and made my way upstairs into the bathroom Lacy and I had shared as children. My sister had a thing for flamingos, and they were everywhere. Toothbrush holder, shower curtain, Kleenex box. You name it and it had a flamingo on it. There was a flamingo-pink rug as well as a matching flamingo-pink toilet seat cover. Two towels hung from a towel rod and each was adorned with—you guessed it—a giant fucking flamingo.

I had just wrapped a towel around my waist and was heading for my dad's closet for some duds when I heard a knock at the door. It'd only been twenty minutes since I'd spoken with one of Seattle's finest, but I wasn't expecting anybody else, so I was led to believe someone of the law enforcement variety was standing on my doorstep. I waddled down the stairs.

I'm not sure who I'd been expecting on the other side of the door, but I can assure you it wasn't this. *This* being a woman clad in a red turtleneck sweater—the tight fitting kind, mind you—black pleated pants, and a standard issue .45 holstered on her right hip. From my experience, oil and vinegar mix better than women and guns. Just saying.

I noticed the car on the far side of the street. It was an unmarked car, tan, probably a Chevy. So she either worked for the IRS or she was a homicide detective.

The woman raised a badge to eye level and said, "Detective Erica Frost, Seattle Police Department."

So I wasn't getting audited after all.

I asked, "Did you guys get new uniforms or something?" If they had, bras were apparently optional. I mean, she looked like she was smuggling honeydews. Not that I was complaining.

She glanced down at her sweater. "I was at a Thanksgiving get-together." Raising her eyes to check out my damp, towel-clad form, she added, "You obviously were not."

"I ordered pizza."

She stared at me.

"I went with the Hawaiian."

No response.

"That's pineapple and Canadian bacon to the layman."

Again, just stared.

"Domino's."

A little nod.

"The kid on the phone talked me into getting the cinnamon breadsticks."

"Sorry I missed it."

"Me too."

I should mention that Detective Erica Frost was attractive in that tongue-hit-your-boot sort of way. Of course, if she'd been ugly, I would have been slightly less annoying. *Slightly*. She had wavy brown hair, light brown, almost hazel eyes, and looked like a poster girl for pilates. I should also mention I was mesmerized by her sweater. It was my hero.

She was eyeing my towel again and said, "Nice flamingo."

I looked myself up and down. "Frank."

She looked confused.

"Frank the flamingo."

Eye roll.

"You came alone?"

She nodded.

"Where's your partner?"

"I didn't see any reason to call him."

"What if I was a bad guy?"

Erica Frost probably felt like I was patronizing her, but I wasn't. At least not completely. A few years back, I'd come across a serial killer who would report a crime, then ambush the first officer to arrive. He killed four officers and two detectives before we caught him.

I couldn't help but notice Erica's hand was now resting on the butt of her pistol. I think she was toying with the notion of shooting me. She wouldn't be the first. Or the last. She asked, "Well, are you a bad guy?"

"No. But people say I can be an asshole."

"Imagine that." Apparently, she'd already come to this conclusion on her own, but she stepped into the foyer nonetheless. "Are you going to tell me your name, or am I just supposed to guess?"

Frosty, this one.

Get it.

I answered, "Thomas."

"Thomas what?"

"Just Thomas. They ran out of last names before they got to my family. We're on a waiting list."

She sighed, a heavy one. "Well, *Thomas*, do you want to show me to this body?"

"Sure thing. But we're going to need flashlights."

"I have a couple in my car."

She ran out to get them and I ran upstairs. I grabbed an old pair of my dad's gray sweat pants and a red, hooded sweatshirt.

Erica was standing in the foyer when I made my way downstairs. She didn't comment on the fact that I looked like an ad for Russell Athletic.

She thrust a flashlight in my hand, and we made our way outside. The storm had subsided, but it was still drizzling, which didn't seem to bother Erica in the slightest. Although, to be fair, to your native Seattleite, drizzle was about as mundane as breathing.

I flopped up the hood on my sweatshirt and said, "Nice night."

She didn't comment on this and I took her silence as agreement. As we started around back, I informed Erica of the options for getting to the body. She lobbied for the quickest path and I went on to explain the dangers. I did a bit of exaggerating, a decent amount of embellishing, and even a couple of outright lies. And yes, when I was finished, route A did carry a remarkable likeness to that of the Fire Swamp from *The Princess Bride*. But I'd already risked my life twice in a day I'd been penciled in to do so zero times.

Again, she thought I was mocking her and started picking her way down the bluff.

I yelled that I'd meet her down there in about half an hour.

She scoffed. "C'mon, it's a little hill."

One, this thing ate *hills* for breakfast. Two, it was pitch dark. Three, it had been hailing for the past thirty minutes. And four, there were quicksand pits and R.O.U.S. Hadn't she been listening?

She shrugged and said, "Suit yourself."

She continued down, and I reluctantly started after her. When I caught up with her, I said, "That's a pretty spiffy sweater. I'd take it off if I were you."

"How 'bout not?"

"Worth a try."

"Stop trying."

"Noted."

I thought perhaps Erica would have let me take the lead seeing as how: 1) I'd done this only hours earlier, 2) this was my backyard, 3) I knew the best path to the water, and 4) I had a penis. She veered off to the left and found a trail. I guess not.

I said, "It's better to stay in the trees." It was more difficult and time-consuming, but if you fell in the trees there was something to hang onto.

Erica cut her eyes at me and said, "Thanks, but if I want your help, I'll ask for it."

Yikes.

After two or three minutes, Erica had a substantial lead on me. I could see the beam of her flashlight bobbing and weaving thirty feet below me. I grabbed hold of the trunk of a large madrone and lowered myself down a couple feet. The soil was slippery, and I nearly lost my footing. When I righted myself, I noticed the beam of Erica's flashlight was no longer visible. I called her name but only a dull echo responded. I'm not sure if she was physically unable to answer or if her pride was caught in her throat.

I picked my way down to where I'd last seen her and continued to shout her name. After a couple seconds, I heard a faint, "Over here!"

I headed in that direction. After about thirty seconds of "Marco Polo," I found her. I shined my flashlight in her face. She squinted her eyes against the light. "You okay, sport?" I tried for my most concerned tone.

She'd slid about twenty feet down and was hanging onto an exposed root jutting from the ground. Half her body dangled off a steep drop-off. I watched as she attempted to pull herself up, but the incline was too steep and she couldn't get a footing.

I inched closer and shined the flashlight down on the terrain below. If she lost her grip she was going to go for quite the tumble. It would go something like *crash, bang, slice, snap, splash, gurgle, eulogy.*

She forced a smile. "Never better."

"Really? Because you don't look like you're all right."

She made a noise.

"Did you know you're dangling off a fifty-foot drop-off?"

"I'm aware of that." She had an underlying defiance in her voice that I didn't appreciate.

"Have you ever seen *The English Patient*?"

"The movie?"

"Yeah, the movie *The English Patient*. The one where the guy goes to the desert and gets sick."

"Sure. Yeah. Sounds familiar."

"Man, does it take him a while to die. What, like, almost four hours?"

"Uh. Yeah, long, uh, long movie." She glanced at her fingers. They appeared to be tiring.

"What do you suppose he had?"

"Who?"

"The guy from that movie. What do you suppose he had? You know, to make him *so* sick?"

She opened and closed her eyes a couple times. I could tell she was really racking her brain for this. Or maybe she was getting exhausted from hanging off a cliff. Probably a combination of the two. Finally she said, "Um, he had cancer. Yeah. Some sort of cancer."

"Cancer, huh? You sure? I'm thinking it was some sort of pox. Chicken or small."

"Could have been." Her fingers were going frantic, slipping, readjusting. She looked up. The defiance was gone, swapped for pure and utter panic. She said, "Um, listen, do you suppose you could lend me a hand here?"

I bent down, grabbed her arm, and pulled her up. She was surprisingly light.

Her flashlight had come to rest about six feet from her. I plucked it from the mud and wiped the lens clean with my sleeve. I handed it back to her, gave her a soft pat on the shoulder, and started picking my way down the bluff. Through the trees, of course.

From that point on, Erica followed behind me.

CHAPTER 5

AFTER A COUPLE MINUTES OF SILENCE, I turned and asked the detective, who was nipping at my heels, "Do you mind my asking how old you are?"

"Yes."

I waited for her to elaborate. She did not.

I turned and stared at her.

She said, "I'll be 26 in two weeks."

"You're 25?"

She nodded.

"Isn't that pretty young for a detective?"

She shrugged. "I guess so. The rule of thumb is usually three years working the beat, but when the position opened up, I was the obvious choice."

I knew the rule of thumb. "And when was this?"

"About ten days ago."

I stopped and turned. "Are you shitting me?"

"Nope."

I wanted to tell Detective Erica Frost what I used to tell my students on the first day of class: "Don't do this. Walk out that door right now and find something else. It will ruin you. It will eat you up from the inside. It will rip out your heart and poison your brain. You've all seen *Ghostbusters*? It's like where they put all those ghosts. You store them in this little part of your brain, a part you can't see, a part they don't have a name for, a part that won't show up on a CAT scan. And you lock them away. Now, it might be thirty years from now, but eventually something is going to flip that switch and let all those ghosts loose. And you can't put them back. You can't ever lock them up again. Do yourself a favor, get up, walk out that door, and never look back." In three semesters only one kid left. He became a real estate agent. Then one of his clients killed him. Life's funny sometimes.

Erica snapped me from my reverie. "And what do you do for a living?"

"I'm retired."

"Well, what is it you used to do?"

"I used to be a party planner."

"Really? You don't strike me as the type."

"Yep. I specialized in Retirement and Going Away."

"You're serious?"

"Yeah. Why? You need something planned? I also do Graduation and Coming Out."

"Not right now. But if I do, you're the first person I'll call."

We made it to the small landing where I'd stopped earlier. We both swept our flashlights over the dark water. The tide had gone out and had taken the white water with it. Erica moved her flashlight to the area just to our right and said, "Is that a wallet?"

She knelt down and pulled my wallet from where I'd hid it just an hour earlier.

"It's probably the killer's." Figured I'd throw that out there.

She ignored me.

She flipped the wallet open and shined her flashlight on the license. She looked from the license to me, then back to the license, then back to me. "Six foot. Brown hair. Blue eyes. 180 pounds." She flipped the wallet closed and handed it to me. Then she said with a smirk, "Consider yourself a suspect, Mr. Prescott."

I smiled, took the wallet from her, and put it in my pocket.

The body was where I'd left it. Erica sidled up to what was left of the woman, training her flashlight on the partially devoured flesh. She went down on her haunches, wrinkling her nose in the process. I guess the smell was getting to her. She looked up at me and asked, "What do you suppose happened to her?"

"Probably some killer whales nibbling on her. There's a bunch of other stuff out there. Sharks, sea dogs, giant salmon. All kinds of weird stuff." Just ask Captain Nemo.

Erica pulled a latex glove from her pocket and slipped it onto her right hand. She grabbed the woman's chin and gently lolled it to the side. She looked up at me, then back at the woman. Her mouth was gaping, and I prodded, "I'm guessing you know who she is?"

"You don't?"

"If I knew who she was, I wouldn't have referred to her as 'the dead lady with the bullet hole in her forehead.'"

"This is Ellen Gray."

"No way."

She nodded, and an evil smile lit her face. I knew that smile all too well. Without her saying a word, I knew she'd just caught the case of a lifetime. A career-maker.

I asked, "Are you sure this is Ellen Gray?"

"Positive."

"I can't believe it."

"Yep. It's her."

"Can I ask you one question?"

"Sure."

"Who the fuck is Ellen Gray?"

She gave me an inquisitive glare. "You *really* don't know?"

I *really* didn't and shook my head.

"She's the governor of Washington."

We both looked at the body, and I said, "You mean *was*."

CHAPTER 6

THE WHEELS WERE IN MOTION. Thanksgiving was about to end for a whole lot of people. The plan was for me to hike back up to the house and wait for the cavalry to arrive. Then play Sherpa. Which of course I wouldn't do. I'd done my part. I'd found the body, called the authorities, passed the buck. My hands were clean. I would have to give a short statement to the crime scene recorder and then I could forget all about my thirty-third Thanksgiving, Erica Frost, and Ellen Gray.

Speaking of Ellen, after Erica had made a couple phone calls, she'd spent the next few minutes filling me in on the ex-governor of Washington.

According to Erica, Ellen Gray had been the governor of Washington the past term and had been up for reelection this fall. Which meant she was first elected four years after I'd bid the Evergreen State farewell.

Apparently, on October 15—roughly six weeks before—the governor went for a Sunday afternoon hike in the North Cascades, a weekly routine during which she allowed no one—not her daughters, her husband, any of her closest friends, not even someone from her security detail—to accompany her. She'd been chided for this repeatedly, but she wouldn't budge. It was her single, solitary block of time away from the public, from the demands of family, friends, and the entire state of Washington.

Governor Gray had not been seen again.

Within hours of her disappearance, the largest search and rescue operation in Washington history was under way: thirty helicopters, a thousand uniformed men, one hundred public officials, and an outreach of citizens so overwhelming they had to start turning people away. Twelve hours into the search, the governor's backpack was found, nestled in a bush at the edge of a glacial ravine six miles deep into the mountains. It contained a Ziploc bag of trail mix, a North Cascades map, a disposable camera, some Benadryl, and a bottled water. No other traces of Ellen would be found.

The search went on for days, then weeks.

She'd vanished.

For the first couple weeks, Erica said you couldn't escape the story. It ran on every channel, every minute of every day. The public demanded answers. Was it an accident? People went missing and died in the treacherous North Cascades all the time. Had she slipped and fallen into one of the many raging rivers? Did she fall into one of the many glacial ravines as her backpack would indicate? Had she been attacked by a bear or a mountain lion?

These were the most logical of answers, but the many conspiracy theorists felt Governor Gray had been kidnapped. Or murdered.

As always, the husband had been the primary suspect. But Adam Gray wasn't your ordinary husband; he was a lawyer. A lawyer who, according to Miss Frost, had just this September been named as one of *Forbes* "100 Most Powerful People."

Adam was used to the spotlight and flourished in it. He had a solid alibi, but the overall consensus from folks was that he was still somehow involved in his wife's disappearance. But over time, as no evidence surfaced, people began to accept that their beloved governor had died in a tragic accident.

Finally, on the second Tuesday of November, a funeral for Ellen Ann Gray was held. A small, private ceremony for friends and family was held, as well as a public funeral at Qwest Stadium. Every seat of the 72,000-capacity stadium was occupied, with another 40,000 watching on the telescreen at nearby Safeco Field. A reported three million people tuned in at home. Schools were canceled. Businesses closed for the day. A city mourned.

Forty-three days after she went missing, Ellen Gray's body was found.

———

A Seattle Sheriff's Department patrol car was parked in my drive when I reached the house. Its red and blue lights danced in the moonlight, and its windshield wipers sloshed to and fro in a losing battle with the returning rain.

I rapped on the driver's side window and two cops stepped out. Both wore blue windbreakers and mustaches. Their names were Bill and Ted. Seriously. I was tempted to ask them where their phone booth was but decided against it.

Ted was the crime scene recorder and he made me sign my name, give a saliva swab, recite my ATM code, and do a ten-second headstand. I'm lying about the last few, of course, but I was officially logged in, subject to deposition, and basically at the county's disposal.

At least Cole Trickle was.

They asked what the fastest way down to the crime scene was, and I told them the gondola. Ted laughed. Bill didn't.

I directed them to where the hill began and said, "It's steep. Don't trip. Have an excellent adventure."

They started down, and I headed for the door. In about an hour this place was going to be a three-ring circus. The patrol car blinking in my drive would be joined by about five of his brethren and God knows what else. Not to mention, if the Ellen Gray story leaked—and it would, and quickly—the news vans might get here before the police cruisers.

After drying off, I went to the kitchen, grabbed another slice of pizza, and retired to the living room, flopping into the black recliner. Twenty minutes passed when I heard the first *thwack* of an approaching helicopter. I could see its light move over my house and disappear into Prescott Cove. The bigwigs had arrived.

I went to the front door and peered through the peephole. I counted five police cars, three unmarked Chevys, and a large van with "Seattle County Forensics" inscribed on the side. No sign of any media moguls. Yet.

I made my way out to the balcony and surveyed the scene below. A series of lights had been erected, and I could make out six or seven people milling about on the small landing five hundred feet below. The rain had softened a bit, coming down at a steep angle through the bright light. It looked like they were shooting a scene in a movie. If I squinted, I could just barely make out Ellen Gray playing the role of Half-Eaten Dead Governor. She committed to the scene like few could. I smelled an Oscar nomination.

A man in a suit leaned over the body. It was immediately evident he was the Leading Man, the actor who commanded $15 million a picture. It was obvious he was calling the shots. Crime Scene Photographer squatted and took snapshots. Hot Detective in Red Sweater conversed with Cop 1 (Bill) and Cop 2 (Ted). Then there were a bunch of stagehands in the shadows.

Crime scenes are far less exciting than people think. Within fifteen minutes, the body had been bagged and most of the people had departed. They left the lights on for the science geeks who would comb over the area with tweezers and ultraviolet lights and Bunsen burners. But by 9:00 p.m., all the major players were playing to the cameras in the street.

On this note, I made my way upstairs into Lacy's old bedroom and to her window. It had a good angle to the street, and I counted five news vans. Lots of prime numbers. Plus CNN. I soaked up the scene for a couple minutes, then heard a knock at the door. I descended the stairs and pulled the door open. There were three of them.

My good friend Erica Frost and two gentlemen. The man on Erica's left had unruly black hair plastered to his forehead, which complemented an untidy beard the same color. He had designer glasses pushed down on his nose and wore a white lab coat over a stained white undershirt. His glasses were foggy from the rain and he pulled them off, lifted his undershirt, and began massaging the lenses. In lifting his shirt, he exposed a thick belly of coarse black hair. He was covered in hair. Hands, forearms, tufts peeking from his shirt. It was like the Cro-Magnon man meets Peter Jackson.

The man to Erica's right was the man I'd seen leaning over Ellen Gray's corpse. The Leading Man. He was a good enough looking fellow with receding blond curls and a heavy ten o'clock shadow. He had two inches on me, twenty pounds, and ten years. Tiny crow's-feet had begun to adhere to the edges of his eyes, but overall he'd aged well since I'd last seen him. His nose had been broken once. I'd know—I broke it.

Erica smiled and gestured at Cro-Magnon-Peter-Jackson, "Thomas, I'd like to introduce Dr. Hans Rebstien, Seattle's Chief Medical Examiner, as well as Detective Sergeant Ethan Kates."

Hans put his glasses back on, then broke into a wide smile. He extended his hand and said, "Thomaz. Thomaz. Zo good to zee you again." Hans was from Germany and still carried a thick accent. Apparently they don't make S's in Germany.

Erica looked on, perplexed. Surely, she was wondering why Thomas the Party Planner knew Hans the Medical Examiner. Her confusion would increase.

I acknowledged Leading Man—Ethan—with a nod. If you

looked up "self-righteous prick" on *Wikipedia,* a picture of Ethan Kates would come up.

I said, "So you're a sergeant now."

Ethan was always chewing gum. In the two years I worked with him, I'd never seen him when he wasn't chewing his cud. Tonight was no different. He took three chomps on the right side of his mouth, then switched sides. Three more chomps.

Erica put her hands up and said, "Wait. How do you know these guys?"

"I'll let you in on a secret: I wasn't a party planner. "

She furrowed her brow. "You were a cop?"

"Detective. Homicide. Same as you."

Ethan took another chomp and said, "Let's cut the bullshit, Prescott. What the fuck are you doing here?"

I raised my eyebrows. "Um, I live here. Usually when someone answers the door and stands in the doorway, it's because they live there."

This guy was a detective?

He nodded to himself and started chomping again, then he looked at Erica. "This is the guy who found the body." It was less of a question and more of an accusation.

She nodded.

Ethan's cell phone rang and he flipped it open. He took a couple steps backward and put the phone to his ear.

Erica took a step forward and said, "How long were you with the SPD?"

"I don't know. I did a year on the beat, then I was a detective for a couple years."

"What precinct?"

"South."

"What happened?"

Ethan was back and answered for me, "He was let go."

Erica stared at me. "You were fired?"

I nodded.

"Why?"

"I stole some office supplies." I'd really needed a hole punch. Life or death.

Ethan smiled. "Actually, he beat a suspect to within an inch of his life. The city was sued for millions."

I kept my eyes on Erica. "He raped and beat a thirteen-year-old girl."

Ethan had testified against me in court. The city was sued for $7 million, and the case against the scumbag was dropped. I, of course, was sent packing the next day. I may or may not have smashed Ethan's face against a locker on my departure.

I locked eyes with Ethan and said, "If I could go back and do it all over again, I would have killed him."

This drew silence from everyone.

Ethan and I were left staring at one another. The two alpha males. There were a couple dozen people on this planet who would relish Mr. Thomas Dergen Prescott ceasing to exist. In fact, I had a note in a safety deposit box somewhere with a list of suspects should I take a bullet in the temple, get pushed in front of a Greyhound, or develop a suspicious case of necrotizing fasciitis. Ethan Kates wasn't at the top of the list, but his name was on there.

Ethan chomped on his gum and smirked. I was tempted to rearrange some more of his cartilage.

Erica finally broke the tension. She touched me lightly on the elbow and said, "Why don't you tell these guys how you found the body?"

I took a deep breath and started in.

CHAPTER 7

AFTER I'D FINISHED the narrative, Hans held up a finger and asked, "One quezion." He paused, smiled, and said, "Do you 'ave any pissa left?"

I laughed. So that's where the S's went. He rubbed the dramatic paunch splitting the seams of his medical coat, and said, "I didn't 'ave a chanze to go for zecondz."

One thing about Hans: he liked his food. I'd once walked in on him during an autopsy. He'd been eating a sandwich and setting it on the cadaver's chest between bites. I think it'd been pastrami. I nodded at the portly German and said, "Sure do."

Erica added, "I could go for a slice. I didn't get a chance to eat."

So the four of us retired to the kitchen and ate pizza. I found some Diet Slice in the cupboard, and we each enjoyed a soda purchased during the Clinton administration.

Erica dabbed at her mouth with a paper towel square, a brand I'm quite positive was no longer in existence, and said, "So the governor goes for a hike in the mountains, and six weeks later she ends up in Puget Sound."

All three of us looked at her. A silence ensued. She took a bite of pizza. As did I.

Ethan, who I suspected was trying to out-profound his colleague, offered, "When murder is involved, there is no duration too long nor distance too great."

I choked on my pizza. I think I'm allergic to the word "nor."

Erica gazed at him like a college student who was infatuated with a brilliant professor. I wondered what, if any, was the relationship between the two.

At any rate, Plato, Aristotle, and Hans turned to stare. Plato asked, "You all right?"

I wrestled the bite down, coughed a half dozen times, beat my chest with my fist, then managed, "I'm fine."

Erica remained focused on the case. "So what exactly are we thinking here?"

Good question. I looked around. You had Erica, who was thinking about how to play Team Manager, how to keep everyone in good graces, and how this case could further her career. Then you had Ethan, who was thinking about my testicles smashed in a vice, as well as the occasional thought about how this case could make him famous, land him on the cover of *Time* magazine, and maybe get him in Erica Frost's pants in the process. And then you had Hans, who was thinking about how long that last slice of pizza had to sit there before he could pick it up. And maybe he was also thinking about forensics, and trace evidence, and ballistics, and defensive wounds, and all that jazz. Of course he was thinking this all in German: *Wie lange diese letzte scheibe der pizza dort sitzen musste, bevor er es aufnehmen konnte und vielleicht er an forensics, und spur-beweise, und allistic, und verteidigungswunden und ganzen diesen jazz dachte.* And then there was me. I was thinking about how the kitchen would look with black tile, and how I was going to fix the brown water problem. And I was thinking about how I *shouldn't* be thinking about how Ellen Gray's daughters were eating Thanksgiving dinner without their mom.

Ethan broke my reverie. He took a drink of Slice, washed

down the image of himself on *Larry King*, and said, "Right now I'm not thinking anything. Today we have a body. Yesterday we didn't."

I inquired of Hans—who had taken the liberty of snagging the remaining slice of pizza—as to the shape of the governor's body.

Hans popped the crust in his mouth, wiped his hands on his shirt, took a swig of soda, and said, "Nod goot."

After a quick disclaimer that the ocean usually eliminated all trace evidence—all that forensics mumbo jumbo—and that he wasn't optimistic the autopsy would hold any apocalyptic findings, he went on to say that by his best judgment Ellen Gray had been in the water for a substantial period of time. And at least from his preliminary findings, she'd been dead for the same duration. Cause of death: gun shot which was consistent with a .32 caliber bullet.

Ethan said, "Adam Gray has a registered .32."

This meant little without the actual bullet. The bullet that, according to Dr. Hans' aforementioned tutorial, ripped through the frontal bone of Ellen Gray's skull, passed through her frontal lobe, fractured her parietal bone, leaving a crater in the back of her head the size of a tangelo, and now presumably rested somewhere on the floor of Puget Sound.

I looked at Ethan and said, "Aren't you some big diver? Why don't you go dredge for it?" Let's see, one bullet, roughly 32 millimeters in length, in a pool of water close to a trillion gallons. Not like trying to find Rush Limbaugh in a kiddy pool. "I'll help. I have a snorkel in the basement."

Hans found this amusing and laughed in German. *Ha-entz. Ha-entz. Ha-entz.*

Ethan, on the other hand, did not. He checked his watch and said, "Well, we should really get going."

"Don't want to miss yourself on the eleven o'clock news."

He did a couple chomps, smiled, and said, "We're going to need you to come down to the station and give a statement in the next couple days."

"I don't really think that will be necessary."

"C'mon, you can say 'hi' to some old friends. It'll be fun."

Right. They were probably still sweeping up the confetti from the day I'd been canned. If you could read between the lines, and I could, Ethan was saying that I'd had my day in the sun. But I was a has-been, a footnote. He was the law around here, and if he wanted me dragged down to the station to answer questions, I would comply. Or else.

I painted my best "fuck you" face and said, "Good luck with that." He wouldn't get me down to the station house with two SWAT teams and Kate Beckinsale in a cheerleader uniform.

The four of us started toward the door. Hans and Erica were a couple paces ahead of Ethan and me. Ethan stopped and grabbed my elbow. This is number eleven on my list of Least Favorite Things, and I swiped his hand away.

He leaned into me, glared with those dark eyes, and said, "I don't know why you're back, and to be honest, I don't really give a shit. But if I even smell you within five miles of this case, I will find some reason to lock you up. You're not the most popular guy in this town, Prescott. Watch your ass, or I'll make sure someone at county watches it for you."

Number six on my list is idle threats by egotistical douche bags named Ethan. I smiled and said, "I'm retired."

He patted me on the shoulder. "Keep it that way." He added, "And do us all a favor and leave as quickly as you came." He winked at me, then meandered to the door and past his waiting colleagues.

I shook hands with Hans and promised to grab a pastrami on rye with him in the near future. He departed, leaving the delectable detective behind. She smiled and said, "What was that all about?"

I assumed she was talking about my interlude with Ethan. "Oh, nothing," I said, losing myself for an instant in her eyes. "Ethan wanted me to put him in touch with my interior designer. We have similar appreciation for feng shui."

I don't think she believed me.

Anyhow, an awkward moment followed, where the two of us just stood there in silence. I mentally put my hands in my pockets and started whistling. Erica made a motion to her hip, and I silently hoped she would pull her gun and put me out of my misery. No such luck. She *did* remove a card from her back pocket and handed it to me.

She said, "Give me a call if you think of anything else. Or if you just want to grab a cup of coffee."

This last sentence could carry multiple meanings. And I wasn't sure if I was ready for any of them. I held on to the card and watched as Erica retreated down the steps. A whirlwind of lights cascaded from the street, and I wondered what time the news stations would pile it in.

I closed the door and surveyed the card Erica had given me. It had all the pertinent information on how to track down Erica Frost should one need to track down Erica Frost. It even had a number written in pen, which I guessed was her private home number. I stuck the card in my pocket and walked into the kitchen.

I picked up one of the discarded crusts from the pizza box and heaved myself onto the center island. I played the last twelve hours over in my head, pondering things big and small. Mostly, I thought about the four women who had touched my life in the last twelve hours: Lacy Prescott, Alex Tooms, Erica Frost, and Ellen Gray.

I saw this radar screen with these four blips. One blip was unwavering, right in the center. One was headed outward to the outermost concentric circle, moving slowly but steadily from the heart. Then there were these two blips just on the outskirts, their pulses weak, barely detectable.

My eyes glazed over and when I shook my head. The clock above the stove hit midnight. My thirty-third Thanksgiving was finally over.

What a day.

CHAPTER 8

I PULLED the thick red curtains in the dining room aside. The window was cold and clammy, and my breath fogged against it. I rubbed the moisture clean with my forearm and peeked out at an angle. It was dark for ten in the morning. I'm guessing this was directly related to the thick cloud cover and persistent drizzle. The big tree in my front yard swayed in the morning breeze, its barren branches clawing at the cold air. Wrapped around the tree's thick trunk was yellow crime scene tape. Death ribbon. It ran across the drive, wrapped around the mailbox, then wrapped around the far post of the gated entrance. I watched as a man with a camera was ushered under the billowing ribbon by a man with a clipboard.

I could make out a throng of onlookers at the far edge of the street. Twos and threes huddled under umbrellas watching the fiasco unfold. Didn't these people have shopping to do?

Seriously, go to Target.

I released the curtain and walked into the kitchen. What I really wanted were some waffles. And some apple cider. And a newspaper.

I was curious what the byline on the front page would read. It could read something as simple as *"Governor Murdered."* Or something clichéd like *"Black Friday."* Or something witty like *"A Gray Day for Washington."* Then again, maybe there was an even bigger story, one that trumped Ellen Gray's murder, and the headline read *"Thomas Prescott is Back."*

I rifled through the cupboards. Slim pickings, unless you liked corn. I did not. The untouched box of cinnamon breadsticks lay on the counter and I ate a couple.

I peeked around the curtains again close to noon and the melee had only increased. The story was now national news, and every affiliate west of the Mississippi had a warm body in the street with a microphone.

The hours crept by. I spent a couple in the basement looking through boxes. I spent a couple cleaning. I ate some corn. I flipped through a couple dusty newspapers my dad had kept. Mount St. Helens is going to erupt in 1980, if you're curious. Many will die. I did some stretching. I ate some more corn. I played myself in chess a couple times. One time I lost. Go figure. I found an old Gameboy and played some Tetris. I ate more corn.

Saturday was much the same. The crowds had thinned in the streets by half. The story was quickly losing its momentum. As for me, I was going stir-crazy. And my thumbs were sore from Tetris. And I was out of AA batteries. And my ass was chafed from shitting corn.

By noon on Sunday, I had a serious case of cabin fever. The street action had died down, like last call at a bar, and only the true diehards remained. I wasn't overly concerned with running into a cop, or even a reporter for that matter. But I didn't want to stumble into any of the curious neighbors. Lots of questions I didn't want to deal with. *What are you doing back, Thomas? Why did you leave in such a rush, Thomas? What's that rash from, Thomas? What's the square root of 632, Thomas?*

I'd rather not.

I went out the back deck and wound my way through the

foliage until I came to route B. From there, I found the frontage road and kept on for a good two miles.

Fisherman's Terminal is a five-block stretch dedicated to fishermen and their boats. The large port is home to over seven hundred ships ranging from 40-footers to 130-footers. The boats fish for anything from sardines to Alaskan king crab. Lined up, side by side, are a half dozen fisheries, a couple boat repair shops, bait and tackle, fill-up stations, anything and everything a fisherman might need. Intermixed are a handful of Seattle's best restaurants and pubs. Everything is built on stilts, and everything hangs out over the water.

One pub is The Flounder, which is ironic considering there are over a thousand different species of fish in the nearby waters and flounder isn't one of them. A decent number of boats were tied up to the dock, and about twice as many cars were parked in the dirt drive.

I walked up the long gangplank, the low tide visibly churning through each open gap in the wood. I pushed through the door and the aroma of stale peanuts overwhelmed my senses. At The Flounder it was standard procedure to fill up a bowl of peanuts from the large barrels near the entrance and proceed to discard the shells on the dusty wooden floors.

I crunched my way across the discarded shells underfoot past a beer-stained pool table, past the quintessential Golden Tee and Buck Hunter machines, and sat down at one of two empty tables.

Forty or so people were scattered about, mostly men. I'd say the demographic was 70 percent fisherman and 30 percent guys stealing away from their in-laws to watch the Seattle Seahawks game. I bet half the guys here were out to get more ice.

A young woman approached my table. She was wearing shorts meant for summer and a small red T-shirt meant for a third grader. The T-shirt read, "I Found Her at The Flounder."

Clever.

The waitress's name was Josie. I ordered a fish sandwich and a beer, watched the game, and ate peanuts. Was I a guy's guy or what?

It was the middle of the third quarter and the Seahawks had the ball. I could name a couple of the more popular players, but most of the names the announcer was throwing out were new to me. My dad, who had been one of the more die-hard Seahawks fans on the planet, would be rolling over in his grave.

The Seahawks made a field goal to go up 31-3, and as they were kicking off to San Fran, my food came. I ordered another beer and asked the increasingly friendly Josie, "Do you know why fish are so skinny?"

She shook her head.

"They eat fish."

Josie thought this was incredibly funny and that I was a regular riot.

I had a third beer and my brain started to wander a bit. Here it was the Sunday after Thanksgiving, and for some reason I was back in Seattle. I was surrounded by the crew of *The Deadliest Catch*, I'd eaten half my weight in peanuts, I'd just flirted with a girl ten years my junior, and the Seahawks were kicking the shit out of the 49ers. Hell, I don't think I could have been more confounded if I woke up at fucking Hogwarts.

The Seahawks game ended at a quarter after five (Seahawks won 38-10), and the five o'clock news came on. A quick post-game locker room report led off, followed by the weather. The TV was muted, but according to the closed-captioning, rain was probable for the next five days.

Weathermen in Seattle were about as necessary as a gall-bladder.

After a commercial break, they flashed to the news desk. A nice looking woman in a tan jacket started spouting. I wasn't really paying attention until the words "Governor Ellen Gray" appeared at the bottom of the screen.

They quickly breezed over the governor's disappearance and

how her body was found. I assumed I was the "local man" who
had "stumbled upon" the governor's body.

I thought "local man who risked life and limb to pull the
governor's body from the raging surf" had a better ring to it, but I
wasn't going to split hairs.

Like all closed-captioning, the words on-screen were three
seconds behind the actual words being spoken, and by the time
the words, "Here are just some of News 5's favorite memories of
the governor," popped up, a photo of Ellen Gray was on screen.
She appeared to be in her late forties. She was beautiful. Dark
hair. Dark eyes. Demi Moore could play her flawlessly in the
made-for-TV movie that no doubt was already in the works.

The photo montage continued. There was a picture of the
governor running in The Race for the Cure. Throwing out the
first pitch at a Mariners game. Cutting a ribbon in front of what
looked to be an enormous library. Astride a horse speaking to a
group of protestors. Reading to a group of small children. Getting
blood drawn at the Health Fair. At a food drive.

The next picture was a shot of hundreds of uniformed men
trudging through the thick brush of a mountainside. Then a shot
of a jam-packed Qwest Stadium which I surmised was the public
funeral Erica had spoken of. The last picture was a shot of the
cove where I'd pulled out her body.

They cut to a young woman walking out of a gray brick building. I recognized the building as the Seattle Police Department
Headquarters. The woman had her hair pulled back in a tight
ponytail and was clad in tan slacks and a blue SPD jacket. She was
what we call "dressed to bust balls." More significantly, she was
Erica Frost. I leaned forward.

*Earlier today, a representative from the Seattle Police Department
spoke to reporters.*

Erica had about ten microphones shoved in her face. She had
just finished a statement and now looked to be taking questions.

Reporter: Is Adam Gray your prime suspect?

Erica: At this time we have no suspects. Adam Gray is just one of a couple persons of interest we're looking into. This is an extremely high profile case and we are looking at all possible scenarios. We'll know more in a couple of days.

Another reporter: When will Adam Gray be arrested?

Erica: Don't get ahead of yourself. He might never be arrested. Like I said, we are looking into all possible scenarios.

I highly doubted this. In fact, I had a strong premonition Erica Frost, the Seattle Police Department, and the State of Washington were putting all their bread in one basket: Adam Gray.

Erica: Rest assured the Seattle Police Department is doing everything in its power to bring Ellen Gray's killer to justice. Whoever they are, wherever they are, they will be found. That's a promise.

She had me convinced. If I killed Ellen Gray I'd be on the red-eye to Guam. The Seattle Police Department could do worse than Erica Frost as a spokesperson. I could relate. I'd done my fair share of P.R. in my day. I think it had something to do with my rugged good looks, soft-spoken manner, and the ability to lie on cue. I'd been good. Erica was better.

It had to be burning Ethan up that Erica was in front of the camera and not him. I wonder what higher-up had made this decision.

Regardless, they wrapped up Erica's sound bite and returned to the female anchor.

Adam Gray was questioned and released after the disappearance of his wife on October 15th.

They cut to a picture of Governor Gray arm in arm with a gentleman, at what I guessed was a fund-raiser of sorts. Or a gala. I'd never been to a gala, and I wasn't exactly sure what constituted a gala, but this had gala written all over it. The gentleman, who I speculated was Adam Gray, was a large man of about fifty. He had thinning salt-and-pepper hair—an emphasis on salt—and a well-trimmed white goatee. He had piercing green eyes, like he'd slipped and fallen on two chunks of green amber. He wasn't attractive, but there was something attractive about him.

They cut to Adam Gray standing in front of an immense wrought iron gate. A colossal gray and baby blue estate was just visible, filling the background.

Adam Gray made a statement at his Bainbridge Island estate just minutes ago.

Adam Gray was holding two little girls' hands, both with brown hair like their mother's. They both wore dresses: one red, one purple. I put one at seven, the other five. Both girls looked rather uncomfortable. I wasn't sure if it was the cameras or if this was the first time they held hands with their father.

After smiling at both his daughters, Adam's mouth began moving. I thought about that old joke. How do you know a lawyer is lying? His mouth is moving.

I read his words at the bottom of the screen:

This has been a trying last few days. Over the last six weeks, I have mourned the tragic loss of my beautiful wife, and these two precious girls have mourned the loss of a loving and devoted mother. Learning that Ellen's death was not an accident, but an intentional and malicious act, has left this family at a loss for words. We are overwhelmed by the outpouring of support from the grieving public. We, as you, demand answers. We demand this vile perpetrator be caught and punished.

By the time I finished reading, the Seahawks coach was sitting behind a microphone on screen.

I downed the last of my beer, over-tipped Josie, and left.

CHAPTER 9

I GUESS you could say Harold Humphries dropped into my life rather unexpectedly.

Early Monday morning, the plumber showed up. The plumber was not Harold Humphries. The plumber's name was Theo. After about two hours of hard labor—seventy-five-dollar hours—Theo had fixed the brown water problem.

Minutes after Theo had left, I heard a distinct ringing. It was a phone. I didn't remember seeing a phone, but the ringing seemed to be coming from upstairs. I ran upstairs and into Lacy's room. The ringing was coming from under her bed. I lifted up the bright flamingo-pink bed skirt and extracted a bright flamingo-pink phone.

I picked up the receiver and said rather timidly, "Hello."

There was a slight pause at the other end. Then in a shallow, hoarse whisper, a man said, "Bobby?"

This would be Harold.

I said, "No. There is no Bobby at this number."

"Oh."

"Sorry."

I'm not sure why I didn't hang up. To this day, I wonder what would have happened if I'd hung up that phone. Would he have called back?

The man—Harold, although he'd yet to give me his name—took five deep breaths, then asked, "Who's this?"

I wouldn't normally divulge my name to a complete stranger, but something about the voice drew it out of me.

I told him my name.

"Is that right?" Old people like to say *Is that right*? At least my Grandpa Prescott had, once upon a time. And this was all I had to go by. If I remembered correctly, it was rhetorical.

I asked, "Who's this?" This would prove to be a grave mistake.

And so Harold Humphries told me who he *was*. In real time. Because Harold's life was really, really long and because Harold talked really, really slowly, this took a really, really long time.

I'd more or less stopped listening when he got up to the Battle of Bunker Hill. Then he said, "I need some things."

Um.

He said, "Grab a pen."

Unfortunately for me, there was a bright pink pen adorned with a flamingo resting on Lacy's bright pink nightstand. I grabbed it.

Harold proceeded to rattle off a list of supplies he needed. When he was done, I looked down at the list on my palm: *Maxim*, Sour Patch Kids, Red Bull, Macadamia Nuts, Big League Chew (Grape), Nestle Chocolate Chip Cookie Dough, and three lotto tickets. In a nutshell, a bunch of nursing home contraband. What were they going to do, add a couple more years to his sentence?

I told him to give me an hour.

I made my way to the garage. There were three cars: my mom's BMW coupe, my dad's Lincoln Continental, and a Range Rover. I found a box of old towels and wiped the many layers of dust off each of the cars. My dad had bought the Lincoln just months before the crash and it still looked brand new, but I opted for the Range Rover.

I made a stop by the local grocery store and picked up Harold's items. Then it took me about twenty minutes to find the Willow Springs Retirement Community. The place was all stucco with a bunch of trees that were not indigenous to the Seattle area, making it look like some sort of all-inclusive club. I think they were trying to trick these old folks into thinking they had come to die in Key West.

I found a parking spot and hopped out. I had no idea what the visitor policy was at Willow Springs, so I'd dressed up a bit, tan slacks and a blue polo. A bit baggy seeing as they were my father's. In addition, I was carrying an old briefcase which contained Harold's nefarious items.

I walked through the double doors and was struck by the stench of old. Antiseptic meets dried apricots. Speaking of dried fruit, I told the prune at the front desk I was here to see Harold Humphries. She eyed the briefcase suspiciously. I had a feeling this wasn't the first time old Harold had tried to pull one over on the headmistress.

I signed in, then was directed to the third building on the left after the fountain. If I hit the hanging lanterns, I'd gone too far.

Was it just me or was this place starting to feel a little too much like Vegas?

I made it to Harold's room and knocked. Two and half minutes later the door creaked open, and Harold peeked out. Harold was probably 5'8" in his prime, but his height was now at a right angle. He had these huge ears—the size of tea saucers—and I imagine if he wasn't bone deaf he could hear for miles. Not a single hair adorned his shiny scalp, which with the age spots looked remarkably like a globe. There was a big brown spot near his crown that could have passed for Australia. He had large glasses perched on a bulbous nose, with lenses that gave the Hubble telescope a run for its money in thickness. The skin around his neck was loose and free-flowing, like his Adam's apple was using it as a hammock. An oxygen tank rested in the front basket of his walker. All in all, I'd have to carbon-date Harold right around a thousand years old.

He took two deep inhales of oxygen and said, "Did you get my stuff?"

I held up the briefcase and said, "Right here." I added, "I forgot the condoms."

He smiled and invited me in.

I walked the small room while he inspected the contents of my briefcase. The room was that of a typical college dorm. Small bed, TV, chair, mini fridge, coffee table, small bath, bong in the corner. Just kidding. It was an oxygen tank.

I surveyed Harold. He had a huge chaw of Big League Chew in his mouth and was flipping through *Maxim* with quite possibly the biggest grin in the history of time. The TV was set on horse racing and I watched three races while Harold devoured the candy and the magazine.

Glipperfoot won the sixth race, but I had my money on Saddlebags. Harold turned his attention to the races and correctly guessed the next four. Then he said, "Come on, I'll give you the grand tour."

The grand tour consisted of the library, a small room with about thirty novels, twenty of which were either W.E.B. Griffin or Nora Roberts. The theater, a 32-inch TV with four rows of chairs and a meager VHS library of classics. The deli which was home to fun portions of sandwiches, bananas, pudding, crackers, cookies, and other assorted goodies. (Harold loaded up his little basket with items, even forcing me to fill my pockets.) The billiard room, which, as far as I could tell, had never played home to any sort of billiard activity. And, of course, the highlight of the tour: the common area. Filling the glorified living room were twenty people in all, broken up into three or four small groups, plus a couple stragglers. A group of six men sat on the couch watching television and bickering about this and that. Harold called them, "The CNN-iles."

Witty.

I was introduced to a group of ladies at a table playing bridge. Two Irises, two Blanches, two Merls, and a Naomi. I think back in the day they must have had a name wheel that parents spun right after delivery. *Come on, one dollar. I mean, come on Evelyn.*

We came full circle an hour later. If I thought I was done with Harold, I was wrong. He told me to sit. I sat. He hit mute on the television and plopped down in his chair. This process took all of four minutes, and I even took the liberty of diving into one of the half egg salad sandwiches in my pocket and a banana half.

He stared at me with those big eyes—about the size of a half dollar behind his half-inch-thick lenses—for a long while. Then he said, "What I'm about to tell you I've never told anyone before. Never told any of my kids, neither of my wives, my priest, nobody."

I nodded.

He said, "I might not be around much longer."

I guess Harold was coming to terms with his mortality.

"I mean, I probably only have a good ten years left."

Then again, maybe not. For the record, it wouldn't have surprised me if Harold had ten breaths left.

He pulled a handkerchief out, blew his nose, neatly folded the handkerchief back up, packed it away, and said, "It was 1942. I'd just turned eighteen, and against my father's wishes I enlisted in the war."

He took a deep inhale on his oxygen tank.

"It was late March. I got up real early. Had to be at the train station by 8:00. Wrote a letter to my Pa, said good-bye to Jessie, our cow, left all my candy out for my sisters, then took Pa's truck."

"You stole your dad's truck?"

"Sure did. But I didn't exactly steal it. Pa would get a ride into town the next day and pick it up from the train station. There was a train station not fifteen miles from our small farm. See, back then, you leased acreage from the owners. We leased seventy-five acres from the Kings. They were old money, had it coming out the wazoo. They lived about seven miles up the road. Big mansion up on a hill. Passed it every time you went into town. There was a lake on their land. A small lake. You could see it from the road. Sometimes, around Christmas, you would see some of the King kids playing on the lake.

"We didn't have the best road into town. After a good rain it would be almost impassable. But the road got better around the King place. It was gravel. Much smoother."

He went on a small tangent about gravel and road conditions. Then he caught himself. "But that's besides the point. As I was driving past the lake I saw this dog, this big dog running across the lake. I slowed down. A girl at the edge of the lake was yelling at the dog. Slapping her legs and such. I'd seen her before. She was one of the Kings. Didn't know her name at the time. But she was a pretty little thing, she was. Brown pigtails. Couldn't have been more than fifteen at the time."

He had this big smile on his face. He patted my hand lightly and I could feel his smile crawl inside of me.

"I couldn't take my eyes off her. Then I see her start screaming. And I look for the dog. Couldn't see him anywhere. Then I saw the break. He'd fallen through the ice."

He took a deep breath and continued, "I pulled the car to the side of the road. The girl was frantic, screaming. I was two hundred yards away and I could hear her screams. I watched her for thirty seconds, then she did the unthinkable. She started onto the ice. I remember shaking my head and praying for her to go back. We'd had an unseasonably warm March—which is why the harvest would prove to be so good—and the lakes had started to thaw early."

I saw where this was going.

"She slowly made it out onto the lake. She made it to the dog and I saw her reach down. But the dog probably weighed more than her. Then she fell. Just disappeared into the lake. I don't know if the ice caved in around her or if she fell in the same hole as the dog, but she disappeared."

He went quiet. Had his eyes clenched tight. The lids of each eye kissing behind his mammoth lenses, looking like two sleeping millipedes. I knew he was back there. For the next few moments, Harold was eighteen again. Harold didn't open his eyes for a couple minutes. Then it was five. Then it was ten. Then the snoring began.

I rummaged through Harold's basket and ate another half sandwich and another half banana. Then I had a pudding. Tapioca. Then I flipped through *Maxim*. I watched horse racing until I correctly guessed a winner. Hollabackgirl in the 10th.

Then I left.

CHAPTER 10

A MAJOR STORM settled in over Seattle, and it poured for the next seven days. Not that I was complaining. I had plenty to keep me occupied inside the house. My first project was the carpet. I ripped out the green shag and replaced it with a cinnamon spice. Next was the kitchen tile. I went with a slate blue which, I must say, really brought out my eyes. The last project on my list was to paint.

Today was the second Monday of December, the eighth. I wanted to get the painting finished up by the weekend. But then I'd be all out of projects. What would I do then? Maybe I would go visit Lacy for a week. Or maybe I'd sign up for one of those singles cruises. Or maybe I'd jump off the Seattle Bridge.

I made it to the Home Depot in downtown Seattle by noon. There wasn't much of a Monday crowd and I was out of there an hour later toting four gallons of Coffee Brown.

Speaking of which, I was craving a Pumpkin Spice latte. I grabbed an umbrella from the trunk of my dad's Lincoln and started walking. You don't have to go far in Seattle to find a Starbucks, and I found one within two blocks.

They were still making the Pumpkin Spice latte, and I ordered a Pumpkin Cream Cheese muffin to complement the beverage.

Just opposite the Starbucks, there was a bus stop with all sorts of advertisements. One in particular caught my eye. It was on the right wall of the enclosure. In fact, it took up the entire right wall. The top copy read "Adam Gray and Associates." Beneath it was a picture of Adam Gray holding a dictionary. Beneath that was the caption "Guilty Isn't in Our Vocabulary."

Barf.

A number of infractions were listed about which you should contact the firm, up to and including DUI/DWI, Drug Crimes, Juvenile Crimes, Parole and Probation, Traffic Violations, White-Collar Crimes, Real Estate, Criminal Law Basics, and Domestic Violence. Some creative persons had added: Sucking Some Dude Off, Fucking a Dog to Death, Lighting a Bitch on Fire, Shanking a Fool, and Pissing on a Kitten.

There was an address and small map at the bottom of the ad—200 Park Avenue—which put the building twenty-five blocks from my present location.

———

The building at 200 Park Avenue is one of several buildings making up Park Avenue Plaza. Ten stories of teal plate glass no doubt housing orthopedists, plastic surgeons, real estate agents, dentists, and probably even a couple competing law firms.

I pushed through the revolving doors and checked the building directory. Adam Gray and Associates was located on the tenth floor. The penthouse. I rode the elevator and stepped off.

The tenth floor had walls a green color that reminded me of sweet pea risotto and plush carpeting a dark plum. Very soothing. Directly across from the elevator was an impressive marble slab with "AGA" stenciled in silver and black. It might well have read

"Welcome to the Big Leagues" or "Almost Makes You Glad You're in Trouble."

I found Adam Gray's office which took up a third of the entire floor, and I pushed through the glass door.

A large desk guarded double doors. An impressive blonde guarded the large desk. When I say blonde, I mean the platinum type, the kind that burns your retinas if you look directly at it for too long. She was wearing an operator-style headset, but I could make out the white cords of an iPod slithering their way up her neck. She had her head down, and as I approached I noticed she was busying herself with one of those Sudoku things. The marble nameplate on the desk read, "Julia."

She didn't look like a Julia. She looked like a Tiffany. Or a Posh.

Posh tapped her pencil rhythmically on the desk to whatever was on her playlist—I'm guessing The Pussycat Dolls—then scribbled in a number. She then proceeded to flip her pencil over and aggressively erase her entry.

I mentally tabulated her SAT score at 700.

Posh was yet to notice my presence. I took two steps forward, bellying up to the desk, my shadow falling over her. She glanced up, yanked out her earphones, and smiled.

I couldn't help but notice Posh's teeth were three shades too white, and it appeared she'd selected her nose out of a lineup. She said, "Oh dear, you startled me. I didn't notice you come in. Welcome to Adam Gray and Associates. How can I assist you?" No, she didn't actually say this.

She did say, "Where'd you come from? You need a lawyer?" Lawyer came out *lawya*.

Make that SAT score 70.

I said, "Is Adam in?"

"Uh, Mr. Gray is in court today. Third day of the Proctor trial. Should wrap up on Thursday. He won't be back for another hour."

I nodded and said, "I'll just hang out if that's okay."

She shrugged.

I added, "You don't really strike me as a Julia."

She looked at me like I'd just predicted her future. *You will go to the bathroom sometime between noon and six-ish.*

She said, "How did you know?"

"I have a sixth sense for these things."

"My name is Sunny."

"And in Seattle no less."

She didn't get it. But maybe Sunny was her middle name. Maybe her first name was Partly.

She said, "They haven't made me a nameplate yet. This is my second week. Julia was the old receptionist. Her mom got really sick and she went to take care of her. I'm filling in until she gets back."

She shrugged and went back to her Sudoku.

I turned and explored Adam Gray's waiting room. Two couches, charcoal, probably suede, were nestled around a giant flat screen. The TV was set to a slide show, and I watched as a handful of Seattle's more picturesque landscapes flashed across the screen: an overhead shot of Qwest stadium lit up at night; a panoramic shot of downtown, the Space Needle just off-center; one of Elliot Bay, a seaplane just barely skimming the water. I watched the entire reel—probably about twenty pictures—until it started repeating.

I plopped down on the couch and picked up a *Forbes* magazine from the coffee table. It was their "100 Most Powerful People in America" issue. Of course. I flipped it open. Number one was Bill Gates, naturally. Two, Warren Buffet. Three, Oprah Winfrey. Four, Lebron James.

I flipped to the back. Gray was number 97. Under his picture was the caption "The Most Powerful Lawyer in America."

It went on to name some of his biggest cases. He got his name defending a fraternity brother from Seattle Pacific who had gone on to become CFO of Sun Microsystems. The accused was charged with vehicular homicide, and the jury returned a verdict of not guilty, for which Gray was rumored to have made upward of seven million dollars in legal fees. He quickly became the must-have defender of the rich and famous. *Forbes* reported that in the last year alone he collected more than $13 million in legal fees and his firm billed clients for more than $100 million. Gray owned eight properties, a multimillion-dollar Bainbridge Island estate (the one he'd been standing in front of on television), a high-rise condo in the heart of Seattle, a lake house up in Edmonds, a condo in downtown Vancouver, a cozy place in the San Juans, a villa in Tuscany, a place in Kauai, and a farm in Virginia, as well as a 32-foot yacht, the *Habeas Corpus*.

And get this, the guy did all his own research. Didn't trust paralegals or secretaries to do anything.

He was licensed to practice in Washington, California, New York, Massachusetts, and Florida, and it was rumored he was in the process of getting his barrister license in England.

The article also mentioned he was married to Governor Ellen Gray, who also happened to make the *Forbes* list. Only she was ranked a baker's dozen higher than her husband. Or lower, in this case. I flipped to number 84. The caption read "Nothing Gray About Her."

The first thing that jumped out at me was Ellen's salary: just over $160,000. This was probably less than the interest Adam accrued on his fortune each month. I found this ironic. And slightly depressing.

I skimmed the article. It highlighted Ellen's rise to power as well as the many contributions she had made to the community. The article likened Ellen Gray to Princess Di not once, but twice.

Adam Gray might be the most powerful lawyer in America, but when it came to his own household, he was second fiddle. A regular Prince Charles.

After twenty minutes, I made my way back up to the desk and said to Sunny, "I'm just going to wait for Adam in his office." She looked at me suspiciously, and I said, "Adam and I went to college together and I want to surprise him. We were frat brothers at Seattle Pacific. Man, was that guy crazy." I tried to look distant, like I was conjuring up images of Adam drinking tequila from a coed's naval.

Sunny smiled.

I got the impression maybe she'd played coed herself. Anyway, she took the bait and shrugged.

CHAPTER 11

ADAM GRAY'S office was contemporary extravagant. Simply rich. Or richly simple. He had two paintings. Watercolors similar enough that they might have been done by the same guy on the same day. A cherry bookcase stretched the length of the near wall. The far wall was glass, providing a scenic view of a wet downtown Seattle. A long couch was nestled up to the glass. Brown leather. A marble bar stood stoic in a far corner. Next to the bar was a giant aquarium. An elegant ceiling fan slowly oscillated twelve feet above an immense desk. If I ever had an office, this would be it.

I went for the bar first. A crystal decanter filled with brown liquid sat beside a few ornate highball glasses. I wrestled the top off the bottle and took a sniff. Scotch. I whipped my head away.

There was a mini fridge under the bar packed with Perrier, and I snagged one.

I bent down and gazed into the aquarium. Ten or twelve exotic fish swam within the blue haven. I tapped on the glass next to a bright purple fish with black stripes. He darted to the far end of the aquarium. I think he was a rare weenie-fish.

I popped the top of the Perrier and made my way to the bookcase. I'd say two-thirds of the books were on law, the other third consisting of classics, motivational type books, and legal thrillers. Each book had a small tag on the back and a number. Either Adam Gray was fanatical about order or he was trying to bring back the Dewey decimal system.

Two black filing cabinets filled the space between the bookcase and the far wall. I gave a tug on a few drawers but they were locked. Above the filing cabinets were Gray's diplomas. Undergrad was Seattle Pacific University. Law school was Columbia.

I continued on.

The back wall was filled with photographs of Gray standing with some very important people, Seattle's elite. Gray with a man in a green apron, both holding what looked to be ventes in front of a Starbucks. I'd read enough tidbits off the side of my Pumpkin Spice lattes to know the guy's name was Howard Shultz. In another picture, Gray was hand in hand with Paul Allen, the cofounder of Microsoft, whom I only recognized because he also happened to be the owner of the Seattle Seahawks. He was like the sixth or seventh richest guy on the planet. Another pic showed Gray canoodling with *the* richest guy on the planet, Mr. Bill Gates.

I continued down the row.

There were a bunch of pictures of Gray getting chummy with some big name athletes: Shaun Alexander, Ray Allen, Gray on the tee box with Tiger, on the putting green with Lefty, Pete Sampras, Lance Armstrong. And then a couple with political figures: Bill Clinton was there, so were both the Bushes.

I wondered if any of these people had pictures hanging on their walls of them with Adam Gray. Probably not. Maybe Bush Jr.

I continued along the wall until I found myself nestled up near the plate glass window. It was a spectacular view. Straight out was a perfectly framed view of downtown Seattle. The Space Needle was just off-center, and it dawned on me that the photograph flashing across the flat screen had been taken by Gray from this exact spot.

So, Adam was an amateur photographer. Good to know.

The white noise of the rain splattering the window sort of put me in a trance and I went away for a long minute. A rumble of thunder cascaded through the building and I shook myself from the city.

There was a long couch to my right. I ran my hand across the tight cinnamon leather. I plopped down and kicked my feet up on the small coffee table. A cork coaster sat in each corner of the table.

One of my legs began to cramp and I stood and faced the couch. I lifted each of the three cushions. The last time I did this at my place in Maine I'd found three dollars in change, two remotes, a CD, a peanut butter and jelly sandwich, and a hamster. Go figure.

Anyhow, the first cushion was in pristine condition, but the undersides of the second and third cushions were covered with dark smears. I'd seen enough bloodstains to know I was looking at one. But then again, maybe Adam was a messy eater and it was strawberry jelly.

I replaced the cushions.

I made my way to Adam's desk and plopped down in his black leather chair. I can only assume the chair was custom-built for Adam's large frame. Nevertheless, I could have slept upright in it. On the side of the chair were three buttons, one of which activated a massage function.

Ahhhhhh.

I turned the massage off and took in the desk. A telephone in one corner. A couple of those kinetic toys in another. A silver rhino paperweight sat on the front center edge.

I started pulling drawers. Gray was a neat freak. Tabs, colors, files, everything in perfect order. I peered around the office. I noticed everything was oddly perfect. Either Adam Gray's interior decorator had autism or Adam Gray had OCD. I put my money on the latter.

Anyhow, there wasn't much left to do but wait. I leaned back in the chair, hit the massage switch, kicked my feet up onto the desk, and closed my eyes.

CHAPTER 12

"EXCUSE ME."

I opened my eyes.

Adam Gray was standing in his doorway. He was bigger in person. He was wearing a well-cut charcoal suit. With his predominantly white hair and perfectly white goatee, he reminded me of the silver rhino at the edge of his desk.

He said, "Mind telling me what you're doing?"

"Whaaattttsoooevvvvveeeeeerrrrrrrrrr dooooo youuuuuu meannnnnnn?"

He took a couple steps forward. He grew exponentially larger. He reached the front of his desk, all six feet six inches, two hundred and thirty pounds of him. He just stared at me for a while. Finally, he said, "My receptionist says you claim we went to college together? I don't remember you."

"Thaaaaaaatttt's causssssssssse weeee—"

I reached down and turned off the massage action, took a deep breath, and continued, "That's because we didn't go to college together."

He nodded confidentially to himself and said, "I'm calling security."

These three words are in the same family as: *Look—a tiger*! *Is that asbestos? Clamp, please*, and *It turned blue*. They demand your attention.

I wriggled out of the chair, stood, and said, "Actually, I'm with the FBI." I walked around the desk, extended my hand, and said, "Agent Todd Gregory."

He shook my hand and said, "Is this about my wife?"

No, moron, it's about that parking meter incident in '93.

I nodded.

"I already told you guys everything I know."

"We just want to go over the details one more time."

He nodded.

He made his way to the doors, poked his head out, and said a couple words to Sunny. Then he closed the doors, flipped the lock, and sauntered to the bar. He picked up the decanter of scotch and looked in my direction. I shook my head. He poured himself about three fingers. He took a step past the aquarium, stopped like he'd been hit with an arrow in the chest, and gazed in my direction. He grabbed a cocktail napkin from the bar, dabbed it in his scotch, and cleaned the smudges on the glass.

I said to his back, "Those are some expensive-looking fish."

He turned and stared at me for a long second. "Quite expensive."

I inquired as to the weenie-fish. Apparently, it was called a "triggerfish." The irony of this was pending.

I asked, "How much does one of those go for?"

"That one, about fifteen."

"Thousand?"

He nodded.

I said, "I hope you got three wishes."

He took a sip of scotch and said, "A better short game, a Seahawks' Superbowl, and a bigger dick."

Never to be outdone, I said, "*The Tony Danza Show* box set, Jessica and Nick getting back together, and a smaller dick."

We both had a good laugh over this. Maybe we *were* long lost frat brothers. Anyhow, I mentioned the photographs on the flat screen and said, "You snap those?"

He took a sip of scotch and said, "Sort of a hobby of mine."

"Like when you aren't defending murderers, rapists, or thugs." I almost added, "Or killing your wife."

He dropped the old cliché: "Everyone is entitled to a good defense."

"Do you really believe that?"

"No."

I nodded. Maybe he had an ounce of integrity after all.

I made my way to his desk and put half my weight up on it. I picked up the silver rhino and said, "Nice desk."

He stared at me. I think he was a tad uncomfortable that I was sitting on his desk and that I was touching his stuff. He managed, "Thanks."

"I think there were Viking ships that used less wood."

"Actually, it's made from one piece of birch."

"Pricey?"

"You don't want to know."

Actually, I did, but I let it go. I placed my Perrier on his desk. In my peripheral I could see Gray take a long sip of scotch to cover his apprehension. I was starting to get the impression Adam Gray wasn't too far off Howard Hughes. Hey, maybe that's what the filing cabinet was for. To hide his milk and pee.

Gray made his way to the coffee table, picked up one of the coasters, and offered it to me.

I took it from him and said, "So why did you do it?"

"Do what?"

Good one.

"Were you sick of living in her shadow? Here you are this big name lawyer, worth millions and millions of dollars, and you are living in your wife's shadow. Has to drive a man crazy."

"Didn't bother me."

Right.

It didn't bother him, just like my smudges on the glass didn't bother him. Just like half my ass up on his big birch desk didn't bother him, or the water ring I left didn't bother him, or how I was playing slinky with his rhino didn't bother him. I mean, I could tell I made this guy's skin itch. The question was *did his wife make his skin itch?* And if so, would he go so far as to kill her to stop the itching?

I backed up a little. "So how did you and Ellen meet?"

"We met at a karaoke bar."

He went on to tell how he was working at some law firm fresh out of college and he and a couple other guys went to some karaoke bar. He was on stage, hammered, doing a horrific rendition of "Baby Light My Fire" when Ellen jumped on stage and rescued him. She'd been attending the college nearby. They got hitched four months later.

I put his rhino down and crossed my arms over my chest. "You're a lawyer, right?"

He looked at me awkwardly. I don't think he knew where I was headed with this line of reasoning. Which would make two of us. My tongue was two seconds ahead of my brain.

"Yes, as an occupation, I practice law."

What a lawyerly response.

My brain caught up and I said, "You have been hired to defend yourself. I'm the jury. Convince me you didn't kill your wife."

"I will not."

"There is a state of more than five million people who are convinced you killed their governor. Now convince me you didn't."

He stared at me for a long second. Then he walked around the back of his desk, removed his jacket, and set it neatly on his chair. He took a sip of scotch, stared at me, set the scotch down, and made his way to the rug centering his office. I watched as he paced back and forth. Then he turned and said, "Did I like my wife? Not particularly. Would I have been happier without her in my life? Certainly. Did I ever think about killing her? Sure."

Not exactly the best opening statement I'd ever heard, but I kept an open mind.

He looked at me and said, "That is exactly how one out of ten men answered an online survey last fall. Of over 600,000 men polled, 1 in 10 men hate their wife and have thought about killing her."

He stared at me with those green eyes and added, "I wasn't one of those 1 in 10."

I fought down a smile.

Gray took a deep breath and said, "Sure, we had our problems. But what married couple doesn't? Only ours were sensationalized, magnified by the media. You get in a yelling match with your wife and next thing you know, according to those vultures, you threw her down a flight of stairs. But we put up with it because deep down, at the core, we loved each other.

"I come from the old school, where the man is the bread-winner and the woman stays home with the kids, cooks, cleans, and that crap. I know it's wrong and I know it's Orwellian 1930s rhetoric, but this is how I was brought up."

I almost objected on the grounds counsel was an ignorant asshole.

"One day, Ellen tells me she wants to run for city council, that she can do some good for the community. Six years later she was the governor. I think part of me loved her for it and part of me resented her for it." He paced back and forth for thirty seconds, then stopped. "On October 15, the day Ellen went missing, I was meeting with a client on my yacht more than two hours from the North Cascades where she was rumored to have been hiking. So I hardly had the means. And although our marriage was not perfect —far from it, actually—I did love my wife. And even if I didn't, I love my daughters, and I would never take their mother from them. So I certainly lacked the motive. There is not one iota of evidence that ties me to her murder. There is not one iota of evidence that ties me to her murder because I had absolutely nothing to do with her murder."

I found myself wanting to clap. But part of me wondered how many times he'd said the same thing to juries when he knew his client was guilty. I mean, who knew if this guy was lying?

I asked, "Do you mind if I cross?"

"Cross?"

"Cross-examine you."

He reluctantly took up a spot on the couch. I cracked my knuckles and conjured the image of Atticus Finch in *To Kill a Mockingbird*.

I took a deep breath and said, "You have a registered .32, correct?"

"I do."

"Where is it presently?"

"It was in the glove compartment of my car."

"So?"

"I told you guys my car was stolen on the Sunday before Thanksgiving."

I tried to mask the fact this information was new to me. I said, "Tell me again."

"Sunday nights, I always go to this bar across the street from here. Sunday before Thanksgiving, I had a couple drinks, left around 10:00. I was walking to my car when something hit me in the leg."

"What was it?"

"Not sure, but it's one of the last things I remember."

"Was it a dart?"

"I have no idea. Could have been."

"Sorry. Continue."

He nodded. "It's all sort of fuzzy. I remember something

hitting me in the leg, then staggering a couple steps. That's the last thing I remember. I woke up the next day in my condo. My keys were gone and I was covered in blood."

"So your keys were stolen?"

He nodded.

"Keys to where?"

I could see him visualizing his key chain, and he said, "The house on Bainbridge, a condo I keep here in town, the Jag, and the yacht.

"What about your office?"

He pointed at the elevator and said, "That's a private elevator from the parking garage. I'm the only one with access. I have a card key and there's a keypad."

"How did you make it inside the condo?"

"I have no idea."

"Does anybody else have a key?"

"I don't think so. I mean, not that I know of."

I smiled. This was the first time he'd lied. I made a chalk mark. I asked, "You said you were covered in blood when you woke up?"

"Yeah. I had a cut on my cheek and a large cut on the side of my head. My shirt was covered in blood. It felt like I had been thrown down a flight of stairs."

"Maybe you were."

"Maybe."

"Did you contact the police?"

"I reported the car stolen."

This would be easy to check, so I had to assume he was telling the truth. I backed up a bit and said, "You said that on the day your wife disappeared you were on your yacht with your client."

"That's correct."

"Is there anybody else who saw you?"

"No. That's why we decided to meet there."

"So, other than your client vouching for you, a person whose life you basically have in the palm of your hand, you don't have an alibi."

He found this amusing. "Do you know how much an hour of my time costs?"

"I dunno. Three hundred dollars?"

"Try two thousand."

I raised my eyebrows.

"We were together ten hours. If he's lying, then it's costing him twenty large." He added, "Plus, my client hates my guts. He'd kill me before he vouched for me."

I tried a different strategy. "So, were you or your wife having any clandestine affairs?" He was. I wasn't sure about her.

He was taken aback by this and stammered, "No. Of course not."

I made another chalk mark.

"Did your wife find out you were fucking someone on the side?"

He stood up. "I think it's time you leave."

I pointed to his couch and said, "Did your wife even know about your condo, or was that where you took your mistress? Or hell, maybe it was Sunny. You know, your receptionist. She's a real smart one. You get her from a temp agency? Or were you sticking it to her and decided to get her a job when a spot opened up?"

Evidently, I'd hit a nerve. He whipped a phone from his pocket and said, "Security."

I pointed to the couch, "Why even go to the condo when you have a couch right here? Hell, you could screw her brains out between clients."

He looked at me and said, "You aren't an FBI agent, are you?"

I shook my head.

"Who are you?"

I was set to say, "I'm your worst nightmare," but there was a knock at the door and a man yelled, "Security. Is everything okay in there?"

Adam started for the door.

I took two steps to my right and hit the elevator call button. The doors opened silently and I slipped inside. The last thing I saw was the door crashing open and three men in black uniforms barging in. Then the elevator doors slid shut.

Twenty seconds later, I was back in the rain.

CHAPTER 13

THE NEXT DAY, I decided to surprise Harold. I stopped by the supermarket and picked up a bunch of items I thought he might enjoy. I went through the same routine with the prune at the front desk, who appeared to have dehydrated even more if possible. Her jowls now had jowls. Just saying.

Harold came to the door. He said, "Where ya been?" He looked five years older.

I handed him his bag of goodies. He smiled, or tried to. His lips no longer appeared to take orders from his brain. But he smiled with his eyes.

He perused his gift bag as I watched horse racing. Harold seemed especially interested in the *Sports Illustrated Swimsuit Issue*. I imagine if he was capable of popping a boner it would have killed him. Anyhow, it was right around lunch time and I sort of hinted that I would like to see what the cafeteria looked like.

The cafeteria was about the size of a small classroom. There were pre-made items—fun size, of course—plus a woman dishing out the meal of the day. According to the calendar at the entrance, it was Salisbury steak and macaroni. Actually, it appeared to be Salisbury steak and macaroni month.

The line moved slowly. This might have something to do with the fact that every other person was using a walker or a wheel-chair, or that the lady who broke her hip was trying to filch an extra Jell-O portion, or that one of the CNN-iles demanded his Salisbury steak be blessed by a rabbi.

When we were almost finished eating, one of the waitresses dropped two pieces of white bread wrapped in cellophane on the table next to Harold. He quickly grabbed the slices and tossed them in the basket of his walker.

After lunch, Harold and I retired to the common area and played a couple games of checkers. Harold played a combination of checkers, backgammon, badminton, chess, and Shoots and Ladders. Needless to say, he won both games. At one point, when he thought I wasn't looking he took three of my pieces and put them in his pocket. I guess when you get to be a hundred and thirty, you no longer worry about karma.

Afterward, Harold told me to follow him. So, I followed him out the back doors and onto a narrow paved path. About a hundred yards down the walkway was a small lake surrounded by large oaks. A fountain was spraying at the far edge of the lake, and two or three groups of ducks paddled in the current. There was a small break in the weather, the sun poking its head through the clouds, but I had the feeling we would be here regardless of the conditions.

We covered the hundred yards in a little under five minutes. Nestled near the lake was a small bench and Harold flopped down onto it. He sat there with his eyes closed and took long deep inhales on his oxygen tank.

I sat next to him.

Harold opened his eyes, took the bread from his walker basket, and unwrapped it. He handed a piece to me. I ripped off a piece of the bread and threw it in my mouth.

"The bread is for the ducks." Harold voiced sternly.

And here I'd been under the impression Harold and I were

gonna eat Wonderbread and talk shop.

So the two of us sat there and ripped off little pieces of bread and tossed them to the ducks. Every time a duck would choke down a piece of bread, the old man's eyes would light up. If a couple ducks fought over the same piece of bread, the old man would laugh and shake his head, only to fall into a coughing fit.

After about twenty minutes, Harold broke the silence. He said, "The lake wasn't much bigger than this."

I wasn't sure exactly what he was talking about for a long second. Then it hit me; we were back in 1942. I turned my attention from the ducks to my friend on my left.

I said, "Right. The girl had just fallen through the ice."

Harold watched as the little girl flapped around in the icy hole. Why was he watching? Shouldn't he do something? He went to open the door on the Model-T Ford. His hand was shaking, but he got the door open.

He remembered seeing a long rope in the trunk of the small truck when he had tossed his bag in earlier that morning. His dad used the rope for this and that. The last time it was used, another truck had to pull theirs from a rivulet in the mud.

Harold leapt into the back of the truck and found the long rope. It was still covered in mud from months earlier, but it would do. He wrapped the rope around his bulging forearm and shoulder, trading quick glances at the frantic girl. He watched as her head disappeared under the water, only to reemerge a second later. Harold couldn't think of a longer second in his life.

He jumped out of the back of the truck, ran across the street, hopped over the small fence, and made his way to the edge of the lake. The girl was no more than forty feet from him. He guessed the rope was much longer than that, probably even double. The girl was facing away from him. He guessed she'd been in the water for thirty seconds, maybe longer.

Harold screamed at the girl. After two or three more yells, she turned to him. Her face was a whitish-blue. Harold could see the fight draining from her body. He had to act fast.

He yelled, "I'm gonna get you out of there!" He couldn't tell if she heard him or not. He yelled, "I'm gonna throw you the rope! Grab it and pull yourself out." Harold found these words silly. How could this girl possibly pull herself out? She'd be lucky if she could get her freezing hands to grip the rope.

He thought about going out onto the ice himself, but if he fell in, then he was dead along with the girl. He let out a long distance of rope and threw it out onto the ice. It made it about two thirds of the way. He cursed.

The girl clung to the side of the ice, her hands frantically moving along the ice's edge. Then a piece of the ice chipped off and the girl disappeared. She met Harold's gaze as she slipped under the water. Harold decided he would not be the last image this young girl saw.

He tied one end of the rope around a fence post, tied the other snuggly around his waist, and ran onto the ice. The ice was thick for the first twenty feet, then became increasingly transparent as he neared the sloshing breach. He came abreast of the hole and stared down into the blackness, then the ice gave way around him.

The sensation was more like being thrown into a fire than anything else. His body didn't know what to do. His brain turned off. Then, a second later, it flickered back on. The girl.

He flipped over in the icy water and kicked his feet downward. He found even the slightest of motions were nearly impossible, like the messages from his brain were rerouted, missing their stops. He opened his eyes, but the blackness he saw was darker than if he had his eyes closed. He clamped his eyes shut and kicked down another couple feet. He moved his hands in every direction, but freezing water is all that touched back. Harold knew he only had a couple seconds left to get to the surface. That's when he felt the touch on his left arm. Just the lightest touch. But a touch that warmed him, filled him with fire.

He found her hand, then her arm, then he had his arms clasped around her. Then he kicked for the surface. Kicked harder than he'd ever kicked in his life. He didn't know how far they traveled, it felt like a mile, maybe two, then his head broke the surface. His first thought wasn't to *breathe, it was the girl. Her head was limp and she was bluer than the sky. He wasn't sure if she was alive or dead.*

Harold was strong as an ox from working fifteen-hour days in the fields, but all his strength had been stripped. He wasn't sure if he would be able to pull himself from the icy waters, let alone the girl. For the first time in a long time, Harold said a quick prayer.

That's when she coughed. Just the tiniest of coughs. But a cough nonetheless. Then her eyes opened.

Harold yelled, "I need you to wrap your arms around my back."

The girl's teeth chattered and she was able to nod just slightly. She made her way around Harold. Two thin arms wrapped around his neck and a head buried itself into his back. Even in such dire circumstances, Harold could never remember feeling so—what was the word—whole. Like a part of him that had gone missing had finally found its way back.

Harold slowly got his freezing hands to wrap around the rope, and centimeter by centimeter he began to reel himself in. He thought it might be easier to pull the truck from a pit of sand than get himself and the girl from the icy pit.

Then he felt the head nestled in his back lift. He heard teeth chattering, and in a shallow whisper the small girl on his back said, "You...saved...me."

In that second, he was already out of the water. He heaved and pulled and inched his way out of the water and crawled the forty feet to safety. Then he turned, collapsed on the rocks, the tiny angel falling into his arms.

I was on the edge of my seat. Literally, sitting on the last half inch of the small bench. I shook my head and said, "How long were you in the water?"

He shook his head. "I don't know. Less than a minute. But it felt like two forevers."

I thought about the freezing Puget. And that water had been 15 degrees warmer than what Harold was dealing with. "And the girl, she was okay?"

"She was blue and she kept saying, 'Pickles.' Pickles was the dog."

I'm guessing that Pickles never barked again. I said, "What then? She was probably hypothermic."

He nodded. "I had some blankets in the car."

Harold returned with the blankets. The little girl was shivering. He gently lifted her up and wrapped the blankets around her. His mom had knitted the blankets, and they were both thick and warm. He massaged the thin body underneath. After a good five minutes of this, the small body stopped shivering. He noticed the girl's eyes were now open. He couldn't remember seeing anything quite like them. They were the color of the caramel his mother made at Christmas. Her teeth were still chattering, but he could have sworn he heard her say, "Thanks."

Harold smiled.

He lifted the small package, surprised at how light she was, probably no more than eighty pounds, and started toward the King mansion. It was a quarter-mile stretch to the enormous house. Harold could fit thirty of his small house within the large estate. Two cars were parked in the gravel courtyard. He had seen the cars driving on the road once or twice. He wasn't sure what kind of cars they were, but they looked awfully expensive. Black and shiny. Nothing like his father's rusted old Ford.

Harold looked down at the small form in his arms. Her eyes were closed and she wasn't moving, but he could feel the rhythmic rise and fall of her small chest under the thick blankets. She was sleeping. He moved a large section of damp hair and kissed her lightly on the forehead.

There was a large brass knocker attached to the door, and Harold lifted it and thrust it against the door twice. After a short time, the door was pulled open. A large black woman dressed in white stood staunchly in the foyer. She smiled warmly, was set to speak, then noticed the bundle in his arms. She said, "Miss Elizabeth!"

Harold looked down at the beautiful, young girl. Elizabeth.

The woman swiftly took the small girl from his arms and turned and ran. Harold didn't know what to do. This isn't how he had envisioned it.

He had saved the young girl. Shouldn't he be praised for his courage? He was a hero. Wasn't he?

The door was left open. Harold could hear feet scampering around and faint yelling in the distance.

He nearly turned to leave when he heard growing footsteps. A man appeared. He was a skinny man dressed in a suit with red suspenders. He had a large mustache and slicked-back hair. Harold found a knot had formed in his throat just at the sight of the man. He eyed Harold and yelled, "What did you do to my daughter?"

Harold tried to speak, but words wouldn't come out. The man said, "You stupid? I asked you what you did to my daughter."

Harold closed his eyes. He knew what he wanted to say. Tell the man that he risked his life to save his precious daughter. But nothing came out. The man said briskly, "What's your name, boy?"

Again, nothing.

A woman appeared. She was cradling Elizabeth in her arms. Harold's old ravaged blankets had been swapped out for expensive linens. Just the idea of having their daughter wrapped in homemade blankets horrified these people.

The man reached his hand back and slapped Harold in the face. "I asked you what your name was boy?"

Harold cringed. He focused and somehow managed, "Harold. Harold Humphries."

The man cocked his head. "You the Humphries' boy from up the road?"

"Uh, yes sir. We lease land from you."

"Seventy-five acres. Yes, I know. Your daddy was late on his payment this year. If he has another bad crop, you lose the land."

This irritated Harold. He wasn't sure if it was because he had just saved this man's daughter and the man was talking about the money his father owed him or because his father hadn't told him about their financial woes. And here Harold was, abandoning his father when he truly needed him on the farm and stealing his truck to do it. A wave of emotion flooded Harold. He nearly began to cry. He looked at his shoes to try and hide his tears.

The man said, "Now, I'm gonna ask you one last time. What did you do to my girl?"

"He saved me."

Both Harold and the man looked at the girl. She locked eyes with Harold, unblinking.

Harold's eyes welled with tears as he smiled at the perfect form.

But then he was struck again by the man. A fierce blow. The man pushed and shoved him. He was yelling, "Get off my property, boy. Get. Get! Before I have you arrested."

Harold stumbled and fell. Arrested? But didn't he just learn that Harold had saved the girl? Harold pushed himself to his feet. He felt the tears streaming from his eyes. Why? Why was this man doing this to him? What had he done?

He pushed himself off the ground and started running. He gave one last look back at the house. The man threw a rock at him and continued to yell. He could see the girl in the doorway. Her eyes still locked on his. She lifted an arm from around her mother's neck and gave a slight wave.

The woman wrinkled her nose, turned, and walked inside.

Now I was off the bench, pacing in front of the small lake. I desperately wanted to find a time machine, go back to 1942, and kick the living shit out of this guy.

Harold watched me silently. Finally, he asked, "Are you okay?'

"Yeah." But, I wasn't.

I'd had a similar experience with a girl's father. He wouldn't let her date me because I was a cop. I still thought about her on occasion. But not as often as I thought about shooting her father in the kneecap.

I asked, "So what did you do?"

He shrugged. "What could I do? I ran to my truck. Drove to the train station and joined the army a day later."

I leaned my head back and sighed. Then I turned and looked at

Harold. He'd gone back to feeding the ducks. He threw a large piece of bread and two ducks jabbed at each other until the bigger of the two choked down the large chunk. Harold shook his head and laughed.

CHAPTER 14

BY NOON ON WEDNESDAY, I had the better part of the upstairs painted. I took a break at one and ate some lunch: PB and J, some Cheetos, a strawberry Fruit Roll Up, three Oreos (Double Stuf, of course), and a tall glass of milk. The perfect combination of protein, carbohydrates, partially hydrogenated vegetables oils, fruit pectin, Red Dye #4, and processed sugar to fuel my second leg of painting.

I'd just started back in—I was finishing up the trim work in Lacy's room—when I heard a rather loud and highly annoying series of wind chimes. It took me a moment to register that it was the doorbell. Oh, how quickly we forget.

I walked out of Lacy's room and across the hall to the guest bedroom. There was a window with white Venetian blinds, and I pushed one of the runners down with my finger. Droplets of water raced down the cold window, embossed over another gray Seattle afternoon. I didn't see a car parked in the slippery drive or one parked on the street.

The chimes settled in for their encore and I decided to wait them out (your average person will give up after two rings). The chimes ended and I waited to see who walked down the drive.

Nobody. The chimes came back on stage a third time. And then a fourth. I waited for the fifth set to mask my steps then crept down the stairs and tiptoed to the door. I peered through the peephole but it was black. Some shrewd individual had a finger over the lens. It was evident we were dealing with a pro here.

I pulled the door open.

Erica Frost was wearing faded blue jeans and a white hooded sweatshirt. Her hair was tucked behind her ears, and she could easily have passed for a student at one of the nearby colleges. I wasn't exactly sure why Erica Frost was standing on my doorstep. Was her visit personal or professional in nature? I had a feeling it was a combination of the two.

Erica decided to clear this little matter up. She smiled and said, "You'll never guess who I got a call from yesterday."

"Ronald Reagan?"

She cut her eyes at me.

"Too soon?"

She shook her head and said, "Adam Gray's lawyer."

I attempted to keep a straight face while I pondered this. It'd never dawned on me Adam Gray would have a lawyer. I mean, they say that a man who represents himself has a fool for a client, but when you're the best criminal defense lawyer on the planet, you might want to do just that. And where exactly do lawyers go when they're in need of a lawyer? Do they just mosey on down the hall and knock on a buddy's door. *Hey, Chuck, howareya? How's that Murphy case going? Good, good. You see Berda got kicked off Biggest Loser last night? Yeah, she half-assed her last-chance workout. At least that's what Jillian said. Hey, listen, I sort of killed my wife. Do you think you could represent me?*

I shook from my reverie and asked, "Why? Are you in some legal trouble?"

"No, I am not in any legal trouble. Actually, a man dropped in on Adam yesterday. Apparently, this man impersonated an FBI agent, asked some extremely sensitive questions, and was escorted out by security."

That sounded like a fair assessment, although I didn't recall being escorted out. I said, "And you're telling me this because?"

"Because the man described fit your description."

"What? Devilishly handsome, charming to no end, and clever like an otter?"

She rolled her eyes. "Actually, the secretary described the man as looking—," she looked down at the pad in her hand and read, "Sort of like Matthew McConaughey, but after a horrible car accident."

Burn.

"I know that guy. He lives in Sarasota. Happy hunting."

"Actually, I think it was you."

I put my hand to my chest. "Me?"

"You."

"Why would I visit Adam Green?"

"Adam *Gray*."

"Right. Why would I visit Adam Gray?"

"Boredom. Curiosity. I don't know. Maybe you just wanted to see the guy for yourself. Maybe you saw the guy on TV, and he pissed you off, and you wanted to kick the shit out of him. I have no idea."

This, of course, was true on all counts. On that note, I said, "I saw you on TV."

Erica reluctantly let me switch the subject to her. "Did you now?"

"You know the camera adds ten pounds."

She looked herself up and down and said, "Are you trying to tell me I looked fat?"

"I didn't say you looked fat. I'm just saying skip a meal every once in a while."

She didn't respond. In fact, she just stood there, no doubt, visualizing kicking my testicles into my throat.

I did some damage control, "Who knows? It might have just been the lens. Maybe it was a fisheye."

I should reiterate that Erica Frost didn't have an ounce of fat on her. I don't make a habit of calling fat people fat. They know they're fat. And they know I know they're fat.

But, if you're wondering why I was acting like such an unconscionable prick, let me explain. I was falling for Erica Frost, plain and simple. That ship had left the pier a long time ago. This scared me. This scared me more than all the death I'd come across in my lifetime. My brain, which I fully understand is slightly less evolved than your average primate, was screaming at me to push her away. And that's what I was doing.

Erica took a deep breath and said, "Well, I should get going here. I have to go throw up my lunch."

She took a couple steps backwards then turned and said, "As for what I said earlier, we'd appreciate if you stopped harassing our suspects. It's making it hard for us to conduct our investigation. Plus, Adam Gray isn't the guy to mess with. He's threatened a lawsuit. Against us and against *you*."

"I still don't know what you're talking about, but thanks for the heads up."

She started down the drive. I stared upward at the ceiling for a couple seconds. I tend to do this before I do—or say—something incredibly foolish. This time would be no different. Erica was halfway to her car when I yelled, "What are you doing the rest of the afternoon?"

She stopped and turned around. "You mean after I go run ten miles, weigh myself thirty times, and order a bottle of *TrimSpa*?"

I was starting to get the impression Erica Frost was sensitive about her weight. Maybe she'd been a porker in high school. Maybe she had a shirt that read, *Fatties Never Forget*. I said, "You looked beautiful."

She cocked her head.

I reiterated. "On TV. You looked beautiful."

Something weird happened to Erica's mouth. Like she was trying to fight down a smile. I've only called a handful of women beautiful in my day, and nothing bad had ever come of it. At least in the short term. Long term was a completely different story. Lots of grief in the long term. In fact, if I had access to a time machine I would have traveled back ten seconds and shot myself in the face.

Erica stood, her hands on her hips, weighing the pros and cons of forgiving Mr. Thomas Prescott. She took her hands off her hips. Forgiven.

She said, "Why? What do you have in mind?"

I had a couple things in mind. But I was a class act. Well, not a class act, but an act of some sort. "Do you want to stick around and help me paint?"

She puffed out her cheeks and looked at the ground. From my recollection, women do this before *they* do or say something incredibly foolish. This time would be no different.

CHAPTER 15

I OUTFITTED Erica in one of my dad's old shirts, then set her up with a roller and a paint tray. After about a minute of silent painting, I asked, "So where did you grow up?"

"Michigan. Just outside East Lansing."

"And how was that?"

"All right, I guess. Normal. Whatever you want to call it."

"What do your parents do?"

"Dad is a professor at Michigan State. Mom teaches preschool."

"What does your dad teach?"

"Shakespeare."

"Ah. The Beard."

"Bard."

"I thought it was *Beard*."

"No. Shakespeare had a beard, but he was referred to as the Bard."

"I guess we'll just have to agree to disagree on this one."

She exhaled deeply, then said, "So, try growing up with William Shakespeare as a third parent. Gets a little old after a while. My dad read me *Macbeth* for the first time when I was two."

Woe is thee.

She recited: "He's mad that trusts in the tameness of a wolf, a horse's health, a boy's love, or a whore's oath."

Tell me about it.

"*Hamlet?*"

"*King Lear.*"

"Which is the one with Mel Gibson and Danny Glover?"

She rolled her eyes at me for some reason and said, "How bout you? Where did you grow up?"

I did a three-sixty and said, "You're looking at it."

"Right."

"Actually, I can't believe this place is still standing. There used to be a few other homes not far from here, but they all slid into the water."

"Really?"

"Really."

She raised her eyebrows and I said, "I think we're safe."

She didn't look like she believed me. After grasping the nearest doorframe to confirm the house wasn't moving, she asked, "And how was your childhood?"

"No complaints." At least from my end.

"Any brothers or sisters?"

"One sister. Lacy."

"*And…*" She did a rolling motion with her free hand.

"And…she's a girl."

"I figured as much."

"She was an accident, although my mother would never admit to it. They had her when I was eight."

"So she's what, thirty-five?"

Zing. "Actually she's forty-two. I exfoliate."

She laughed and said, "Really? She's what, twenty-three?"

"Twenty-five."

"Is she here? In Washington, I mean?"

"She's working at an art gallery in France."

I bragged about her painting, told a couple Lacy anecdotes, and played Thomas Prescott M.D. for ten solid minutes. I explained what multiple sclerosis is, what it does, how Lacy was diagnosed, and how the disease is treated. I finished with, "The last time I talked to her, she said she was thinking about staying in France."

I think Erica detected the angst in my voice. She asked, "And if she does decide to stay, what then?"

This could have been a fishing question. Maybe someone looking into the future. Maybe someone doing some long-term planning. Maybe this was someone who wanted to stop writing her five-year plans in pencil. Then again, maybe it was nothing.

"I'll move to France." And I would.

"Really?"

"Sure. Compared to the French, I come across as a nice guy."

She laughed.

Time to change the subject. "How 'bout you? Any siblings?"

"Two brothers."

"*And...*" I accompanied this with the *please tell me more* head bob.

She smiled. "One a year younger and one three years older. Paul, the younger one, is Mr. Outdoors. Rock-climbing, kayaking, hiking, camping, skiing. He's saving up to climb Everest. I love him to death."

"And the older one?"

"James is your typical firstborn. Thinks he has all the answers. Let's just say we don't see eye to eye. I haven't talked to him in more than five years."

Evidently, Erica was good at holding grudges. Two demerits. "What about your parents? How often do you talk to them?"

She cringed. "Three times a year. Like clockwork. Christmas, Easter, and on my birthday. I haven't been back to Michigan in three years." She switched things back to me. "What about you? When's the last time you saw your folks?"

"A little over eight years."

"Eight years? Is there a riff between you?"

"If you can count a pulse as a riff."

She turned. All the color had drained from her face, her gigantic faux pas sinking in.

"My parents died in a plane crash eight years ago."

"I'm sorry. I mean, I should have known. I mean, this is their house and all. Oh my God."

"It's okay." I went on to narrate the last couple hours of my parents' life. Rolling Stones concert in California. Coming back in my dad's company jet. Engine failure. Crash landing in the Sierra Nevadas. No survivors.

"After the funeral, Lacy and I both left. Lacy had just graduated from high school and was headed to Temple. And I didn't have a job, seeing as I was 'let go' from the force. A week after the funeral we looked at each other, packed up, and left. Three days later we were sharing a two-bedroom loft in Philadelphia."

"How did you keep busy?"

"A guy I went to college with was a lieutenant in Philly. He found out I was living in town and asked me for my input on a case every so often. Then he started coming to me with every case. Then I started taking three-, sometimes ten-day contracts. Couple serial killers, couple cold cases. The Feds got wind of some of my triumphs, and next thing I know, I've gone from working with angry Italians to working with tight-assed, tight-lipped, WASPs."

"So it was basically the blind following the deaf, dumb, and blind."

"More or less."

She cocked her head to the side and said, "That's why your name sounds familiar. Weren't you involved in that case up in Maine about a year ago? The MAINEiac, I think they were calling him."

"If by 'involved' you mean 'was shot and nearly killed by,' then yeah, I guess you could say I was involved."

She raised her eyebrows.

I pulled the collar of my shirt down to expose my left shoulder. A patch of dimpled scar tissue there resembled the bottom of a cork. I said, "Another one just like him on my right thigh."

"No wonder you retired."

I wasn't sure if she was being sincere or goading me. With this small break in the conversation, Erica dipped her roller and started on a new section. Then she said over her shoulder, "So, you ever been married?"

Only a matter of time.

"Nope. I got close once." She, of course, ended up in thirty pieces with her eyes nailed to a wall. It would have been a messy wedding. I kept this to myself. "It didn't work out. She said I was premature."

"Are you sure you don't mean *immature?*"

"That too."

She shook her head and laughed. It was gut-wrenchingly cute.

"How 'bout you. You ever get hitched?"

"Nope."

"Ever come close?"

She shook her head, and I said, "Clock's ticking."

"You're worse than my mother."

We hit a conversation standstill, so I started in a new direction. "How 'bout you bring me up to speed on the Ellen Gray case?"

She didn't respond. She just continued painting. After about ten furtive glances and five or six applications of paint to her roller, she gave. She turned and said, "You know I shouldn't be telling you any of this."

I was tempted to point out she was yet to tell me anything, but I didn't want our first fight to be over semantics.

She took a deep breath and said, "We're picking him up tomorrow."

I assumed she was referring to Adam Gray. "Tomorrow?"

She nodded and said, "Ethan is at the courthouse getting an arrest warrant as we speak."

"What changed?" Last I'd heard—which was directly from the lion's mouth—they didn't have anything to hold him on, least of all charge him with murder.

"We found Adam Gray's yacht."

"You found the *Habeas Corpu*—"

Erica froze. "How did you know the name of his yacht?"

I took a deep breath and said, "I was flipping through *Forbes* magazine and they had a write-up about him. They mentioned the yacht." What I failed to mention was that I was flipping through the magazine while sitting in Adam Gray's waiting room, just before I broke into his office and later interrogated him. I should also mention that I was toying with the idea of telling Erica about the blood I'd found on the underside of the cushions, but it would appear they already had enough against him. Not to mention that this information would place me in Gray's office. I kept quiet.

Erica eyed me but appeared to buy it.

She continued, "We'd searched practically every shipyard, port, and slip this side of the Everglades, but Gray's yacht was MIA. Then yesterday, we get a call from a guy in Edmonds. He'd been on vacation for the last three weeks. Comes home and finds a yacht tied up to his dock. He takes a quick peek and notices a couple puddles of pink water on the deck that could have been blood. So, he called the cops."

I remember Adam saying something about having a house somewhere in Edmonds. I wondered if Erica was working with the same information packet as me. I said, "I read somewhere that Gray has a place up that way."

"Just three houses from where we found the boat."

"You guys didn't think to check that area?"

"We checked his property, of course, and we did a spot check on a couple neighbors. Somehow it slipped through the cracks."

"So you got a warrant?"

"We didn't need a warrant because the blood was in plain view."

"Let me guess, you found a gun?"

She smiled. "A recently fired .32."

"And the blood?"

"The DNA on the deck was inconclusive. Something to do with the saltwater. But it was female and type AB."

AB was the rarest blood type. This wasn't nearly as concrete as DNA evidence, but it was enough that a judge would allow it to be entered as evidence.

She was holding back and I gave her a look. She said, "We found traces of Ellen Gray's blood on a washcloth in the galley."

This, of course, was conclusive.

"What about prints?"

"Adam Gray's prints were on the gun."

"What about the boat?"

"We lifted three sets. Two male: Adam Gray's and one of his clients."

This would corroborate Gray's alibi for the day Ellen went missing. "Who was the third?"

"Not sure, but they were female. They weren't from Ellen Gray, and they weren't in the system."

So, Adam *did* have a woman on the side.

Erica said, "We had some of our computer geeks hack into his navigational system. Records everywhere the boat goes on GPS."

"Let me guess. Adam took a late-night trip into Puget Sound leading up to Thanksgiving."

"Four days before, actually."

That would make it Sunday. When, if you believed Adam—and I was starting to have my doubts that I did—he had been drugged and his keys were stolen. I couldn't comment on this, being that I had never met Adam Gray.

Erica went on. "He took the yacht out at 11:25 a.m., drove about 70 miles out to the middle of the Sound, stopped for exactly two minutes, then at 3:17 a.m. drove the boat to where we found it in Edmonds."

A textbook timeline for the disposal of a body.

On paper, this was what you call an "airtight case." Although, if this had been my case, I would have been contemplating the following questions: Why would Adam Gray—who is an absolute perfectionist—plan such a sloppy murder? Why hide the gun when you could just throw it overboard? Why not wear gloves and risk leaving fingerprints? Why leave the bloody cloth in the galley? And why leave the yacht tied three houses from a property you own? Adam Gray didn't get to where he was by making mistakes. But, according to Erica, he made four. Four biggies. You make four mistakes in a big court case and you're toast. End up with your client strapped to a chair with a needle in his arm.

I surveyed Erica. I was wondering if the same questions were running through her head. Was she a skeptic? I hoped so.

We painted for another twenty minutes before Erica's cell went off. She left the room for a couple minutes. When she came back she was holding the shirt I'd given her. She handed it to me and said, "That was Ethan. There's a problem with the arrest warrant. The judge won't sign it. Turns out Gray went to school with one of his cousins or something."

It didn't surprise me that Gray had a judge in his pocket; he probably had many. Adam Gray was one powerful man. *Forbes* might have him listed at 97, but he was #1 when it came to his home turf. Even though this particular judge might not have signed the arrest warrant, eventually a judge would. There was too much evidence. An overwhelming amount. Still, I'd always thought of evidence like a bell curve. Too little, or too much, and you needed to reevaluate the case.

Erica's phone rang a second time and she had a thirty-second conversation. She flipped the phone shut and said, "Ethan found a judge to sign the arrest warrant, but not until Friday. The judge doesn't want the Proctor case to go to mistrial. They're giving their final summations tomorrow."

I nodded.

I walked Erica to the door. I wasn't sure if I was supposed to shake hands with her, give her a hug, or give her a hundred bucks for her labor.

I told her I'd be in touch. I had her card.

I opened the door for her and she started down the drive. She took two steps, then turned. "Oh, by the way, Gray's lawyer sent over the security tapes from Monday."

Security tapes?

She said, "You sleep with your eyes open. It's kinda creepy."

"I'll remember that next time I take a nap on camera."

She turned and started down the drive. When she was about halfway, I said, "He didn't do it."

She turned around. She just stared at me for a long minute. A thousand-yard stare. Finally, she said, "Then who did?"

"I don't know."

But I was going to find out.

CHAPTER 16

THE SEATTLE MUNICIPAL COURTHOUSE was located in the heart of downtown Seattle. I parked in the Space Needle parking lot and walked the three blocks west to the courthouse. The pervasive rain was unable to deter the protestors from showing up; close to a hundred people congregated near a series of barricades girdling the courthouse's stone steps. Most were decked out in ponchos and holding some sort of sign.

I tapped a man wearing a bright blue poncho on the shoulder and asked him about the case. He said a guy named Proctor was accused of strangling a young black prostitute. Now, Seattle is one of the more liberated, and liberal, cities in the United States, and the fact that the girl was black wasn't an issue for the protestors. But Adam Gray had made a career of getting these deviants off without a slap on the wrist, and it was beginning to upset some folks.

I read a couple of the ink-blurred placards as I skirted around the melee. "No O.J. For Adam Gray." Another was more direct: "Proctor? Gray? Who Cares. Kill 'Em Both."

Well put.

Camera crews hovered around and I saw a handful of

reporters readying themselves to go live for the noon editions. I slipped past one of the barricades and started up the stone steps. I didn't expect to just waltz into the courtroom; I had concocted a little tall tale for the occasion. Stepbrother of the accused. Two cops stopped me as I approached, and I fed them my line. They sneered at me but let me through.

I pushed through the large doors and into a feeding frenzy. The foyer of the courthouse was packed with more cameramen, more reporters. The combination of the high profile Proctor case, Gray as his counsel and also as suspect *numero uno* in his wife's death was too much for the media. It was one big clusterfuck.

I tapped a well-dressed woman on the shoulder and said, "Do you know what's going on in there?"

"Prosecution just rested. Recess until 12:30, then summations." She added, "They're not letting anyone else in. I heard there's a viewing room in the east wing."

I nodded my thanks, then made my way to the courtroom doors. The bailiff gave me a once-over and said, "We're filled to capacity. There's an extra viewing room set up in the east wing."

I think this may have been the woman's source of information, but I wasn't positive.

I said, "I'm brother of the accused. I flew in from the Netherlands to be here."

He raised his eyebrows. "The Netherlands?"

Sure. Why not?

"Yep."

He looked from side to side then opened the door and ushered me in before anyone saw. It was standing room only. I wiggled my way through until I had a spot up against the far left wall.

It was a large courtroom. The jury box was on my side, twelve empty seats. The gallery was twenty rows of seats filled to capacity. Both the prosecution and the defense tables were empty. No doubt both sides were getting their ducks in a row for their final summations.

I'd only been inside a courtroom a handful of times. I had to testify twice in official investigations, and there had been three or four times when I'd been involved in a case and stopped in to watch the action. Speaking of which, I could make out Erica and Ethan sitting in the third row behind the prosecution table. I wondered how they got such good seats. Did they Fandango?

Anyhow, ten minutes later, the prosecution team rolled in. Four of them. All dressed sharply. The lead prosecutor was a balding man of about fifty with circular spectacles, sort of a middle-aged Harry Potter.

All chatter stopped abruptly as they walked in and sat. The defense came next. It was just Adam Gray and his client. I recognized the defendant. I hadn't put it together until now. Proctor was in actuality Daniel Proctor. Daniel Proctor was a couple years younger than me, a decent looking guy—compliments of an excellent plastic surgeon—with dark eyes and jet-black hair. He reminded me of that really snaky Baldwin brother. William, I think. Daniel and I had crossed paths eight years earlier. He'd been my last arrest. In fact, the last time I'd seen Mr. Proctor he'd been connected to all sorts of tubes and his face had been swollen shut. The last time he'd seen *me* had been twelve hours prior to this when I'd stripped him of all his clothes and repeatedly smashed my fist into his face. This, of course, led to my immediate dismissal from the Seattle Police Department and Proctor suing the city for seven million dollars. Which he would go on to win.

The jury was led in, and a moment later the judge entered. Everyone stood, then sat. I didn't recognize the judge, but he was a strict old codger. Within a couple short minutes, the district attorney was out of his seat and delivering his summation.

Harry Potter was a tad long-winded, but he was good. The State had about as solid a case as I'd ever heard. Cut and dry. Proctor picked up the girl, took her to a shitty motel, had sex with her, strangled her, then threw her in a dumpster. They had his semen, her blood, his blood, one witness who saw him pick her up, the motel manager who saw him enter the motel with the girl, and a third who saw him exit without the girl.

This wasn't exactly the grassy knoll.

After the prosecution rested, I'd say everyone in the court-room was convinced Mr. Proctor was a killer. And I didn't think there was anything Adam Gray could say to convince me other-wise. I was wrong.

The judge nodded at Gray that it was time for his closing statement. He whispered into his client's ear, then stood.

A hush fell over an already-hushed crowd. Gray brushed a couple stray pieces of lint from his arms. He walked in front of the jury and locked eyes with each person for a brief moment. Two jurors had to look away, Gray's piercing green eyes simply too much.

After a long minute the judge had had enough. "Please proceed, counsel."

Gray gave him a dismissive glance. This was Gray's court-room, and everyone, including the judge, knew this. He would proceed at his own pace.

He turned his gaze to the prosecution, stopping in front of each of the four attorneys. It was the definition of smug, and I found myself smiling, rooting for the asshole.

Gray turned to the gallery. He swept his gaze over the family of the accused, then the family of the victim. He locked eyes with Erica and Ethan. I wondered if he knew they would be arresting him sometime in the next twenty-four hours. If he did, he didn't show it.

He then gave one last look around the courtroom. He swept his eyes past me, then snapped them back. I offered a soft wink.

Guess who?

He took a deep breath but continued to stare me down. After ten seconds, everyone in the courthouse began craning their necks to see who he was looking at. Soon every eyeball in the large courtroom was trained on yours truly. So much for anonymity.

Gray's client, Daniel Proctor, sneered at me. I guess some of his long-term memory had come back. I thought I detected the faintest of smiles flash across his thin lips, but he turned before I could be sure.

Anyhow, after another long second, Gray turned and faced the jury. I gave a quick look in Erica Frost's direction. She gave me a tiny wave with her fingers. Ethan shook his head at me, then faced forward.

Gray coughed into his hand. It was show time. The crowd collectively leaned forward as Gray said, "Ladies and gentlemen of the jury, my client is a murderer."

Everyone gasped, including his client. Gray pointed at Proctor and said, "That man sitting right there has killed before, and if he walks out of here a free man today *he will kill again.*"

Proctor was out of his seat. I'm quite certain he didn't know his attorney would be playing the *murderer* angle. Proctor screamed at his attorney, "I'm gonna kill you first, you stupid sonofabitch!"

Adam smiled and said to the jury, "See what I mean?"

There was a bit of uncomfortable laughter from the gallery, even a couple jurors cracked smiles. The prosecution was grinning ear to ear.

The bailiff got Proctor under control, and Gray continued as if nothing had occurred. "But ladies and gentlemen, there is one small problem." He paused, stared at his client, and said, "No matter what you think of my client, no matter how many women he's killed in the past or how many women he will kill in the future, you can't hold this against him. The law will not allow it. Because when my client left Amanda Peters that night, she was alive. Sure she was a bit banged up, but she was still very much alive."

Proctor gave his counsel a cockeyed look.

Gray went on for a short ten minutes. He quickly discredited all three witnesses. The witness who saw him pick up the girl was in a liquor store across the street and had himself a bad case of cataracts. The manager, who was the most important witness, had been swigging on a bottle of Angry Times whiskey (they found it in the trash can) during his shift and had a blood alcohol level of .18 when they questioned him six hours later. And the final witness, the witness who testified she saw the accused leave the motel alone, at 3:30 in the morning, was a prostitute herself. And, if this wasn't enough, she had a little crack problem.

Gray shook his head and said, "The medical examiner concluded the victim died by asphyxiation less than six hours before she was found, putting her time of death at 3:00 in the morning. Which is all fine and dandy, except my client's car went through a tollbooth thirty miles away, heading in the opposite direction, at just after midnight."

The jury of course knew all these details, but for most of the spectators, these details were fresh. People in the gallery jabbed one another and whispered.

Gray said, "Traces of my client's semen were found inside the victim, but so was that of three other gentlemen. Who's to say there wasn't another fellow after my client? Or two? Or all three? We don't know these things and we never will."

A black woman stood and cried, "He killed her! He killed my baby!"

The judge slammed down his gavel and said, "I will not allow outbursts in this courtroom."

The woman shrank back into her seat.

Gray looked at the woman and said, "I'm sorry for your loss. Truly, I am. But my client did not kill your daughter. Somebody did. Maybe someday we will find him."

Gray turned back to the jury. He went on to narrate how the Seattle Police Department had made mistake after mistake while gathering the evidence, and if they had only widened the suspect pool beyond his client they may have found out who had committed this "horrible, irrefutable, ungodly crime."

Adam walked to the defense table and the judge said, "Will that be all, counsel?"

Adam took a sip of water, shook his head, and said, "No."

He cocked his head to the side, took a deep inhale through his nose, and turned to face the gallery. There was something majestic about the way he held himself, as if he were a black hole sucking in the gaze of everything around him.

Again, he swept his eyes over the collective audience. And again, his eyes settled on me.

He said, almost as if he was talking to me and me alone, "The system is corrupt. It is. We live in a country governed by laws written hundreds of years ago. We look to a Constitution that has remained unchanged for nearly two centuries. It states that all men deserve a fair trial. But do they really? Does every man deserve a fair trial? Does my client? A playboy with an unlimited supply of the city's money, who has never worked an honest day in his life. A man who has hurt, killed, and God knows what else. Does he deserve a fair trial?"

Adam shook his head. "Surely he does not. He deserves to have his face beat in. Scum like him doesn't deserve a jail cell. He deserves to feel all the pain and suffering he's caused in his life-time. Really, he deserves to die."

The audience jeered and a handful of people even started clap-ping. Proctor was gritting his teeth. The bailiff eyed him to stay put.

The judge banged his gavel and said, "I don't know where you're going with this, counsel, but please tread lightly." He turned his gaze to the gallery. "And if I hear so much as a peep from any of you spectators, you will be removed from my courtroom."

Gray continued unfazed. "And don't get me started on a fair trial. There is nothing fair about this trial. This case has always been stacked in my client's favor."

He walked to the prosecution table and said, "These four attorneys did an amazing job. Really. They are hardworking lawyers, working for slave wages, who have been working tirelessly for the past three months to put my client behind bars."

The prosecution team didn't appear to know how to take the praise, and all four appeared markedly uncomfortable. Harry Potter stood and said, "I object, Your Honor."

The judge laughed and said, "On what grounds? That you were given a compliment? Sit down, Counsel."

He sat.

Gray continued. "But they had little to work with: three witnesses that could hardly be considered reliable, two detectives that mishandled evidence at every step of the investigation. And, most importantly, they had me."

Everyone in the courtroom was shaking their heads. And from what I could see, most were fighting down smiles.

"I'm expensive. I'm expensive because I'm the best. Had my client been guilty, had my client killed that young woman, would I still have taken the case? You're damn right I would have. And I would have gotten him off just the same."

I looked down at my arms. I had chills.

Adam said, "But when my client looks into my eyes after telling me about all the pain and suffering and death—yes, *death*— that he's caused in the past and swears to high hell that when he left that girl she was a bit bruised but very much alive, well, I believe him."

He turned to the jury and said, "Hopefully, someday they can tie my client to one of his horrendous crimes and put him away for a long time. In fact, I hope they sentence him to death. I really do. But today he is charged with the murder of Amanda Peters. A murder he didn't commit."

He walked up to the jury box, placed his hands on the railing, and said, "He didn't do it. He didn't kill Amanda Peters. Someone else did. And for this very reason you have to find my client not guilty."

He added, "It's your duty."

———

The jury recessed for twenty-six minutes before returning a verdict of not guilty. The gallery, reconvened quickly from the courthouse hallways, collectively gasped.

Proctor let out a long sigh, then turned to shake hands with his lawyer. But Gray was already on his way out. He threw a quick glance in my direction, a look similar to the one MJ threw Spike Lee at the Garden after he put up sixty-three. And I, much like Spike Lee, nodded in respect.

The courtroom emptied, and I followed the herd until I was in the courtroom foyer. I was making for the exit when I felt a tug on my shirtsleeve. I turned. It was Ethan. Erica was at his side.

Ethan said, "You're still the same little punk you were eight years ago, Prescott. I told you to stay away from this case."

"I was here clearing up a traffic violation. I was doing 260 in a school zone."

He glared. "If I see you again, just *see you*, I'm gonna have you arrested." He stormed off.

Something about the way he said it made me not doubt him.

Erica leaned in and said, "What'd you think about Gray's little performance?"

I told her it was quite impressive. She concurred.

She smiled and said, "Still think he didn't do it?"

"It doesn't matter what I think."

"You're right. It doesn't."

She winked at me and followed after Ethan.

CHAPTER 17

I KNOW VERY little about politics. In fact, I'd go so far as to say that I know absolutely nothing about politics. Hell, the last time I voted it was for Carrie Underwood.

So about the time Adam Gray was being hauled away by Ethan, Erica, and company, I was in Olympia trying to find a parking spot on Capitol Hill. If I was going to find out more about Ellen Gray, I thought this the best place to start.

I should mention that I looked slightly presentable. I'd shaved, threw on a pair of my dad's jeans and a light blue button down. I think the style was in J. Crew as Detective Chic.

Anyhow, I covered my head and ran through the torrential downpour. It wasn't coming down in sheets, it was coming down in comforters. I'd said that to Alex once. She didn't laugh. And she did break up with me three days later. Coincidence? Maybe not.

The streets were lined with school buses and it dawned on me that the only time I'd been inside the capitol building was in fourth grade.

As for the building, it looked like the White House's ugly step-cousin. It was gray concrete, and although they might use different jargon in *Architectural Digest*, I'd describe it as column-y.

The compulsory steepled dome was there, as well as the American flag and Washington state flag. Throw in a couple hardworking state employees clambering down the stone steps, and you've got yourself a Norman Rockwell painting.

I trudged up the thirty or so steps and pushed through the large double doors. I walked to the standard information booth, where a white-haired lady sat behind a high desk. She had the glasses with the necklace and looked like she should be in the enormous library across the street. She had a name tag that read "Milly."

Milly said, "Help you?" Her voice took me off guard. It sounded like that of a child, sweet and buttery.

I said, "Hi. I have a couple stupid questions for you."

She smiled, revealing perfect pink gums and flawless teeth. I guessed she used Efferdent and not the generic. Anyhow, she remarked, "I'm sure they're not stupid questions."

Au contraire.

I said, "What exactly is a governor?"

She gave a look as if to say, "You're right. That is a stupid question," then said, "I'm not sure I understand the question."

That made two of us. I tried again, "What is a governor in charge of?"

"Oh. Well, that's not *that* stupid." She sat on the word *that* like it was her favorite porch lounger.

I smiled.

She took her glasses off and let them hang around her neck. "The governor is in charge of the state. Making sure the state runs smoothly."

"And how long is a governor's term?"

"Four years per term. Up to two terms. Just like the president."

"And who does the governor spend the most time with?"

She furrowed her brow, and I clarified. "I mean, who is the governor closest with? People-wise?"

"Oh. It differs. When a new governor is elected, they bring in their own cabinet."

Apparently, I looked confused.

She said, "You do know what a cabinet is, don't you?"

"Sure, I put my groceries in them. In fact, I'm thinking of having mine redone." For the record, I knew what a cabinet was. And, to come clean here, I knew the basics of what a governor did. But when people think you are incompetent and a tad slow, they tell you things they wouldn't tell the average person. Just look at Geraldo, he made a career out of it.

She pushed her glasses up. "A cabinet is basically an elected official's team. Think of the governor as the coach and the cabinet as the players."

I nodded my understanding. "Just out of curiosity, who is the present governor?"

Her eyes immediately glazed over. She said, "Well, the acting governor is Bill Eggers. He took over about two weeks ago. He won't officially be governor until the first of the year. Unfortunately, the *real* governor was killed. Her name was Ellen Gray."

I nodded and said, "Oh." Like I'd caught it on the news recently. After a moment, I asked, "Who was she closest with? Who did she confide in?"

"Her press secretary, Kim. Kim Halloway."

Bingo. "Does she still work here?"

"Not a her. It's a him. And yes, he's still around. One of the few that survived the changing of the guard." She inched up in her chair, gave a small nod, and said, "In fact, that's him right there."

I looked over my shoulder. A tall gentleman was strolling into the café attached to the back of the building. He had one of those Blackberry things in his hand and one of those wireless things in his ear—the ones where from one side you look like a cyborg and from the other side you look like you just escaped the asylum.

Milly smiled and said, "If you hurry, you can catch him."

I gave a wry smile, turned, and followed after Kim Halloway.

CHAPTER 18

THE CAPITOL BISTRO was half coffee shop, half restaurant, half retail shop, and half asleep.

Kim had opted for the coffee and sandwich bar, and I fell into line three people behind him. He was clad in a business suit with a pink dress shirt and complementary pink striped tie. It takes a rare specimen to be able to pull off the pink ensemble, and Kim did it flawlessly. He had thick black hair with some of that pomade stuff in it, designer glasses, and the aforementioned metal earwig. I'd put him in his mid to late thirties.

He ordered a wrap of sorts and a complicated beverage, then found a seat at a table near the window. I ordered a piece of banana bread and some apple cider. Kim was playing with his Blackberry when I approached. The drab Seattle day pressed hard against the bistro's glass walls, and condensation had built up between the layers of the double-paned window.

I stood behind the chair opposite Kim and waited for him to acknowledge me. He had one of those touch screen Blackberrys, and he did a couple finger jabs before finally looking up. He had light blue eyes with long eyelashes. Girls would kill for these lashes.

I motioned to the seat with my apple cider and said, "Do you mind?"

It was immediately evident he minded. He said, "Actually, I'm expecting someone."

"Great. I'll leave when they get here." I sat.

He looked around the restaurant then said, "There are plenty of open tables."

I ignored him. I popped a chunk of banana bread in my mouth and garbled, "Nice tie."

He looked down. "Thanks."

"It's pink."

"It is."

"So is your shirt."

He nodded.

"*Bright* pink."

"You're a keen observer of color."

I shrugged and said, "It's a gift." I added, "I could never wear pink. But it looks good on you."

He glanced down once. "Thanks, I guess."

I popped another chunk of banana bread and took a long swig of apple cider. Kim had gone back to his Blackberry. He was probably writing a memo to himself to avoid wearing pink so as to stop getting hit on by strange men. I tossed back my last chunk of banana bread, wiped my hands, and said, "Word is you were Ellen Gray's press secretary."

He looked up. "Maybe I was."

"Well, you either were or you weren't. Which is it?"

"Depends on who's asking."

"I am."

"And who are you?"

"I'm me."

I don't think Kim was in the mood for my Abbot and Costello routine. He started to gather his stuff, and I said, "Hold on." I told him how I'd been the one to pull her from the surf.

He asked to see my ID and I suppose he found it satisfactory because he started yammering away. "I've already told the police everything I know. They came looking for me a couple days after she went missing and put me through the ringer. I was one of the few people that knew where she'd been that Sunday."

"Hiking?"

"Yeah. Other than me, and the guy who heads up her security detail, and maybe her husband, she never told anybody when she went hiking."

"Describe the guy you talked to."

"Big guy. Curly blond hair. Not quite as good looking as you, but close."

I gave him a look.

"Yeah, I am."

I mentally shrugged. What did I care if this guy liked to go *mano a mano*?

I said, "So they say you two were close."

"Who?"

You and Sir Elton. "You and Ellen."

"I suppose we were. I think she was drawn to me because I was the first guy in her life that didn't want to get into her pants. I mean, how many guys can you have *Sex and the City* night with?"

Not many.

I explained to him I thought her death might be tied to her job. I asked him what her last couple motions had been as governor.

He said, "Well, as anyone who lives here knows, the freeway system is a nightmare."

I was tempted to tell him that at one point today I went negative ten feet in forty-seven minutes. I let him continue.

"She wanted to institute a tax on all alcohol, tobacco, and firearms that would go directly to reconstruction of the freeway system. It would raise close to $10 million annually. It's actually in the last stages of legislation. Should be on the docket come next session. Looks like it will pass no problem."

That would have angered a decent number of people. One out of three drink alcohol. One out of five use some sort of tobacco product. One out of ten own a firearm. But would anyone go so far as murder for a two-cent tax increase? I guess I'd have to take a straw poll at the next NASCAR race.

I asked, "Anything else?"

He told me about a couple of her highest priorities. Basically all your standard stuff, the big five—education, environment, crime, water, and transportation—among others.

I wasn't exactly sure what a press secretary was in charge of, and Kim spent the next couple minutes titillating me with the intricacies of his job. Basically, he was in charge of making sure Ellen Gray said all the right things at all the right times. Sounded fun.

I asked, "So do you have any suspects?"

"You mean besides that asshole she married?"

"Yes. Besides him."

"No. Everybody adored Ellen."

"No threats?"

"None. At least nothing that got back to me."

"She was a celebrity. And she was beautiful. There had to be a couple nutjobs who were in love with her."

"Oh, there was the occasional love letter. A couple that got a little creepy, but nothing we ever took seriously."

"What about stuff related to work? She had to piss off someone. What's the cliché? 'It's harder to fit half a camel through the eye of a needle than to teach a man to fish all day?'" I added, "Carpe diem."

He looked at the table, then looked up, "Promise me you'll never say that again."

I promised.

He said, "I think the cliché you're thinking of is more like, 'You can only please some of the people some of the time.'"

I pointed at him and winked. "That's the one." Although I probably shouldn't have winked. Leading the poor guy on and all.

"Ellen alienated her fair share of people. She was pretty conservative."

"Was there any hot-button issue in particular that resonated with her?"

He leaned back in his chair, then brought it back down. "I wouldn't exactly call it a hot-button issue, but Ellen felt strongly about agriculture. She grew up on a ranch in Wisconsin in the sixties. I think they sold mostly livestock. So she was always looking out for the farmers and ranchers. She pushed for more subsidized money from the state, better irrigation laws. She held a huge fund-raiser every year that benefited the Washington Ranchers' Society. Raised about two hundred thousand annually."

I nodded. Then I leaned back in my chair. "What about men?"

"What about them?"

"Was Ellen seeing anyone? Any clandestine affairs?"

He shook his head. "She didn't have the time. Hell, she couldn't make time for one man, let alone two."

"What about him?"

"Adam?"

"Yeah, Adam."

"She never mentioned anything, but I wouldn't put it past him." Neither would I. Or had I.

I asked, "Did she ever talk about her marriage?"

"Every once in a while."

"Did she hate him?"

"No. But she married him when she was too young. Too naïve." He leaned in and said, "She was divorcing him."

Adam hadn't mentioned this. I gave Kim a quizzical look. He leaned even farther in and whispered, "After she got elected this term she was going to file."

I knocked this around for a while. It would have been the

perfect timing to file for divorce. She couldn't have filed while she was campaigning. No matter how strong her poll ratings were, a divorce would have ruined her. She might have carried the female vote—although she would have lost a substantial portion of even those—but the male vote would be irrevocably lost.

I said, "So she gets reelected and files for divorce."

He nodded.

"When did she tell you this?"

"Beginning of October, about two weeks before she disappeared."

"Do you know if she had a prenup?"

"I never asked her about it, but I would highly doubt it. When they got married, Gray was scraping to get by. He started amassing his fortune about the sixth year of their marriage."

"So she stood to take a pretty penny with her in the settlement?"

"That would be an understatement."

"When's the last time you saw her?"

"We did *Sex and the City* night the week before she disappeared. We were working our way through Season Three."

He started to get choked up and dabbed at his leaking eyes with his pink tie. I visualized Kim setting Season Four on her casket still in the cellophane.

He continued. "I got a call early the morning of the sixteenth. Head of her security detail, Hank Praud, asked if I'd talked to her. I hadn't. She usually made a day out of hiking. She'd pack a lunch, get there early, and hike like ten or fifteen miles. But she was usually back in her car by 4:00 or 5:00, and she'd call Hank first off. He didn't start worrying until the following morning."

"When did he drive up there?"

"He found her car around noon on Monday." His eyes started to water and I had a feeling we were on the verge of some Niagara Falls-type weeping.

Surprisingly, he fought back the currents and said, "I knew right then that she was dead."

"So you think Adam had something to do with it."

"That's exactly what I think."

"Give me a scenario."

He didn't hesitate. "Adam gets wind that Ellen is going to divorce him. He knows she's hiking, away from her cell phone, away from her security detail. What better time to get rid of her?"

"But he had an alibi."

"Yeah, I know, he's meeting with his client on his yacht." He rolled his eyes. "Even so, he could easily have paid someone to do it for him. They didn't even have to kill her, just abduct her, and then he could do the rest."

I shrugged with my mouth. I hadn't thought about this angle. Murder for hire. And Kim was right, they didn't even have to kill her. It was kidnap for hire, which I'm sure with all the shady characters Gray knew, and the money in his bank account, was not inconceivable. Shit, how many guys had Gray gotten off without a hitch? He could have just called in a marker. But my instincts told me Gray was hands-on. He didn't outsource anything, didn't have any paralegals. He was a loner. If he killed his wife, he did it alone. And he did it with his bare hands.

I asked, "What about the new governor?"

"Bill Eggers?"

"Yeah."

"Well, he was the Democrat running against Ellen." He laughed to himself and said, "Ellen had been missing for nearly three weeks, you know, before the November elections, and she still carried over 60 percent of the vote."

"He lost, despite her being presumed dead?"

He nodded.

"Why was her name still on the ballot?"

"Most people vote by mail these days, so they'd already mailed out all those. Plus, it would have been impossible to reprint all the ballots in such a small time span."

He looked at me like I should know these things. Unfortunately, I'd never voted. I came close once. I had this one girlfriend who liked to do—well, *it*—in some rather odd places. I remember her wanting to vote for some Republican guy. I voted she stop voting and take her shirt off. My campaign won out.

I asked, "And then what?"

"Something like this had never happened before. So, the state legislature put it to a vote. They could either leave Ellen's cabinet in place and let the vice governor take over, or by default they could usher Bill and his people in. They voted to leave Ellen's cabinet in place until the first of the year. But when her body was found, the legislature took a revote and ushered in Bill and his people."

"Think he had anything to do with it?"

He shook his head. "Doubt it. He had a speaking engagement in Tacoma the day she went missing."

I nodded.

We chatted for another couple minutes, then I asked, "Is there anybody else that might know anything? Anybody else I should talk to?"

He tilted his head back and said, "The nanny."

"Who?"

"The nanny. Resmelda or something like that. Been with them for like the last eight years."

"Does she still work for them?"

"As far as I know."

"How do I get in touch with her?"

"Ride the ferry."

I put my hand up. "Slow down there, cowboy. We've only just met."

He blushed and stammered, "I didn't mean—"

"I know you didn't."

When his face had returned to its natural color he said, "They, well, Adam, has a large waterfront property on Bainbridge Island."

Adam had mentioned the place. So had the *Forbes* article.

Bainbridge Island is an island twenty miles due west of Seattle. The waterfront properties, with views of both Seattle and Mount Rainier, were rumored to go for upward of $10 million. Both Steve Allen and Howard Shultz owned properties on the water.

I asked, "Do you know the address?"

He hit the Blackberry a couple times and told me the address.

I thanked him, apologized for being such a jerk-off, and left.

CHAPTER 19

THE FERRY STATION was a short forty-five minute drive north. A barrage of rich businessmen, real estate developers, software moguls, and Seattle Seahawks were coming into Seattle, but I was just one of a handful going out. A single ride cost $11.85, a twenty-ride card, $189.60. I opted for the former.

I drove the car onto the platform then hopped out and found the sitting area on the top deck. It was still early, before the afternoon storms, and there wasn't a touch of blue in the sky. It was chilly, probably hovering around fifty, and I had traded out the blue button-down for a gray, hooded sweatshirt.

Six other people were scattered about, decked out in coats, scarves, the whole nine yards. I looked out of place in my sweatshirt and jeans. I caught a couple hard stares, the Seattle elite wondering why the shoddy figure before them was going to their forbidden island. One lady in a fur jacket threw me a strained look, and I mimed clipping hedges. She gave a nod as if this made perfect sense.

I walked down a flight of stairs and grabbed a coffee at the small café. This is where most of the people congregated, and there was airport-type seating as well as five or six small TVs. One of the TVs was tuned to the news, and a red Breaking News banner ran across the bottom of the screen.

I assumed I knew what was coming next.

They cut to footage of the courthouse steps, and a voice-over said, "Just hours ago, authorities arrested Adam Gray in connection with his wife's murder."

Seconds later, the courthouse doors opened and a handcuffed Adam Gray emerged. By his side, none other than Ethan Kates, Erica Frost, and two uniformed officers emerged.

I shook my head and took a step forward.

Ethan was holding one of Gray's arms. His long fingers choked Gray's biceps like five baby anacondas. He was standing tall, shoulders back, his jaw working double time on the Juicy Fruit lodged in his cheek. He reminded me of Kevin Costner from *The Untouchables*.

Erica was holding the other arm. She looked almost the antithesis of Ethan; slouched, eyes down, touching Adam's elbow as if she might contract a deadly disease.

As for Gray, he appeared stoic. Eyes forward. Head up. I imagined he would look no different being escorted to the first green at Pebble Beach.

I found it a bit tacky that Ethan had decided to arrest Adam at the courthouse. Usually with these celebrity types, they have the decency to *arrange* an arrest, whereby the cuffs usually stay on the belt, and the celebrity can dress dignified and say rehearsed statements. Today had been a publicity stunt. No doubt an anonymous phone call had been placed to one of the networks that something was going to happen at the courthouse around noon.

The voice-over came back on. "Gray was at the courthouse finalizing documents concerning the Proctor case, which had wrapped up just yesterday. Until today he had simply been considered a person of interest in the death of his wife, Governor Ellen Gray. Reports from the Seattle Police Department indicate that he is now their prime suspect."

They didn't have much else to go on but promised more during the five o'clock edition. They began recounting the saga, and I turned and made my way up the stairs and back to the top deck.

The rest of the brave souls had called it quits, so I had the entire deck to myself. The ferry plowed through the water, and a slight breeze came off the ocean.

I flopped up the hood on my sweatshirt and walked to the edge of the boat. No whale tails, no shark fins, no mermaids, just miles and miles of open water. A distant land mass stood regally amid the vast blue. The island carried that gray-green color that screams, "Pristine and Untouched." At least that's what it said on the billboard. Five to one, there was a Starbucks somewhere on the island.

Thirty-five minutes later we hit Bainbridge Island. And ten minutes after that, I was pulling up to the Gray mansion.

As I approached the gated entrance, a black man in a uniform put down a magazine and stepped from the security booth. I noticed a surveillance camera pointed in my direction.

I rolled down my window.

The security guard asked, "Can I help you?"

I whipped out a badge and said, "Todd Gregory, FBI. I'm here to see the nanny, Resmelda." The badge was legit. Agent Todd Gregory wouldn't need it where he was.

He surveyed the badge for a moment before handing it back to me. He walked back to his booth and returned with a clipboard. He informed me I was not on the day's list of scheduled visitors.

I said, "I don't know if you heard, but Mr. Gray was arrested this afternoon."

He nodded. The guy signed his check; of course he'd heard. I added, "We just have a couple more questions for Resmelda."

He eyed me suspiciously, then walked back into the booth, hit something that started the gate opening, and picked his magazine back up.

So much for hired help.

I pulled through the gate. The estate was marked by finely manicured gardens, densely packed with flowers that should have read their obituaries six weeks earlier. There were two fountains, a few statues, and a bunch of other stuff that looked out of place on a private residence. As for the house, it was a behemoth. It was all angles and sharp edges. White columns supported baby-blue eves. Gray brick fed into gray shingled roofing. Off to the far right looked to be a greenhouse. To the left was a putting green and a sand trap. I assumed the stable was somewhere in the back.

There was a buzzer box near the door and I pushed the middle black square. After about a minute, the door opened. Standing in the doorway was a well-fed woman of around fifty. She had dark hair held up in a bun and dark skin, looking more Spanish than Mexican.

I asked, "Are you Resmelda?"

She gave a slight nod. "Si."

"Can I ask you a couple questions?"

"Si."

"May I come in?"

"Si."

She seemed a bit nervous and I said in my best Spanish, "I'm-o not-o with-o immigration-o."

She brought her hand to her forehead and said in perfect English, "Thank God. They might send me back to Toronto."

El bitch-o.

She stepped out onto the front porch and said, "Can you make this quick? I have some vacuuming I need to finish up."

"Sure thing. Just a couple questions concerning Mr. Gray."

"Mr. Gray's secretary called less than an hour ago saying he was arrested."

"That's true. This is just standard follow-up. No stone left unturned and all that."

She shrugged and said, "I'll tell you what I can."

This, of course, was somewhere between *I'll tell you what I know* and *I'll tell you what will make you leave the quickest.*

I asked, "How often did Mr. and Mrs. Gray fight?"

She rocked her head from side to side. "Seldom. But then again, they seldom saw each other."

"Were the fights bad?"

"No worse than other married couples, I suppose."

"Anyone ever get hurt?"

She stalled, then said, "Once."

"He beat her up?"

"Other way around."

I stifled a laugh. "What happened?"

"They were arguing. Mrs. Gray threw a glass at him. I don't know if she meant to hit him, but she did. Hit him right in the back of the head. He had to get six stitches."

"Why were they fighting?"

"They were fighting over this house. Mrs. Gray had the governor's mansion at her disposal, but she only stayed there a couple nights a week. She hated taking the ferry here, then back to the city, plus a forty minute drive. She couldn't understand why they couldn't all live in the governor's mansion like past governors. But Mr. Gray wouldn't have it. He found it proletariat. His words. But to be honest, I think Mr. Gray dreaded the commute just as much as his wife. But he'd never admit it. He sleeps at his office half the time anyway."

Actually, he slept at his condo and he didn't sleep alone. I kept this to myself.

I asked, "So why didn't they sell the place? There are plenty of other rich neighborhoods. Mercer Island is right there in the city." Mercer Island isn't really an island, connected to the heart of Seattle by a half-mile-long bridge. It was even a step up from Bainbridge if that's possible. Bill Gates had a $30 million estate somewhere on the island.

She smiled and said, "The girls. They love it here. The schools are good. And the girls love riding the ferry into town. I think if it weren't for the girls, they could do without the house."

From the tone of her voice, I got the impression the girls were the only thing holding the marriage together. I wondered if Resmelda knew Mrs. Gray was thinking of leaving Mr. Gray. I would get to this later.

I said, "Tell me about the girls."

She beamed. "Adrian is eight and Shelly is five."

I nodded.

"Poor things. Mr. and Mrs. Gray worked so hard that I practically raised them myself." She paused for a moment. "They're staying with my parents in Toronto for a couple weeks. Get them away from it all."

"What about Ellen's or Adam's parents?"

"Ellen's parents still have the farm in Wisconsin. They were never close with their granddaughters. They never once came here, and Mrs. Gray only made it back there once. For Christmas, I think. And Mr. Gray's parents died when he was just a kid. He was raised by one of his aunts."

"Was there ever any talk of divorce?"

"Not that I ever heard."

After a slight pause I asked, "Do you think he did it?"

She went silent. After a brief couple seconds, she said, "I think deep down, Mr. and Mrs. Gray loved one another. There were times you could see it in their eyes. I think it was more the situation than anything else. Two high profile people, high profile jobs. They just didn't make the time."

"You didn't answer the question."

"No. I don't think he did it."

I wasn't sure if she was saying this out of loyalty or if she truly felt this way. The way she eyed her feet told me it was the former.

I said, "There's quite a bit of evidence that says otherwise."

She nodded, but said nothing.

I asked if there was a number I could reach her at in case I had any more questions, and she gave me one. Then I said, "Well, I'll let you get back to your vacuuming. Thank you for your time."

She nodded, then receded back into the house. I started down the brick path, counted to twenty, then turned and made my way back to the door. I pressed my ear against the wood and heard the faint thrum of the vacuum cleaner.

I turned the door handle and pushed it inward. It opened. The noise from the vacuum cleaner was coming from somewhere on the ground floor. Your average person will vacuum from the ground up, and I hoped Resmelda was just getting started rather than wrapping things up. From what I could see, the ground floor was mostly hardwood, whereas the second and third stories would be mostly carpeted.

I wasn't exactly sure what it was I was looking for. If Adam was going to hide something from his wife, he would either keep it in his office or his condo. Or apparently—in regards to his gun —on his yacht. But that was now safely tucked away in the Seattle Police Department impound. Ellen wouldn't have it as easy. I wasn't sure what her level of privacy was in the governor's mansion, but my gut told me she would be reluctant to hide anything there. I had a feeling if she were hiding something, it would be here. I was thinking maybe photographs of Adam intertwined with another woman.

Anyhow, from my experience, when you aren't looking for anything at all, you are usually apt to find something. Deep, I know.

I made my way up the stairs, the thick burgundy carpet absorbing every inch of sound. There were three bedrooms and two baths on the second floor. Both the girls' rooms, plus a guest bedroom. I took a quick peek inside each, then continued up to the third floor. The third floor housed a second guest bedroom as well as the master bedroom.

I poked my head into the guest room. It was empty. There was a sliding glass door on the far wall. I slid the door open and stepped out. The balcony looked out on the water and had a clear view of both Seattle and Mount Rainier. The view was priceless, or maybe *pricey* is more accurate.

I scanned the water and noticed each house had a pier jetting out into the dark water. Docked and lapping idly against each was either a yacht or a speedboat. Some had both. The pier directly below me looked freshly stained, a dark brown that gleamed under heavy clouds. Thick white ropes lay silently on the wood. A yacht—more specifically, the *Habeas Corpus*—had been tied up to that small pier just days before I'd pulled Ellen Gray's remains from the water. Were the two events connected? Had Ellen's body been aboard that yacht at one time or another? And if so, had Adam been at the helm?

I wasn't sure anymore.

I shut the balcony doors and made my way across the long hall. About halfway there the vacuum cut out and I stopped in my tracks. Seconds later, I heard the clambering of a vacuum being lifted up the stairs. I waited for Resmelda to appear, see me, most likely have a stroke, fall down the stairs, and break her neck. Or she would run and call the police, and I would end up arrested and have a breaking and entering charge added to my rap sheet. But Resmelda stopped on the second floor, and twenty seconds later the soft whir of the vacuum started back up.

I took a deep breath and made my way into the master bedroom. The room looked much like you would expect of a married couple's room. Large bed (unmade), dresser for his clothes, closet for hers, couple paintings on the wall, attached bathroom with a large walk-in shower and Jacuzzi tub.

I riffled through a couple drawers: Adam was a whitie-tighties guy, he was reading some Grisham book, and he brushed with Aquafresh. I got on my hands and knees and looked under the bed.

Nada.

I picked up his book, *The Innocent Man*, off the night stand and read the back copy. Didn't sound half bad. Something slipped from the pages of the book and fluttered to the bed. It was a photograph, a four by six. A shot of fall foliage, a snowcapped mountain range just off-center. It was a nice shot. Good lighting. Probably early morning.

I shrugged. But this wasn't the only thing hidden within the book. I noticed a small bulge and flipped it open to four folded sheets of paper. I unfolded the crisp pages. The letterhead atop the first page read, "Seattle First National."

It was a checking account statement.

I flipped through the statement. Actually, it was two separate checking account statements. The Seattle First National statement was three pages. Then a single page statement from a bank called Bank of Victoria.

I checked the dates. Both statements were for November. I perused the First National statement first. Three pages' worth. According to the statement, Gray's balance was over $2 million. His liquid assets. He no doubt had millions more tied up in his portfolio, stocks, bonds, whatever was the latest trend. And if he'd gotten suspicious that his wife was divorcing him, he might have been trying to diversify even further. If you get my drift.

I flipped to the back page of his transactions and read the total at the bottom. Gray had spent nearly $217,000 in the month alone. I flipped through the pages, noting some of the bigger transactions. A couple were in the low four figures. Both looked to be for furniture. He had six transactions in the fifty-dollar range to Shell Corp. So he filled up his tank about every five days. He had four separate mortgage payments to Allied Morg. All totaling nearly $80,000. The biggest charge, more than $52,000, was to SUFH, which as life goes, I knew stood for Seattle United Funeral Home.

I laid the pages on the bed and picked up the Bank of Victoria statement. Gray had over $13 million in the account. There were four charges for the month of November, including a $22,000 mortgage and a $42,000 mortgage. The first charge was to the same mortgage company as the other four. I wasn't sure which place this was. The second was to a different mortgage company. This, of course, was his condo in the city. That he didn't pay for the condo in cash meant that Ellen didn't know about this particular bank account.

This started me thinking and I checked the name on the account. And surprise, surprise, there was no name. It was a numbered account. The Swiss and Caymans did it best, but the Canadians were a close third. I checked the mailing address: it was a post office box. I had a feeling not too many people knew about this account. Maybe not even the IRS.

The next two charges were even more intriguing. One for $17,345.22 to SPU and another for $200,000 charge to GPI Inc.

I was almost positive SPU was Gray's alma mater, Seattle Pacific University. The logical assumption was that this was a donation check. But why on the numbered account? And why such an odd amount? But I'd never given a donation before so I wasn't sure if they took these out in installments. As for GPI Inc, I wasn't sure what the "G" stood for, but 90 percent of the time PI stood for "private investigator." But most defense attorneys, especially the big-hitters, have a private investigator on the payroll, so I took this with a grain of salt.

I heard a soft squishing sound and froze.

A moment later a voice from the doorway said, "Hey."

CHAPTER 20

I SLOWLY TURNED my head in the direction of the voice. Resmelda had lied; the girls weren't at her parents. The small girl had shoulder-length brown hair and was holding what looked like a Barbie doll. I surmised this would be the younger of the two.

Shelly.

She asked, "Whatcha doin?"

"Oh. I'm just looking around." I folded the picture up in the pages and slipped it in the front pocket of my sweatshirt.

The small girl cocked her head to the side and said, "What are you looking for?"

"I'm not sure."

"Can I help?"

I ignored her question. I placed the book back on the dresser, walked to her, and got down on my haunches. Shelly had her mother's big brown eyes, but that was all. She had her father's nose and lips. She was at that age where everything still looked perfect. A doll herself. As for the doll she was holding, it was one of those 80's Barbies—Punk Barbie or something—hair back in a ponytail, the token headband, tights, jean jacket—collar up—and neon armbands. Reminded me of a girl I dated in high school.

I asked, "What's her name?"

She looked at the doll and said, "Deidra."

"That's a pretty name. What's your name?"

"Shelly."

"That's even prettier. I'm Thomas."

She repeated, "Thomas."

"How old are you, Shelly?"

She clamped the doll to her chest with her elbow so her hands were free and made a five with her left hand. Then she asked, "How old are you?"

I made my fingers into an eight. Shelly opened her mouth wide and exclaimed, "That's *old*."

You're telling me. "Do you go to school?"

"I'm in kindergarten."

"Yeah?"

She nodded. She peeked around my shoulder and said, "This is mommy and daddy's room."

"Is it?"

"Mommy's in heaven."

I didn't know how to respond to this so I kept quiet.

Shelly asked, "Are you looking for the bad man?"

I hope this wasn't her nickname for daddy. "Who is the bad man?"

"He yelled at mommy."

"The bad man yelled at mommy?" I skipped the day they taught how to question a five-year-old, but I remembered something about repeating their statements.

She nodded. Three times. Slowly, the way kids do.

I asked, "Where did the bad man yell at mommy?"

"By the fish."

By the fish? That could mean just about anywhere in Seattle. "What fish are you talking about?"

"They throw them." She threw her doll in the air about six inches, then caught it, cradling it back to her chest.

They throw the fish?

Then it hit me. In the heart of Seattle is a glorified flea market —*glorified* because, unlike a real flea market, things are not cheap and rarely negotiable—about a mile long. Basically, Pike Place Market is a throng of shops selling anything and everything: flowers, fruit, jewelry, shirts, belts, honey, carvings, paintings, salt and pepper shakers, knitted caps, I Love Seattle gear, and everything in between. The most renowned of all the shops is the Pikes Place Fish Company. Whenever there's an order they throw the fish about forty feet, then chop its head off to the delight of the onlookers.

I asked, "Do you mean Pike Market?"

She nodded.

"What did the bad man say?"

She shook her head.

"You don't remember?"

She shook her head again.

"But the man was yelling at her?"

She nodded.

"What did he look like?"

She shrugged.

"Was he older than me?"

She shrugged again. Great time to get shy, kid. She cocked her head to the side and I knew she'd remembered something. She said, "He had a red face."

I wasn't exactly sure what this meant. Did the guy have his face painted? I'd been to Pike a handful of times, and they always had a booth were the kids could paint their faces.

I asked, "He had red paint on his face?"

She shook her head. No paint.

"Was he an Indian?" Sorry, but all political correctness gets thrown out when you're dealing with a five-year-old. Plus, there were at least a dozen Native American shops at Pike.

Shelly thought this was funny and said, "Like Squanto?"

She'd probably just finished learning about the first Thanksgiving in kindergarten. "Yeah, like Squanto."

She shook her head, a smile clinging to the edges of her small mouth.

Shucks. That would have narrowed down the suspect pool. *Um, excuse me, I'm looking for Chief Red Face.*

I asked, "Do you remember anything else?"

She thought for a moment, then said, "He had a big sign."

I thought about this. This could mean one of two things: either he had a booth at Pike or he was picketing. But more importantly, this meant that he might make a habit of hanging out down there.

"Did you know what the sign said?"

"I can't read yet." She added, "But I know the alphabet."

"Do you?"

She proved that she did indeed know the alphabet.

I'd already pushed my luck on time and said my good-byes to Shelly. She insisted I say bye to Diedra, and I was happy to oblige. I was on my way down the hall when I heard footsteps pitter-pattering behind me. I turned.

Shelly was standing behind me. She said, "He had a doggy."

The vacuum cut out. I stood still. A door opened and Resmelda yelled, "Shelly, honey, who are you talking to?"

I put my finger up to my mouth and pointed to her doll. She smiled and said, "Diedra."

Resmelda laughed and said, "Okay, sweetie."

The door closed and the vacuum started back up. I took a deep breath. I whispered, "Who had a doggy?"

"The bad man."

"What did the doggy look like?"

She said he was big and white and that he was a "scary doggy."

I asked her a couple more questions, but she went back to the shrugs. I said, "Can you keep a secret?"

She nodded.

"Don't tell anybody about me, okay? Our little secret."

She nodded. I made her cross her heart. She did. She made me say good-bye to Diedra again, then I quickly descended the stairs. I could see the cord from the vacuum slithering under one of the girl's bedroom doors. I vaulted down the steps and silently slid out the front door. I ran down the cobbled path and exited through a side gate, then hightailed it to my car. For all I knew, Shelly had already spilled the beans, and the police were on their way.

I made it to my car, pulled a U-turn, and drove to the security booth. I was rehearsing the lines I was going to feed to the security guard, but to my delight, the gate swung open automatically. Once I'd made it down a couple blocks, I allowed myself a few calming breaths. On my third exhale, a black Jaguar, with a darkly tinted windows, screeched through a stop sign and zoomed past me. I watched in my rearview mirror as the black blur turned left onto Gray's block. The car's license plate read "NTGLTY."

Adam Gray had made bail. And a killer was on the loose.

CHAPTER 21

"G47."

I looked down at my card.

G50. G48. G46. G59. G53.

No G47.

I glanced to my left and watched Harold. He was hovering an inch over his card, slowly moving his head down the column. I couldn't help but notice he was hovering over column B. At this point it might be better just to be completely blind.

Anyhow, I noticed he had G47 on his board. I took my stamper and stamped it for him, covering the number in an inky green.

He looked at me and said, "I thought she said B411."

I didn't have the heart to tell him this wasn't possible.

We'd been playing Bingo for over an hour and no one had won. I think it was a combination of the twenty people playing being either deaf or blind, the lady yelling out the Bingo numbers having been a recent recipient of a tracheotomy and using one of those electronic vibration thingies—making her sound like Robocop—and two-thirds of the participants being either asleep or dead.

I'd first gotten Bingo an hour ago. My entire sheet had been blacked out for the last thirty minutes. I should also add that I was starving. And cranky.

I leaned into Harold and whispered into his Cinnabon-sized ear, "When is the game over?"

"What game?"

Right.

I asked, "You hungry?"

He nodded.

Thank God.

We made our way to the cafeteria and ate the same things we had eaten and talked about the same things we had talked about on my last visit. Near the end of our meal, like before, the waitress dropped off two slices of white bread wrapped in cellophane. And, like before, twenty minutes later we were sitting on the bench, tossing small pieces of bread into the still lake. The bread would land softly on the glass water, tiny rivulets spreading outward from it, small foothills on a desolate blue.

The ducks never came. Gone south for the winter. I looked at the old form taking the deep inhales from the oxygen tank beside me. I think a part of him knew he would never see the ducks again.

He took a deep breath, the oxygen tank letting out a light puff, and said, "War is terrible."

Harold's first weeks at Fort Bragg were miserable. He'd had little interaction with other men his age, and he found himself uncomfortable in his new surroundings. He didn't mind the commanders, the yelling, or any of the physical hardships. In fact, he quickly rose to the top of his class. He learned early on he was a great deal stronger than his peers. And faster. And smarter. The very reasons many of his fellow infantry mates despised him.

Six weeks in and one of the larger kids, a bully type everyone called "Harker," knocked Harold's tray over in the mess hall. The meek Harold

quickly grabbed a broom and cleaned up the spill, apologizing for what-
ever he'd done.

He was jeered for his cowardly act. They called him everything from
"yellow farmer boy" to "the cowardly lion."

Harold began to doubt his resolve. If he couldn't stick up to a kid his
own age, how could he be expected to kill another soldier in battle?

A week later, a similar confrontation occurred. He was returning his
tray when he felt two hands on his back. The violent shove sent him reel-
ing, sending the contents of his tray onto a group of five soldiers eating
nearby. The five jumped to their feet, and Harold was soon outnumbered
six to one. He brushed himself off, trying to stop the tears in their tracks.

He failed.

Tears began to drip from his cheeks.

The hulking Harker stepped forward and slapped him across the face.
For that split second, Harold was back on the Kings' doorstep. He could
see the precious Elizabeth watching him. In fact, it was as if she was
watching him that very second.

Harker and two other boys spent the next five weeks in the
infirmary.

I shook my head, "You kicked the shit out of all of them?"

"Just three of them. After I kicked in Harker's knee, I smashed
two guys' heads together. The other three ran away before I could
get to them."

I looked at Harold/Rambo and let out a laugh. "I bet no one
ever messed with you again."

"No. No, they didn't."

Harold's unit was Company E, 16th Infantry, 1st Infantry Division.
Harold had quickly moved up the ranks to lieutenant.

On June 6, 1944, Harold and his fellow troops stormed Omaha
Beach, facing the recently formed German 352nd Infantry Division.

He had become close friends with many of his soldiers, but he was closest with one named Thad, whom, incidentally, Harold had put in the infirmary just a little over a year earlier. The two had watched as half their regiment was either killed or badly wounded in three separate battles preceding D-Day. But nothing could have prepared them for the onslaught they would see this day. Fifty thousand Americans stormed Omaha beach on D-Day. Five thousand of them would never return. Thad would be one of those five thousand.

While sitting in hiding, not more than seven feet from his best friend and commander, Thad had taken a piece of shrapnel in his side. His good friend had held his entrails in his hands as he took his final breaths.

I let out a long breath and said, "Fuck."

Harold nodded. "Yeah. Fuck."

Harold didn't eat for a week. Then two. He relinquished his position as lieutenant. He became even more reserved. He wondered how he could possibly get through another year and a half of watching people die. Watching his friends die.

Harold was moved into Poland to do patrol, one of the safer positions at the time. Neither he nor the U.S. Army believed Harold Humphries was still capable of pulling a trigger. Harold vowed he would never take another life. Unless it was his own.

It was a Tuesday in August of his third year. He had less than nine months left in his enlistment. The soldier in charge of mail delivery came into his barracks and began dropping letters and packages on people's beds. In his two and a half years, Harold had received three letters from his parents and three letters from each sister. Normally, Harold received the letters eight or ten weeks after they'd been postmarked. So when the soldier stopped in front of Harold's bed and dropped off a thick stack of letters, Harold was more than taken aback.

He unbound the letters and stared at the top one. It had "Harold Humphries, U.S. Army" scrawled in tight cursive.

He opened the letter and read it. It was from the young girl.

Elizabeth.

My cheeks hurt from smiling.

I said, "She wrote you a letter?"

"She wrote me 129 letters."

"129?"

"One a week for two and a half years."

"What did she say?"

He patted my leg and said, "Everything. She said *everything*."

Harold read the letters every day for a month. All 129 letters. Every day for a month. Then he finally wrote her back, poured his heart out. Told her a day hadn't gone by that he hadn't thought about her. That he wanted to come back to marry her. That he loved her.

The delivery soldier walked by his bed for eight weeks. Eight weeks without stopping. Then the ninth week, he stopped. Harold's heart leapt. He picked up the letter but he couldn't bear to read it. What if she didn't feel the same way?

He kept the letter for a week before reading it. Then he did, with tears running down his cheeks. She felt the same way. She desperately wanted to marry him. She couldn't think of anything that would make her happier.

Harold kept the letter in his pocket while he did his patrols, slept with it under his pillow. He read it every day, sometimes twice. It became his mantra. His reason for living. He could utter every word under his breath like a favorite poem.

Harold paused for a brief moment. Then he slowly began hiking up his right pant leg, exposing a grotesquely white leg. Blue, black, purple, and red veins spider-webbed across the pasty flesh. A black sock was pulled taut halfway up his calf. There was a small bulge at top.

Harold reached his arm down, slid his fingers into his sock, and pulled out a folded piece of paper. The paper appeared soft and supple. Reopened and refolded so many times, the fibers had broken down. It had streaks of brown running across it.

Harold unfolded the letter, and I watched as his large eyes pulled in every word. About halfway through he took two quick inhales through his nose, something I'd yet to see him do.

I felt like I was watching, seeing something I knew I shouldn't be. Like when you accidentally flip to something in the 660s on television.

Harold finished the letter, the folds practically doing themselves, and stuffed it back in his sock. He gave it two quick pats then released the bunched fabric of his pant leg. He gazed across the still lake, hands clasped together on his lap. I watched as he slowly moved his hand from his lap and laid it silently on the bench just to my left.

I stared at the long fingers, bony and brittle. I imagined those fingers working the fields for hours and hours, those fingers wrapped around the butt of a gun, those fingers slinking around a pen and moving briskly across the page. Truly, those fingers had been through war.

I reached out my left hand and slid it beneath the cold fingers. They slowly awakened, intertwining between mine. We held hands like that for a while, waiting for the ducks to return.

CHAPTER 22

WITHIN A SQUARE MILE was the Seattle Convention and Visitors Center, Westlake shopping center, the Seattle Symphony's Benaroya Hall, the Seattle Art Museum, the Pacific Science Center, waterfront shopping along Elliott Bay, Safeco Field and the Seahawks' Qwest Field, yet the Pike Place Market remained the number one tourist attraction in the state of Washington.

I'd come to Pike for two reasons. One, Christmas was less than two weeks away and I had yet to buy Lacy a present. I'd never sent anything overseas, but I imagined I wouldn't be able to overnight it as per my usual method. Second, Shelly's "bad man" might be in attendance. I wasn't overly optimistic, but it was one of those rare Seattle sunny days—there wasn't a cloud in the sky—and I had a feeling people would be out in record numbers.

The place was a zoo. And I use the word "zoo" both literally and figuratively. Seriously, some of these people belonged in cages. I'm not talking about the bums and the beggars who were ever-present. I'm talking about the street performers. Seattle was a hub of culture—art, music, and dance—and the street performers came in hordes.

In just the first block alone, I encountered about ten street performers. Let's see, there was Disco Dancing Guy, Mannequin Guy, Multiple Instrument Guy, Piano Playing Bum, Old Chinese Guy with String Bow-Type Instrument, Hippie Band with One Too Many Sleeping Dogs, Blind Musician Guy, and countless others vying for your shiny quarter or crumpled George Washington.

My first objective was this Polish pastry joint. The line was out the door, but I remembered it moved fast and I hopped in back. I ordered an apple cinnamon roll—they had a special name for it, of course, probably an eight-letter word with no vowels like "plztkjvc"—then moved on to Coffee Shop Alley.

There were about twenty coffee shops, including both the first Starbucks and the first Seattle's Best. I chose Starbucks because I am loyal and they need the money. Plus, they had the Pumpkin Spice latte, which in two months when it was discontinued would land me in rehab. I sipped the beautiful drink and made my way over to watch the Piano Playing Bum.

About sixty people huddled in a half-moon around the man and his dwarf piano. The guy was unkempt and probably hadn't showered in a week, but he was simply amazing. Beethoven meets Gary Busey. He was the one guy who always had a thick crowd and his tip jar was always full. He had long white hair flowing from beneath a knitted cap, a ragged, green army jacket, and knitted gloves. The fingertips had been cut off the gloves, and you could see his fingers flittering away. On the side of his piano he advertised his CD was only $19.95 and he did private parties.

Good to know.

I listened to him play two songs, then stuffed a five-dollar bill in his tip jar.

Saturday was always the busiest day at Pike, at least for the picketers. They congregated nearest the north entrance where a huge park was nestled up on the water. Six or seven different groups congregated on the grassy knoll leading into the market. Some were picketing the war (for and against), some the current traffic problems, some for candidates that I'd never heard of (for positions I'd never heard of), and even one that was picketing *picketing*.

I read a handful of the various signs: *Bush Wants Your Son Dead, Let's Invade Canada, Make I-5 19 Lanes (Both Directions), Vote Balsky Second Vice Treasurer,* and *No More Picketing at Pike.*

Maybe there was an irony convention in town.

Anyhow, I didn't come by a red-faced man with a pooch so I decided to take my chances with the booth owners. Nobody caught my eye in the front half of the market, but I did start and finish my Christmas shopping. I bought Lacy some earrings, a cool bracelet, and a couple pieces of local art she would love.

About the midpoint of the market is the Pike Place Fish Company. Thousands of pounds of fish were displayed behind thick glass as well a hundred feet of shelved ice covered in every fish imaginable. I read some of the handwritten signs: *Fancy Alaskan King Crab, We Pack Fish for Travel, Local Live Mussels, Fresh Catfish, We Deliver to ll Downtown Hotels for Free, Wild Troll King Salmon is Finally Here,* and various others. One section was littered with enormous fish: giant salmon, marlin, swordfish. I guessed some of these weighed upward of sixty pounds.

About a hundred people waited around the wraparound for the four employees, decked out in bright orange jumpers, to start throwing fish. A timid young woman stepped forward from the crowd—she looked like one of those shy kids who steps in front of the microphone at the National Spelling Bee—and asked for a particular kind of fish. The four orange-clad men yelled in unison, "Fish in!" One man went around the ice and grabbed an enormous fish about three feet long and heaved it into the air. The crowd "oohed" and "ahhed" at every toss until the prize fish's head was chopped off and it was neatly packaged. The woman paid for the fish and returned to the sanctity of the crowd.

I watched the ruckus for twenty minutes then started the second leg. I perused for another two hours, making my way down to the far south end. I was watching a young man airbrush a hat when I noticed a man a couple booths down. Or I noticed the big dog perched in front of his booth.

I made my way over. The dog was big and white, a husky. He had those light blue husky eyes. I'm not sure if the dog had a metabolism problem or if his diet consisted entirely of honey and jam—as the two empty jars beside him would indicate—but he was like the Jabba the Hutt of dogs. He didn't seem all that scary and I gave him a rub behind the ears. As for the booth owner, he was more or less a kid, maybe eighteen, maybe twenty. He had dark brown hair and a generous amount of raw acne which gave his face a red cast. Worth a try.

He was working a booth that sold honeys and jams. The young man was just finishing up with an older woman with a cane, packing her many jars into a box.

I sidled up to the table, set the bag holding Lacy's gifts on the ground, and leaned the two paintings I was lugging against the table legs. A bunch of samples were laid out and I picked a straw of honey, which turned out to be peach, and sucked it down. It was heavenly.

The kid wrapped up the transaction with the woman and turned to me. On closer inspection, the kid's face was a mess. Like one of those "before" pictures on the Proactive infomercials.

He smiled and said, "Whaddaya think?"

I thought about telling this kid he needed to invest in some tetracycline honey, but I still had the straw in my mouth and garbled, "Tastes like honey."

The kid found this amusing then said, "Yeah, the peach is one of our best-sellers."

I cocked my head to the side and asked, "That your dog?"

"Yep. Larry."

I looked down, but Larry had moved into the center of the walkway and appeared to be licking up the remnants of a dropped wafflecone. Yeah, that's just what he needed.

I turned back around. The kid was fishing around under the table. He emerged with a honey stick from some secret supply and said, "Give this one a try."

I took the straw from him and squeezed it into my mouth. It was hard to describe, tart but delicious. I gave him a slight nod and he said, "Pomegranate."

He had me taste several of his other flavors, all the while rambling about the quality of his honey, its origins, why it was better than the competition, and so on and so forth. Then he went in for the kill, "So how 'bout we do one of each?"

The kid was good.

I'd forgotten why I'd stumbled to his booth in the first place. I said, "Sure."

He was packaging up my items when I said, "I have a couple questions for you." I added, "And they aren't about honey." I should mention that at this point I had my badge out and dangling in front of me.

Pimply Face's eyes registered the badge and his jaw literally dropped. His Adam's apple went up twice, and I thought he might actually throw it up. Two actions that rank extremely high on my list of suspicious behaviors.

Pimply Face went back to packing up my order then in one quick movement lurched in my direction. I didn't have time to react, the entire contents of a jar of honey blasting me in the face.

For the record, it was the peach.

I'm not going to go into the particulars of honey and its struc-ture, but it's heavy and it's sticky. I had honey in my hair, my nose, my eyes, my ears, my mouth, honey all over my chest, huge globs of it dripping off my chin and into my shirt.

I was not a happy camper.

I did a quick swipe of my face and turned on my heel. My vision was a bit blurry on account of the honey glaze on my contacts, but I could still make out the back of the kid's head as he darted through the crowd. I figured he had a ten-step head start. I tore through the crowd screaming for people to get out of my way. Most people did. I turned a corner and smashed into a man strumming a guitar. I had just enough time to see that he was wearing dark sunglasses and a top hat. I struck the man hard and we both tumbled to the ground in a heap. I fell on the man's guitar case and pushed myself up.

I said, "Sorry. I told you to watch out."

The man said, "I'm blind."

Right. I guess watching out wouldn't be his strong suit.

I turned. The kid was now about ten booths ahead of me, screeching around a large booth filled with flowers. I resumed the chase.

At some point I noticed something clinging to my chest. I glanced down. There were five or six quarters, three one dollar bills, and one ten dollar bill sticking to my honey-drenched sweatshirt. The blind guy must not be half bad.

I made it to the flower booth. It was one of the longer booths, covered with bright bouquets. People were backed up four deep, sniffing and poking at the flowers. I needed to make up some ground on the kid, and before I knew what I was doing, I'd leapt onto the closest table. The table wobbled but held. There were four Asian women working the booth, and they all began screaming. One of the women grabbed a broom and swung it at me as I darted across the long booth. I'm not going to sugarcoat it; many a plant died that day.

I hopped off the platform, pulled the $14.25 off my sweatshirt, and plopped it on the counter. Karma and all.

A second round of screaming ensued, and I peered down the length of the table. At first I thought it was a polar bear. It wasn't. It was Larry. He had decided to join the chase and had somehow jumped up onto the wobbly tables. I watched rapt as Larry slowly, methodically, knocked over—or ate—every flower in sight. Had I not been in the midst of a chase, I imagine I would have been rolling around on the ground in hysterics.

But back to the chase.

Less than twenty yards behind me, there was a stairwell and I figured the kid probably went down. I took the stairs four at a time. When I reached the bottom I could make out Pimply Face going up the stairs at the opposite end. A couple dozen people were waiting in line for the restrooms, but for the most part the corridor was barren. I sprinted the stretch and vaulted up the stairs and into the sunlight.

I could see the kid huffing and puffing in the middle of the street. His eyes bugged out when he saw me, and he took off. He bolted left, crashing through a booth selling an assortment of multi-colored pepper mills. The kid ran through the back of the booth, knocking over a beam in the process, and the entire booth came crashing down.

It was a good move; the kid put some distance between the two of us. I ran around the booth and entered into a densely packed walkway. We were nearing the Pike Place Fish Company where the crowd had quadrupled in the last hour.

I could see the kid weaving his way through the people. I decided to make up some ground and darted behind the ice shelving to where the men in orange jumpers were standing, thinking if I could cut through the back, I would come out before the kid, then just wait for him to emerge. At least that's how I figured it in my head.

I heard the first "ooh," then a loud "ahh."

I never saw the fish coming. It hit me hard in the chest. It felt like a truck. Apparently, someone had ordered a sperm whale.

I lay flat on my back, eyes closed, gasping for a breath that would never come. The last thing I remember was the sensation of a tongue running down the length of my face.

Larry.

Then I blacked out.

CHAPTER 23

I LOOKED up at the doctor. He was all white. White hair, white mustache, white coat, white face. His name was also White, Dr. White. Dr. White was holding something black. On closer inspection, it appeared to be X-ray film. He shook his head from side to side. I hate it when they do that

He said, "It looks like you've suffered a collapsed lung, Mr. Prescott."

I readjusted myself on the bed—a blinding pain shooting through my chest—and managed, "Is that bad?"

"It isn't *good.*" He added, "We actually thought you'd suffered a heart attack until we looked at the X-rays. You were reaching oxygen levels in the ninety-eighth percentile with your right lung alone."

To my knowledge, I'd never reached the ninety-eighth percentile in anything in my life. "Can you call my tenth grade Trigonometry teacher and tell her that?"

He threw me a half smile, probably his thirtieth of the day. He turned and said, "Well, what we're going to have to do is pump up that left lung of yours."

Sounded easy enough.

"It will take about twenty-four hours. And I'd be lying if I said it was pleasant."

Not exactly the words a patient longs for. But I guess it's better than "It's malignant" or "It's going to have to come off" or "I hope you didn't buy any green bananas."

He explained what exactly would be taking place, and he was right, it didn't sound pleasant. They would make a small incision just under my armpit and insert a hose. The hose would vacuum out all the air surrounding the outside of my lung. In a sense, they were *sucking* my lung back open. The doctor walked to the doorway, then turned and said, "A nurse will be in shortly to get things started."

Twenty-seven minutes later, there was a knock at the door and Patty walked into my life. How would one describe Patty without invoking the gag reflex? I think she might have been a patient and won some *be a nurse for a day* sweepstakes. She had two moles. One on her forehead and one just under her chin. Let me tell you about these two moles. First off, they had a combined surface area of a tennis ball. Second, these two moles could have been the "after" picture on a Hair Club for Men infomercial. And third, they jiggled. Like Jell-O molds.

If Patty wasn't scary enough, she was pushing this huge machine. Using my uncanny detective abilities, I deduced that this was the machine I would soon be attached to, ergo, it was the machine which would *suck* my lung open. Seriously, get Wes Craven on the phone.

Patty slipped this little thing on my finger—she called it a pulse oximeter—that monitored my oxygen levels. She was putting an IV in my arm when it happened. I'm fine with needles, stick one in my eye if you please. But I was *not fine* with the proximity of Patty's mole. As she was leaning down to insert the needle, Patty's mole danced in the breeze like a Sugar Ray Leonard punching bag. Just as she found my vein, Mr. Mole brushed my shoulder. My arm flew up, Patty screamed, and I gagged—all within a nanosecond of one another. Patty covered her face and ran from the room.

I was confused until I looked at my finger. There, on the plastic contraption on my left pointer finger, was Patty's mole.

I may have screamed.

Two nurses barged through the door and asked what was wrong. I told them. One of them turned white. The other picked the contraption off the floor thirty feet away—where I'd thrown it —and outfitted me with a fresh one.

The doc came in twenty minutes later. He asked if I wanted to be put to sleep or if I wanted a local anesthesia. I told him to run the operation by me a second time. He said the surgery was simple enough; he would make a small incision under my armpit, insert a "chest tube" into my "pleural cavity," and the "chest tube" would be attached to the "suction device" which I would be hooked up to for "the foreseeable future."

Anesthesia, please.

I woke up two hours later in a fog. The sterile post-op room slowly came into focus, as did the small child in the bed directly opposite mine. Apparently, I'd booked a double. And here I thought I was getting a suite. Looking back on it, I'm fairly certain Patty was responsible for this decision. I must have ripped off her *favorite* mole. I did her a favor if you ask me. A dermatologist would have charged a hundred bucks to lance that atrocity. If he charged by the ounce, it would have been twice that.

The kid's name was Danny. Danny was twelve. Danny had just had his tonsils removed. Because Danny couldn't talk, Danny had a big pad and Danny would write messages on his big pad and Danny would wave his big pad at Thomas until Thomas read it. This is how Thomas would learn all the aforementioned data about Danny. Thomas would also learn that Danny liked to play basketball. And draw. And fish. And annoy the hell out of Thomas.

After about an hour of this, young Danny picked up some little video game thingy and started playing it. Thank God.

I watched the clock for twenty minutes. Then I watched my heart beat for twenty minutes. Funny thing is, when Danny was annoying the shit out of me, the time went considerably faster.

I asked, "What is that thing?"

He put the game down, scribbled on his pad, and held it up. It read "Nintendo DS."

I'd never heard of it. "What game are you playing?"

He wrote some game I'd never heard of.

I asked, "Do you have Tetris?"

He nodded. Then he wrote, "Do you want to play it?"

Oh, sweet, sweet Danny.

Danny walked the thing over, and with a bunch of jostling and cajoling he showed me how to play it. Needless to say, they'd made drastic improvements since the days of the Gameboy. Danny watched me play a game then retired back to his bed.

I was just getting the hang of things when I noticed Danny's pad being waved in my peripheral. I looked up. Written on his pad was, "Can I have it back now?"

I smiled and said, "Ten more minutes."

He wrote ferociously, then held his pad up again. It read, "That's what you said two hours ago."

Actually it was three hours ago. I smiled at him and punched the button on the side of my bed. Thirty seconds later, a nurse came bursting through the door. She ran to my bed and said, "Is everything okay? You tripped your panic button."

"I'm fine. But he won't stop screaming." I pointed at young Danny.

She looked at Danny. She did the Poor Baby headshake then proceeded to pull a syringe from her waist and stick it into Danny's IV.

Danny looked confused. I smiled at him and waved. Night, night, Danny. Three minutes later he was out cold.

I played the video game until it ran out of batteries. I tossed it to Danny and it landed on his chest with a thud. He didn't budge. Still out. Speaking of which, the medicine they'd given me was wearing off and I called the nurse for another dose. She obliged, and a couple minutes later, I too was in a narcotic-induced slumber.

I woke up a couple hours later in a groggy stupor. I sat up. Danny was awake and had a message waiting for me, "Rise and shine, sleepyhead."

I looked for something to throw at him, but everything in reach was bolted down.

Thirty seconds later Danny had a new message, "Grumpy. Paging Dr. Grumpy."

I closed my eyes and mentally shoved Danny's pen and pad down his throat. When I opened my eyes, a lady was standing in the doorway, and it wasn't Patty. I glanced at the heart rate monitor. Luckily, it was facing away from the woman in the doorway's field of vision. The red numbers jumped from 63 to 83 to 97 to 106 to 118.

Not a good sign.

I said, "Are you here for your measles, mumps, and rubella shot too?"

Erica smiled and said, "Got mine last year."

She took a couple steps toward my bed. For the record, she was wearing blue jeans and a tan jacket. She had a pink hat pulled down low on her forehead. Not to mention, she *looked* like she *smelled* good. If that makes any sense. I glanced at the heart rate monitor.

115.

127.

135.

Erica plopped down in the chair nearest my bed and grabbed my hand. She smiled and said, "Howya feeling?"

She was directly underneath the heart rate monitor which was now reading 161 in big red numbers. If I didn't get my heart rate under control here in the next couple seconds, three nurses were going to come crashing through the door.

I slipped my hand from hers and said, "Like Brett Favre on Monday."

She flashed an uncomfortable smile. At my slipping my hand away or my dumb joke, she didn't specify.

I asked, "How did you know I was here?"

"I have my ways."

I raised an eyebrow.

She said, "I heard honey was involved."

She must have read the police report. I nodded. "Peach."

"They ended up catching the kid, you know." She paused, then added, "How did you know?"

"How did I know *what*?"

"About his secret stash?"

"The pomegranate? He let me sample it. Tastes a little like a mango wrapped in seaweed."

"I'm talking about the *other* stash."

I tried to sit up. "Drugs?"

"Yeah. He had a couple boxes of honey that was infused with methamphetamines."

Meth honey. No wonder he freaked when I showed him my badge.

Erica studied me for a second then said, "If you didn't know about the drugs, then why were you chasing him?" She stood up. "Please tell me this doesn't have anything to do with Ellen Gray."

I put up my hands. "Settle down there. Now, who is this Ellen Gray you speak of?"

She shook her head from side to side. Like she had Parkinson's. She looked like she belonged on the eighth floor.

She stammered, "I thought you said you weren't going to get involved."

"I'm *not* involved. I'm sitting in a hospital bed with a big tube in my side getting my lung sucked open."

She sat back down.

"But for the sake of argument, why don't you tell me how the case is progressing?"

"You promise you won't get involved?"

"Scout's honor." I failed to mention the closest I'd ever been to a scout was playing Stratego.

She took a deep breath. "As you know, we arrested him last Thursday. He spent a total of forty-five minutes behind bars. This guy has connections like you wouldn't believe. People are scared of him. Cops don't want to go near him. Judges are ducking and covering like a field full of prairie dogs. I've never seen anything like it. Anyhow, a grand jury is convening starting Monday. They'll decide if there's enough evidence against him to mandate a trial."

"And?"

"And what?"

"And is there?"

"An overwhelming amount."

I laughed. This was inconvenient and I nearly threw up from the pain that coursed through my chest. Erica patted my arm and asked, "You okay?"

Her touch was electric. The pain shooting through my chest was the last thing on my mind. I took a deep breath and said, "Yeah, I'm all right."

What I wanted to say was, "Come on, kid, get a clue. Why would Adam Gray, a man who reached the pinnacle of his profession by making a habit of not making mistakes—*any*, *ever*—leave a trail of cookie crumbs? It was an obvious setup. Such an obvious setup that I was starting to think that Adam Gray had set up his own setup. But again, he was too smart. Lawyers are the experts of persuasion and mind molding. And they do it without the jury knowing. Adam Gray was a master of manipulation. That's what made him the best. If Adam Gray had committed this murder, Ellen Gray's body would never have been found. This I knew for certain.

I stared into Erica's deep hazel eyes. She had these tiny little green flecks, like little chunks of ivy growing from her perfect pupil. There was an intelligence in those eyes, the same intelligence I saw in the back of a spoon. She'd get to the truth eventually. I just hoped it was before I caused myself any more bodily harm.

There was a knock at the door and Patty popped in her head, or popped in her mole if you want to get technical. She said, "Visiting hours are over."

I scratched my chin and said, "Thanks, Patty." She didn't find this humorous and disappeared.

Erica stood up, gave my hand a final squeeze, and said, "See ya round, Mr. Prescott."

"See ya round, Miss Frost."

She walked from the room, giving me a quick glance and a smile, then slipped through the doorway.

I took a calming breath and laid my head back. I could see Danny waving his stupid pad at me and I read what he'd written.

I smirked.

Yeah, kid. I did.

CHAPTER 24

I WIPED the sleep from my eyes and licked my teeth with my tongue. A yawn tickled the inside of my nose and began crawling down my throat. I tried to fight it off, but in the end my body relented to the yawn, invoking muscles I had no control over to flex. It felt like someone had a crowbar wedged between my third and fourth ribs and was trying to pry them apart, a pain just a notch below the one emanating from my left lung.

You know that guy from *Indiana Jones and the Temple of Doom* who gets his heart ripped out then gets lowered into the lava pit? Well, he could *maybe* relate to what I was going through. I mention this because the only movies my father owned were the *Indiana Jones* collection, and I had watched each movie three times in the last five days. I'm still a tad puzzled by the end of *Raiders of the Lost Ark.* I mean, did Spielberg sleep with the special effects guy's wife or something?

Seriously.

Anyhow, I lolled my head to the left and peered at the glass coffee table. It was littered with peanut butter and jelly debris, a half-finished bag of Oreos, and a barrage of juice boxes. Talk about déjà vu. For a split second I was back in Maine, it was

Thanksgiving morning, and I had just woken up from a horrible nightmare.

I pondered sitting up, but the thought was fleeting.

I'm not sure if it was the fact I hadn't seen the sun for over three weeks. Or if I was in withdrawal from the Vicodin. Or if it was because I hadn't been able to exercise in over a week. Or because I hadn't talked to Lacy in the past couple days. Or if it was Ellen Gray's death. Or Adam Gray's guilt. Or my incompetence. Or if I was falling in love *again*. Or if I had some residual feelings for Alex. Or a combination of all of these. But I was having a slight bout of depression. And by slight, I mean severe. And by depression, I mean wanting to jump off the Space Needle. But that would involve getting off the couch so I was at a bit of a crossroads.

Maybe I needed one of those seasonal depression lamps.

I pushed myself off the couch, made my way to the VCR, popped out *Indiana Jones and the Temple of Doom*, and slipped in *Indiana Jones and the Last Crusade*. (On a side note, after much deliberation, I had decided that I needed to buy a whip. Just saying.)

I was halfway through the movie—the part where Sean Connery scares all the birds with his umbrella and they fly into the plane's propeller—when it happened. I'd made a peanut butter and jelly sandwich and decided to throw a couple Oreos in the mix. It wasn't half bad. But I did get overly aggressive with the jelly, and a huge blob of it leaked out the top of my PBJ&O and landed between my legs on the sofa.

Just when you think you've hit rock bottom.

I cleaned it up using the powerful spray of a juice box, sort of a lazy man's power wash—which worked surprisingly poorly—and I succeeded in turning a small purple stain into a large, wet, pink stain.

I finished the sandwich, licked my fingers, stood up, picked the cushion up, flipped it over, and put it back down. I turned to sit but caught myself. I just stood there staring at the cushion. It was a bit dusty, but for the most part in pristine condition.

I shook my head and smiled.

Going up the stairs was harder than I expected, and by the time I reached Lacy's room my newly inflated lung was wheezing and I was seeing constellations. Once Orion's belt disappeared, I picked up Lacy's pink phone and dialed information. I asked for the number for Adam Gray and Associates and decided to pay the extra seventy-five cents for them to dial the number for me. No one answered. I thought about trying "Adam Gray," but there would be multiple listings in the Seattle area and surely the Adam Gray I was seeking had an unlisted number. I searched my brain for the number the nanny had rattled off on my visit. The first three numbers I tried were unsuccessful. I swapped a couple numbers around and hit pay dirt.

She picked up on the third ring.

I asked, "Is this Resmelda?"

"This is she."

"This is Agent Todd Gregory. I hope I didn't get you in any trouble the other day."

She made a *hmmph* sound, then said, "First, your name is Thomas something or other. And two, you only got me fired, deported, and sued is all. And I'm never allowed to see the girls again." She started sobbing.

I leaned my head back, took a deep breath, and said, "What happened?"

After she composed herself, she said, "Mr. Gray came home not long after you left. He burst through the door screaming. He fired the security guy, Ralph, on the spot. Poor Ralph. His wife is due with twins in January. I told Mr. Gray we only talked for a couple minutes, then you left. But he wouldn't believe me. He thinks you were inside the house. Something about drawers being opened."

If I remembered correctly, I'd made a conscious effort to leave everything precisely as I'd found it. I had a feeling maybe Shelly had done some drawer pulling after I'd left. Or maybe he'd noticed that his bank statements were suddenly MIA. Either way, it didn't matter. Adam Gray had been suspicious enough that he'd gone to look at the security tapes at the security booth and knew it was me. Hopefully he didn't have any tapes of me breaking and entering. But if he had, I suspect I would have been arrested. Or worse.

By the end of Resmelda's narrative, I started to feel partly responsible for her getting fired. And deported. And sued. But only partly.

I said, "I need to talk to Mr. Gray."

"Haven't you done enough?" The inflection in her voice denoted that I had, in fact, done enough.

I said, "I'll get you your job back."

She was silent for a moment, then said, "How are you going to do that?"

"I can prove Mr. Gray is innocent."

"How?"

"A couch cushion."

"How is a couch cushion going to prove Mr. Gray is innocent?"

"You're just going to have to trust me."

She was silent.

"If you ever want to see your girls again, you're going to have to trust me."

"Okay. But I don't know his cell phone number. It was programmed into the phone they gave me and he took it back."

Damn.

I could try him at his office on Monday, but I had a feeling if I walked through his office doors I might not walk out. Resmelda interrupted my thoughts, "He'll be at the Ritz Carlton tonight."

"The Ritz Carlton. Why?"

"The office Christmas party. The Daisy Room. I think it starts at 7:00. I was supposed to attend." She choked up, "I was going to take the girls."

I tried to console her, telling her in eleven different ways that everything would turn out just fine.

She sniffed. "So you'll get me my girls back?"

"Do peanuts grow on trees?"

"No."

"I thought they did."

"I don't think so."

"Never mind. I'll get you your girls back."

I could feel her smile on the other end. I looked at the clock above the stove: it was 6:47 p.m. I hung up with Resmelda.

I had a party to crash.

CHAPTER 25

THE RITZ CARLTON is located in downtown Seattle. As far as hotels go, the Ritz is top of the line. It doesn't get much swankier. The average room goes for three bills, suites for five, and presidential suites are in the low four figures. Ballrooms are rumored to be reserved years in advance. The main ballroom, a decade.

I pulled my car into the valet area and stepped out. A kid dressed in a white shirt and black vest opened my door. He looked me up and down and tried to stifle a laugh.

I hadn't had much to work with in the wardrobe department and I was clad in some of my dad's snazzier dinner wear. I was guessing the Adam Gray and Associates Christmas Extravaganza would be black tie. I was dressed in one of my father's old tuxedos, circa 1985, and I imagine I looked like I'd just walked off the set of the last episode of *Dynasty*.

I made my way through the revolving doors and into the mezzanine. A large sign listed each of the four ballrooms. The Rose Room was the Starbucks Christmas party. The Tulip Room was the Oracle Christmas Party. The Daisy Room was the Adam Gray and Associates Christmas Party.

The Daisy Room was located on the seventh floor. I stepped off the elevator and followed arrows until I heard the party.

A woman sat at an antique writing table at the entrance. She had a name tag: Tracy. Tracy asked my name and I gave her one. She asked how to spell it and I guessed. She wrinkled her nose and said, "I'm not seeing you here."

I told her I was a special guest of Adam's. She scribbled on a name tag and handed it to me. She smirked and said, "Here you go, *Percival*." She added, "Table 62."

"How many tables are there?"

"Sixty-two."

Ah, the leper table. Just my luck, I get stuck with the secretary with the lazy eye and the lawyer with halitosis.

"Just out of curiosity, how many are you expecting tonight?"

She said including lawyers, paralegals, secretaries, plus guests they were expecting close to three hundred.

As I entered the ballroom, I noticed half the people were sitting, the other half making small talk or congregating near the bar. Two couples had already made their way to the dance floor and they slow danced to the smooth styling of Eddie Money.

As I guessed, most men were decked out in penguin suits and the women were clad in recently acquired dresses. If Gray's lawyers were anything like him, most of these wives hadn't had a reason to dress up, well, probably since the last Christmas party.

Waiters zoomed in and out of the crowds with trays filled with champagne, wine, and hors d'oeuvres. I surveyed the crowd for any sign of Gray. I didn't see him, but I did spot his receptionist, Sunny. She was wearing a black dress, cut low, showing off her plastic Tetons. She was surrounded by no less than seven different guys.

Men are pigs.

Needless to say, I headed in that direction.

Just kidding.

I made my way over to the bar and the bartender rattled off a bunch of beers. I told him to bring me whatever was the coldest. He brought me a Sam Adams. It tasted a lot like beer. Which I like in a beer.

The guy next to me struck up a conversation. He asked what year my tuxedo was from. I told him I took his wife to the prom in this tuxedo. He found this hysterical and slapped me on the shoulder. His eyes were already starting to glaze over and he said, "I've always liked you, Percival."

I didn't have the heart to tell him that he met me close to sixty —no, seventy—seconds earlier. His name was Max. Max had a story for everything, and whether or not they were true, they kept my attention for three more beers. A public service announcement here, if anyone ever starts off a story with the words "So I'm at this donkey show...," do yourself a favor and rip off your ears.

Around 8:30, I spotted Mr. Adam Gray. He had just started making the rounds. He got about halfway through the tables when they started asking people to take their seats for dinner. Max attempted to drag me to his table, which was table 7, only three tables from Adam's. I respectfully declined. I didn't want to get thrown out before I got my hands on some chicken cordon bleu.

I retired to table 62.

There were three open seats and I took one with my back to the center of the room. The secretary with the lazy eye was actually the secretary without a chin. There was no definitive spot where her neck ended and her face began. So you had Chinless, then you had Stutter, Third-Person Paul, Wig Lady, Manic Depressive Asian, Hook Arm, Adult Braces, and 80s Tuxedo.

All and all, the who's who of birth defects, personality disorders, and vagabonds off the street.

Go Table 62!

We made small talk and I lied quite a bit.

The chicken cordon bleu was excellent. Hook Arm didn't want hers and asked if I wanted it. I said yes and she proceeded to slide her chicken onto my plate using her hook. I did not eat it. Dessert was carrot cake and I had two slices.

Adam stood up and gave a toast about the past year, how proud he was of his team, that the year ahead looked even more promising, and for everyone to enjoy themselves. He failed to mention that in the new year he would probably go on trial for his life.

Moot point, I guess.

After a champagne toast, the music started back up, plates were cleared, and people started to mingle. Women huddled around tables, men flocked to the bar, a dozen couples headed for the dance floor.

I bid farewell to my comrades at table 62, albeit with a strong sense that Chinless and Third Person Paul were going to make some poor decisions. I overheard Paul say, "Paul doesn't care about chins."

I made my way to Adam's table and sidled up to the group of six guys, including my friend Max, that had congregated there. Adam was telling a golfing anecdote, and I worked my way into the inner circle. I was two people to Adam's left.

Adam was saying, "...sand trap was thirty feet deep. Michelson bets me fifty large he'll get up and down. I tell him he's on. He reaches into his bag, and I shit you not, he takes out his seven wood. He takes a half swing, the ball runs up the thirty-foot lip, drips over, and ends up three inches from the cup. Best golf shot I've ever seen."

I leaned in and said, "I once saw this kid hit a ball through a windmill."

A couple guys gave a slight chuckle. Max found this hilarious. Adam looked at me directly and smiled. "Enjoying the party. Mr. Prescott?"

"I am. Chicken was a bit dry, but I'm sure you didn't cook it."

"I'll pass that on to Wolfgang."

After an awkward second, he said, "I'm glad you stopped by so

I can tell you in person that I drafted up a civil suit for trespassing. I plan to enter it into court tomorrow morning."

I could have denied ever being there. I could have concocted a story. I could have done a lot of things. I went with, "Calvin Klein, huh?"

He cocked his head to one side.

"I was surprised. I would have taken you for a Fruit of the Loom guy."

He took a deep breath. Exhaled. "Please leave before I have you thrown out."

No one moved or said anything for a good three seconds. I took a long sip of beer.

Adam waved over a couple of gentlemen, and they politely asked me to leave. Then they asked me impolitely to leave, which involved my arms being wrenched behind my back.

The entire room went quiet.

The DJ had even killed the music.

As I was being dragged out I yelled, "I know you didn't kill your wife."

A hush fell over the crowd.

Adam locked eyes with me, and I said with a smile, "And I can prove it."

CHAPTER 26

THE SECURITY GUARDS let me go. The only sound was that of Adam storming in my direction. He turned me around and pushed me forward through the double doors and into the hallway. We made our way to the elevators, called for one, and stepped inside. Adam hit the emergency stop button and said, "This better be good."

Just to clear the air, if I was to go toe-to-toe with Adam Gray, I wouldn't win. But then again, neither would he. There's a good chance we'd both end up paying for the other's reconstructive surgery.

I brushed my tuxedo smooth and said, "I came here as a favor."

"You call crashing my Christmas party and embarrassing me in front of my employees a *favor*."

I laughed.

Adam didn't.

I took a deep breath and said, "You said the night your car was stolen, you were across the street getting a drink, and were drugged, beat up, and had your keys stolen."

He nodded.

"Then the next morning, you woke up in your condo. You had no idea how you got there."

"Right."

"According to the navigational system on your yacht, it was taken out that night at 11:25 p.m., driven seventy miles out to the middle of the Sound, stopped for exactly two minutes, then driven to where it was found in Edmonds at 3:17 a.m."

"That's what they tell me."

"According to you, you can't account for your whereabouts from ten that evening until nine when you woke up the next morning."

"Again, correct."

"So, technically, you could have been on your yacht."

He took a deep breath. Let it out. I could see him visualizing twelve of his peers digesting this information. Finally, he said, quite objectively, "Technically, yes."

"Now we're getting somewhere."

I smiled.

Gray lurched forward and hit the emergency stop button. He said, "I think you've wasted enough of my time."

I moved in front of him and slapped the button. "If you'd give me one more fucking minute, I'm about to give you your life back."

He squinted at me, as if he might be able to read my mind if he tried hard enough.

"When I was in your office that day, I noticed a stain on two of your couch cushions."

He raised his eyebrows. "Stain? That couch is worth twenty-five large. I think I'd know if it had stains."

"I'm sure you would. It'd been scrubbed then flipped upside down."

"I would never do that."

"I know you wouldn't." That's how I'd put it together. I had no problem flipping the cushion over, but OCD Adam could never. "The stain was blood."

"Blood? On my couch?" He looked queasy just thinking about it.

I helped him along. "You made it back there that night."

"What do you mean?"

"I'm guessing you were drugged. Probably some sort of tranquilizer."

"Okay."

"Here's my theory. October 15, someone abducts and kills your wife. They dump her body in the ocean, but somewhere they have access to. Maybe they weight her body down in a shallow area, or tie her up to a pier, could be anywhere. I think this nut has it out for you too. Maybe he wants both Grays tied up to his pier. So, come the Sunday before Thanksgiving, he waits for you outside the bar and hits you with some sort of tranquilizer. But you don't go down. You put up a fight and get away, but not before you sustain a couple injuries. Somehow the guy gets your keys—maybe they slip out of your pocket during the struggle. The guy finds the gun in your glove compartment and has this brilliant idea.

"Maybe he can't kill you, but he can put you away for life. He retrieves Ellen's body from wherever he has it stashed, takes out your yacht, dumps Ellen's body overboard, and plants the gun. As for you, you're drugged up, bloody, moving on instinct alone. You're close to your office building. By some miracle, you make it to the garage, the private elevator, and into your office. Then to the couch."

Gray went quiet. His brow furrowed. I could tell he was running this through his head, weighing its plausibility. Finally he said, "If this is true, then I would be on the surveillance camera in my office."

"Right. Which you have done by a third party. They store the images on a hard drive. And, if I'm correct, then you can't alter any images."

"Nope. But I can log into my account and watch the live feed from my office or I can go into the archives and watch any point in time."

I cocked my head.

He hit the emergency stop button once more, then hit the button for the twenty-second floor. He said, "Business center."

We stepped off the twenty-second floor and Adam slid a card in a conference room door lock. He pulled the door open and the lights went up. At the head of a large conference table sat a laptop. He flipped the top up, turned it on, and was on the Internet in a matter of seconds. After a couple of quick clicks, the image on the computer monitor was superimposed on the projection screen on the wall behind us.

I watched as he typed in his security company's website, then his account number and password. The page refreshed and nine separate images popped up; his desk, the bookcase, the bar, the aquarium, the filing cabinets, the elevator, the doors, the couch, and the back wall.

He clicked on Archives and typed in "November 19"—the night his yacht was taken out and presumably Ellen's body was thrown overboard—then moved numbers around to start at 8:00 p.m. The page refreshed but looked identical. The plant was smaller.

I said, "Fast forward."

He hit the double arrows and we watched as the time moved quickly. By 9:00, nothing had happened. Then 10:00. Then 11:00. Then the date moved to the twentieth.

Adam looked at me.

Shit.

He shook his head, "Happy?"

He started to flip the laptop closed when I said, "Wait."

He turned and watched the big screen. The clock read,

"12:11:54 a.m." The light over the elevator had just lit up. I pointed to it. "Someone's on their way up."

He clicked the play button on the computer screen. We looked at each other, then back to the screen. After about six seconds the elevator doors opened and a body flopped out.

It was Adam.

———

We watched the rest of the video.

A bloodied and disoriented Adam crawled on his hands and knees to the couch. Nothing else would happen for seven hours.

At exactly 7:12:06 a.m., a head peeked into the office. It was an older woman with white hair.

I said, "Who's that?"

"June. She cleans the office every Monday morning."

The white-haired woman on the screen took another step into Gray's office. Maybe June saw the blood or smelled it. Either way, she made her way to Adam and shook him. When he didn't respond, she became agitated and frazzled. She attempted to flip him over. After a couple tries, she got him on his side. He was covered in blood. She started crying.

After composing herself, she dragged him off the couch, laid him on his back on the floor, then walked out of the room. She returned with two bottles of cleaning supplies, a sponge, and a couple towels. She began scrubbing the cushions.

Adam was fighting down a smile. I couldn't blame him. This wouldn't exonerate him completely, but it would put a large dent in the State's case against him.

We fast-forwarded as June scrubbed for ten minutes, then flipped over the cushions and replaced them on the couch. Adam hit play. June exited, then returned. She attempted to wake Adam for over a minute. He appeared to open his eyes once or twice, even murmur a couple words, but he was still very much under the influence of the drug. In an impressive display of strength, the tiny woman reached under Adam's armpits and fireman-dragged him into the elevator. Then the two disappeared.

I said, "I'm gonna take a stab in the dark here and guess that June also cleans your condo?"

He nodded.

"So she would have keys to the condo?"

"She would."

"And I'm guessing she's been with you a long time and is loyal to a fault."

"Correct."

So June thought he killed his wife. But she kept quiet. I think it was safe to assume June had a substantial Christmas bonus coming her way.

Adam stuck out his hand and said, "I don't know how to thank you."

I told him he could start by dropping the civil suit and giving Resmelda her job back.

He told me to consider it done. He removed a card from his pocket and handed it to me. He patted me on the shoulder and said, "If you ever need anything at all, don't hesitate to call."

I stuck the card in my pocket. I wouldn't.

CHAPTER 27

THEY CELEBRATED Christmas on the twenty-second, which I found odd seeing as how it wasn't Christmas, or Christmas Eve, or even Christmas Eve Eve for that matter. But they were old, and if they wanted to celebrate Arbor Day in August, then I'd plant my tree in August.

Harold had mentioned on my last visit that none of his family was going to make it out for the holiday. And it's not like I had much else to do.

I knocked on the door and Harold answered. He was wearing a red turtleneck and a Santa hat. Sort of like what Santa would look like if he was eighty-six pounds, had *extensive* electrolysis, and had died three or four years earlier.

I wasn't exactly sure what one buys for someone who can say the words "So me and Patton are shooting the shit when Lee comes in . . ." and be completely serious, but I'd decided on a gift certificate for Lasik. Just kidding. I got him a subscription to *Girls Gone Wild*.

He took the two videos from me, looked around his small room for a good minute, then slid them under the couch cushions. Good thinking.

Harold told me he had to go to the bathroom and to "sit tight." Fifty-five minutes later, he returned with a small gift in his little basket and held it up. It was about the size of a coffee mug and haphazardly wrapped. A large white bow was stuck to a crumpled section of wrapping paper at top. Harold held the gift out and said, "For you."

Lacy had bought me tickets to the upcoming Seattle Seahawks playoff game, but the presents she'd sent wouldn't arrive until after Christmas. So there was a good chance the small package before me—which I was almost certain *was* a coffee cup—would be the only present I opened for Christmas. I ripped off the wrapping paper and revealed a coffee mug stuffed with half a banana and a Tapioca Snackpack.

I thanked him for his generosity, and the guy waved me off like he'd just bought me a brand new Lexus.

We retired to the Christmas celebration, and Harold and I ate at a table with two of the CNN-iles and their families. It was a mix of young and old. Daughters, sons, nieces, nephews, and even a couple babies. The meal was good, and after they'd cleared our plates, we played reindeer games for over an hour. Then a couple old-timers jumped on the piano and we sang Christmas carols and danced or—in the case of three couples in mobility scooters—played bumper cars.

At around 7:00, the party fizzled. Apparently, colostomy bags don't empty themselves. But I wasn't ready to leave. I wanted to hear some more of Harold's story.

I followed behind Harold on the way back to his building. He stopped, turned, and said, "You know what I really want?"

I shook my head.

"A Slurpee."

"A Slurpee?"

"Yeah. A Slurpee."

So Harold and I went for Slurpees.

———

Harold was buckled in the passenger seat, his walker lying across the whole of the backseat. When we'd first made it to the car, Harold had asked if he could drive. I told him if it was up to me he could drive the car off a cliff, but according to the seven documents I had to sign and the urine sample I had to leave with the prune at the front desk, he wasn't allowed to drive.

There was a gas station two miles up the road, and I stopped, ran in, and grabbed a couple Slurpees. Back in the car, I handed Harold his Mountain Dew Kryptonite Ice Slurpee and said, "Where to?"

He took a long slurp and said, "Just drive."

So I just drove.

After ten minutes of just driving Harold had slurped up the majority of his Slurpee, which after only a couple sips had given me a nice little hand tremor, heart arrhythmia, a headache, a toothache, and the sensation I was falling.

Harold took one final slurp, set the cup between his legs, and said, "She was to meet me at the train station."

After three years, Harold was finally set to go home. He had traded letters with Elizabeth for the last nine months. In one of her last letters, Elizabeth had sent him a picture. A black and white that just barely fit in the envelope. It was of her, her two brothers, her mom, and her dad. Harold couldn't believe how much she'd grown. She was wearing a white blouse and a long black skirt. Her dark hair was long, disappearing behind her back. Harold didn't know the right word to describe her. Perfect simply didn't do her justice.

In the picture, her father had his right hand resting on Elizabeth's shoulder. Harold remembered that right hand, remembered it striking him in the face. But if he could make something as beautiful as Elizabeth, then he couldn't be all bad. Could he? Plus, he would soon be

Harold's father-in-law. They would be forced to get along. He decided then and there to forgive the man.

In April, the day finally came. Harold hadn't slept in four days. In her last letter she had told him she would be waiting at the train station for him. That she couldn't wait to hold him in her arms. She couldn't believe she was actually going to see the man she so deeply loved.

After two days of traveling, Harold was back at Fort Bragg. He hopped on a train and three days later found himself arriving at the same train station he'd departed from over three years earlier. He thought about the young man—boy, really—who had left on that train. A boy who was now returning a man. And he had Elizabeth to thank.

The train ground to a halt and Harold pressed his nose against the glass. His train was filled with a handful of soldiers and a large mob— fathers, mothers, brothers, sisters, grandparents, and girlfriends alike— was waiting on the platform.

Harold's hands were shaking so badly he was having a hard time holding onto his dufflebag. He stepped off the train, the commotion thundering.

She had told Harold she would be wearing her favorite red blouse and a white skirt. Harold walked up and down the small walkway. He scanned the masses, saw a girl in a red blouse. He ran up to the girl, but when she turned, it wasn't Elizabeth.

The train emptied and slowly the throngs of people dissipated. Soon, the only person remaining was Harold. Harold holding onto his bag. Harold, the tears dripping from his eyes.

"She never showed?"

Staring straight ahead, he said, "She never showed."

"But she had a good reason. You went to her house and she gave you a good reason."

He looked at me, but said nothing.

I said, "You went to her house, though. Didn't you?"

"Oh, I went to her house all right."

Harold began walking in the direction of the King mansion. There had to be a good reason Elizabeth hadn't shown. Had she simply forgotten? He didn't see how. Harold's stomach lurched. What if she was sick? Or what if it was something worse? It had to be terrible, just awful, if it would keep her from him.

He dropped his duffle bag and began sprinting the seven miles to the King mansion. He came abreast of the house and slowed. He looked out over the small lake, the turquoise water whipping in the light breeze. That spring morning played over in his head in slow motion. The dog. Elizabeth screaming. The light touch on his arm. The soft whisper. Elizabeth never taking her eyes off him.

He ran up the drive and to the house. He noticed there wasn't a single car parked in front of the house. No shiny black automobiles.

He set his bag down and began banging on the door. He must have banged for an hour. He banged against that door until his hands started to bleed.

He tried to tell himself they were at church. Or on a vacation. These rich people were always taking vacations. But he knew. He knew they were gone. Knew she was gone. Knew he would never see his sweet Elizabeth again.

CHAPTER 28

THE KID who delivered my pizza on Christmas was the same kid who delivered my pizza on Thanksgiving. I asked him if this made him a bigger loser than me. He laughed and we decided to call it a tie. I tipped him a hundred bucks and told him I'd see him on Easter.

Lacy called later that night and we chatted for a couple hours. Her boyfriend, Caleb—one of my past students and an altogether good guy—was visiting and had popped the question. The two hadn't set a wedding date, but they were shooting for spring of the following year.

After I hung up with Lacy, I went for a long run. It'd been almost two weeks since the fish incident and I was ready to give my lung a try. I did my usual routine of push-ups and sit-ups before setting out into the drizzle. My chest was tight for the first couple miles; then like everything else, my lung seemed to loosen up.

As my feet slapped against the wet gravel, I found myself getting introspective. Which I normally avoid like the plague. It might have had something to do with my sister's engagement. Here she was, eight years my junior, and she'd found the one thing she was passionate about and the one person she wanted to spend the rest of her life with.

Then you had me.

At the present juncture, I was unemployed, I was up to my ears in a case that I shouldn't be involved in, I was a phone call away from spending a couple months behind bars, I hadn't had sex in three months, and yesterday, I'd found a gray hair. And not on my head.

Something had to give.

———

I woke up early on the twenty-sixth.

It was still early, around ten, and the library parking lot was half full. I walked into the large building, followed a couple signs, and thirty seconds later I was sitting in front of a computer. I brought up Google and typed "Ellen Gray."

There were half a million results. I clicked on the third result down: "The official website of Governor Ellen Gray."

The page came up, but all it said was, "Governor Ellen Gray, 1960—2010. She will be missed."

I clicked back to the results page, scrolled down a couple hits, then clicked on the Wikipedia page for Ellen Gray.

Ellen had graduated from the University of Washington with a bachelor's degree in speech and sociology. She'd been president of her sorority. She, like her husband, had a law degree, graduating from Gonzaga. From here, she quickly moved up the ranks of the political arena.

I scrolled down.

Ellen Gray was elected governor four years earlier, beating out the incumbent by a mere percentage point.

There was a section marked *priorities*, followed by a bulleted list.

- Building a Safe and Effective Transportation System
- Educating to Compete
- Taking charge of our health
- Reducing our dependence on foreign oil
- Caring for our environment
- Holding our government accountable
- Strengthening Families
- Supporting Washington farmers and Ranchers

There was a small blurb for each.

I scrolled down to "Building a Safe & Efficient Transportation System" and began reading.

The first legislative session ended with Gray brokering new bipartisan transportation legislation. The package included a 0.5-cent-per-gallon gas-tax increase to help repair many roads in Washington, particularly around Seattle, such as the Alaskan Way Viaduct, Interstate 405, and the Route 520 Bridge. This proposal was initially rejected by the House but then passed with a re-vote the final day of the 2008 session.

The tax package was met with mixed reviews. While she was praised widely by Democratic and Republican leaders of the House and Senate for her leadership skills regarding the passage of this deal, several legislators disagreed about the merits of the tax. Their reasons included the heavy emphasis on funding Seattle-area projects and the already high price of gas. An initiative to repeal the tax, Measure 912, was part of the November 2009 ballot but was rejected by the voters.

It seemed that Ellen alienated more than her fair share of

concerned citizens. But would anyone go to the extreme of murder over a half-cent tax hike?

I read a couple more blurbs but nothing jumped out at me. I made my way back to the results page and clicked on "Images."

About thirty images popped up and I scanned the lot of them. One particular picture caught my eye. It was the same shot shown in Ellen Gray's picture montage on the news. She was speaking to a small crowd of mostly men, outdoorsy types. A couple were holding signs that read "Vote Yes on 217."

Half the people were wearing shirts that read "Defenders of Wildlife."

"U.S. Fish and Wildlife Service" was visible on a brown building in the background of the photo.

I Googled "U.S. Fish and Wildlife Service" and "Washington state," and was directed to the Washington Division homepage for the agency.

I clicked on "Field Office," and a picture of the building from the photograph popped up. It looked bigger without the hoards of people surrounding it. I noted the address: 23 North Cascades Highway.

I MapQuested the address and surveyed the map. The building was a mile from the entrance to North Cascades National Park.

Where Ellen had gone missing.

I hadn't been to the North Cascades since I was a kid. I decided it was time I went back.

CHAPTER 29

NORTH CASCADES NATIONAL Park is located about two-thirds of the way between Seattle and Canada, the last great divider between "The Land of the Free" and "Those Who Guard the Land for Thee." And, of course, cheap prescription drugs.

The park is mystical in its beauty, characterized by steep mountains, snaking rivers, subdued falls, lively brush, brazen wildlife, and cavernous glaciers.

However, I had little fondness for the North Cascades. I still had distant memories of being wrestled from bed at the crack of dawn to go hiking and fishing. These, my two least favorite activities united together in some sort of evil father/son liaison, typically climaxed with me falling into a freezing lake, getting attacked by a porcupine, getting a tick, or getting scarlet fever. I would forever associate the North Cascades with terror.

Anyhow, I headed up Route 2 northbound. The traffic was light. It was early, meaning it was before noon.

The ubiquitous Seattle drizzle turned to a light snow as I entered the mountains. The rains that had plagued Seattle for the last thirty days and thirty nights had come in the form of snow in the elevated areas of the state, and the mountains were covered in a thick blanket of white.

I followed the signs, made some treacherous curves, went through two tunnels, and half an hour later I was parking in a narrow lot piled high with brown snow.

In the far west corner of the lot were two Jeep Cherokees. One was simply a Jeep-shaped cloud of snow. The other had a light dusting of flakes and "U.S. Fish and Wildlife" embossed on the side.

As for the building, it resembled something of a leasing office, inviting yet dismissive. It was brown brick and brown aluminum siding. Two windows, set evenly apart, were both a frozen blue and filled to half capacity with snow. As for the roof, the snow was packed high, patiently awaiting a gunshot, a car backfire, or even the slightest vibration to prompt an avalanche. Huge icicles hung from the eves like clear stalactites.

I hopped out and trudged to the entrance. For the record, I looked rather foolish. Because I had failed to pack any winter items when leaving Maine, I was once again relegated to wearing some of my father's old gear. He—like many a Seattleite—was a diehard Seahawks fan. So I was wearing a puffy Seahawks coat, Seahawks beanie, and Seahawks gloves.

Thomas Prescott, Seahawks Super Fan.

As I neared the building, I noticed two snowmobiles sleeping: one two-seater and another more compact model. I headed up the angled walkway and rapped on the thin door. No response. I knocked a second time, and the door swung inward revealing drab orange, industrial carpet. A rush of warm air washed over me.

I squeezed my head through the opening and yelled the customary, "Ahlo? Anybody home?"

The prelude for any good breaking and entering.

I waited for a response, received none, then pushed the door open and entered into a wide room. To my immediate left were two doors: one I guessed led to an office and the other to a lavatory. Soft light shone through the windows. I hit a light switch and surveyed my surroundings. There were a series of displays set up within the room, and posters and maps covered most of the walls. I moved to one of the displays. It was a plaster slab of a fish. I read about it. This particular fish was best known for its ability to swim as well as breathe under water.

I spent the next few minutes reading about the various types of wildlife that roamed the North Cascades: mountain lions, mountain goats, black bears, grizzly bears, lynx, moose, wolverines, cougars, elk, deer, beavers, raccoons, bats, you name it.

According to a large topographical map, North Cascades National Park covered more than 685,000 acres. The majority of the mountain peaks were under 10,000 feet, save for one, Mount Baker, standing tall at 10,778.

I made my way to the hall and pushed the first of two identical doors inward. It revealed a functional bathroom. A single toilet with no lid and rusty pipes. A soon-to-be-retired roll of toilet paper sat atop the tank. A solitary light dangled from the ceiling. It swayed in a tight circle from an unknown source. I pulled the door closed and moved on.

The second door led to a compact office with a small desk at center. Sitting atop a clutter of paper was an open Tupperware container, the fork and knife resting peacefully on the bottom, the lid askew. Directly behind the desk was a black filing cabinet with two of its four drawers pulled out at different distances. A pair of skis crisscrossed in one corner and a rifle catnapped in another.

The walls were covered with maps, notices, memos, things tacked to *things tacked to* the wall. A Deep Rock water system gurgled just feet from me. It was filled with light blue pebbles and green vegetation. I leaned down for closer inspection and noticed two fish floating at the surface. I visualized Adam Gray standing in the doorway, his thumb in his mouth, rocking lightly back and forth.

I glanced at a couple different documents strewn on the desk. Mostly gibberish. Stuff starting with "Section 7, Code 12, Clause BB" and ending with a long list of "Contributors."

No thanks.

I went for the filing cabinet. It was alphabetized. A through F in the top bin, G through L in the second, and so on. The second drawer from the bottom was open. I fingered the manila folders. Pulled out P. Opened it. Thumbed through a folder marked "Precipitation Records." Lots of line graphs. I replaced the folder. Over the next few minutes I checked W for "Why Ellen Gray was killed." No go. I searched S for "Secret" and T for "Top Secret." No and no. I searched M for "Murder" which did contain a Sue Grafton novel, but little else. I was searching E for "Election" when I stumbled on a folder marked "Endangered."

It was a bright red folder. The only red folder I'd yet to encounter. I flipped through a couple pages. Lots of small print. The fifth page was orange and had "Ballot Measure 217" written at top.

I recalled the photograph of Ellen behind a podium, the man in the audience with the Defenders of Wildlife T-shirt holding a sign that read "Vote Yes on Measure 217."

The top sentence read "Ballot Measure 217 is a repeal of Bill SE 1670, thereby granting reintroduction of the *Canis lupus* to the North Cascades National Park."

So Ellen Gray was an animal rights activist.

Another dead end.

"Ahem."

I looked up.

A woman stood in the doorway. She had a tan jacket with the U.S Fish and Wildlife logo on the left breast and a black headband with the same logo. She had short brown hair and blue eyes. She reminded me of the cute girl from Northern Exposure, Maggie O'Connell. Most importantly, she looked substantially annoyed.

She scowled at me, then said, "Did you eat that?"

I raised my eyebrows.

She pointed to the Tupperware container. "My lunch. Did you eat my lunch?"

"That would be a no. It was sitting out like that when I broke in and started snooping."

She shook her head. "I swear, if that bastard eats my lunch one more time, I'm gonna cut off his balls."

"Who?"

"Other guy doing rounds today. Herb." She stared at me for an awkward moment. "What are you doing in my office?"

It's always best to tell the truth in a situation such as this and I said, "I'll level with you. I'm a bounty hunter."

"You don't look like a bounty hunter."

I looked myself up and down. No, I sure didn't. I looked like a crazed Seahawks fan that had just broken out of an institution. But I was already committed to the lie and so began the stupidest story in the history of time.

Seven minutes later, when I concluded my ridiculous tall tale, the bewildered park ranger said, "And you think after he jumped out of the plane he landed somewhere around here?"

I nodded.

"Well, I hope you find him."

"Me too."

"I can take you around on the snowmobile if you want."

It's not like I had anything else to do. This trip had been a considerable waste of time, and I wasn't about to turn down a snowmobile ride with the increasingly cute park ranger. "That would be great."

As we were heading for the door I said, "Just out of curiosity, what are *Canis lupus*?"

She turned. "*Canis lupus*?"

"Yeah."

She paused, then smiled. "Wolves."

CHAPTER 30

I MENTALLY GULPED AND SAID, "Did you say *wolves*?"

In fourth grade I was on a field trip to the zoo, and let's just say there was an incident involving a seven-year-old Thomas Prescott and the wolf exhibit. I vaguely remember a teacher screaming, "Thomas, how did you get in there?" I believe I responded, "I want to pet the doggies." Long story short, I ended up on television, the zoo was closed "indefinitely," my teacher was fired, I got seventeen stitches, a wolf was "put down," and I wet my bed every other night until I was twelve.

She nodded. "Yep, wolves."

I thought back to all the wildlife exhibits in the adjoining room. There had been no mention of wolves. I asked, "Why wolves?"

"There used to be lots of wolves in the North Cascades. But over the course of the last sixty years they have slowly been eradicated."

No thanks to me.

She added, "They're an important part of the ecosystem."

"I didn't think they were still endangered."

"Well, in Canada and other parts of the Americas they're thriving. There are more than 50,000 wolves up in Canada, and they have made a comeback in Wisconsin, Minnesota, and Idaho. And most recently they were reintroduced to Yellowstone National Park. But here in Washington and a couple other states where they used to roam free, wolf populations are nearly depleted."

I nodded along.

"Wolves became nearly extinct in the lower forty-eight states in the early part of the twentieth century because settlers believed wolves caused widespread livestock losses. They were constantly targeted by large-scale predator-eradication programs sponsored by the federal government. By the time wolves were finally protected by the Endangered Species Act of 1973, they had been exterminated from the lower forty-eight states."

I did not know that.

She nodded along to herself and said, "Wolves—more than any other species—can be credited with keeping the other hunters in check. They are what we call a super-predator, which means they eat other predators. They keep the deer population down, elk, caribou. There are countless other animals that rely on wolves to eat. Birds, small rodents, and other carnivores that aren't capable of kills on their own."

"Why do people have to vote for whether or not they can be reintroduced to the area?"

"Wolves are—and always will be—an extremely controversial animal. There's an old saying: 'Wolves can live with people. People can't always live with wolves.'"

She was preaching to the choir on this one.

She continued, "Wolves have always had a mystique about them. Think about it, *Little Red Riding Hood*, *The Boy Who Cried Wolf*, even *The Three Little Pigs*. It's more myth than anything else, but it's ingrained in each of us at such a young age that it's hard to separate the animal from the lore."

"You missed the part about the werewolf."

She smiled. "That one started in Europe. They believed the

devil was personified in the form of a werewolf: half-man, half-wolf. These terrifying creatures were supposed to live in the forests and to feast on human flesh at night."

"Can we talk about Ebola?"

She laughed. She had a big dimple in her right cheek.

"It isn't all bad. Wolves are revered by many cultures. In Native American mythology, the gray wolf represents the figure of the master and sage; its teeth are a talisman, ensuring courage and liberty. There is a dual aspect to the symbolic value of the wolf; on one hand it is dark and terrifying, on the other hand, benevolent and life-saving. In some cultures it accompanies souls to the hereafter. Hades, the Greek god of the Underworld, wore a wolf skin. And Etrusan, the god of death, had the ears of a wolf."

I nodded like I'd known Etrusan personally.

She asked, "Are you familiar with Etrusan."

"I follow him on Twitter."

She laughed again and I switched the subject before she got going about the Aztecs. I said, "So tell me about Ballot Measure 217."

"After they reintroduced wolves to Yellowstone and parts of Idaho, there were some ramifications on the surrounding communities. In the following years, a few states passed bills that would prohibit the introduction of the gray wolf. Washington was one of those states. A bill was passed in 2006. Defenders of Wildlife and other such organizations have been fighting to have it repealed each of the last three years."

"So the repeal passed?"

"In November. Third try."

Ellen Gray must have felt strongly on the issue to get it on the ballot on three separate occasions.

I took a step forward and said, "I didn't catch your name?"

"Riley. Riley Peterson."

I introduced myself. Then I added, "I'm not really a bounty hunter."

"Yeah, I sort of figured as much."

I smiled meekly.

Riley said, "I'm about to go feed them if you want to tag along?"

"Feed who?"

"The wolves."

Well, that depended entirely on if she wanted to watch a thirty-three year old man piss himself. But I was just the least bit curious to know if I'd conquered this little phobia of mine. Plus, Park Ranger Riley made me tingle. Well, not me. It.

I said, "Why not?"

She walked past me to a wooden cabinet and opened one of the doors. She slipped a couple things in her pocket, then turned around. She had two PowerBars in her hand and said, "Want one?"

"Sure."

She handed me a bar, which was Banana, and asked, "So do you, like, play for the Seahawks or something?"

———

I followed behind Riley until we reached the snowmobiles. Another snowmobile was parked near the other two now, only facing the opposite direction. A faded bumper sticker on the front read, "I love Chachi." I'd only known Riley for going on eleven minutes but I still found this fitting.

I wasn't sure if I was supposed to ride shotgun or if I was expected to drive one of the other sleds—as Riley referred to them. Riley took it upon herself to clear up this matter. She turned and said, "Are you just going to stand there or are you going to hop on."

I hopped on.

The fit was tight. There wasn't anywhere to put my hands, so I folded them in my lap. Riley tilted her head up and said, "Better hold on."

I shrugged and wrapped my arms around her midsection. She was just a tiny little thing underneath the large jacket. Riley turned around and said dryly, "I meant hold on to the *hand holds*."

Whoops.

I undid my hands and looked down at the thin bar jetting from both sides of the snowmobile. I took hold of both and said, "Sorry."

She turned her head around and said, "Don't be." Then she gave me a soft wink.

Riley hit a red button, the engine coughed, caught, then purred. She gunned the throttle and the snowmobile shot forward, slicing through the open area behind the building criss-crossed in fresh tracks and day-old tracks nearly wiped clean by Mother Nature. Riley followed an invisible path, zipping around trees, plowing through valleys, skirting around boulders.

Over the course of the next fifteen minutes, I would learn a substantial amount of information about Park Ranger Riley Peterson. For one, she wasn't a park ranger at all. She had her master's degree in biology. She had thought about becoming a vet but didn't think she would thrive in an office building. And two, she was a diehard Seahawks fan. She rambled on about their season, who was playing well, who was dogging it, why the front office was "a bunch of morons," why they should have "just kicked a field goal," why Hasselbeck should get hair plugs, and so on and so forth.

We came within a stone's throw of a raging river and stopped. Riley hopped off the snowmobile and said, "I'll just be a second." She started trudging through the snow. She came back two minutes later with two vials filled with river water. She said, "We check the pH a couple times a week."

I nodded, then asked, "What's the name of that river?"

"The Skagit. It starts up in Canada, runs for about a hundred miles, and eventually empties into the Sound."

I found this interesting, but I wasn't sure why.

She continued on for another couple minutes about the different species of fish and other animal life that inhabited the river. I felt like I was on a field trip and I would have to fill out a handout when we finished.

We picked our way through a dense portion of trees then popped out into vast whiteness. Literally a lake of snow. The only thing breaking the horizon was tall metal fencing girdling the perimeter. The fencing was about eight feet high, with the top couple feet curving inward, resembling something of a lowercase "f." Within this haven, sitting at the far back right corner, was a small brick building.

Riley brought the snowmobile to a halt and said over the engine, "This is the den."

Impressive.

"And exactly how big is the den?"

"Well, it isn't actually a den—that's just a stupid name Herb came up with. The fencing extends into those trees down there and down the slope. About seven acres. We want the wolves to have as realistic an experience as possible before we release them into the wild. It increases their chances for survival dramatically."

"When did the project start?"

"December first. We're doing a soft release with this pack, mainly because there are pups involved. We plan to release them into the park the second week of January."

She explained that a hard release was when you simply took the wolves and literally dumped them in a new area. A soft release let the animals acclimate to their new climate in an enclosure, usually between one and three acres (theirs was larger than normal), with the full release several weeks later.

"Who's in charge of the project?"

"Well, once the red tape was cleared, it was basically me, Herb, and the Professor. Herb and I are in charge of the feeding and the tracking. The Professor pretty much does everything else."

"Who is the Professor?"

"Professor Koble. Guy in charge of the project. Half these wolves he had a hand in rescuing. He's different."

I nodded.

She decided to elaborate. "These wolves are his life. He used to be a professor, but he quit and tracked wolves for fifteen years. I don't think he ever felt accepted by humanity. But the wolves, I think he felt like they never judged him. You should see him interact with them; it's like he's one of them. It's incredible, really. I don't know what he would have done if the repeal hadn't passed this year."

Well, he had Ellen Gray to thank for that. I hope he sent her a thank you card.

Riley lifted up in the seat. She released the throttle with her right glove and leveled it against the horizon. She lifted her chin with a smile and said, "There they are."

I followed her gaze. There were eleven in all. A couple were snow-white, two were black, and the rest were a different shade of gray. The sight of them sent shivers down my spine.

Riley slowly eased the throttle and we started forward. The wolves were positioned on a ridge a quarter mile into the enclosure, and all eleven heads snapped in our direction. Twenty-two eyes watched our every move. Just studying. Watching. Scouting. Strategizing. Planning. To kill me.

Riley parked the snowmobile outside a gated entrance and we hopped off. I looked back over my shoulder to the wolves, but there was no trace of them. They'd vanished.

Riley unchained the fence and pulled the large gate aside. She drove the snowmobile through the opening and to the small brick building.

I asked, "What is this place?"

"It's the barn."

"The barn?"

"This used to be a bunker of sorts for soldiers during the war. A refuge, really. They traversed these mountains on cross-country skis way back when. The place hadn't been used for years. We converted it into a holding stall for the project."

"A holding stall? For what, the wolves?"

"Not exactly."

We entered the building, a musty draft washing over us. The smell was strong, similar to what a petting zoo might smell like. A small outer room was filled with equipment. I guessed it was used to track the wolves. Riley confirmed this.

Two sets of cross-country skis leaned against the wall. Riley noticed me eyeing them and said, "Sometimes it's easier to get around on the skis than a snowmobile. The trees are pretty thick in this area."

I nodded. A gun was lying on one of the small counters, and I picked it up.

Riley nodded at the gun. "That's a tranquilizer gun. Darts are filled with Ketamine, low level animal tranquilizer."

"Are these hard to get?"

"In the state of Washington you need to have a license, but according to Herb, they're readily available on the Internet."

Isn't everything?

We pushed through a second door to the sound of clattering hooves. There wasn't much for light, but you could hear the deep inhale and exhale of wildlife. Stalls were lined up on both sides of a dirty walkway, and I guessed half of them were occupied.

I looked at Riley and asked, "What are they?"

Her lips flexed into a thin smirk. "Deer."

CHAPTER 31

MY EYES HAD STARTED to adjust to the soft light, and I peered over the top of one of the stalls. A deer huddled in the corner. He looked like a Dave. Dave the deer. Dave's eyes bulged and his ears sat back like two perfect isosceles triangles.

Riley walked to the far end of the building and propped a door open. The bright light fed into the small room. She moved on down the row, stopping at the last stall on the left. Then she pulled open the stall door and stood back. The deer didn't take much prodding. After about three seconds, it shot from the stall and into the sunlight. Riley said, "Feeding time."

She pulled the door closed and said, "Let's go watch."

We went out the way we'd entered, hopped on the snowmobile, and followed the deer tracks leading from the building's far end into the trees. Riley parked the snowmobile at the tree line and said, "It won't be long now."

She shut off the engine and we were left in simple silence.

"Aren't we going to follow the tracks?" I found it odd that I was genuinely intrigued to watch this poor deer be slaughtered.

She shook her head. "The deer has the advantage in the trees. The wolves will chase it out into the open."

I nodded.

She was right, it didn't take long. From deep within the trees, came a soft rumbling and a sheet of snow fell from a large spruce. Emerging through the white was the deer. It was about a football field away, but I could see a look of panic on its face. Like John Elway scrambling out of the pocket. The wolves bounded behind the prancing deer, teeth gritted, kicking up snow like exhaust fumes. The deer shot out of the tree line about forty feet ahead of us. The wolves came three seconds later—four in a tight group, then a group of five, then a couple stragglers.

The two of us swiveled in our seats.

The wolves made up the ground quickly in the open as Riley had predicted. The lead wolf was stride on stride with the deer, cutting off his path to the right. The deer started to its left where, unbeknownst to him, another wolf had materialized. The wolf tangled up one of the deer's legs and the deer lost a step. That's when the third wolf made its lunge. It latched onto the deer's neck, where it hung for a split second. Then the deer went down and it was over. Dinner for eleven.

I felt my head shaking from side to side. It was one of the more amazing feats I'd ever witnessed. Equal to, if not greater than, watching Bob Ross paint some trees.

Riley started the snowmobile and we slowly crept toward the feasting wolves until we were less than fifteen yards away. A couple of the wolves traded glances our way, but for the most part their attention was on the deer.

Riley said, "We really shouldn't be doing this. The less human contact the better, but you probably won't get another chance to see wolves this close in your lifetime."

"Promise."

She laughed and slapped my leg.

I asked, "How long have these wolves been here?" On closer inspection, only five wolves looked full-grown, the other six markedly smaller.

"Well, the two big white wolves are an alpha pair from up in Wisconsin. Initially, we were going to wait for the pair to mate and have a litter, but it just so happened three weeks after we transported them here, the Professor rescued a wolf in Canada that birthed a litter. But the mother died during the pregnancy. Six cubs. Then three transports."

"And you just throw them all together?"

"Basically. The alpha pair didn't seem to mind the three transplants, but they didn't want anything to do with the pups. Wouldn't go near them. The alpha pair is responsible for the feeding, protection, training, and socialization of its members. It was the alpha male, which is rare, that finally came around. I witnessed it firsthand. We'd just finished feeding the pups—they were still on formula at that point—and Cujo came and nuzzled one of the pups with his head. From that day forward, they've been like a family."

"Did you say Cujo?"

"One of Herb's stupid names. Herb named the five adults. I got to name the pups." She paused. "Want to hear their names?"

"Do I ever."

"Well, there's Cujo. He's the big one, the lead wolf in the chase. He's big by even wolf standards. Somewhere around 165 pounds."

I looked at Cujo. He was watching the others eat. I didn't like being terrified by something that I outweighed by twenty pounds. But then again, I wasn't too hip on spiders either. It was slowly donning on me that I was sort of a pussy.

She continued, "The alpha female is J-Lo. She's the big white one on the right. The three transplants are the two gray ones, Quagmire and Carmen Electra, and the black one off to the side, Cartman." She rolled her eyes and said, "I don't know where he gets these names."

I couldn't wait to meet this Herb character.

Cartman was thirty yards from the others, a large chunk of

deer draping from his snarling snout. He was perfect black against the perfect white. He trained his eyes on me.

Riley laughed. "He doesn't seem to like you."

"No, he doesn't."

"He was the one wolf that never really meshed."

"Like the weird uncle that shows up to Easter brunch with his friend Jake."

"More like the weird neighbor who kills his family." She added, "There used to be another wolf. Cartman killed him the first week."

Double gulp.

I looked at the rather small pups trying to eat the meat, biting at the air, and said, "What are the pups' names?"

"Ross, Chandler, Joey, Monica, Phoebe, and Rachel."

I wondered if she was a huge *Friends* fan or if this was a weird coincidence. She gave a little giggle and said, "Yup, *Friends.*"

Matter solved.

So I watched Cujo, J-Lo, Cartman, Quagmire, Carmen Electra, Ross, Joey, Chandler, Monica, Phoebe, and Rachel devour Bambi.

After about ten minutes, the pups started playing. They would rub their heads together and Riley explained they were nuzzling, an important show of affection.

At one point, two of the pups made their way in our direction. Riley whispered, "The one on the right is Monica. The one on the left is Phoebe."

"Where's Phoebe's guitar?"

I don't think she heard me. Or she decided to act like she didn't hear me. I'm guessing the latter.

The wolves came right up to us. Could have just been a pair of Labradors. Dark blue-black eyes against their fluffy gray fur. Jet black noses. Truly gorgeous animals. They both had thin collars around their necks. I assumed these were the tracking devices.

Riley reached out her hand and scratched Monica behind the

ears. Phoebe waited patiently for me to do the same. She bobbed her head from side to side and lifted her ears. She sensed my hesitation and took a couple more steps in my direction, burying her head in my lap.

Riley said, "Somebody likes you."

I gently scratched the wolf behind the ears, Phoebe wrestling her head from side to side in obvious enjoyment. Then, in a flash, both pups took off back to the pack.

I looked at Riley and said, "They seem pretty tame."

"The pups are usually pretty tame for the first year. As they get older they slowly lose it. But you never know."

She took off her glove and showed me her right hand. She had seven small scars on the fleshy skin between her thumb and pointer finger. She turned her hand over and revealed similar scars on her palm. "The wolf has an incredible bite. Their jaws can exert a pressure of more than 400 pounds per square inch. Ross did this to me three weeks ago. I was petting him and then he just chomped down on my hand, wouldn't let go. Forty-seven stitches." She paused. "The second you stop respecting them as wild and vicious animals is usually one second too late."

Touché.

A hollow, throaty bellow snapped my attention back to the wolves. One of the darker wolves had its head snapped back and was howling at the heavens. I think it was Quagmire. Within seconds, all the wolves had their heads reared back and were doing the same. The pups' noise was higher, something between a howl and yelp. A holp. The cumulative noise was a deep thunderstorm rolling through the mountains.

I looked at Riley and said, "I thought they only howled when there was a full moon." Did *Underworld 2* teach us nothing?

"They howl for lots of different reasons. Basically it's to show fellowship to one another and strength to others."

"I thought that's what chugging beer was for."

She thought this was incredibly funny.

I noticed movement to my left and turned. Just at the edge of the tree line was a man on cross-country skis. He was dressed from head to toe in white with one of those white masks covering his face so only his eyes and mouth were visible.

I cocked my head at him, and Riley said, "That's Professor Koble."

"He just follows them around on his skis?"

"Pretty much. If we weren't here, he would probably be eating with them."

"He'd eat raw deer?"

"I told you he was a little different."

I don't know if I would classify a guy who thinks he is a wolf as different. I'd file that under off-his-fucking-rocker.

We watched the wolves for another couple minutes, then Riley started up the snowmobile and we headed back the way we'd come. I watched the Professor at the edge of the trees. He held his gaze on us, much like the wolves had earlier.

Halfway into the trip, Riley stopped the sled and asked if I'd like to drive. I scooted up and she slid in behind me. I hit the switch and said, "Hold on tight." I added, "And not to the handholds."

She wrapped her arms around me and dug her head into my back. Ten minutes later, I parked the snowmobile where we found it and turned off the ignition. We were about to hop off when I turned and asked, "What are you doing tomorrow?"

"I've got to do a quick round in the morning, but that's about it. Why?"

"My sister got me tickets to the Seahawks' playoff game on Sunday. I wasn't going to use them, but since you're such a die-hard fan and all." Actually, I'd been planning on taking Harold, but when I'd asked him if he was a Seahawks fan, he told me that, aside from all the pooping, he supposed they were okay.

Anyhow, Riley pursed her lips and said, "Are you asking me out on a date?"

"It would appear that way."

"I'd love to go to the game with you."

And then she kissed me on the cheek.

CHAPTER 32

A SOFT CREAKING noise jarred me awake and I opened my right eye. The bathroom door was ajar, and a steamy fog slowly dissipated into the bedroom. Riley was standing in the doorway, a lime green towel wrapped around her. She had another towel and was drying her hair with it. Needless to say, at this point I decided to open my left eye. She noticed me eyeing her and said, "Hey, sleepyhead."

I smacked my lips a couple times. "What time it is?"

"I don't know. A little before 8:00."

"a.m.?"

She nodded.

"Can I ask you a question?"

"Of course."

I smacked my lips a couple more times before asking, "Are you by chance a morning person?" I'd heard these people existed but had never actually seen one in the flesh.

She nodded again.

Ten demerits.

She continued drying her hair. I continued to stare at her. She asked, "Did you have a nice sleep?"

I raised an eyebrow. "Sleep would denote having one's eyes closed and resting."

"I guess there wasn't much of that last night."

"No. No, there wasn't."

I closed my eyes and said, "Can you put some clothes on so I can go back to sleep."

"Maybe I don't want you to go back to sleep. Maybe I want to have my way with you."

I pulled up the sheets and looked down. Paddington was in a sex-induced coma. I said, "I don't know if that's going to be possible."

She sighed and continued drying her hair.

As I stared at her, a barrage of thoughts raced through my head. How they got there and why, I have no idea. Did I regret sleeping with her? I didn't think so. Of course, if I ended up asking my local pharmacist some rather peculiar questions the following week, then I might. But it went deeper than that. It was like having eggnog before Thanksgiving. It's always there on the shelf, and it always tastes good, but you know it will taste that much better if you wait until Thanksgiving. Then again, I hadn't gotten a whiff of eggnog this year. No, I was fishing dead women out of Puget Sound. So maybe this, Riley, was my eggnog.

If you want to dig deeper, and I did, it all came back to Alex. But I wasn't thinking about Alex. I was thinking about someone else. But I was starting to give myself a migraine and there was a very attractive woman standing half naked in my bedroom.

I lifted up the sheets and whispered, "*Psst. Psst.* Wake up."

He rolled over but said nothing.

Lazy dick.

Riley finished drying her hair, then walked up to the edge of the bed. She slowly unraveled the towel and let it fall to the floor. She had small, firm breasts, a perfectly toned stomach, and a thin strip of chestnut brown pubic hair. She raised her eyebrows.

I pulled up the sheets and Paddington winked at me, which is always a good sign.

———

An hour later, I was walking Riley downstairs. She was wearing the same jeans and sweater she'd worn to the game. I was wearing a plaid comforter, toga style. My plan was to walk Riley to the front door then proceed to the couch where I would sleep for the better portion of the day.

That is, until the doorbell rang.

I would have preferred if it'd been the mailman. Or one of those annoying kids selling holiday wrapping paper. I wouldn't have minded if it'd been one of my nosy neighbors dressed up as Bryant Gumble. Or Ethan with a sawed-off shotgun. Or an Arab holding a can of Anthrax. Or a ten-year-old kid holding a blood test. Or James Patterson holding his latest novel. It wasn't.

Erica was wearing dress slacks and a black sweater. She smiled and said, "Do you even own clothes?"

I think she was referring to the fact that two of the three times I'd opened the door, I'd been clad in linens. I gave a goofy smile and said, "I'm waiting for Kohl's spring clearance."

She laughed and said, "Can I come in for a minute?"

I mentally pulled out a grenade and stared at it. "Um." I pulled the pin with my teeth. "I, um." I put the grenade in my mouth. "I don't know if—"

Riley poked her head out and said, "Hi there."

3....2...1...

I opened the door all the way. Riley sidled up next to me, stuck out her hand, and said, "I'm Riley."

Ka-BOOM!

Erica threw a shifty look my way, then took Riley's hand and shook it. "Sorry, um, I'm Erica."

A long silence ensued. I mentally dug the large piece of shrapnel from my throat and said, "Cold today."

Riley and Erica glanced at each other, then looked back at me. They both nodded. I looked up, then said poignantly, "Might rain later."

They both kept quiet.

"Just saying. It might."

Erica did a half turn and said, "I'm gonna take off. Good to see you, Thomas." She turned to Riley, gave a little head bob, and said, "Nice to meet you."

Riley nodded at her and said, "Actually, I have to get going anyhow." She gave me a peck on the cheek, flashed a smile at Erica, then walked briskly to her car and drove off.

Erica and I both watched as her green Jeep pulled onto the street. Erica looked at me and said, "She seems nice." She actually said this to the invisible person standing to my left.

"She's my favorite cousin."

Erica narrowed her eyes. I'm not sure she bought the cousin bit. And I'm not exactly sure why I was selling it.

"Do you sleep with all your cousins?"

"Just first cousins."

She didn't seem to know how to take this. Anyhow, it was chilly outside and I said, "So do you still want to come in?"

I didn't wait for a response. I walked inside, leaving the door open behind me. I made my way into the kitchen and grabbed a box of waffles from the freezer. As I popped four waffles into the toaster, I heard the front door close. I waited for footsteps but heard none. She was gone.

I took a deep breath. How could I have handled this encounter with Erica differently? And why did I care? The last thing I wanted—*needed*—was to fall head over heels for another woman. I shook my head. I wonder if I could take legal action against Alex for screwing me up so badly.

The waffles popped up. Two were perfect and two were barely

cooked. I took the cooked ones out and transferred the uncooked ones to the working slots. Then let out a scream. A long one that had almost nothing to do with uncooked waffles.

"Are you okay?"

I turned to my left. Erica was standing in the doorway to the kitchen.

I cleared my throat and said, "These waffles are taking forever to cook. It's very frustrating. I think it has something to do with the chocolate chips."

"If you say so."

The waffles popped up a second time, a perfect golden-brown. I drenched the waffles in syrup.

From the doorway Erica said, "How do you feel about murder-for-hire?"

It took me a moment to process her question. I was also processing a quadruple-decker bite and garbled, "Noda gance."

She took a seat at the kitchen table and I joined her. I offered her a bite of waffles but she respectfully declined. That she was here spoke volumes. I guessed that their case—and by *their*, I mean, Erica's, Ethan's, and the entire state of Washington's—had folded since I blew the whistle on the videotapes.

I asked her about this.

She said, "Gray met with the judge that next morning and showed him the tapes. It's obvious he was in his office when his yacht was being taken out. It's a third-party video surveillance so there's no way the dates and times could have been tampered with. It's about as solid an alibi as you're gonna get these days."

I nodded.

This didn't grant Adam Gray absolution from his wife's murder, but it did put a large dent in the prosecution's case. There was still the matter of his fingerprints on the gun, the gun itself, and motive, which, the more I uncovered about the couple, only seemed to intensify.

Erica finished, "The judge dismissed the case on the spot."

Ergo, she was asking me, aka the grand poobah of cunning and wizardry, to do some information gathering. For the first time, I wondered if she was here of her own accord or if she'd been prodded by my pal Ethan. Or more logically, she was here to make certain that I was staying clear of the henhouse as promised.

On this note I asked, "And you are here because…?"

She moved backward a couple inches as if I'd physically pushed her. She stammered, "Because I respect your opinion and I wanted to know what your thoughts were on Adam Gray hiring someone to kill his wife."

"I thought you wanted me to keep my nose out of this."

"I do. But I've pretty much accepted the fact that you aren't going to."

Acceptance is the first step to recovery. Speaking of recovery, I was having what my psychiatrist referred to as trust issues. As in, I didn't trust people who weren't named Thomas. I didn't even trust all of these. Especially that Bjorn guy.

After a few awkward seconds, I said, "Well, I'd have to say the odds are slim Adam Gray would outsource his dirty work."

She nodded.

"I mean, this guy refuses to send a paralegal to research any minute detail he may need for a case. He's hands-on, start to finish. If Gray killed his wife, it would have been done perfectly, and you and I wouldn't be here right now because Ellen's body never would have been found and Adam would smell of roses.

"Seriously, this guy has an unhealthy relationship with order that hovers around OCD. Now, I'm not saying he's Howard Hughes, but he isn't far off. The only thing Adam Gray is guilty of is being an irrational neat freak, an awful husband, a negligent father, and a prick. Somebody wanted him to go to jail for his wife's murder. You find whoever had it out for the two of them, Ellen and Adam, and you've found your murderer."

"Makes sense," she said dryly. She stood. "Well, I'd better be going."

I walked her to the door and had my second awkward foyer moment of the day. My record is three.

Erica stuck her hands in her pockets and glanced up at me. I had an overwhelming urge to grab her face and kiss her softly. Almost as if something was bubbling inside of me and the only way to release it was to press my lips flush with hers. I'd never felt the bubbles with Riley. In fact, I'm not sure I'd felt the bubbles with Alex. At least not to this level. But I have a rule that I don't kiss two different women in the same twenty-four-hour time period. I'm a class act like that.

I patted her on the shoulder and said, "Thanks for stopping by."

I'm quite certain these were not the parting words Erica was seeking. She did sort of a half-smile and said, "Do me a favor and tell—Riley, is it?—that I'm sorry if I was rude earlier. I'm sure she's wonderful."

"I'll be sure to do that."

She added, "I mean, she is your *favorite* cousin."

We both gave a forced laugh.

She opened the door and started down the drive. She gave a little wave as she headed in the direction of her car. I almost called to her. I almost ran to her. I almost turned her around and kissed her…the kiss I'd played over in my head since the day I laid eyes on her.

Almost.

CHAPTER 33

FOR SOME REASON they celebrated New Year's Eve on the thirtieth. Seriously, it was like they operated on some different calendar altogether. They probably celebrated Easter the sixth Sunday after the first Joseph died, and Labor Day two weeks after the first hip broke.

Harold was decked out in his Sunday best. He looked sharp. Dead, but sharp.

I could describe my wardrobe selection in one word. Camelhair. I looked ridiculous so, needless to say, I fit in perfectly.

We retired to the cafeteria, which had been decorated a la millennium party and I felt like I was in my seventh-grade gymnasium. A table near the door was strewn with cheap top hats, plastic tiaras, noisemakers, and kazoos. I visualized all these old-timers blowing on kazoos at midnight. I hope they had a couple defibrillators handy.

Dinner was prime rib, potatoes, and cornbread. Most of the old-timers had a glass of wine. Harold had his, plus mine, and his Titleist-sized eyeballs had glassed over by the time we did a champagne toast.

A couple dustbusters stood, or attempted to at any rate, and gave toasts. Mostly they toasted to still being alive, to loved ones that had already moved on, that we lived in such a great country—one lady toasted to cats—but more or less their toasts put life in perspective, and I was pretty choked up by the end.

They did a mock countdown at 7:00 p.m. and the party raged until 7:13. Harold and I were the last to leave.

Sitting just outside the cafeteria was a piano and Harold stopped to rest. We generally stopped every hundred yards, so naturally I thought nothing of it. He sat on the small bench and took deep inhales on the oxygen tank.

It might have been the wine, or the champagne, or the fact he was up an hour past his bedtime, but he looked especially old. Old and tired. He reminded me of one of those old trucks you see parked on the side of people's houses. Rusted, dented, weathered, what's left more spare parts than originals. But every time you turned the key, it would start. It would cough and sputter, it would choke and wane—almost as if it was on its hands and knees begging *not* to start—but eventually it would always turn over.

The old truck swiveled and faced the piano.

Harold stretched out his fingers and laid them gently on the keys. I wasn't sure if his fingers were hovering over the thin white keys or if they lacked the weight, and he the strength, to elicit sound. And then suddenly his fingers became music. The notes were deep and long, hanging in the air above the piano like London fog.

I watched—mesmerized, really—as Harold played snippets, small delicate pieces of songs long forgotten. His eyes were closed, his head swaying from side to side. I wondered where Harold was. And what year it was. And who he was with.

Somehow I knew.

Harold stopped playing. He laid his hands by his sides, opened his large eyes, and said, "I walked past the King house every day for a year."

For the first month, Harold walked past the King place two, sometimes three times a day. After a twelve- to fifteen-hour day in the field, he would walk the seven miles to the King mansion. Sometimes he would walk up the stone path and bang on the door a couple times, but mostly he would just toss rocks into the thin lake.

The long days in the sun gave him plenty of time to ponder what had happened. Had she fallen out of love with him? Had he said or written something horrible that he didn't know about? How could someone say the things she said, say the things she felt, then just up and disappear?

These questions ate at him as the hours crept by. On more than one occasion, Harold found himself huddled between the stalks of corn, legs curled up to his chest, tears dribbling down his cheeks.

His life had been nearly perfect. He couldn't have asked for anything more. And then, just like that, just like Thad's final breaths, it was all gone.

Harold decided Elizabeth's father had to be at fault. He visualized the skinny man dragging Elizabeth from the house kicking and screaming. Her yelling at him how much she loved Harold. That she had to be with him. That he was coming for her. That she wasn't whole without him.

Harold hated the man, a hate he didn't think he was capable of, a hate that during the throes of war he would have thought utterly impossible.

He would think about Mr. King, then he would think about his own father. When Harold had walked through the door the night he'd returned, he'd tried to be strong—after all, he was a soldier—but when he'd seen his mother and his sisters, his I had broken. His mother and sisters cried with him. As for his father, he didn't say a word, simply stuck out his hand and Harold shook it. His father might not be the smartest man, but he was a good man, and he worked hard. His father was nothing like Elizabeth's father.

He'd started back in the fields the very next day. It was a large planting and Harold kept busy. The days slowly turned into weeks, and the weeks into months.

Harold had asked around, local merchants, other farmers, even his father, and no one knew where the Kings went. Just that they were gone. His father was especially elated. If a year went by and no one heard from the Kings, the land would become his.

And it did.

It was late August of the following year. They were in the middle of the second harvest and Harold's father even thought they might squeak out a third if the weather stayed the way it had been. Harold had just finished up a twelve-hour day in the field. His back felt as though it might never again be straight, his arms as if they were destined to stay at his sides for the rest of eternity, his feet as if there was a nail driven through each heel.

He overheard his mother tell his father that while coming back from town, she'd seen a bunch of cars at the King place.

Harold didn't waste a moment. He jumped off the rocking chair and started running. Barefoot. His three sisters called after him, asking what in the devil had gotten into old Harold, but he didn't hear them. His Elizabeth had returned. He knew she would come back. They'd probably been on vacation. Maybe they'd gone to California. Or Florida. Or even overseas. But it didn't matter where they'd been, or why. They were back. His Elizabeth was back.

Harold's feet pounded against the gravel for seven miles, but he didn't feel a single solitary step. As he closed in on the house, he could see four cars parked in the drive. The cars were larger, newer, shinier.

Harold ran up the drive. It never occurred to him what he looked like or what he was wearing. Harold never stopped to think what it would look like when a boy ran up to the house in overalls, no undershirt, covered in two days' worth of sweat and grime, barefoot, feet calloused and spurting blood. No, Harold was too preoccupied with the image of twirling his precious Elizabeth in his arms and telling her he would never let her go. That he would die before he let her go.

As Harold neared the front door, a black man removed a large box from one of the cars. The man dropped the box and blocked Harold's path to the front door. He said slowly, with almost an air of superiority, "This here is private property, young lad."

Harold asked to see his Elizabeth. The black man shook his head and told him that no one named Elizabeth lived there.

The family that moved into the King estate was the Grangers. They'd bought the property from the Kings.

Harold could feel his heart, which just minutes earlier he was sure would leap right out of his chest, fall into his stomach. He doubled over and vomited.

The black man told him to run along, giving him a slight push in the direction of the road, and began kicking dirt on Harold's mess.

Harold wiped his mouth and turned on his heel. His head lowered, he slowly made his way down the dirt road. He could hardly lift his raw bloody feet, more of a scraping than walking. When he was halfway down the long drive, the black man yelled at him.

Harold turned. The man's outline was hazy through his stream of tears. From what he could tell, the man was no longer angry. Then the man said one word. One word that would forever change Harold's life.

"Seattle?"

He smiled. "*Seattle.*"

I had a cramp in my right cheek from smiling. "And let me guess—you moved to Seattle."

"I hopped on a train the next day."

It was 1947. Harold had some money saved up from his days in the Army, plus his father now owned the land and had given him some money on his departure.

Harold found a small apartment in the city. He'd been in big cities before—he'd had to make train transfers in both Chicago and Pittsburgh, and he'd seen the ruins of major cities in Europe—but this was the first time he'd been part of a city.

There were so many people, people in cars, people on bikes, people walking about. How was he ever supposed to find his dear, sweet Eliza-beth with so many people around? He tried the phone books, but there were quite a few Kings, and the hours he spent on the phone were wasted hours.

He spent a month searching for her, walking around the city day and night. After five weeks, Harold was beginning to run out of money. He saw an ad in one of the papers for airplane builders. Harold was skilled with his hands and he had a good understanding of airplanes from time in the army. He started three days later.

The hours were long and hard, but nothing could compare to a sixteen-hour day in the field. As the days passed, Harold found himself thinking of Elizabeth less and less. It was slowly donning on him that it wasn't meant to be.

Walking around one evening, Harold stumbled across a movie theater. In all of his twenty-three years, he'd never seen a cinema. He was quickly addicted. The Lady of Shanghai, The Bicycle Thief, Unfaithfully Yours, Letter from an Unknown Woman, Moonrise, Force of Evil. *Harold saw them all. His favorite was* Fort Chief *with John Wayne.*

In December of his first year in Seattle, he'd been grocery shopping. He hadn't been paying attention and bumped into a young woman. She'd called him a "doofus." He'd never been called a doofus before and found himself laughing uncontrollably. The woman quickly apologized for the remark. They had dinner two nights later. Harold and Gwen didn't spend a day apart for the next six months.

He had a good job. He'd bought a car, a brand new Chevy. He had a great girl. Life was good.

Harold, along with nearly everyone else, had been waiting impatiently for the next John Wayne film. She Wore a Yellow Ribbon *opened on a rainy night in February of 1948.*

It was the best movie he'd ever seen, Harold remarked to Gwen as they were leaving the bustling theater. There was something about that John Wayne. Something magnetic. You couldn't take your eyes off him. Gwen held his arm and whispered softly in his ear, "He's almost as handsome as you."

But Harold was a million miles away. And if it weren't for the dark corridor, Gwen would have seen that Harold was white as a ghost. She did notice his body had gone stiff and asked, "What's wrong?"

Harold shook his head and continued to stare at the raven-haired woman ten feet in front of him. She was with a group of six or seven other girls. All their hair was done up the same, curled up and under, and they were giggling as they moved through the doors and into the drizzle. Harold didn't know how he knew, but he did.

Without a word, he unhooked his arm and pushed through the crowd. Gwen asked where he was going, but he didn't hear her. He pushed into the drizzle, spotting the group of ladies starting up a side street. He followed behind them. The group—huddled beneath a collection of umbrellas—stopped. One of the girl's shoes had fallen off. It was the girl Harold hadn't taken his eyes off for the past sixty seconds.

She knelt down, grabbed her shoe, and hopped around trying to put it back on her foot. Then suddenly she stopped, the shoe dangling from her hand, her right foot hanging in the air. She was staring directly at Harold.

One of the girls in the group said, "What's wrong? Elizabeth, what's wrong?"

It was her.

Harold ducked behind a post. Why hadn't he run to her? Why hadn't he picked her up and twirled her? What would John Wayne have done? Would John Wayne have hid behind a street lamp until she left. Harold smacked his head backwards against the post, then peeked out. The girls were getting into a car. His Elizabeth was the last to get in. She gave one final look in his direction before getting in the car.

Harold watched as the car sped away.

I yelled, "You didn't go talk to her?"

Harold shook his head. "I couldn't."

"You big weenie."

He smiled.

"So what did you do?"

"I ran to my car and followed them."

"You followed them?"

"Sure did. Alcove Academy, a private women's college."

"What happened to Gwen?"

He hit a piano key down with his finger, its soothing sound rumbling through the small room, and said, "I never saw Gwen again."

I laughed so hard my knees buckled. Luckily I was sitting down.

Harold turned to me and asked, "You like polka?"

CHAPTER 34

I TOOK a long run in the rain.

Back at the house, I grabbed a glass of water, gulped it down, then went back for a second. Days earlier, I'd noticed a phone jack underneath the cabinets just to the right of the faucet, and I'd taken the liberty of transplanting Lacy's pink phone. Then while rummaging around in the basement, I'd stumbled across an antique answering machine. I'd hooked this up to the phone. A large button at the bottom right corner of the machine was blinking red. I hit the button then went back to the faucet for a third glass of water.

The mechanical voice said, "*December 31st, 2:36 p.m.*" A moment later Lacy's voice came on. "*You got an answering machine! Yay! So, I haven't talked to you since Christmas. Hope you enjoyed the game. Saw that they won. Anyhow, I'm headed out; we're hosting a party at the gallery. Starts in about half an hour. Just wanted to wish you a Happy New Year. No need to call me back. Talk to you next year.*"

I smiled at the sound of her voice.

The answering machine wasn't done. "*December 31st, 2:47 p.m....Hi Thomas, it's Riley.*"

I didn't recall giving Riley my telephone number. But then

again, she did do a couple things to me for which I would have given up Anne Frank's hiding spot. *She's in the attic. Don't stop.*

"*...anyhow, I thought if you weren't busy this evening you might want to join me for some New Year's festivities. I'll cook us dinner, we could drink some wine, nothing too glamorous. I know this is sort of last minute, and if you already have plans then no worries. Talk to you later. Go Seahawks.*"

I could think of worse ways to ring in the New Year. I'd planned on ordering pizza, drinking a six-pack, and maybe doing a back flip off the balcony.

A third message began to play. "*...31st, 3:12 p.m....Hey, Mr. Prescott.*"

It was Erica.

"*...if you aren't doing anything tonight, a bunch of us are going over to this bar over on Third called Markey's.*"

I hit pause. I knew Markey's. It was an Irish pub with an identity crisis on Cherry Street. It had changed hands so many times all that was left of its original heritage was a Guinness mirror and a couple shamrock urinal cakes. Of course, this was eight years ago. I remembered the place usually having a decent crowd, and I'd even spent a couple New Year's Eves there.

I hit play. "*...it should be fun. Anyhow, if you're looking for something to do tonight, that's an option. See ya.*"

Interesting.

I wondered if Erica was just being polite or if she was trying to secure a midnight kiss. I'd heard of women who lined up three or four backup plans just in case one didn't work out. No woman wanted to be the girl stuck kissing her brother, or her friend, or worse yet, no one at all.

I blew out a long breath and made for the refrigerator. The mechanical voice came on one last time, and I turned around.

Talk about Mr. Popularity.

The message played, "*...4:45 p.m.*"

I looked at the clock above the stove. 5:23 p.m. Whoever it

was, called right around the time I hit mile three of my jog. A voice came on. This time it was a man's. *"Thomas, sorry I missed you."*

It was Ethan.

"...Hey, I never got a chance to thank you for that little piece of detective work you did with the surveillance tapes. Top of the line, Thomas. Top of the line. Although I briefly remember telling you that I didn't want you coming near this case. Do you remember that conversation, Thomas? Do you? It went a little something like this: 'You better watch your ass, Prescott, or I'm gonna make sure someone at county watches it for you.' Ring a bell?"

I hit pause. I remember him saying this. I also remember wanting to rip out his larynx after he said it.

I hit play. *"...I'm just calling to make sure that in the new year you don't do anything stupid. I've got the go-ahead from the boys upstairs to arrest you for just about anything. You fart and I smell it, and you're finished, you piece of shit. I told you to leave as quickly as you came. You should have listened to me. Oh, and one last thing, you prick. Stay away from Erica. You come near her, I'm not going to arrest you, I'm gonna shoot you...Hey, Happy New Year, pal."*

I wanted to call Ethan and tell him that the last time he threatened me he ended up with a broken nose, but then I'd be buying into his macho bullshit.

I made a peanut butter and jelly sandwich and contemplated my four phone messages. Then I took a well-deserved nap.

CHAPTER 35

RILEY'S CABIN was tucked back deep in the Cascades seven winding roads past the U.S. Fish and Wildlife building. It was made of logs and was square. I think I'd built the prototype with Lincoln Logs when I was seven.

I parked behind Riley's Jeep, grabbed the bottle of wine off the passenger seat, and strode to the door.

I hadn't known exactly how to dress for the occasion so I'd gone with a sweater. And a bad one at that. It was between my dad's holiday sweater collection—of which three lit up and one sang—and his Cosby collection. I'd chosen one from the latter and my sweater looked like it was sewn by a blind lady with an affinity for triangles.

I knocked on the door and Riley pulled it inward. She looked me up and down and said, "Nice sweater."

I brushed at it and said, "Dr. Huxtable at your service." I would have gone directly into my Cosby Pudding Pop bit, but I was a tad rusty.

Riley got a giggle out of this and said, "Did you find the place okay?"

This question really annoys me and I was tempted to say, "Um, if I didn't, I probably wouldn't be here," but Riley wasn't wearing much, and I put my wiseass remarks on screen saver. I said I found the place just fine.

For the record, Riley was wearing an apron. That's it. The apron was pink and said in wide lettering, "No Bitchin' in My Kitchen."

I told her I liked her apron.

She lifted the bottom of its skirt and twirled.

I nearly dropped the bottle of wine. Not to mention poking a hole through my favorite sweater.

I followed her inside and set the brown bag holding the wine on the counter. Two fish were laid out on a white cutting board. The scales were still oily and the eyes glassy. Come to think of it, they looked a lot like those stupid fish people hang on their walls that sing "Take Me To The River."

I commented, "Nice looking fish."

"Bass."

Billy Bass.

She said, "Caught them this morning."

"Give a man a fish, he eats for a day. Teach a man to fish, he eats every day."

"Right. Which are you?"

"I eat waffles."

She laughed. Then she opened the refrigerator, bent down (gulp), and handed me a Miller Light. I took it from her, we clinked beer necks, and both took a drink. Riley scooted me out of the kitchen, demanding that I take a look around while she filleted Billy and Bonny Bass.

She took out a large knife and said, "Beat it."

She was really living up to that apron.

So I walked the small cabin. And I had that stupid song in my head, which is quite possibly worse than an arrow.

Take me to the river.

Throw me in the water.

Stick a gun in my mouth.
Blow my brains out.

The cabin was small: one bedroom, small bath, living room, small dining room. I walked into the small bedroom and pushed my hand down on the bed. It wasn't a Sleep Number by Select Comfort, but it would do. There was a small window and I peeked out at an angle. It was a darkness only known to the deep mountains. I thought I saw a sputter of light in the distance and pushed my face against the cold glass. It'd been just the faintest of glows, like the flickering of a lighter. I watched for another minute but didn't see the anomaly again.

I was a bit on edge. I thought I'd seen a car following me on the highway. I'd been expecting Ethan to put a tail on me at some point, but I didn't figure too many guys would be volunteering for overtime on New Year's Eve.

Anyhow, by the time I made it full circle, the bottle of wine was open and breathing. I couldn't help but notice Riley had taken the liberty of pouring herself a small glass.

I said, "Thanks for waiting."

"I'm not really the patient type."

I, of course, had learned this firsthand.

She slid two large seasoned fish fillets into a pan and they began sizzling. She looked up at me and said, "They take about six minutes a side."

"Six minutes, huh?"

Funny. That was my average.

She picked up her glass and chugged the remaining inch. Then she undid her apron and let it drop to the floor. It was the couch the first time. Then she went to flip the fish. Then it was the kitchen floor.

After we'd eaten, Riley said she wanted to drink wine and watch me do the dishes. Kinky, I know.

At 11:30 we cuddled up on the couch and watched Dick Clark's New Year's Rocking Eve. Which had actually been over for nearly three hours, and no doubt Dick Clark was already under the covers, or in his hyperbolic chamber, or frozen, or hanging upside down in his cave.

We were under a blanket, Riley lying backward against me. I rubbed her firm belly with my right hand. She scratched my arm.

I was in lust. Again.

At 11:59, Riley jumped up, ran to the kitchen, and emerged a second later with a bottle of bubbly.

They released the ball and it slowly started to move down the pole. The crowd started chanting and Riley began counting down with them. At six seconds she pinched my leg and in my best Hans impression I said, "...funf...vier...drei...zwei...eins...Happy New Year."

After she shook her head in utter dismay, we kissed. And at that moment, in those first few moments of the new year, Riley Peterson was my only thought. She stuck her arm through mine and we both chugged our glasses of champagne. Then we kissed some more. Then we rang in the New Year.

Riley didn't have a kazoo, so we improvised.

CHAPTER 36

I OPENED my eyes and craned my head off the sofa. I wasn't sure who would be knocking at my door at 9:00 in the morning the first day of the year, and I was in no mood to find out.

The knocking subsided and I laid my head back down and closed my eyes. I'd left Riley's at some time around 3:30 a.m.—considerably tuckered out—and I was yet to get my eight hours of required shut-eye. Riley had to get up early, not my early but her early, and I was happy for the excuse to sleep on my own couch.

The knocking started back in, and I rolled off the sofa and walked to the door. I looked through the peephole. Whoever was out there was standing just inches from the lens and I couldn't decipher much. But it did appear to be more than one person. Whoever they were, they were *persona non grata* on my doorstep. I smoothed out the sweater, went to unlock the door—but it was already unlocked—and pulled it open.

I stared at Erica and Ethan through half-open eyes. I looked from one to the other, licked my lips, yawned, took a deep breath, yawned again, slammed the door and locked it, walked back to the couch, and flopped back onto it. This was about the time the knocking started back up.

It lasted five minutes. After ten, I decided they weren't going anywhere. Maybe Ethan had come to congratulate me in person on my outstanding detective work. Then again, maybe he'd bought me some huge sunglasses, a bomber jacket, and a plane ticket to South Korea.

I rolled off the couch and made the trek to the door a second time. As I pulled it open, I said to Ethan, whose hand was still in a fist and in the upright position, "If you stop banging your hand against the door, it will stop making that annoying knocking sound."

He sneered at me and took a step back.

Erica stepped forward and said, "We need to talk to you for a few minutes if that's okay."

Ethan threw her a strained glance. I don't think he appreciated her soft-spoken manner or the fact she was asking my permission. But it was obvious from their body language that they had planned on Erica leading the attack, whatever that might be.

I could think of only a handful of reasons that would put Ethan Kates and Erica Frost on my doorstep nine hours into the New Year. One, I was being arrested. For what? Well, there was the breaking and entering at Adam Gray's place, but I found it hard to believe he would press charges after what I'd done for him. Then you had my overall involvement in the case, which in some circles they might call "hampering an investigation." But I hadn't done much hampering in the last couple days. In fact, since I'd taken my trip to the North Cascades, I hadn't done much hampering at all. But Ethan had it in for me, and we all know when someone has it in for you, all the rules are thrown out the window. Which led to the only other thing I could think of: there had been a break in the Ellen Gray case, and Ethan and Erica were here to ask my advice. This option was slightly less believable than Scientology. So, in a nutshell, I had not the slightest clue, not an inkling, why an asshole, Erica, and two cops standing off in the distance were all staring at me like I had deviled egg all over my face.

I raised my eyebrows and said, "And what exactly do you need to talk to me about?"

"We just have a couple questions."

The quicker I answered their questions, the quicker I could get back to sleep. I said, "Fire away."

Ethan said, "Where were you last—"

Erica held up her hand, and he stopped midsentence. She nearly smiled and said, "So how did you spend your New Year's Eve?"

I wasn't sure I wanted to divulge to Erica that I spent the majority of my night playing hide the pickle with Park Ranger Peterson. But I'd also asked variations of this question enough times to know that if you aren't going to tell the truth, you need to say something that is nearly impossible to verify. So I said, "I didn't do much. Didn't leave the house. In bed by 1:00."

Ethan said, in a matter of fact tone, "Does the name Riley Peterson mean anything to you?"

I took a step back. I gave a slight nod and said, "Rings a bell. Why?"

I noticed Erica staring at her feet in my peripheral. I also noticed for the first time that Ethan was holding a manila envelope in his right hand. He opened the envelope and extracted a glossy photo.

He held out the photo and said, "She was found early this morning."

The words "was" and "found" rattled around my brain. I snapped the photo from Ethan's fingers and glanced down at it. Riley lay on her stomach on her kitchen linoleum. Blood pooled around her naked body.

My heart was caught in my throat. I couldn't believe Riley was dead. I'd seen her, all of her, every inch, just hours earlier. Now she was just a cold shell, lying in a pool of her own blood.

I said through clenched teeth, "Who found her?"

Erica was still looking down and spoke quietly. "Some guy she works with. When she didn't show up for work and didn't answer his calls, he drove to her cabin."

"What time?"

"A couple hours ago."

"What *time*?"

"7:23 a.m."

Ethan couldn't stand it. "If you don't mind, we'll ask the questions."

I wanted to tell him to go fuck himself but held it in.

After a slight pause he asked, "Were you with the victim last night?"

"Would you be here if I weren't?"

"No."

Evidently, Ethan had put a tail on me.

"You had me followed, you piece of shit."

"First off, if I wanted to put a tail on you it would be well within my jurisdiction. But, no, I didn't."

If Ethan hadn't had me followed, then who had been following me, and more importantly, how did they know how I rang in the new year?

Ethan sensed my thought process and said, "We found a receipt for a bottle of wine in the trash. You used your MasterCard."

Right.

I looked at Erica and said, "Isn't this a little out of your guys' jurisdiction?"

Ethan said, "I pulled some strings."

I bet he did. I bet once he heard my name, he called in every marker he had out there. But then again, some of these smaller counties don't even have a homicide detective on the payroll and wouldn't hesitate to pass the buck.

Ethan broke my musings. "Why did you lie about being with

the victim?"

"Because it's none of your business how, or with who, I spend my New Year's." And I was trying to be somewhat of a gentleman in front of Erica Frost.

"This is true. But when a women ends up dead and you were the last one to see her alive, then it becomes my business."

Touché. But since I didn't kill her, I highly doubted I was the last one to see her alive.

Erica asked, "You mind telling us about your night?"

Ethan gave Erica another harsh stare. He didn't like that her approach ended with question marks. He was right. You don't ask questions. You demand answers.

I shook my head and said, "Not really."

Ethan took a deep breath and said, "Account for your where-abouts from the minute you left the house last evening to when you returned home."

"No thanks."

"Then you wouldn't mind if we took a look inside."

I took a step to the side and said, "Be my guest."

He waved the cops forward and they strode past me. One of the cops snarled at me as he passed. I grabbed his arm and dug my fingers into his small biceps and said, "Be careful. I wouldn't want to have to break anything valuable of yours."

He ripped his arm from my grasp, threw me a look, then ambled past me. That left Erica, Ethan, and me standing on the stoop and more or less twiddling our thumbs. You had Ethan who hated my guts and had a good suspicion that I was a murderer. Then you had Erica who was interested in Mr. Thomas Prescott but was a bit circumspect now that he might have killed a woman. And then you had Thomas Prescott who could give half a shit about the two people standing on his porch because a woman he cared about was dead and she was never coming back.

Anyhow, no words were said.

After about thirty seconds, Ethan said to Erica, "I'd better get in there and make sure they aren't breaking any of Thomas's valuables."

He walked past me. I wondered if it was coded in his DNA to be such an unconscionable prick.

At present, Erica was checking her shoes for scuffs. She looked up and said, "I'm sorry."

She didn't specify what exactly she was sorry for. But I assumed it was an all-inclusive sorry about Riley, sorry that we had to come here today, and sorry that it had to be like this. Or maybe it was a pre-sorry for what was still to come, my arrest, the sentence, and the prison anal raping. Then again, it could be a post-sorry, a sorry we ever met. Regardless, she was just doing her job. I gave a little nod.

Fifteen minutes later, Ethan emerged. He made eye contact with Erica that said they hadn't found anything.

I asked, "Did you stumble across my Gameboy?"

Ethan ignored me.

I asked, "Where are Tweetledee and Tweetledum?"

He smiled and said, "Just tidying up a bit."

They were probably taking a whiz in my ice trays and giving me an upper decker.

Five minutes later, the first of the officers walked out. He gave me an odd stare. Three feet behind him was his buddy. He shook his head at me and smiled. In his right hand, shielded by his body, was a clear evidence bag. He walked up to Ethan and said defiantly, "We found this in the flamingo room."

Ethan held up the baggy. In the evidence bag was a long, curved knife. I recognized it. It was the knife Riley had used to fillet the fish.

Eight eyes trained on the knife. Then moved to my chest.

Oh, bugger.

CHAPTER 37

INTERROGATION ROOMS HAVE CHANGED over the years. The concrete bunkers, one-way mirrors, bolted down tables, garage lighting, and heat lamps were a thing of the past. Leave that stuff to the KGB. Nowadays, most everything was glass. Studies showed suspects were measurably more cooperative when they were on display.

Today, however, this would not be the case.

I rested my elbows on the thin, rectangular table and watched Ethan, Erica, and a handful of others confer through the tinted glass. This went on for over an hour. Different people would come and go, there would be a quick conference, sometimes something would be passed from one person to another, and always a quick glance in my direction before leaving.

Twenty minutes later, Ethan pushed through the door. He feigned reading a document, then looked up. He looked almost surprised to see me. Like he hadn't expected me to be in the room he'd locked me in.

He asked, "How you doin?"

"I'm super."

He sat down and I noticed for the first time since I'd met him that he wasn't chewing gum. At that moment, he pulled a pack from his coat pocket—that stuff you push through the foil—and popped a piece. He offered the pack to me and I respectfully declined.

"I've been off the stuff for three years now," I said.

He didn't find this amusing. I almost told him to lighten up. I mean, you would have thought the guy was a suspect in a homicide investigation or something. He had a bunch of paperwork spread out in front of him, including the manila envelope containing the crime scene photos of Riley. This might be my only chance to view the pictures and I asked, "You mind?"

He shrugged and slid the envelope across the table. This would have been a later tactic on his behalf—make the suspect study the pictures. Sometimes the reality of the crime would hit home and then the suspect would crack on the spot. I'd seen it happen before my very eyes. I'd even had one suspect look at the crime scene photos of an eleven-year-old girl he murdered and smile with pride. I may have accidentally smashed his face into the picture. Accidents happen.

I slid the envelope off the table and stared at it. I'd seen hundreds of these crime scene photographs and it's never easy. If you know the person intimately, as I knew Riley, it was nearly impossible. Some people could flip that switch, turn off their emotions. Take Ethan, for example. He had looked at these pictures and he hadn't seen Riley; he hadn't even seen a woman. He saw a case. He saw a picture of someone behind bars. He saw a picture of me, maybe with a needle in my arm. Or maybe he saw a picture of me tossing some big black guy's salad. Whatever he saw, he didn't see death.

I'd never been able to flip that switch. I was emotionally involved in every case I ever worked. It separated me from them. It's why I was the best. Or had been.

I extracted a stack of seven glossy photographs. The top photo was the one I'd already seen. I gave this a quick glance then shuffled it to the back. The next was a close-up of Riley's head and neck. Her short brown hair fell over her face, but her left eye was visible, open about half way. There was a dark gash in her neck, and dried blood was caked around the wound like dried lava. The blood pooled around her neck in about a foot radius, and the surface had just begun to harden into a blood pudding.

I flipped to the next picture. It was the whole of the kitchen. Blood spatter covered the white linoleum, a couple of the cabinets, and half the white cutting board.

I glanced at the remaining four pictures, slid them back in the envelope, and slid the envelope back across the table.

Ethan said, "Admiring your work?"

"Fuck you."

He paused for a few moments, then said, "So tell me how it went down."

"I told you, when I last saw Riley she very much alive."

He nodded.

He riffled through the papers, not looking at anything in particular, then glanced up. "Here's what we got. We can put you at the scene. You and no one else. So you had the means. You lied to us about your alibi. That's never good. And we found the murder weapon hidden under your sister's bed." He shook his head. "Now if you were me, would you arrest you?"

Was this guy born in Pronounville?

I asked, "If I were me, would you arrest I?"

"You think this is funny?"

"I certainly do not." And I didn't.

After a long moment I answered his question. "First, I'm not you. If I was, I would have done the world a favor, checked the organ donor box on the back of my license, and jumped in front of a Greyhound years ago." Ethan's nostrils gave a slight flare and I continued. "Second, yes, I would probably arrest me."

He grinned.

"But only if you were me."

The grin faded. He'd had about enough of me. I'm better in doses.

He stood up and said, "I'm gonna go grab a drink. You want something?"

I was parched and said, "A blue Powerade. The one with the sports top." There was a vending machine on the third floor that sold such things. At least there had been eight years ago.

He waved me off and said, "Nothing, then."

Jerk.

I watched through the glass as Ethan conversed quickly with Erica. I could make out the last words he said: *Are you up for this?*

She nodded. Then she stared at me through the glass. Ethan gave me one last look.

I mouthed, *"Blue Powerade. Sports Top."*

He mouthed two unmistakable words before walking off.

Erica had turned around—no doubt to take one last calming breath—then pushed through the doors. I didn't take my eyes off her as she pulled out a chair and sat. She raised the left side of her mouth and said, "How you doing?"

I shook my head. This was going to be far more difficult than I had anticipated. Ethan had been a cinch. This tore at my heartstrings.

She gave a quick smile, then her right hand shot forward a couple inches. She caught herself and drew it back. After a lengthy pause, she said, "So, I've been talking to the D.A."

I knew where this was heading and I began shaking my head.

"Hear me out. Please." Her voice was trembling. "I've been talking to the D.A. and I think we can plead this down to Man Two. That's less than fifteen. Hell, these days you wouldn't do more than six or seven."

I reached out and grabbed Erica's hand. I said slowly, "I... didn't...do it."

It might have been my touch, or the fact that tears were starting to form in the creases of my eyes, but I saw it. Erica had walked through those doors under the presumption I was a killer. No longer.

If Ethan hadn't entered then, I might have leaned over the table and kissed her.

Ethan pulled up a chair and said, "Am I interrupting something?" I noticed he just happened to be holding a blue Powerade. With a sports top.

Erica shook her head.

"Good." He flipped the top on the Powerade, threw me a wry smile, brought the bottle to his mouth and squeezed. Nothing came out. He raised his eyebrows, shook the bottle, and squeezed again. Again, nothing came out.

I laughed.

Three shakes, five squeezes, and thirty seconds later, Ethan unscrewed the top and peeled off the safety seal under the cap. This took my mind off the fact I was being investigated for murder for a split second. That is, until a woman in a lab coat pushed through the door and handed a printed document to Ethan.

Ethan perused the document, then handed it to Erica. She gave it a quick glance before handing it back to Ethan.

He shook his head and said, "Bad news, Thomas. Very... bad...news."

"Aren't you supposed to ask if I want to hear the good news first?"

"There is no good news."

That *was* bad news.

He slid the document across the table. He said, "We were able to lift a set of fingerprints from the knife. Full thumb and partial right index." He paused and added, "Both are exact matches to your prints on file."

I picked up the document. The document was six separate images. There were images of both sides of the knife. The knife was about eight inches long, slightly curved. Like a quarter moon.

Small amounts of dried blood speckled both sides. You could see the thumbprint on one side of the blade and the partial index on the opposite side. Then there were two blown-up images of the fingerprints, as well as two blow-ups of my prints that were on file. Both were positive matches.

I slid the document back over the table and said calmly, "I did the dishes."

He looked confused and I repeated, "I did the dishes."

"You expect me to believe that you left those prints while washing the dishes."

"I don't give a shit what you believe. That's what happened."

"If you were washing the dishes then it makes sense that you would have washed off your fingerprints as well."

"Wrong."

"Wrong?"

"I must have confused you. By doing the dishes, I meant that I put the dishes in the dishwasher." I heard some people gave the dishes a quick rinse before placing them in the dishwasher, but this always seemed silly to me. If the dishes aren't clean after their first go-round, you do a second. I ran a load once—after eating only peanut butter and jelly for a week—eleven times.

Ethan said, "You said before that the victim filleted the fish."

"True."

"Then why aren't her prints anywhere on the knife?"

"Maybe you've heard of this thing called Teflon. Many consumer products are made from this material, like the handle of the fillet knife, for instance. Teflon, by virtue of its slipperiness, repels oil and would make a fingerprint nearly impossible to come by."

Was this guy still cooking in clay pots?

He nodded.

Point, Prescott.

I wasn't done. "And if you look at your little printout there," he picked it up, "Those fingerprints are on the blade."

I mimicked picking up the blade with my thumb and right index finger. "That's how I picked up the knife and set it in the dishwasher. You don't grab a knife in that fashion if you intend to use it to take someone's life."

"That's not to say that you didn't handle the knife by the handle. You said yourself that Teflon repels oil so fingerprints would be hard to come by."

"Actually, I said, '*impossible* to come by.'"

"Regardless. Technically, you could have handled the knife without leaving a print."

My friend Ethan was starting to piss me off, and I mentally took an invisible two-by-four out of my pocket and smashed it across his face, which, surprisingly enough, made me feel much better.

He was about to start talking and I interrupted him. "But—"

He raised his eyebrows.

I leaned forward and said, "That knife that you have a picture of—" I paused so he could pick up the printout, "—isn't the knife that was used to kill Riley."

He looked at the image. Erica leaned over for a better look. I'm not sure either of them bought what I was selling.

Ethan said, "And why exactly do you think this?"

"For one, those prints are set in fish oil." Fish oil was thick and it had sheen to it. I continued, "Can we agree on this much?"

Erica said, "We'd have to run a test, but I'd say that is accurate."

Ethan gave her a harsh stare, but he too seemed to concur with this analysis. He said nothing to contradict this statement. "So if my prints are set in fish oil, it's safe to say that these prints were imprinted prior to the death of the victim."

Erica nodded. I looked at Ethan. After a long pause, he nodded.

I continued, "Look at the amount of blood on the knife. Not much at all. Barely any, actually."

Erica's and Ethan's faces were just inches from the document, nearly touching. They both surveyed the knife for a long minute. Erica said, "You're right."

Of course I was right.

I added, "The victim died from a laceration of the neck, more accurately the carotid artery, which we all know is the biggest artery in the body. I mean, look at the crime scene photos; there's blood spatter six feet from the body. How, then, is it possible that there is almost no blood on the knife? No, if this knife was the murder weapon, there would be so much blood that those perfect fingerprints of mine would be long gone."

Erica was smiling.

Ethan was stewing.

In case I hadn't already convinced the pair, I said, "Also, if you look at the size and shape of the laceration on the victim's neck, it isn't consistent with the knife found under my sister's mattress. The knife that killed the victim was serrated." Fillet knives aren't serrated.

Erica shuffled through the photos until she found the close-up of the laceration. She looked up, "You're right. There's too much blood coagulated near the wound. If this was the knife used, it would be much cleaner."

Thatta girl.

Ethan took the photo from her and returned it with the others. He said, "Well, that's enough for today."

He left the room for a brief moment, had a quick conversation with a man in a suit, then returned. He had a piece of paper in his hand. He walked behind me and said, "Thomas Prescott, you are under arrest for the murder of Riley Peterson."

Erica's eyes bulged but she said nothing. Evidently there had been enough evidence to convince a judge to sign an arrest warrant.

I couldn't really blame them. But I did.

I turned to him and said, "If you think I'm going to jail, you're fucking crazy."

He laughed.

"I want my phone call."

"Sure thing."

He gave a quick chuckle, and he and Erica walked from the room. A moment later a uniformed officer pushed through the door with a phone. He asked me the number and I told him. He dialed, then handed me the phone. The cuffs made it difficult to talk and I was forced to hold the phone up to my ear using both hands. I had a minute-long conversation, then handed the phone back to the officer. He left as quickly as he came.

Ten minutes later, Erica and Ethan strolled back in. Ethan had a shit-eating grin on his face and asked, "So who'd you call?"

"My lawyer."

He got a kick out of that. "Oh, I can't wait to see this guy." He picked up his blue Powerade and shot a stream into his mouth. He kicked his legs up on the table and said, "I made a special request that you be in the same cell as Joey Valeno. You remember him?"

Joey Valeno was a guy I busted my first year. I may or may not have accidentally shot the tip of his dick off.

Ethan added, "I told him you were on your way. He said he would start stretching."

If this was true, I could kiss my ass good-bye. Literally.

Ten minutes later, my lawyer showed up. He walked through the door and laid his briefcase on the table. I watched as Ethan's jaw slowly dropped and the gum he'd been chewing spewed onto his lap.

Adam Gray looked at me and said, "Don't say another word."

CHAPTER 38

ETHAN AND ERICA left the room, and Adam and I conferred. After twenty minutes, Adam waved the detectives back in.

They walked through the door and sat. The cocky Ethan of earlier was nowhere to be seen. It was hard to believe that, only weeks earlier, Ethan had led a handcuffed Adam Gray down the courthouse steps. And now, here he was, an innocent man, representing quite possibly Ethan's least favorite person on the planet.

Ha.

Adam was dressed immaculately in a three-piece suit. Navy blue and probably cost what most people pay for a secondhand KIA. He lifted his right foot up onto the chair next to me and feigned tying his shoe. His shoe was tied, and I guessed it was more posturing than anything else. He stayed in that position, half leaning, right foot up on the chair, and stared at the two detectives. Finally, he said, "After conferring with my client, it would appear there are a couple of small kinks in your investigation."

Both Erica and Ethan sat upright.

Adam took his foot off the chair and began pacing the small room. He said to no one in particular, "It would appear to me your case is based solely on the murder weapon. Is it safe to assume that if the murder weapon was not discovered in my client's sister's room, under the sister's bed, then my client wouldn't be here right now?"

Ethan said, "We can also place your client at the scene."

"My client doesn't deny that he was with the victim."

"Actually, he did."

"What do you mean?"

Ethan's back straightened just slightly, and he said, "When we first questioned him about his whereabouts last night, he lied. He said he didn't leave the house, when in actuality he was with the victim."

Adam looked at me and said, "My client failed to inform me of this."

Whoops.

He turned his gaze to Erica, then back to Ethan. He then said, "Did it ever occur to you my client didn't want to discuss his New Year's Eve blowjob in front of your partner here?"

Ethan looked at Erica than back to Adam. He didn't have an answer. Erica gave a hesitant look in my direction, then broke away.

Gray added, "And is it not true that when you did reveal the identity of the victim, my client volunteered freely that he was indeed with the victim on the night in question?"

Ethan said nothing. Erica chimed in, "Yes."

"Thank you, Detective Frost."

She gave a thin nod.

"But this isn't what concerns me. What concerns me is the murder weapon. The knife found under the sister's bed."

Ethan said, "As it should."

"You found the murder weapon in the sister's room, under the sister's bed. Is this correct?"

"Where the weapon was found is moot. Your client consented to the search of the entire property."

Adam said perfunctorily, "See, that's the problem."

Ethan sat up. Erica leaned forward.

I crossed my arms and smiled.

Adam trained his eyes on Ethan and said, "By property you are referring to the residence of 14 Magnolia Lane, Seattle, Washington, 98199."

"That sounds right."

"That residence belongs to my client's sister, a one Lacy Prescott."

Ethan went limp.

My father had named me sole executor of his will. After all the red tape was cleared, debts paid, taxes remunerated, and stock options settled, what was left over was a healthy inheritance, not to mention two properties. My parents also owned a home in San Diego. My father was all but retired, having to sit in on a board of directors meeting every couple months, and my parents spent the majority of the winter in San Diego. The inheritance went into a joint bank account accessible to both Lacy and me. The deed to the San Diego property was under my name. The deed to the Magnolia house was under Lacy Ann Prescott.

Adam said, "Only the owner of a property can consent to a search of said property. This would make the knife inadmissible in court."

Ethan blew out a long exhale, the weight of his blunder almost visible on his slouched shoulders. "The property deed will have to be verified."

I said, "It will be on file at the King County Recorder's office."

Ethan was down but not out. He said with a smirk, "Unfortunately, it's a holiday weekend and the recorder's office is closed until Monday." He turned to Adam and said, "Looks like your client will be spending a couple days in the county jail after all."

I looked at Adam and shook my head. "Have him call the judge."

I knew enough about the law to know that if the judge who signed the arrest warrant saw fit, he could dismiss the order.

Adam said, "I think that's a terrific idea." He turned to Ethan. "Who signed the arrest warrant?"

"Judge Harden."

"Call him."

"I would, but we barely caught him at his home. He and his wife are headed to the San Juans for the holiday weekend." He tried to give the impression there wasn't anything he could do.

I said, "Call his cell."

Ethan scoffed and said, "Harden doesn't believe in cell phones. He says they make people easy to find."

Adam laughed. I had a feeling he'd heard these exact words from the mouth of the lion himself. He looked at me and said, "Don't worry, Harriet should have hers with her."

"Harriet?"

"Yes, Harriet. His wife."

Adam whipped out his cell phone and dialed.

Ethan stared on with horror.

After a long couple seconds, Adam said, "Harriet, how are you?...Happy New Year to you too...So, I hear you're headed to the San Juans...Lovely this time of year...Listen, can I have a quick word with Bob?...I know, but it's important...will do."

He looked at me and winked.

Ethan was slowly turning a shade of green.

Adam started back up. "Slow down, Bob...I'm doing you a favor here...Will you listen to me?...About the arrest warrant you signed...Yeah, well, it wasn't his property...No, I'm not shitting you...You have to dismiss the charges...Yeah, right here...You want to talk to him?"

Adam handed the phone to Ethan, who took it as though it were made of enriched uranium. Meanwhile, Erica was trying to hide a widening grin.

After taking what must have been a two-minute tongue-lashing, Ethan handed the phone back to Adam.

For a moment, I thought he was going to cry.

My lawyer listened for another minute, then said, "Yeah, yeah, no problem...Yes, that could have been embarrassing...Next Thursday...I'll make the tee time."

Ten minutes later, I walked out of the Seattle Police Department a free man.

CHAPTER 39

I SPENT the better part of the holiday weekend feeling sorry for myself. Now, I'm not saying if you're a woman and you let me into your life you are destined to meet an untimely death, but my record was pretty grisly. Just over a year before, the last case I worked, my ex-fiancée was brutally murdered. And both my sister and Alex came very close to being killed.

That's why I'd run from that life. That's why I was back in Seattle, to escape it all. Mind my own business and maybe, just maybe, stop getting people killed. But there are some things you can't run from. Just ask Riley Peterson.

But now I was involved. I no longer had control over my actions. I was like that big boulder in *Indiana Jones and the Temple of Doom*. Riley's death had set me in motion and I wouldn't stop, couldn't stop, until I crushed whoever had killed her.

I was about to snap. I needed to go running. I laced up the old Asics and started into the drizzle.

After about a half mile, the crime scene photos of Riley flashed through my mind. I tried to blink the images away, but they didn't waver. I knew from past experience that these images would play over and over until I found out who killed her, who robbed her of her life.

If Riley had just been murdered, I might've been able to write this off as a terrible coincidence, just another victim of the ubiquitous black cloud that had shrouded my life for the past decade. But I'd been framed for her murder. Someone either wanted me locked up or they wanted to send a clear message that I was snooping around in something I shouldn't be. Was this the same person that framed Adam Gray for his wife's murder? I didn't see how it could be anyone else. Ellen and Riley's murders had to be connected.

Speaking of Ellen, the more I thought about her, the more I was convinced whoever killed her wanted her body to be discovered. I thought about where Gray's yacht had been driven that night and how her body had been dumped. This particular channel of the Sound was probably the most highly-trafficked waterway in all of the Pacific Northwest. You had multiple ferries crisscrossing through the water every thirty minutes. You had boats coming in and out of Fishermen's Terminal at all hours. Not to mention a Coast Guard station, one of the five largest shipping piers on the West Coast, and four tourist overlooks. There were more eyes scanning this particular area than possibly any other waterway in the United States. I mean, the chances of Ellen's body *not* being found were astronomical.

But why? Why would someone want her body found?

Obviously, they wanted to frame Adam for her murder. But this seemed almost after the fact.

Maybe I was looking at this all wrong. Maybe I needed to start looking at this from a new perspective. Not Ellen. But Adam. Maybe one of Adam's clients. I'm sure he represented his fair share of shady individuals. But from what I'd read, he'd gotten most of them off scot-free, so they should be sending him fruit baskets, not framing him for his wife's murder.

Then you had Riley. What was her role? She was peripherally

connected to Ellen through the North Cascades. Had Riley seen or heard something and kept quiet? She didn't seem the type. Maybe she knew something without knowing it. And maybe whoever killed her thought I would be the one to drag it out of her. Or maybe they killed her just to piss me off.

Which brought us back to me.

Once again, I'd found myself tangled up in a sticky web of death. Was I an innocent fly that had been caught unexpectedly by the trap? Not really. But Riley had been. Ellen, possibly, as well. Even Adam hadn't intentionally been prodding and poking at the web as I had. I'd been the one to awaken the spider. I'd been the one flying around, watching as the spider silently crept up to his captive and sank in his teeth.

But who was the spider?

I didn't have the faintest idea.

My gut had always told me it had something to do with the North Cascades. This was the only point where Riley, Ellen, and I connected. I had a feeling Ellen Gray's relationship with the North Cascades went a bit deeper than hiking and leisure.

I had a couple more questions I wanted to throw at Kim, Ellen's press secretary. But my mind was sapped. I needed to set it all aside for a while.

I needed to see Harold.

———

As per regulations, I stopped at the front desk to sign in before I made my way to Harold's room.

The woman at the desk was new—maybe a couple hours younger than the dug-up corpse I was used to seeing—and she picked up the clipboard after I signed it. I'm guessing the other lady had made the move from employee to resident. Anyhow, the lady raised her penciled-in eyebrows and said, "Who's CH?"

"Cretaceous Harold."

Her eyebrows nearly touched, or overlapped, and I said, "That's what he told me to call him."

She checked a ledger and her face fell. Uh-oh.

She said, "I have some bad news."

I took a deep breath. I wasn't stable enough to handle the old coot kicking the bucket. I mean, I know sometimes old people die. But Harold was really, really, really old. He was nearly mummified. It had never registered that he was, in fact, pushing his luck.

I asked, "Dead?"

She shook her head, "Not yet."

Yet?

She added, "He's in the hospital wing. Took a pretty bad fall a couple days ago. Broke both his wrists."

I tried to hold in a laugh but was unsuccessful. The image of Harold with a cast on each wrist was too much. But the good news was I wouldn't have to hear any more polka any time soon.

I asked, "Can I see him?"

She said I could and gave me directions.

I made my way to the hospital wing, which should have been called the morgue wing. In the hallway, I passed two black bags or, as we referred to them in my past life, two "deadies."

I found his room and peeked through the small window in the closed door. I could see Harold sitting upright in the bed, his casted arms crossed over his chest. He had an IV in one arm and an oxygen mask over his mouth. A nurse was standing in front of a large machine with a clipboard. My stomach tightened. I think there was more to the story than just two broken wrists.

I pushed through the door.

The nurse, an attractive black woman, glanced at me and smiled. I smiled back and said, "How is he?"

She leaned her head to the side and said, "He's stable."

"What happened?"

"Well, they initially brought him here for two broken wrists.

Poor guy thought he had his walker in front of him and leaned forward to take a step. Fell face-first. Snapped both wrists."

I glanced down at Harold. The oxygen mask over his mouth filled with fog as his chest fell. His glasses were off and sitting on a small tray just to his left.

I asked, "What's with all the tubes?"

She put the clipboard down, uncrossed Harold's arms, and set them at his sides. She looked up and said, "While they were setting his wrists he had what's called an emphysema attack. Basically, it's just a violent coughing attack, but it can easily cause a heart attack or stroke or internal bleeding. Luckily, he was in the hospital wing and we could give him something to quell it right off."

I nodded.

On a small side table were six or seven cards, a couple bouquets of flowers, a coffee mug, two AA batteries, a blue Sharpie, a stapler, and a Snackpack of tapioca pudding.

The nurse noticed my gaze and said, "They steal things, then send them to each other as get-well presents."

I laughed. Maybe I could get a job here as a security guard. Patrol the halls. Catch one of these guys stealing the batteries out of a remote and send him to a week in the hole.

The nurse started for the door and said, "The meds we gave him should wear off here pretty soon, so he might wake up." She waved the clipboard at me and walked out.

I read a couple of the cards while I ate the pudding. Then I made my way to the window at the back of the room and peered out. There was a clear view of the lake. The shallow parts near the shore were frozen, but the water in the deep center still carried a soft ripple.

I heard a cough and turned. Harold was awake. I could see him fidgeting with the mask with his two white club hands. I walked over to him and lifted the mask off his face. His usual oxygen tank was sitting beside the bed, and I helped him get it situated. Then I took his glasses off the side table and slid them over his large nose. His eyes widened when he saw me.

I said, "I'm the new nurse."

"Where's Oprah?"

"Oprah?"

"Yeah, the black lady."

I laughed. "She said she'd be back in a bit."

His eyes lit up. I think he liked her. I imagine through those thick lenses, she did look a lot like Oprah.

I said, "You want to play Frisbee?"

The joke was lost on him.

We chatted about his injury for a couple minutes. I told him he was made of balsa. He thought this was funny and had a small cough attack. I made a mental note to take my hilarious antics, quips, and witticisms down a couple notches. I mean, if I so much as farted, Harold could be a goner. Plus, Ethan would probably arrest me for homicide.

I don't know if Harold sensed his time was running out, but he didn't waste much of it. He leaned his head back, staring at the ceiling, and said, "After seeing Elizabeth, I was a mess."

Harold couldn't think. He kept putting things on backwards. He could barely hold a screwdriver. He was constantly sweating. His muscles ached. His stomach was in knots. He couldn't eat. He lost ten pounds. Finally, he was forced to quit his job.

His boss was loyal to a fault and told him it was a shame to lose him and there would always be a job for him if he wanted to come back. Harold appreciated his boss's kindness, but he wasn't sure if he could ever work another day of his life. He was having trouble breathing enough times to get through each day.

It was worse. It was worse than three years earlier. How was that possible? Wasn't time supposed to heal all wounds? How could he feel this way after three years? How could he feel this way about a girl he'd never had a conversation with in person?

The first time Harold went by the school, he just did one quick pass. There was a high wrought iron fence surrounding the small campus, with a gate in the front for cars and people to come and go. Three large buildings stood on the well-manicured grounds. Three stories of dark brick each. He saw a single girl walking on campus on his first pass. She was dressed in a black skirt and white blouse. It wasn't Elizabeth.

Harold made a second pass a half hour later. He didn't know much about the goings-on of a college campus, but he assumed the girls got a break between classes. The courtyard filled up with the young women. All dressed the same. Black skirt. White blouse. He saw thirty girls that could have been Elizabeth. It was impossible to tell.

Harold did the same the next day. And then the next. He took to wearing different clothes. A hat one day. Carrying an umbrella the next. He would walk slowly and scan the masses. The group of girls sitting in a circle giggling. The lone girl sitting against a tree reading. The three girls eating lunch at the picnic table.

This went on for days, then weeks. Harold would go at different times. Sometimes early, sometimes late. Sometimes he would get a newspaper and sit on the bus bench across the street. He never saw her. Although he wasn't exactly sure what he would do if he did see her. Just run up to the fence and scream how much he loved her? How he couldn't eat? Couldn't sleep? Couldn't live without her?

Harold noticed the men on a Wednesday. There were a handful of them, maybe six or seven. The men were roughly the same age as he was, a couple looked to be even a tad younger. Three of them were mowing the lawn of the large grounds. Others were trimming hedges. Two were planting flowers. Another was on a ladder washing the windows.

Every once in a while a group of the girls would approach one of the men. They would talk to him and blush and giggle. Then one of the teachers would walk over and chastise the girls, and they would continue giggling as they walked away.

Harold shook his head. It never changed. These girls were the elite. They weren't allowed to talk to the groundskeepers. It's just the way it was. Maybe that's how it would always be. Harold watched this dynamic of the grounds crew, the young women, and the teachers for three Wednesdays.

On the fourth Wednesday, Harold got up early. He put on a ratty pair of jeans and a white T-shirt. He hadn't shaved in a couple days and he had a bit of stubble. He looked in the mirror and smiled.

Harold wasn't sure how early they arrived. He guessed they got there pretty early to beat the heat, so he got in position at 5:30.

The men arrived promptly at 6:00, each carrying a box. Harold wasn't sure what was in the boxes. They came to the gate and it was unlocked by a well-dressed fat man. His hair was slicked back and he greeted them with a sneer. He looked familiar. Like one of Harold's commanders from his days in the army. He stuck a key in the large gate lock.

Harold made his move. He crossed the street and bellied up to the back of the group. One by one, they walked past the man at the gate. When Harold passed, the man put his arm out. He said, "Never seen you before, boy."

Harold managed, "I'm new. They decided to add a man so we can get out of here quicker."

The large man contemplated this then let Harold through. He locked up the gate and Harold followed the men to a shed. One of the guys—a kid around Harold's age with a shaved head and a thin mustache—turned and said, "Don't mind him. That's the dean of the school. He's an asshole." The guy stuck out his hand. "I'm Jimmy."

Harold stuck with Jimmy, who was in charge of washing windows. There were 117 in all. Jimmy liked to talk. And two hours in and twenty-eight windows later, according to Jimmy's count, Harold had almost forgotten why he was there in the first place.

At 9:00, the rooms started to fill up. Jimmy said, "Just ignore 'em."

A couple of girls made small waves at them. Or winked. Harold blushed a couple times. He thought if he saw Elizabeth he would most certainly fall off his ladder.

At 11:00, the grounds filled up with the young women. Harold peered around every so often, but for the most part he concentrated on the job at

*hand. He was having trouble keeping up with the speedy Jimmy. A half
hour later, the rooms filled back up, and Jimmy said it was time for a
break. The seven men, plus Harold, found a spot in the shade, and each
opened up the box they'd been carrying. Lunch.*

*Harold couldn't believe he forgot to pack a lunch. For the first time in
a long time, he was starving. One of the other guys, Harold was pretty
sure his name was Robby, asked, "Why ain't you eatin?"*

*Harold grinned sheepishly. "Forgot my lunch on the kitchen table.
And on my first day, of all things."*

*The guys took a laugh at this. Jimmy ripped a large chunk of sand-
wich off and handed it to him. Each of the other six men did the same.
Harold felt an instant camaraderie he hadn't felt since the army. The
eight of them ate and talked shop for an hour. Harold mostly listened.
Someone brought up the war and Harold chimed in. When the guys
found out Harold had been in the war, D-Day even, they peppered him
with questions. By the end of the day, he was just one of the guys.*

*They broke for the day and Harold asked Jimmy, "Where are you
guys going tomorrow?"*

*They were doing another college on the other side of town. Harold
was there. With a lunch box. They did another college on Friday. Harold
was there. Harold walked by the school twice over the weekend. Girls
came and went, but Harold didn't see Elizabeth. They did a large private
estate on Monday and Tuesday. Harold was there. The next Wednesday
came fast.*

*Harold quickly became friends with all seven guys: Jimmy, Robby,
Marky, Jake, Ben, Jerry, and Perry.*

*Harold saw a couple girls he thought might have been Elizabeth.
There was one girl he was sure was her, but after tapping the glass, she
turned and it wasn't.*

*On Friday, Jimmy handed Harold an envelope. When Harold opened
it and found it filled with cash, he looked surprised. Jimmy said, "I
thought something was fishy about you."*

Harold was silent.

Jimmy shrugged, "I don't much care. I told the boss I hired another guy to help with the windows. Said he preferred to be paid in cash if that was all right. Boss shrugged and said he didn't much care as long as the job gets done."

Harold and the guys hit a bar after work on Friday. Harold didn't remember ever having so much fun.

Summer came and the school cleared out, so he didn't have to worry about seeing Elizabeth. In August, the girls came back.

It happened the first week of September.

It was about a half hour before the girls would break, and Jimmy and Harold were working on the south building. They usually did the north building second, but the sun had moved over the months and they kept the shade the longest if they got the south building out of the way early. Harold had for the most part stopped his incessant scanning of the classrooms, but every once in a while he would sneak a peek.

He'd never seen the group he saw that day as he peered into the small classroom. On the blackboard behind the teacher he could see some scribbles that he thought looked like poetry. Every once in a while, a girl would come to the front and read from a notebook. Harold watched as one girl sat down and another stood up. She walked to the front and turned.

It was Elizabeth.

Harold couldn't breathe. He watched as she read from her notebook.

Jimmy said, "What's wrong? Come on, we're laggin' behind here, Harry."

He ignored Jimmy and watched Elizabeth. Her chest heaved as she read, and he could see tears running down her cheeks. She was crying. Elizabeth walked back to her seat, head down, never looking in his direction.

Later at lunch, Harold ate his ham and cheese in silence as the others told stories. Robby asked, "Why you so quiet over there, Harry?"

Harold looked around, and then he told them. He told them the whole story. An hour break turned into a two-hour break. No one spoke. They hung on his every word. When he was done, Marky asked, "What are you going to do?"

Harold sighed and said, "What can I do?"
Jimmy smiled and said, "I have an idea."
And so the eight of them hatched a plan.

"Hatched a plan?" I shook my head. "What are you, a bunch of bank robbers?"

Harold laughed. And then he coughed. And then he coughed some more. By the time I returned with the nurse, Harold was coughing so violently I thought he was going to break in half.

The nurse injected a syringe into his IV, removed Harold's glasses and put the mask over his face. His coughing slowed. A minute later, Harold's breathing had stabilized.

I took a deep breath.

The nurse, Oprah, came over to me and said, "You okay?"

I nodded.

She patted me on the arm and said, "Don't worry, he'll be all right."

After she left, I watched Harold for a good ten minutes. Then I grabbed the Sharpie off the counter and signed Harry's cast.

CHAPTER 40

THE SEATTLE FREEWAY SYSTEM, for the most part, is a never-ending logjam; however, today, the first Monday of the New Year, it teetered on undriveable.

I looked at the dash: 9:27 a.m. I'd started merging onto the on-ramp at 9:03. I was maybe a third of the way up and I hadn't moved in five minutes. Things started to loosen up an hour later, and I made it to Capitol Hill right around 11:00.

These government types were creatures of habit, at least the ones I'd come across, so I took up a seat in the small café. At exactly 11:20 a.m., Kim made his way into the café and took up a spot in the sandwich bar line. Today he was decked out in lime. Lime dress shirt, lime tie. He looked like a Popsicle. A very gay Popsicle.

He paid for his sandwich and coffee and made for a table in the rear. He didn't notice me, or pretended not to, and I made my way over to his table. He was just about to take a bite of his wrap when he looked up at me.

I patted him on the shoulder and said, "You mind?"

He choked down the bite and said, "Sure. But I'm meeting with Bill Eggers in about ten minutes."

I sat. "So did Ellen go hiking often?"

"Not really. She'd just recently gotten into it. She'd driven to the North Cascades sometime in early September. Then she'd gone pretty much every weekend after that."

Hmmm. "And she just liked the outdoors?"

"I guess."

He paused and I said, "What?"

"Well, sometimes I'd talk to her after she was done hiking and she'd always seem depressed. Like she'd just spent ten hours at a press conference."

Odd.

A thought struck me. "The backpack that they found?"

"What about it?"

"Wasn't there a camera?"

"It was one of the disposable jobbies."

"Were there any pictures on it?"

"Only had two shots on it. One was of a fox. The other was of a footprint."

"A footprint?"

"Well, an animal track."

"What kind of animal?"

He paused, then said, "It was a wolf track."

Back to the wolves.

"What was Ellen's infatuation with wolves?"

He looked around the small coffee shop then said, "She detested them."

"Detested them? Then why was she lobbying for people to vote yes on Ballot Measure 217?"

"She wasn't."

I was confused. "I saw a photograph of her standing in front of a group of people and they all had signs that read, 'Vote YES on 217.'"

"Those were *protestors.*"

It took a moment for the shoe to fall. "So Ellen was *against*

Measure 217."

"Fervently against."

He paused, then said, "Measure 217 was a repeal of SE 1670."

"What's SE 1670? Is that the new Lexus?"

"SE 1670 was Ellen's first bill put into law."

He messed around with his Blackberry, tapped a couple buttons, then turned it to me.

SENATE BILL REPORT
SE 1670

As Reported By Senate Committee On: U.S Fish and Wildlife
Committee, April 3, 2007
Title: An act relating to gray wolf management
Brief Description: Prohibiting the introduction of the gray wolf
into the State of Washington
Sponsors: Governor Ellen Gray
Committee Activity: U.S. Fish and Wildlife Service: 2/25/06,
3/3/06

SENATE COMMITTEE ON U.S. Fish and Wildlife Service
Majority Report: Do pass
Signed by: Senators Okey, Chair; Sheahnan, Vice Chair;
Doumite, Eser, Mortin and Stecker
Staff: Victor Mooney (786-7469)

I looked up. "Okay, so she hated wolves. Why?"

He took a deep breath and said, "Wolves have always been a sensitive topic, by and large the most sensitive of any animal in North America."

"I've heard that."

"When they reintroduced wolves to Yellowstone National Park

a couple years back, it started all sorts of conflict. There's a saying—"

I quipped, "Wolves can get along with people, but people can't always get along with wolves."

"Right."

"But with all the other things going on, how did Ellen Gray make time to protest wolves returning to Washington?"

He licked his lips and said, "What I'm about to tell you only a handful of people know. Ellen once told me she never even told her husband."

I nodded.

"Ellen rarely talked about her childhood. She left home when she was sixteen. She kept in contact with one brother, but for the most part she erased her family from her past. She grew up on a ranch. Her parents raised livestock, which back then—in the '60s—wasn't a bad way to make a living."

"Wisconsin, right?"

"Right. Anyhow, she had three older brothers and one younger brother. The younger brother adored her. Went everywhere she went. One day, Ellen is home alone with him. They aren't allowed to leave the house because in the last weeks they'd lost over a third of their cattle to a wolf pack. Happened a lot back then."

I saw where this was going.

"Ellen didn't go into the details, but she was playing with her brother and he went outside. They were running around and next thing she knew, three wolves pounced on him and ripped him to shreds."

I leaned back.

"Her family blamed her. She blamed herself. She never wanted it to get out because no one would take her bill seriously if they found out." He paused then said, "Ellen Gray has single-handedly kept wolves out of Washington for the last four years."

"Until now."

He nodded. "Until now."

CHAPTER 41

KIM and I chatted for another ten minutes, then I borrowed his Blackberry and put in a call to Hans. After a couple minutes, the portly medical examiner came on the line.

"Ahlo?"

"Hans, it's Thomas."

"Thomaz, zo nice to hear your voize."

I could hear him chewing and said, "What are you eating?"

"How'g you know?"

"Easy. You're always eating."

He laughed. "Dis is true. Egg zalad stoundi."

My stomach rumbled.

I said, "Listen, I need a favor."

"Zure thing."

I told him what I was after.

———

I walked to the enormous library across the street and found an empty computer. I Googled "Ellen Gray" and clicked on the web page I'd browsed a couple weeks prior. I scrolled down the page until I came to her priorities and clicked on "Caring for Washington Ranchers and Farmers."

The first couple paragraphs concerned the Washington Ranchers Society and their annual fund-raiser, then there were links to legislation that affected ranchers and farmers. Of the three ballots measures listed, I clicked on "Ballot Measure 217."

A small write-up confirmed what Kim had said: Ballot Measure 217 was a repeal of Bill SE 1670, which, if passed, would allow the introduction of the gray wolf to Washington.

A hyperlink was marked "Wolf Speech" and I clicked on it. A media window popped up, and a clip buffered then began playing.

Governor Ellen Gray was behind a podium. A giant sign behind her read *"Vote NO on 217."*

The camera panned to the audience. I hit pause. The frame went still. The majority of these people were holding signs that read "Vote YES on 217" or "Let the Wolf Return." One sign read "Stop Playing God With our Wolves." Quite a few of the people were wearing shirts that read "Defenders of Wildlife." It was almost identical to the picture I'd seen the first time I'd researched the governor at the library. I'd thought these people were there to support the governor, but, in actuality, they were there to protest.

I hit play.

Ellen said, "We are here today to call attention to the economic impact wolves would have on our great state."

There was some heavy booing.

One person yelled, "Give us back our wolves!"

I heard a couple jeers, and I could also see that there were a few supporters intermixed with the protesters.

After some light introductory remarks, the governor said, "In 1995, the U.S. Fish and Wildlife Service began wolf recovery efforts in Idaho with the release of fifteen wolves. The Idaho wolf population has steadily increased to an estimated 661 in 2007.

I could hear some soft cheering in the background.

"In 1996, after the first fiscal year of the wolves' reintroduction, Wildlife Service expenditures were an estimated $16,000 in state funds for addressing wolf-related issues, conducting predation investigations, and wolf-control actions.

"In 2001, these expenditures had risen to over $150,000, almost a thousand percent increase. In 2007, these trends continued and wolf expenditures had risen to nearly $1.5 million. If these trends continue, by 2020 these expenditures will rise to over $100 million dollars."

For the most part, everyone was quiet.

She took a breath and said, "Nearly 30 percent of all farms and ranches in Washington are within a fifty-mile radius of the North Cascades and Olympia National Parks. With the close proximity of these ranches, costs in Washington would far exceed those of Idaho, threatening the very livelihood of many ranchers. Even if annual losses are as low as 10 percent, this 10 percent may seem insignificant, but in this time of very tight agricultural margins that amount of added costs is critical."

A thundering applause arose from the supporters.

The governor waited for quiet then said, "I'd like to introduce Barry Steadmore. He owns a ranch in Montana."

A man in jeans and a plaid shirt stepped to the podium. He had black hair swept across his forehead, almost like this was the first time he'd styled his hair. He said, "I own a ranch, or I guess I should say I *used* to own a ranch near Bozeman, Montana."

He spoke for a couple minutes, talking about how Bozeman-area ranch families have taken heavy hits to their bottom line due to wolves killing and maiming their cattle. Over the course of three years, wolves killed nearly 15 percent of his annual cattle production, and just recently, not six months earlier, his land was seized by the government.

He ended with, "Ranchers are losing their calves. Wolves are killing them. The ranching economy bears an unfair portion of the costs. If America wants wolves back, why are we paying for it?"

Again, heavy applause erupted from Governor Gray's supporters.

The man stepped off the stage and the governor returned. The camera panned to the audience and I noticed that a good portion of the protesters had lowered their signs. You could see it on their faces: seeing the actual effects on this simple man had impacted them.

The governor stepped to the microphone and said, "My sole purpose today is to remind everyone that, while we all have an opinion on wolves, ranchers are the ones that are dealing directly with the impact of their presence. I just want everybody to understand that there is a cost involved with the reintroduction of wolves. And I urge you to vote 'no' on Measure 217 come November."

The clip ended.

I noticed the date in the bottom right corner: 10/25/2009.

Ellen had given this speech the last week of October last year. And the repeal failed to pass. I had a feeling she would have given the same speech this year had she not been killed. But she had been, and the repeal had passed. And wolves had returned to Washington state.

———

The deli was called The Pickle. It was six blocks down the street from the Seattle Police Department Headquarters.

I spotted Hans sitting in the back booth. He looked to be about two-thirds of the way through his sandwich.

I slid in the opposite side of the booth and asked, "Didn't you just eat?"

His mouth was full, but he puffed his cheeks into a sort of smile.

"Did you do what I asked?"

He garbled, "I did, I did."

"And?"

He wiped a large drop of mustard from the side of his mouth and said, "The resultz are quide stounding."

"Cut the accent crap, Hans."

He nodded and said in perfect English, "Sorry. The results are quite astounding." He could control his accent when he wanted to. I mean, the guy grew up in Detroit.

He continued, "I cross-referenced the teeth marks on Ellen Gray with a number of different submarine animals."

I hadn't told him much, just that I wanted him to run the bite marks from Ellen Gray's body through his mainframe and come up with a match.

He started back in, "I'd actually taken an impression of two of the bites during the autopsy. I hadn't looked into it much deeper than that, just assumed it was a killer whale or a barracuda or something. I figured when you have a hole in your forehead, it doesn't much matter what's been nibbling on you."

"Right."

"Anyhow, the curvature of the teeth didn't match any fish in the system. These teeth were big and differently sized. Most fish have small teeth, roughly the same width and diameter throughout, save for sharks. I thought perhaps it might have been a smaller species of shark simply because in many places the tissue was ripped from the body as opposed to bitten."

"Go on."

"So, I scanned the impression plate I'd made, loaded it into the computer databases and ran it against our known animal index."

I said, "I bet I know what came up."

"Do you now?"

"*Canis lupus.*"

He laughed and said, "Right. Ellen Gray had been attacked by a wolf."

———

I asked Hans to keep a lid on this for a couple days. He said he would, and I thanked him and left.

I thought it was time I had a chat with the Professor.

CHAPTER 42

AS I DROVE to the North Cascades, a rather fuzzy picture started to come into focus. I couldn't believe it'd taken me so long to piece it altogether. It's funny, you make all these small notations: *The river empties right into the Sound. She was hiking in the North Cascades.*

You record these small snippets of conversation: *She detested wolves. He had a doggy.*

You make all these little chalk marks: *Right, she'd been attacked by a wolf. I don't know what he'd do if the repeal hadn't passed.*

They mean utterly nothing all by themselves. But when grouped together, they tell a story. Or in this case, a murder.

I looked at the picture sitting on the seat beside me. At the library, I'd done a quick Google of the Professor. He wasn't hard to find. These nutjobs never are. His name was Theodore Koble. Grew up on a houseboat out in the Sound in the early '70s. Received his doctorate in Animal Behavior from Seattle Pacific University and went on to teach the very subject at the very university.

In 1993, he'd taken a research trip to Canada to study wolves. Apparently, he had fallen in love with them, even—get this—after he was attacked by one of the wolves and his trachea and larynx were ripped from his neck. Barely survived. But after surgery, he spent the next fourteen years living with the wolves.

I picked up the picture I'd printed of him and stared at it. It was a close-up of him standing in front of a chalkboard.

According to the article, the birth defect Koble suffered from was called a congenital hemangioma. Taking up the better part of the left side of the Professor's face was a reddish-purple birth-mark. It looked like an ink stain running down the length of his nose, blanketing his left eye, the edge of his mouth, his entire cheek, and running down into his collar.

———

At some point on the drive, I checked my rearview mirror and noticed a black sedan keeping pace a quarter mile behind me. I wondered how long they'd been following me. In all probability they had been with me since I left my house this morning, so they knew I went to the capitol building. Did they know I met with Kim? I had to assume they did.

I thought about turning around, but if I hadn't been arrested yet, I wasn't sure I'd be arrested at all. Or maybe, Ethan wanted me to get as deep into the shit as possible before he made his move. He'd already arrested me once and that hadn't worked out in his favor.

The only thing that worried me was that Ethan would put together the connection between Ellen Gray, Riley Peterson, the North Cascades, the Professor, and wolves. I didn't want him to get credit for the bust. Old habits die hard. But, I had a hard time believing he would put two and two together. I mean, the guy could barely figure out how to work a Powerade bottle. Plus, I could always tell him I was paying my respects to Riley. No one could question this.

I went over a small hill and pulled to the shoulder. Thirty

seconds later, the black sedan flew by. I waited. One Mississippi. Two Mississippi. Three Mississ—

The brake lights flashed and the car pulled to the side.

I laughed, threw the car in drive, and flipped off the two goons as I passed.

———

The U.S. Fish and Wildlife building once again appeared vacant. As I was parking in the dirt lot, a Jeep pulled in and parked not far from me. An extremely large black man stepped out. He was wearing the same tan outfit Riley had been when we met, as well as a brimmed hat. He had a remarkable likeness to Smokey the Bear. I suspected this would be Herb.

I stepped from the car and approached him. He had a toothpick dangling from the left corner of his mouth. He was one of the few black men I'd ever seen with freckles. He muttered, "What can I do for ya, chief?" He had a thick accent. Cajun meets Scottish. William Wallace meets Mardi Gras. I really wanted him to say, "Only you can prevent forest fires," just to see what it sounded like.

I didn't particularly want him to know who I was, but I did pass on my condolences as to his partner's passing.

He didn't ask how I knew her or who I was. He just started talking about Riley. How great she was. Always smiling. Always acting mad when he ate her food, but he knew she packed it just for him. I didn't have the heart to tell him that she didn't pack those lunches for him. He still seemed pretty broken up about her death. This would make two of us.

Finally he said, "If you'd 'scuse me, I've got some paper to push. Just me to do it all now."

I asked, "Do you mind if I take one of the sleds for a spin?"

"Those are government property."

"Yeah, that's what Riley said."

He raised his eyebrows. "Riley take you out on one of the sleds?"

"Sure did."

He shrugged. "Hell, if she trust you, I trust you. Keys are'n the 'nition."

I told him the sled was in good hands. He nodded, but I don't think he cared if I drove the sled into the river. After we shook hands, he headed into the building and I made my way over to the snowmobiles. I plopped down on one of the two-seaters and I hit the red starter button.

The route to the den was easy enough and the tall fence came into view after ten minutes. I crept to the edge of the tree line and cut the engine. The wolves were out in the open about two football fields from the small field house.

A handful of the wolves weren't doing much, standing stoic, gazing across the whiteness. But about half were playing, wrestling around. It took me a moment to register that one of the wrestlers was a man.

He was dressed in the same white snowsuit, same white beanie pulled down over his face. Professor Theodore Koble. I watched for a good five minutes as this idiot rolled around with these wolves.

From this far away you would have thought it was a man playing with his dogs. I waited for one of the wolves to go Siegfried and Roy on him, but it never happened. It would appear he was one of them. Or the pack had accepted him as such.

I drove the snowmobile up near the fence. The wolves stopped playing and stared in my direction. The Professor was on his hands and knees doing precisely the same. I had little doubt this man, or wolf, werewolf, or whatever this guy thought he was, killed both Ellen Gray and Riley Peterson. I waved him over.

He reluctantly stood, strapped on his cross-country skis, and made his way over. Even if he thought he was a wolf, he was still in charge of this project and had to play the part of human every once in a while. At least for another week, until they released the wolves. Then I had a feeling no one would ever see this whack job again.

He skied up to the fence and stopped. The wolves never took their eyes off him. Not for a second. Only the Professor's eyes and mouth could be seen, the red plague visible over his left eye and a bit of his mouth. His left eye, a white oasis in a sea of red, carried a pink cast.

It was impossible not to feel a bit of sympathy for the guy. But my sympathy glands were a bit fatigued, and I couldn't muster much.

I said, "Are you Professor Koble?"

He nodded.

"Can I ask you a couple questions?"

He nodded.

"Can you speak?"

He shook his head and made a coughing sound. I took the combination as a "no."

I hopped off the snowmobile and trudged to the fence. We were only inches from one another. "Okay, then you stand there and you listen. I know you killed Ellen Gray and I know you murdered Riley Peterson. And I don't give a shit what's growing on your face or that you think you're a fucking wolf."

He didn't move.

"I know how it all played out. You've been pushing to have these wolves reintroduced for the past three years and each year you fell short. Why? Because Governor Ellen Gray strongly opposed wolves. Did you know why? Because one of your buddies over there ate her little fucking brother. Yeah, slaughtered him right in front of her. That's why your repeal never passed. And you knew with Ellen in the picture, the bill would never be over-turned. Never had a chance. But you tried to convince people that wolves were harmless. You even took one with you when you went to Pike Place Market."

He made no reaction.

I felt my voice rise. "You know what I think? I think you've secretly been bringing wolves here for years now. That's why the governor would come here every Sunday. She was spotting for any sign of wolves. She just knew. So when you saw her, you knew what you had to do. You put a bullet in her forehead, then you let your friends munch on her, then you threw her body in the river. This starting to sound familiar to you?"

I thought I saw the tug of a smile on his lips. Or maybe it was a snarl. If there hadn't been a fence between us I would have knocked his birth defect off his face.

I took a breath and said, "With the governor out of the way, there was no one to protest the repeal, no one to call attention to the ramifications of wolves on the local ranchers and surrounding communities. And what do you know, the repeal passed.

"After you got the go-ahead, it dawned on you that somehow, some way, this would be traced back to you. And if it was, it would be so long wolves. So you decided to frame her husband for the murder. You grab the tranquilizer gun, follow Adam from his office, shoot him, rough him up, steal his keys, take his yacht out. You're familiar with boats; you grew up on a boat. And you knew if Ellen's body ever did surface, it would have been carried out by the raging river and would surface somewhere in the Sound."

I leaned into the fence, the cold steel pressing deep into my cheek. "But you didn't count on me. And when you saw me that day, you knew that I was closing in on you and that I was going to put a stop to you and your little wolf factory. So you decide Riley has to go, and you figure you'll frame me for her murder. Ellen's dead, Riley's dead, and I'm going away for two lifetimes. Is that right? Is that how you planned it out?"

He didn't move.

"Well, it didn't work. 'Cause here I am. And you're the one

who's gonna be locked in a cage for two lifetimes, buddy. That's right, shitbag, locked up. A caged animal."

He remained impassive.

I wondered what he was thinking. Was he thinking about living in an eight-foot by six-foot cell the rest of his life? Could he survive?

I looked at this frail man who'd had, if not a horrible life, a hard one, and decided he wouldn't last an hour.

My options were limited. I could hop the fence, but he was on skis and I wouldn't stand a chance. If I had the forethought to bring a gun I would be at the advantage, but I didn't see the guy just putting his hands behind his back and surrendering. He was, at least in his deranged brain, a wild animal, so there's no telling what he would do. I could see him tame one second, then latched onto my neck the next. But in order to pull off Ellen Gray and Riley Peterson's murders, not to mentions Adam's and my framing, he also needed to be cold and calculating.

It dawned on me that I was glad there was a fence between the two of us. Professor Koble was a different scary than I'd ever come across.

A deep, hollow echo broke me from my reverie, and both the Professor and I turned. The wolves, all eleven of them, were back on their haunches howling at the spirits above or maybe they were calling to their buddies who roamed freely.

I looked back at the Professor. He was gone. Skiing back to the pack. As the Professor neared, the howling subsided.

The pack jumped up and started for the trees, the Professor just a step behind on his skis.

It took a moment for it all to register, for the gravity of what I'd just witnessed to sink into the bloodstream, to be sucked into each and every cell in my body. Riley had also said the wolves howl to call the pack together.

The wolves had been calling to the Professor.

CHAPTER 43

I HADN'T EATEN anything all day and I was starving. And, to be brutally honest, I needed a drink. In fact, I needed a couple drinks.

I pulled my car into the dirt lot and stepped out. The taxpayers' hard-earned money followed me into the lot and parked. I saluted my buddies and made my way down the steep hill.

The Flounder was still awash with Christmas lights, and its bright neon sign lit up the narrow walkway. High tide would be in the next half hour or so, and the cold black water whished five feet below. A dozen boats of different makes and sizes were tied up to the pier, and my car was one of about ten in the small lot. Eleven if you counted Ace and Gary.

There was a healthy crowd and it was loud for 6:00 on a Wednesday night. I found a table and looked for Josie, but she wasn't running around in her skimpy little outfit.

Darn.

I flagged down a waitress and told her I had a medical condition and if I didn't get a beer and a shot of tequila in the next minute, I would start frothing at the mouth. She laughed and I started counting.

Two minutes later I had a shot of Don Julio and half a beer

rumbling around in my empty stomach. I ordered three burgers with fries and another beer. The waitress gave me a quizzical glance, and I told her I was training for one of those dog-eating contests.

She said, "Don't you mean hot dogs."

"No, I mean terriers."

She left in a rush. To get my beer or call animal control, it was a crapshoot.

Anyhow, I sipped on the beer and watched the local news, which was mostly weather and football. The Seahawks were playing the Arizona Cardinals in the NFC Championship. The Seahawks had home field advantage and the game would be played in Qwest Stadium come this Sunday. I stared through my half-empty glass and thought about super fan Riley Peterson for a long minute.

When I looked up, they were doing the weather. Some huge storm was funneling down from Alaska. The storm had already punished parts of Canada with up to three feet of snow, and it looked to be getting stronger as it moved across the Pacific Northwest. According to the annoying man on the television waving his hands at the map, the snow would start sometime on Friday and continue through the weekend. They were calling for parts of the city to get over twenty inches and parts of the high country to get anywhere from three to five feet.

So much for Old Man Winter getting lost in Canada. I guess someone bought him one of those tracking bracelets.

My food came and I grabbed two of the baskets and made my way outside. Ace rolled down the window as I approached and I handed the food through. They both thanked me and Gary asked me for some ketchup.

I told him to go jump off the Seattle Bridge.

The burger soaked up the beer and the tequila, so I ordered another beer and another tequila.

I was having a rather difficult time trying not to think about the case. Point in fact, I was now thinking about it in terms of *the case.*

I wasn't sure how I wanted to play this with the Professor. It could get tricky. If I killed him—and don't think I hadn't discounted the possibility—I would probably end up in jail. I could always go to the police. But for one, I didn't think anyone would believe me. And two, they would ask why I was sticking my nose into things I should not be sticking my nose into. Such things as tampering with an official investigation and countless other trivial charges in the general vicinity of jaywalking could be used against me. And I couldn't forget that I still had a murder charge hanging over my head.

Of course, I did have one other option. I could pick up and leave. Which just so happened to be my favorite of the options, and the one I was most proficient at. Whenever I had been confronted with something awful, I picked up and left. Parents die. Bon voyage. Get dumped. See ya. My sister called it "arrived-erci syndrome."

Speaking of which, that's where I would go. I could pack up and be in France in less than a day.

But I was sick of thinking. I just wanted to turn my brain off for a couple hours. I ordered myself a pitcher and picked up the box of cards sitting on the table. They were old Trivial Pursuit cards, so I spent the next hour playing myself in trivia and guzzling Miller Lite.

I was in the midst of doing all the history questions when a man approached my table and took the seat across from me. After staring at him for a good second, I said, "What year did Panama purchase the Panama Canal from the United States?"

He took two or three chomps and said, "1963."

"I say 1967."

I turned the card over. "1963."

Ethan raised his eyebrows.

I said, "Isn't that the year you graduated high school?"

Ethan, who was only a couple years older than me, ignored this remark. Currently, he was flagging down a server. One came over and he ordered a scotch and water.

He said, "So, what did you do today, Thomas?"

I had a good suspicion Ethan knew exactly what I did today. I'm sure Ace and Gary had briefed him of my daily activities.

"I spent the day looking for Seattle Memorial. I wanted to ask Dr. McSteamy a couple questions about my prostate."

He showed no reaction to my jest, and come to think of it, I don't know if I'd ever seen the guy laugh. But then again, maybe he didn't watch *Grey's Anatomy*. Maybe he was a *Big People, Small World* kind of guy. He smirked and said, "Actually, I heard through the grapevine that you went to the capitol building, had a little sit-down, made a pit stop at the library, then took a little trip to the mountains. That sound about right?"

"I went to Arby's too. Got a Beef n' Cheddar and a Jamocha shake."

He ignored this and asked, "Now, what interest could you possibly have in the U.S. Fish and Wildlife building?"

That, of course, was the million-dollar question. "I'm writing a paper about the mating rituals of the musk ox."

He took a sip of scotch, smacked his lips, and said, "Did you know that Riley Peterson—the woman you may or may not have brutally murdered—worked for the U.S. Fish and Wildlife Service?"

"It never came up."

"That's hard to believe."

Outlandish lies usually are. I was starting to get fed up with my buddy Ethan and I said, "What the fuck do you want, Ethan?"

"I want you to pack up and leave, Prescott. Shit, I don't care if you did kill that poor girl. You get out of town and I'll make sure the whole thing disappears."

He noticed my reaction and said, "Don't think I've put that case to rest. And if I wanted to, I could arrest you right now for sticking your nose in an official investigation. But I'd rather see you locked up for a while, see you do some real hard time. I spoke with one of the district attorneys not ten minutes ago. He found a case, actually *multiple* cases, where evidence found in a relative's house was deemed admissible. You can expect to be arrested in the next forty-eight hours, and there isn't a fucking thing your piece-of-shit lawyer can do to help you this time."

I drained half my beer and thought about what Ethan had said. Now, I did not think for a second I would get convicted of murder. Especially when I knew exactly who *had* committed the murder. But this was my ace and I wasn't sure if I wanted to play it at all, least of all now, being that I was considering killing the man with my bare hands who killed Ellen and Riley. But I didn't like the thought of being arrested a second time, or sitting in the interrogation room, or standing trial if it came to that.

Ethan downed his scotch but said nothing. Then he grabbed for the pitcher and filled up his rocks glass with *my* Miller Lite. He smiled and said, "I'll get the next one."

Wow. Just like college. Although the thought of splitting a pitcher of beer with Ethan Kates ranked right up there with getting my dick caught in my zipper.

But the idea of leaving town still beckoned. "So you're saying if I just disappear, I'm clear."

"You're clear."

"Of everything?"

"Of everything. Wipe the slate clean." He smiled. "You just have to promise not to come back. Put that house of your sister's up on the market and never come back. My cousin is a real estate agent; I'll give you his card."

He had quite the sales pitch. I could tell him what I knew about the Professor, let him run with that, and I'd be on the next plane to France. Shit, the market was good, the house would go upward of a million, and I could forget about Washington forever.

There was an easy solution to this. "I'll play you eighteen holes for it."

"Golf?"

I cocked my head at the Golden Tee machine in the corner and said, "Eighteen holes right now. You win, I pack my bags and catch the next flight out. I win, I stay. I do my job. You do yours. And fuck all the rest."

He knew exactly what was on the line here. I was saying, if I won, I could find out who killed Riley and deal with it myself. And I would. I would go home, clean off my dad's old shotgun, drive up to the mountains again, shoot the Professor in his gross-ass face, and feed him to his friends. And if he won, I would be on the next flight to France.

Ethan had a bit of a competitive streak in him. We used to play on an intersquad basketball league on Tuesday nights. Everybody else was just out to have a good time and Ethan was running around like he's friggin Richard Hamilton.

He winked at me and said, "You're on."

———

Ethan picked the course. It was somewhere in Maui and there were a bunch of orange spots on all the holes.

I pointed to one of the orange blobs and said, "What are those?"

"Lava pits."

Great. The third time in my life I play Golden Tee, I'm playing for the right to *not* move to France, and he picks the course with lava pits.

The first hole was a long par four that doglegged right. Ethan went first. He hit a perfect drive down the middle of the fairway a good 300 yards. I had a feeling Ethan had played his fair share of Golden Tee.

Hello, Air France, it's Thomas. S'il vous plaît.

I noticed that if you cut across the lava pits you could reach the green in one. I took two steps back and hit the ball as hard as I could. My ball landed perfectly on the green, then bounced off, hit the lava rock, then went into a lava pit. The screen notified me of a Two-Stroke Penalty.

Ethan took a long drink to mask his smile. He went on to get a birdie. I got an 11. Yeah, I decided I wanted to see what the lava was like twice more. For the record, it's hot. Like magma.

Over the course of the next seventeen holes, Ethan and I polished off two more pitchers. Ethan went in the lava once. I went in the lava thirty-two times. My player even fell in the lava once, which I didn't know was possible. I incurred a five-stroke penalty and had to put in another dollar.

When it was over, I shook Ethan's hand. He pulled out his cell phone and handed it to me. After about ten minutes, I had booked a flight to Charles de Gaulle Airport. One-way.

Ethan called his cousin and we spoke briefly about the property. He said he would take care of everything. I knew Lacy would be okay with it. Ethan and I took a shot of expensive scotch and clinked glasses to my departure.

I'm not sure who was happier.

Ace and Gary drove me home. They were coming back at 8:00 in the morning to take me to the airport. I flopped down on the couch and passed out.

CHAPTER 44

THE KNOCKING WAS BACK.

I pushed myself off the couch with a grunt. I was no longer drunk. And I was yet to be hungover. I was in that limbo period, like when Billy Joel wakes up inside the house. Inside his car.

I walked into the kitchen and took a long drink from the faucet. It wasn't quite as satisfying as a blue Powerade with a sports top, but my tongue no longer felt like it was wearing a turban.

The clock above the stove told me it was 4:00 in the morning.

As I shuffled to the door, the events of the previous evening started to slowly come back. I vaguely remembered playing a game of Golden Tee for my right to stay in the great state of Washington. A game I believe I went on to lose by forty-seven strokes.

Friggin lava.

I had a feeling it was either Ace or Gary on the other side of the door. Or both. Ethan had probably sent them over to help me pack my bags.

I pulled the door open. It wasn't Ace. Or Gary.

I gave a quick nod and said, "Hey."

Erica gave a little smile. "Heard you were leaving."

I pondered asking her how she'd come across such sensitive information, but the odds were that she either called Ethan, or Ethan called her, or she read my blog.

"My flight is in about six hours."

Erica was wearing tight jeans and a gray sweatshirt, as well as her pink ball cap. She had her hands stuffed down in her pockets and her head cocked to the side. My mouth went dry and my stomach churned. Was it her? Was it the alcohol?

I wasn't certain what words I wanted to say. Or what words she wanted to hear. I decided upon, "I was going to call."

"Were you now?"

"Yeah, from the airphone." I mimicked sliding my credit card, then dialing, then wrapping the long cord around the guy coughing incessantly next to me.

She tried not to laugh, but it was impossible because I am hilarious. The next few minutes were going to be tricky. For one, I was still slightly tipsy and I tended to make bad decisions when I was slightly tipsy. That's how I'd ended up engaged. That's how I'd fallen for Alex. That's how I'd sat through *The New World*. That's how I'd ended up with a timeshare in Arkansas. And that's how I'd ended up with a one-way ticket to France.

We stared at each other for a couple long seconds. I took a step to the side and said, "Do you want to come in?"

She hesitated for a second, then walked past me into the house. I said, "Can I offer you something to drink? I have hot water or cold water."

"I'm good, thanks."

About halfway to the kitchen Erica turned and said, "I'm off the case, you know."

I did not know.

"Ethan said he didn't think I could handle the magnitude of this case. Then he went and told the chief that somehow you were clouding my judgment. That my naiveté was cause for both you and Adam Gray having charges dismissed against you."

I took a step forward and said, "Well, is he right? Have I clouded your judgment?"

There are few times I've found myself being serious, and this was one of those times. I needed to hear it from her. Needed to hear how she felt. This was Thomas Prescott at his very worst. I could feel my heart, my brain, my insides seeping out from my pores. Okay, so there's a good chance it was ethyl, but you get my drift. Girls call it "wearing your heart on your sleeve." Dr. Phil calls it "being vulnerable." Guys call it "being a pussy."

She shook her head. "You never clouded my judgment. Not for a second. It was always about Ellen Gray. It still is. And concerning Riley, I told the chief you may be a moron, but you weren't a murderer."

"Thanks for the endorsement." I did a U-turn, walked to the door, and held it open, "I'll send you a postcard."

She stood in the foyer. I think she was waiting to see if I was serious. I was.

It took a moment for Erica to take her first step. After the first, the second and third came quickly.

I yelled, "Wait a minute."

She turned.

"I have something I need to tell you."

She took a couple steps forward. I had two separate things I wanted to tell her. It was one or the other. If I told her one thing, I would end up staying and staying meant jail time and possibly some man-on-man time, which the more I thought about, the less I was enthused about. And if I told her the other thing, I put into concrete that I was getting on a plane in five hours.

I mentally flipped a coin.

It was Heads.

I said, "Wolves."

She wrinkled her nose and said, "Wolves?"

I nodded.

She raised her eyebrows.

"This whole thing was about wolves. Ellen, Riley, Adam, me. It was all about wolves."

She took a step forward.

I spent the next ten minutes walking Erica through what happened, or what I was nearly certain happened. When I finished, her head was shaking. "Holy shit."

"Yeah."

"What are you going to do?"

"I just did it."

"You're leaving this up to me?"

"Not a whole lot I can do from France."

"You could always stay."

I told Erica about the bet. She found this just the least bit ridiculous. She asked, "Why would you make such a stupid bet?"

"Seemed like a great idea at the time."

"And what? You suck at Golden Tee or something?"

"My guy kept falling in the lava."

"Lava?"

"Long story short, I lost."

She took a deep breath and said, "What should I do?"

It took me a moment to realize she was talking about the Professor. "That's up to you."

"But I'm off the case."

"So you say."

She was quiet for a minute, biting into her bottom lip. She looked at me and I knew the question before she asked it. "What would you do?"

"You really want to know?"

She nodded.

"I'd rip out what's left of his throat and shoot him in both kneecaps."

"That's a big help."

"I'm a problem solver."

She spent the next five minutes trying to convince me to stay, that the two of us could do it together.

When she was done, I said, "I can't."

She nodded.

I could see her eyes getting all misty and I told her I should really get packing. Although, in reality, all I had to do was grab my wallet. Mostly, I wanted Erica off my doorstep. I wanted her to stop looking at me with her perfect eyes, her devious smile. And I needed her to stop biting her lip.

She told me to look her up when I got back, and I broke the news that, according to the small print of the aforementioned ridiculous bet, I wasn't ever allowed back.

We said our good-byes, the way people do when they know they'll never cross paths again.

CHAPTER 45

THE AIRPORT WAS busy for a Thursday morning. I found the line to the security checkpoint and looked at a wall clock. I had an hour before the flight boarded. I glanced around at families and friends waiting on the outskirts to say their final good-byes. I half expected to see Erica. I didn't. I did happen to see Ace and Gary, both drinking coffees and throwing glances in my direction every so often. I guess they'd been under orders to see this through till the very end.

I saluted them and they saluted back. Project Prescott was finally over. I wondered what they were going to do to celebrate. Wrap it up, boys.

An hour and a half later, I watched as the city I flew into just six weeks earlier disappeared beneath me. I could have gotten introspective, thought about the irony of the situation, pondered how I had come to Seattle to escape a problem and now I was leaving Seattle for the same reason. But I was too tired to get introspective.

I fell asleep before the cart lady came around.

———

As I was killing two hours at Cincinnati International, it dawned on me that if I showed up on Lacy's doorstep without Christmas presents, she would flip. I'd explained to her about how I'd lost her presents in a melee that concluded with me having a collapsed lung, but I'm not sure she bought the story.

So I checked out a couple of the shops in the airport. I got her an Ohio Landscapes calendar, an Ohio State hoodie, and an Ocho-Cinco jersey.

As I boarded the plane for the ten-hour nonstop flight to France, I noticed the passenger makeup was predominantly French and American businesspeople coming and going. A handful of college kids filled the other seats, no doubt heading to Europe to do a couple weeks of backpacking, hostel jumping, and poor decision making.

I was sandwiched between a businessman and a young girl with about seventy piercings. She had a beanie, an iPod, and a black hooded sweatshirt to complete the punk look.

As the plane took off, I found that I wasn't as excited as I thought I'd be. Or should be, for that matter. Here I was headed to one of the most exotic cities in the world, about to be reunited with the only family I had left, about to get a fresh start, and all I could think about was Erica Frost.

I couldn't see her taking the information I'd relayed to her and passing it on to the proper people, specifically, Ethan Kates. But then again, that's exactly why I'd told her and not him. I'd wanted her to get the bust. But, Erica was a rogue—one of the very reasons I was drawn to her—and I highly doubted she would alert anyone to the course she set. Which, if it were me, would be to drive directly to the North Cascades and haul that shitbag in.

I pulled out the airphone and tried all four of Erica Frost's phone numbers. I got four no answers.

I placed the receiver back and let out a sigh. There was a solid chance the only person who knew Erica Frost's whereabouts was about halfway over the Atlantic Ocean.

———

We landed at Charles de Gaulle Airport at 1:04 p.m. local time. Or about 5:04 a.m. Seattle time.

I walked from the plane and into the corridor. I spotted the punk girl leaning against a wall. She was now wearing a large backpack covered with different buttons and patches. She threw me a dismissive glance as I approached. I mimed taking off my headphones. She did.

I said, "Hi, I was wondering if you could do me a favor."

She scoffed. "I'm not going to blow you if that's what you're wondering."

I looked around. I thought about turning and running.

She added, "At least not here."

I raised my eyebrows and said, "Not the favor I was thinking of, but thank you."

I told her what I wanted her to do and handed her the bag. I took out a pen and wrote the address on her hand. Then I took five hundred dollars out of my wallet and handed it to her.

As I turned to leave she said, "My offer still stands."

I told her maybe next time and found the nearest ticket desk.

I spent the better part of the next day sleeping and brushing up on my celebrity relationship knowledge.

Sixteen hours later, the pilot came on the intercom and said, "Welcome to Seattle. The local time is 9:23 p.m. The temperature is 18 degrees and it's snowing."

He paused, then added, "Actually, it's blizzarding."

———

They grounded all outgoing flights as of 10:00 p.m. and began redirecting incoming flights to smaller airports in parts of southern Washington and northern Oregon as of 10:30 p.m. This, of course, was according to 1090 AM, the station my taxi driver, Bernard, had the stereo tuned to.

The snow was coming down in drifts, the traffic at a near standstill, and it took two hours for the taxi to reach my house.

Sitting just on the outskirts of my gate, partially blanketed by a fresh coat of snow, was a For Sale sign.

Wow, this guy didn't mess around.

I pulled the sign out from the frozen earth and laid it on the ground.

Inside the house, I checked my machine. There was one message. It was from Lacy. She was a tad confused when a punk rocker chick had showed up at her doorstep and handed her a bag of presents, which all appeared to be purchased in the great state of Ohio, and said that they were from her brother. Needless to say, she wanted me to call her back *immediately.*

Unfortunately, there were more pressing matters at hand. I picked up the phone and tried all four of Erica's numbers. All four went unanswered.

I found myself saying out loud, "Where are you, Erica Frost?"

But again, I knew exactly where she was.

I only hoped she was alone.

CHAPTER 46

WHEN I SETTLED in behind the wheel of the large four-wheel drive it was closing in on 1:00 a.m. The snow was coming down at a steep angle, an endless sea of large, white flakes.

I turned on the radio, tuned it to 1090 AM, and listened to the forecast. The system was moving down from the mountains, and they were calling for at least another foot in the city. They listed a number of road closures and counties on accident alert. It sounded as if the entire city was making arrangements to shut down for the next couple days. They were even predicting the NFC Championship game would be postponed, seeing as how the Arizona Cardinals' flight had been canceled. On a side note, State Road 20, also know as North Cascades Highway, had been listed among the roads closed. This, of course, could throw a hitch in my rescue mission.

The plows were running on the highway and I drafted behind one of the large trucks. I wouldn't exactly quantify the storm as a white-out, but visibility was down to about twenty feet.

After an hour of averaging speeds between seven and fifteen miles per hour, I came to the junction to the North Cascades

Highway. Three snow plows, their lights blinking, blocked off the incoming traffic.

I pulled up near the trucks. A man setting up roadblocks walked over. He had a thick jacket on with the hood pulled up and ski goggles.

I rolled the window down and the man said, "Road's closed, pal."

I yelled into the wind, "Listen, I have to get up there." I made up some story about my wife going into labor.

I took out my badge—well, Todd Gregory's badge—and flashed it to him.

He said, "I wish I could help you, pal, but your car just isn't going to make it. This is the first wave of the storm. The second wave is rolling down from Canada as we speak. They think this one could set records. Calling for like four or five feet."

This was what I was afraid of. I was little help if my car got stuck, or if I drove off the side of the mountain or got caught in an avalanche, which weren't exactly rare in these glacial mountains.

The guy seemed genuinely concerned. Far more concerned than I would have been for a total stranger.

He asked, "How far up you going?"

"Not too far."

I could see he was contemplating driving me up there. He knew the roads and he knew the weather. But was he going to put his ass on the line? I was starting to think he might.

I was wrong.

He said, "Sorry, pal. I can't help you."

Wrong answer.

I opened up the glove compartment and pulled out my father's Smith and Wesson. I pointed the gun at the man's face. "I'm not asking anymore, *pal*."

He actually softened quite quickly. He handed me the keys, walked me over to the plow and gave me a quick crash course. I was set to leave and I said, "One more thing."

He looked at me skeptically.

"I need your goggles."

————

The plow ripped through the snow and I made decent time. Every half mile or so, I would come across a car on the side of the road. There were even two cars parked in the middle of the road. I wondered where the occupants were. If I weren't on a time crunch, I might have stopped and made sure no one was trying to stave off death inside the vehicles.

As I persevered up the mountain, the snow continued to let up. But you could see the damage the first wave had done. More than a foot of fresh snow as far as the eye could see.

An hour later, the U.S. Fish and Wildlife building came into view. There were two cars. One was parked where Herb had parked his Jeep the day we'd met, and I assumed this was his car. The other was parked on the far side of the lot, and the snow cloud it was in resembled a sedan.

I ran to the car and brushed off the license plate. It was Erica's. I wondered how long the car had been parked there. Probably close to thirty-six hours.

Shit.

I grabbed my things from the plow and made my way into the building. I called out to Herb, but I had a feeling he wasn't around. He was either snowed in somewhere or with Erica. Which, if the latter was true, means there was a good chance Herb was dead.

I changed into my winter gear. It was slim pickings. My father's old ski gear was a pretty ridiculous old full-body snow-suit. Lime green, magenta, and yellow stripes ran down the length of the arms and legs.

I went into the office and snagged the remaining PowerBars and a couple bottled waters and stuffed them in one of many zippered pockets. I pulled open a locker and found an emergency rescue kit. I opened it and pulled out a flare gun, which I stuffed snuggly beneath the belt of the snowsuit. I also took one of three flashlights and stuck it next to the flare gun.

As I was leaving, I eyed the rifle resting in the corner. The snub-nosed revolver I'd used in my plow-jacking hadn't been loaded. Guns without bullets only get you so far.

I picked up the rifle and checked the barrel. Loaded.

I made my way to the door and opened it to a wall of white. The second wave of the storm had arrived.

CHAPTER 47

TWO OF THE three snowmobiles were missing. I wondered what Erica's plan had been. Had she planned to escort the deranged Professor back on the snowmobile? Or make him ski in front of her while she trained her nine millimeter at the back of his head? And what about Herb? Had he chaperoned Erica on her endeavor? And if so, were either of them still alive?

I wiped the excess snow off the snowmobile and found the key in the ignition. A bungee cord was attached to the back of the sled and I secured the rifle as best I could.

I hit the ignition and the machine roared to life. I pulled my goggles down, pulled back on the throttle, and the snowmobile lurched forward.

The snow was falling at an incredible pace. I could barely see my own hands in front of me. After twenty minutes, I figured I was about halfway there. Then I heard the unthinkable: the engine beneath me sputtered.

I wiped the dash and peered at the gas gauge.

Empty.

The snowmobile coughed, waned, then died.

I may have cursed.

I hopped off the sled and into the snow. The snow came up to above my knees. I figured that at the rate it was falling, in an hour it would be up to my waist.

There were a large set of boulders to my right and I remembered the den was about a mile in that direction.

After ten minutes, my chest was heaving. I'm not sure if it was the material the snowsuit was composed of or if I'd accidentally lit myself on fire with the flare gun, but my body temp was hovering around five thousand degrees.

I kept on for another twenty minutes, then stopped. I looked in every direction. It was a sea of white. I was lost. I thought about doubling back, but I wasn't really sure which way back was. And over the course of the last ten minutes, the snow had intensified, if that was possible.

I put my head down and forged ahead. I didn't see the fence until it was literally a foot in front of me. I followed the fence with my hands until I came to the gate. It was open.

I took ten trudges through the gate, half expecting a wolf to latch onto my throat at any moment. I continued through the snow, the faint outline of the barn slowly coming into focus. As I approached the barn, I noticed a silhouette of something thirty yards in front of the small building. I came abreast of it. It was a snowmobile. I instinctively dusted off the gas gauge and took a peek. Nearly full.

I took a step past the sled and stopped. My mouth went dry. A large pile of pink snow was directly underfoot. Sitting amid the pile was a brimmed hat.

My stomach fell. If Herb was dead, it didn't bode well for Erica.

My throat tightened as I trudged the final steps to the barn. It was unlocked. It was at about this point that it dawned on me I'd left the rifle attached to the snowmobile.

Awesome.

I figured if I did come across the Professor, which was a long shot—I had a feeling he was skiing around with his wolf buddies —maybe I could smash him over the head with a PowerBar or something. And I did have the flare gun. But if you've ever seen a flare gun, you know they aren't the most reliable of devices, or accurate. Even so, I pulled it from my waist and pushed the door open. The acrid smell of wildlife filled my nostrils and I gave my head a stiff shake.

It was dark, and I pulled the goggles up. I let my eyes adjust, then pushed through the door leading to the holding cells. The sound of hooves and deep breathing echoed through the small chamber. The clatter grew louder and louder as the animals thrashed about. The small room was an acoustical chamber, the sounds echoing through the soft wood. It was deafening.

I held the flashlight up high with my left hand and the flare gun in front of me with my right. On each side of the room were five holding pens. Ten places for someone to hide. Ten places for someone to spring from and send a cartridge of Ketamine into my back or neck.

I said, "Hey, Professor, I saw this infomercial the other night. It was for this cream that covers up disgusting abnormalities like the one growing on your face."

He didn't respond. Because he wasn't in the room or because he didn't want to blow his cover or because he had seen the same infomercial, I wasn't sure.

I leaned over the first stall, but other than two or three large piles of shit, it was empty. I turned around and did the same with the stall on my right side. Again, nothing.

I took a deep breath. Eight to go.

I shined the flashlight on the second stall on the left and peered over the edge. Empty. I could hear deep rustling from the stall on the right. I peered over the edge of it and saw a large deer huddled in the far corner. I shined the light in its face and its eyes disappeared into two white chasms. I watched as its ears fluttered and nose flared.

I said, "It's gonna be all right, buddy. I'm not here for you. I'm here for the Professor. You don't happen to know where he is, do ya?"

The deer cocked his head to the right and said, "I saw the Professor duck into the last stall on the right. Hey, I haven't heard from Dave in a while."

I didn't have the heart to tell him he wouldn't be getting a Christmas card from Dave come next year.

Due to the intense heat of the snowsuit, compounded with the high stress level of my present situation and the fact that Herb was dead and Erica had most likely met a similar fate, and multiplied by two days of jet lag, these all added up to my having an imaginary conversation with a fucking deer.

I shook my head and moved up to the next row.

Both vacant.

I could hear movement in at least two of the last four cubbies. I checked the one on the left. I saw something scurry across the floor, but it was either a rat or a mouse, which, other than bringing to mind a Discovery special I'd seen on the Hanta virus, didn't overly concern me.

I turned to the right and stared at the second to last stall. Something was definitely behind that wall. I took a deep breath, fingered the trigger on the flare gun, and took a step toward the wooden door. My face was inches from a line of sight when something sprang up on the door. I fell backwards, instinctively pulling the trigger on the gun.

The flare erupted, whizzing from the gun, filling the small room with supernova quality illumination. I shielded my eyes and pushed myself backwards on the dirt floor. I pulled the goggles down to block the light and crawled to the edge of the stall, slowly climbing up the wooden planks. I gingerly peeked over the edge. A large elk lay on its side thrashing about. The flare was sticking out of its chest spurting white-hot flames. Both the elk and half the stall were on fire.

Good grief.

Not one to dawdle, I peeked over the stall next to the burning elk. Empty. Then I moved quickly to the other side and gazed into the last stall. I took a deep breath. In the back right corner was Erica. Her eyes found mine. There was duct tape over her mouth, but I knew she was smiling.

On closer examination, I saw that she was handcuffed, the cuffs slinking beneath a piece of wood framing that divided the stalls.

I pulled the door open and crawled to her. She raised her eyebrows. I pulled the tape off her mouth gingerly. I could have mouthed the words with her. *You're my hero. You saved my life. You came back for me.*

She said none of these things.

She did say, "Who are you?"

I lifted the goggles.

Her eyebrows rose. After a short pause, she said, "Why are you dressed like that?"

"It's a long story."

She sniffed a couple times. I thought she was starting to get emotional. She said, "I think I smell smoke."

Then again, maybe not.

I brushed a strand of hair out of her eyes and said, "I accidentally lit the place on fire."

Her eyes widened.

I could feel an intense heat on my back and I turned. I'd say two-thirds of the place was engulfed in flames.

This could get messy.

I asked, "Where are the keys to the cuffs?"

"Do you really think if I knew the answer to that question I would be in this position?"

Valid point.

The smoke was starting to get thick and I said, "Lie down."

She did, her hands outstretched. I took two steps back and kicked the wooden divider with my foot. Nothing happened.

I kicked three more times. I was getting dizzy from the fumes and I was having trouble keeping my balance. I kicked a fourth time and felt a slight shudder. On the seventh kick there was a loud crack and the divider fell six inches. My eyes had started to water and I could barely breathe. I figured we had about a minute left before we both passed out from the carbon monoxide.

I took three steps back and smashed into the divider like Steve Atwater into Christian Okoye. A loud crack echoed through the room and the divider fell to the floor. I stamped on the two-by-four until it snapped in half.

Erica pulled the cuffs around the wood, then stood.

We both turned.

The flames were everywhere. A wall of fire. I knew there was a door just to the left where Riley had ushered out the deer, but we were going to have to go through the fire.

I said, "Get on my back."

She wrapped the handcuffs around my head and hopped on my back.

"Ready?"

She dug her head in my back. I covered my face with my arm, ran into the flames, smashed through the door, took three large steps, then dove into the snow.

After we both exhausted our coughing fits, I mustered, "Are you okay?"

"I think so."

We lay there for a couple seconds, gathering our breath. The heat was intense. We both stood and began trudging away from the billowing building. The snow had let up by half and visibility was fifty or sixty yards.

We were closing in on the snowmobile when I looked at Erica and said, "Now, tell me what happened."

"After you left—"

There were two loud cracks.

I dragged Erica to the snow. The bullets just missed us, cutting through the base of the snowmobile.

Erica said, "What was th—"

I put my finger to my lips, then peeked over the edge of the snowmobile. Through the blur of the snow, just outside the fence, was a man. A man dressed in all white. A man holding a very familiar-looking rifle.

The Professor.

CHAPTER 48

I CLIMBED on the large snowmobile and yelled, "GET ON!"

Erica jumped on the back and once again draped her arms over my head, the metal cuffs settling in around my waist. As I started the snowmobile I gave a quick look over my shoulder, but the Professor was gone.

I took a deep breath. Relaxed. Tried to formulate some sort of plan. That's when I saw the light. It moved slowly through the blanket of snow in the direction of the gate. It was blinding and moving fast. It appeared the Professor had swapped out the skis for a snowmobile.

Uh-oh.

Erica pinched me and said, "GO!"

Riley had mentioned a second gate at the far edge of the den. If that was open we stood a chance. If it was closed, we would be dead.

We zipped through the deep snow. The far side of the fencing came into view. It took a moment to locate the gate. It wasn't easy to spot because it was closed.

I looked over my shoulder. The Professor was gaining on us, maybe fifty yards behind. I thought about cutting it into the trees or circling back around to the other gate, but he'd cut us off at the angle either way.

I yelled, "HOLD ON!"

"WHY?"

"JUST HOLD ON TIGHT!" I didn't want to tell her that I was going to bash through the gate.

In the movies, this would be no problem. But this wasn't the movies. If the gate was locked with a thick chain and padlock as the other gate had been, then this wouldn't end pretty. Lots of loose steel, loose parts, and loose limbs.

I was banking on the hinges. They were relatively cheap on metal fencing, and with the intense cold, I was hoping they would snap easily.

The gate was twenty yards away.

Erica yelled, "THERE'S A FENCE!"

Then ten.

"ARE YOU CRAZY?"

Five.

"WHAT ARE YOU—"

I closed my eyes and stiffened.

There was a loud crack, then a jolt.

I opened my eyes and was surprised to see that I was still alive.

Erica yelled, "ARE YOU FUCKING SERIOUS? YOU COULD HAVE WARNED ME!"

"I DID. I TOLD YOU TO HANG ON."

I looked behind us. The gate hung limply by a single hinge. And more importantly, the Professor had slowed to maneuver around the gate.

Take that, *Die Hard*.

We started down a steep hill. We were in a valley and it was white as far as the eye could see. The snowmobile was making an odd clicking sound. I brushed my hand over the control panel and noticed for the second time that the snowmobile was running on empty. One of those bullets must have ripped through the gas tank.

I said, "We have a problem."

"No shit, Sherlock."

"Okay. We have a couple problems." I leaned forward and said, "We're about to run out of gas."

"Find a hill."

She must have taken auto mechanics in high school. Most gas tanks have their drip in the rear. That's why when you run out of gas, it's usually on something of a decline.

I leaned forward. "Here's what we're going to do." I laid the plan out for her. She nodded. It was our only hope.

We hit a trough and started up an incline. The crest was about two hundred yards away and littered with pine trees.

I asked, "Where is he?"

I could feel her turn around, the cuffs tightening around my waist. She turned back. "I can just barely see his shadow moving down the hill."

We were fast approaching the crest, fifty yards away, when the engine first coughed.

Erica leaned back and yelled, "Left or right?"

The engine coughed twice more.

I yelled, "LEFT!"

We both situated ourselves on the left side of the snowmobile. We hit the crest. I had just enough time to take in the outlay of the hill; a steep decline with very few trees. We had a fighting chance that the snowmobile would make it to the bottom of the long hill and then some. We just had to pray the Professor didn't notice it didn't have any occupants.

I screamed, "NOW!"

We dove left.

The deep powder cushioned our blow and we sank deep. We dove near a series of trees, and the snow shaken from the branches gave cover to the large hole amidst the untouched powder. Erica's arms were still wrapped around my waist so she couldn't do much.

I said, "Count to ten."

"Okay."

I started digging, covering us with as much snow as possible. Within two short seconds it was pitch dark. I pulled snow from beneath us and packed it above us, entrenching us in an ice cavern.

Erica whispered, "Ten."

I stopped.

I could feel my heartbeat thudding against my ribs. My throat began to tighten. I took deep breaths through my nose. I wasn't exactly claustrophobic, but I wasn't too fond of close quarters.

Then I heard the slight vibrations. A quivering that ran through the ground. Erica's hands clenched to my chest. The soft tones of the motor came next. Slight at first, then strong and swift. I could feel the snowmobile inch its way up the crest of the small hill. The sounds carried through the cold snow like a boat's propeller through a silent pool.

Just when I thought the sounds, the reverberations, had reached their pinnacle, they grew louder, stronger. I could visualize the Professor taking stock of his surroundings. We weren't being followed. We were being *hunted*.

The seconds ticked by. Why was he still here? Why hadn't he started down the hill? Had he noticed the snowmobile was empty?

The noise was deafening. The vibrations numbing. He couldn't have been more than a couple feet away. Then the snowmobile went quiet.

I clung to Erica.

A thud.

The Professor was off the snowmobile. He was behind us and to the right.

I whispered, "He must have seen something."

"Shhhhhhhhhh."

"Right."

"Be quiet."

I paused for a second then said, "You be quiet."

The *squish-squish* of the Professor's footsteps came steadily closer. He was walking around his snowmobile. He took two steps and stopped. Erica's fingers clawed at my chest and I could feel her body stiffen.

He took another step. I flexed every muscle in my body so as not to move.

I could feel his leg drive downward in the snow. His foot came down on my foot. I slinked my foot up as far as possible. I could hear his foot moving around searching for whatever he'd stepped on. I wouldn't have been surprised if he just started firing into the snow.

He stood there for three seconds, then five.

I thought about using the element of surprise and going for him. In fact, if his leg had been anywhere near one of my arms I would have. But I had a 110-pound bag of potatoes strapped to my back.

Then his leg slipped from the snow. The squishes faded. The engine fired. The Professor was gone.

CHAPTER 49

WE WAITED a good minute before we moved. Erica whispered, "You think it's safe?"

There was a fine line between not waiting long enough and waiting too long. If the Professor did come back, I wanted to put as much distance between us and the surrounding area as possible. It was only a matter of time before he noticed that wherever the snowmobile did come to rest, no footprints led away from it. And he would begin to backtrack. When he did, I wanted to be at the closest Comfort Inn.

I said, "Yeah, I think we're good."

I swept the snow from above us and we sat up. I peered down the mountain. Two sets of fresh snowmobile tracks shot directly down and out of sight. I let out a long sigh. Although, as I think the cliché goes, we weren't out of the woods quite yet.

We stood up.

The cuffs were still wrapped around my waist, and I turned so they were now around my back. It was a tight fit and Erica's large chest was squishing into my stomach. Erica was staring at my chest. Afraid to look up. I leaned my head down until it was touching hers. I gave her cheek a light nudge. She slowly lifted her head until her magical eyes were staring into mine. Her lips flexed into a meek smile and her chest moved slowly in and out.

In.

Out.

In.

Out.

I moved my cheek gently across her neck. I ran my lips near her perfect ear, across her soft cheek. She tilted her head up, and I brushed lightly against her supple top lip. Time stopped. She moved the cuffs up my back until her hands found the back of my head. Her lips welcomed mine, her silky tongue timidly exploring every inch of my tongue. I don't know how long the kiss lasted. Nor did I care to know.

We stayed that way for a while. At one point, Erica pulled away and licked her lips.

I was in love.

Again.

Erica broke away and said, "Not that I don't thoroughly enjoy this, but I think we should get moving."

"Oh, right. That guy is trying to kill us, isn't he?"

She nodded silently. I think she said a quick prayer that the kids would get my eyes and not my personality. Or maybe she was having kisser's remorse. Either way, she was right.

Erica pulled the cuffs up and over my head. Then she pulled me down for another kiss. Just a quick one. They say it's all in the first kiss. They're wrong. It's the second kiss that matters most. And in this case, the Earth shook.

We gave one last look around us and took off.

Trudging through the deep snow took its toll and we were forced to take a break after twenty minutes. We worked our way into a deep set of trees, which would be nearly impossible to negotiate on a snowmobile, and plopped down.

I extracted the bottle of water and two PowerBars from zipper pocket #7E. I handed Erica a bar and said, "You want to tell me what happened?"

Erica took the bar and ripped off the wrapper. She took a huge bite and forced it down, then gobbled up the remainder. She eyed the half eaten bar in my hand and said, "You gonna eat that?"

I had been thinking about it. I handed over the bar and said, "I had a Cinnabon thirty hours ago. I'm stuffed."

She ignored me, attacking the second PowerBar. I thought about telling her she was almost out of her Atkins points for the day, but I typically like to date girls for at least a month before I give them dieting advice.

She polished off the bar, swigged down the bottle of water, let out a deep breath, and said, "Much better."

I nodded.

She closed her eyes for a second, as if remembering. "So after I left your house, I was pissed off. Actually I was really pissed off. At you. At myself. At the world."

She paused. I think she wanted me to chime in that I shouldn't have let it end the way it had. I said no such thing.

She started back up. "My plan was to call Ethan, tell him everything you told me, then go to the grocery store and clean out their Ben & Jerry's section. Ethan answered, and before I could tell him anything, he told me he knew that I'd just come from your house and that he just got off the phone with the chief. I was officially on probation. This put me over the edge, and I told him that he and the chief could go to hell for all I cared."

"Let me guess. You didn't tell him about the wolves."

She shook her head. "I went home, slept for a couple hours, then drove to the mountains. I got up here and thought it was a dead end. There wasn't anybody around. I sat in my car for a good hour, then this car pulls up and this big black guy steps out."

"Herb."

"You met him?"

"About six-six, two-fifty. Talks like an Oxford educated Bubba Gump."

She nodded.

"I hate to tell you this, but Herb was...how do I put this...devoured."

Erica gulped.

"And I have a feeling if I hadn't come to your rescue, you would have met the same fate."

She smiled, crawled the two feet to me, and planted a fat one on me. She said, quite sarcastically, mind you, "My hero."

"So you met Herb—"

She crawled back. "Right. Then I pretty much told him what you told me. When I mentioned Riley he got sort of choked up."

She paused for a second. I think she wanted to see if I would have a similar reaction.

The crime scene photo of Riley flashed across my eyes and my stomach tightened. Not at the sight of her dead, but at the idea of what I was imagining doing to the Professor. I won't bore you with the details, but I will tell you that the Professor's testicles were no longer dangling peacefully from his scrotum.

"You all right?"

I was anything but all right, but Erica wanted to hear that I was all right, so I told her I was.

She eyed me suspiciously, then continued in stride. "We hopped on his snowmobile and drove to the den."

I nodded.

"There were a bunch of wolves and this man watching them. Herb tells me the guy is the Professor. As we got closer, you could see that something was wrong with his face."

"Congenital hemangioma."

"Is that what it's called?"

I nodded.

"A girl at my high school had something similar. Hard way to go through life."

I concurred. Going through life like that, everyone staring at you, kids calling you a monster, it would be difficult. I could see why he chose the life of a wolf. Wolves didn't judge him, didn't cross the street when they saw him, didn't see him and thank God they didn't have what he had.

You deal with enough of these sickos, and I'm not saying that you understand—to understand is impossible—but you can see why. Your dad locks you in the basement, or your uncle wants to play hide the pickle, or your mom makes you stick your hands in boiling water, or one of your foster parents likes to make you watch *Full House* reruns, you're going to end up fucked up. There wasn't a day in the Professor's life that he didn't think about the red plague taking up the better side of his face. He probably considered just ending it a hundred times. A million times. But he hadn't. He'd decided to end Ellen Gray's life. And Riley Peterson's. And for those two reasons I was going to kill him. For those two reasons, I was going to make him suffer.

"Thomas."

I looked up.

Erica was staring at me.

"Sorry. Keep going."

"Well, Herb, he yelled at the Professor. He looked our way, then finally walked over. I told him who I was."

"Did he say anything?"

"No."

"Yeah, he doesn't talk much."

"No, he doesn't. I told him I needed him to come down to the station for questioning. He nodded that he understood, then walked to the small building. He was in the building for about five minutes, and I was set to go check on him when he walked out the front door. You could tell right away something was off. It happened so fast. Before I knew it, Herb had a dart sticking in his chest, and I had one in my thigh."

Erica weighed about a buck ten, about the same as an adult wolf.

She probably was out like a light within ten seconds. But it couldn't have had much effect on Herb. Probably made him a little dizzy. Or high. But a single dart wouldn't have knocked out a 250-plus-pound man. Which is exactly the reason Herb was dead. He'd probably been hit by the dart, started to get dizzy but shook it off, then made for the snowmobile. That's when the wolves had pounced.

I asked, "How long were you out for?"

"I have no idea. When I came to, I was handcuffed in one of the stalls. I've been there for a day and a half. I think you know the rest."

"Thomas Prescott saves the day and gets the girl."

"More like Thomas Prescott lights the barn on fire, gets shot at, hides in snow cave, gets hypothermia, then gets eaten by hungry wolves."

"Spoil the ending, why don't you?"

We both got a good laugh out of this.

I asked, "But does he get the girl?"

"Of course he gets the girl."

This led to another round of kissing. I was rounding second when a heart-stopping sound rolled through the mountains. A deep guttural howl. Chills crept up my spine.

They were out there.

And they were hunting us.

I said, "Let's go."

She nodded.

We stood and started picking our way through the trees until we came to a large clearing, a valley, not a tree in sight. Erica and I glanced at one another. I think the same thought filled both our heads. The last thing we wanted to do was get caught out in the open and be run down by a pack of wolves. It would be certain death. Here in the trees we at least stood a fighting chance. Not to mention we could always climb a tree. But who knew how long we could be out here before we were saved. I didn't want to get treed by these wolves only to have the Professor come pick us off like the first level of Duck Hunt.

I was weighing the pros and cons when another round of howls filled the cold night air. When the echo ran its course, Erica said, "They haven't moved."

I agreed. They sounded as if they either hadn't moved or were headed in the opposite direction. I looked out on the large clearing and made some quick tabulations. I figured if we did it at a reasonable pace, we could traverse the clearing in ten minutes. Six or seven minutes if we really hustled.

I looked at Erica. She nodded.

And we started across.

———

The snow was the deepest we'd come across and it took us ten minutes to reach no man's land, or more accurately, the point of no return. I turned around. The sun was just beginning to wake and everything was cast in a perfect gray. If not for the incredible glare coming off the snow, I would imagine it was a breathtaking landscape.

We hit the three-quarter mark and I started to relax a bit. We had, give or take, the distance of a short par three until we reached the haven of the thick trees. Erica looked my way and gave me a little smile. I smiled back. That's when we heard it. A noise far more frightening than the howl of a wolf. It was the whir of a snowmobile.

I turned and looked over my shoulder. Under the cover of the sun's glare, I could just make out the snowmobile's running light moving diligently through the trees. The Professor would reach the edge of the clearing in a matter of seconds, and in the open field he would be on us in well under a minute.

I looked at Erica and screamed, "RUN!"

We ran. If you could call it running. It was like trying to move through three feet of molasses.

I could hear the snowmobile closing in. I looked over my shoulder again. The Professor had reached the clearing. I turned back around. The trees were still fifty yards off. I heard a slight puff to my left and saw Erica was face first in the snow. I yanked her up, giving the Professor a quick glance in the process. He had started into the clearing, and the bright running light of the snow-mobile was coming at us fast.

We trudged on. My heartbeat was running somewhere in the low 400s. The snow's depth was receding slightly, plus there was a small decline, and we made good time the next fifteen seconds.

With just twenty yards left, I could feel the snowmobile rumbling through the snow, the whir coming from directly behind me. I visualized the gun trained between my L4 and L5 vertebrae and I waited for the bullet to come. It never did.

I turned around just in time to see the snowmobile blow past me. I pulled Erica behind me as it skidded ten yards ahead of us and stopped. The front running light and snow glare were blinding, but I assumed the Professor had the gun leveled at our chests.

The engine on the snowmobile cut, carried away by the wind. Then the Professor said his first words. "DON'T MOVE!"

I looked at Erica.

I didn't think the Professor could talk.

The running light on the snowmobile flicked off and the man yelled, "LET HER GO!"

Erica and I looked at one another, then at the man standing on the snowmobile holding his .45 pointed at my chest.

It was Ethan.

CHAPTER 50

ERICA TOOK a step forward and said, "What are you doing here?"

Ethan hopped off the snowmobile, the gun pointed somewhere between my left ventricle and my right atrium. He shouted, "Walk to me, Erica!"

She looked at me, then at Ethan, and it finally dawned on her that Ethan Kates was under the impression the strange man in the neon leotard had kidnapped her. Although there's a good chance Ethan would still be leveling the gun at my chest had he known it was me.

Erica said, "I'm fine." She pointed to me and said, "That's Thomas."

"Thomas?"

I lifted my goggles and said, "Remember me?"

"I thought you went to France."

I couldn't help but notice that he hadn't lowered his gun. Well, actually, he'd lowered it from my chest to my balls.

"Technically, I did go to France." I added, "If you ever go, make sure you check out the gift shop in the east wing of the airport. It's a thing of beauty."

Ethan looked at me and said, "You reneged on our deal."

"I did."

"I'll be speaking to the D.A. tomorrow, and I can assure you that you will do jail time."

I had pretty much come to terms with this already. Maybe six months in county would be good for me. I mean, my knowledge of petroleum jelly was negligible. "Hey, you gotta do what you gotta do."

He nodded.

Ethan said, "So this whole thing was about wolves."

Erica and I both gave him a strained glance.

"Oh, it wasn't that difficult. After I put together why Thomas had visited the U.S. Fish and Wildlife building, it all came together quite nicely. I even did a bit of background on Ellen Gray. Talked to her folks. Apparently, she once had a little brother. They actually didn't know about all the great strides their daughter had taken to ensure that wolves were never relocated to the great state of Washington. Mom even choked up a little bit.

"And I did a bit of background on this Professor Koble. Ellen actually had a restraining order against the man after an altercation at Pike Market. He wasn't allowed within a hundred yards of her. And he had a record. He bit one of his students during his last year teaching."

I scoffed, "Did you say he *bit* one of his students?"

"According to the report, one of his students called him a freak, and the Professor latched onto his shoulder. Kid had to get five stitches. Professor resigned two days later."

Erica asked, "How did you find us?"

"I've been driving around on the snowmobile for about six hours. When I saw the smoke from the fire, I headed in that direction."

I said, "And then you started shooting at us."

"I thought you were the Professor."

How ironic. And here I'd thought *he* was the Professor.

"Well, I'm glad we got that little misunderstanding resolved."

He grinned. I'm not sure he felt the same way. I think he would have preferred the county coroner to point out this small error.

After a cleansing breath, I asked, "So do you still think I killed Riley Peterson?"

"No, I don't. I think the Professor saw that you were poking around too closely and wanted to get you out of the mix. So I figure the Professor killed her and framed you for the murder." He paused. "This doesn't mean that you're off the hook. I told you the second I saw you to keep your nose out of this business. You hampered an ongoing investigation."

"Would you be here right now if I hadn't?"

"That's neither here nor there."

"No, actually, that's here. Actually, you, me, and Erica are *here*."

He shrugged, then said to Erica, "So how did you put it all together?"

Erica spent the next five minutes narrating the events that led up to her involvement, kidnap, rescue, and chase. She left out a couple parts, or one part, or the best part, which is probably a good thing seeing as how Ethan could still shoot me and no one would ever be the wiser.

Ethan nodded along as Erica wrapped things up. Then the three of us stopped. Froze. A howl filled the silence. It was much louder than before.

All of us turned and squinted at the tree line where Ethan had just come from. A shape darted from the trees into the open, quickly followed by several others.

They'd found us.

———

We watched as the wolves moved fluidly through the thick snow, their outstretched bodies gliding, then spraying up snow, then gliding once more. We had maybe two minutes.

I pushed Erica forward and said, "Let's get out of here."

Ethan jumped behind the wheel of the snowmobile. As Erica and I approached the sled, it quickly became evident the snowmobile was the compact model. Two people would be pushing it. Three would be utterly impossible.

Ethan turned to Erica and said, "Get on."

She looked at me and I nodded.

She didn't move.

I looked over my shoulder. The wolves were at about the quarter mark, kicking up all kinds of snow.

Ethan repeated, "Erica, get on the snowmobile."

I moved her to the back of the sled and said, "Don't worry about me. I'll be fine." For the record, I would be dinner. "I'll climb a tree or something and you can come back for me." I had another PowerBar I hadn't told her about.

I glanced in the direction of the wolves. Some of the pups had lagged behind, but the adults were in a tight formation. Five big wolves. Coming to eat me.

I said, "Please get on the snowmobile."

She shook her head and I saw tears form in her eyes.

I grabbed her shoulders and yelled, "ERICA, GET ON THE FUCKING SNOWMOBILE!"

She reluctantly started to move. She settled in behind Ethan and wrapped her arms around him. Then she said to Ethan "Give him your backup piece."

He shook his head, "I didn't bring a backup."

I could see by the bulge of his ankle that he had indeed packed his backup. But I only had about a hundred, maybe a hundred and fifty heartbeats remaining and I didn't want to spend them quibbling over such trivial matters.

Erica grabbed me around the neck and whispered in my ear.

Had I not been about to be eaten by eleven angry wolves I might have said it back. I broke away from her and said, more to Ethan than her, "DRIVE!"

Ethan nodded and hit the gas. Erica gazed at me as they took a sharp right and went quickly down the mountain. I turned. The wolves were about two football fields away. I could see Cujo out in front leading the pack.

I started running.

CHAPTER 51

I MADE my way into the trees and immediately started looking for a tree to climb. The majority of the trees were covered in snow and would be impossible to get a foothold. I found what seemed a suitable tree and stopped. I wrapped my arms around the back, but the bark was wet and there wasn't a chance in hell I would make it up in time.

I gave a sideways look and yelled, "Shit!" Cujo was close enough that I could see his snarling teeth. He would be in the trees in the next ten seconds.

I whipped my head back and forth, surveying the trees for any haven. Anything I could climb in or climb up. There was a small clearing twenty yards away with a large white mound at center. A big boulder covered by the snow. If I could somehow find my way up the rock I might be safe.

I noticed a good-sized stick on the ground and picked it up. I broke it in two and took off in the direction of the rock. My legs were pumping at an impossible pace.

The mound was ten yards away.

Then five.

I made it to the boulder. It was larger than at first glance, about ten feet high, with nearly straight sides. A giant square. I dug my hands into the thick snow and tried to find a fingerhold. The rock was smooth. I gave a couple halfhearted leaps, but the effort was futile. Finally, I took a long deep breath and turned around.

Cujo was already in the air, his large mouth open, his huge white teeth agape. He hit me in the right shoulder, clamping down four-hundred pounds of pressure into my deltoid.

If it weren't for the rock behind me, I would have been knocked back ten feet. I hit the rock hard, the back of my head taking the brunt of it. A flash of white light played over my eyes and I prayed I'd just died. But death was a long way off.

I envisioned the deer. Bambi. Basically eaten alive. The deer's heart beating, its eyes and brain taking in everything as it lay there conscious. Until finally one of the wolves had ripped out its jugular. Only then had it died. I thought of Ellen Gray's ragged corpse. Nearly ripped to shreds. And then Herb. Herb was relegated to nothing more than a couple bones and a hat.

The snarling of the wolves brought me back. I had the two sticks in my hands and I pondered jamming one into my temple. Ending it on my own terms. The thought was fleeting.

Cujo was latched onto my shoulder, ripping this way and that. I squeezed the stick in my left hand and screamed. A scream that shook the trees. A scream that momentarily took Cujo off guard. His bite relaxed ever so slightly and I rolled over and plunged the stick into the side of his head. There was a loud squish, followed by a yelp, and the intense pressure on my shoulder loosened.

As I shook off the dead Cujo, two separate wolves clamped down on my left thigh and my left forearm. I still had the stick in my right hand and tried to bring it up.

Every tendon and muscle in my right shoulder was torn and my arm didn't respond.

I opened my eyes for a split second. The wolf on my left arm was the only thing I could see. I had suspected it was one of the pups, and it was. I brought my right leg up, wedging it between me and the pup. I pried him loose then shook my left arm free.

I rolled over and grabbed the stick out of my right hand. As the pup lunged for my face, I leaned back and drove the stick upward, plunging the harpoon into the wolf's neck. He fell on me and I rolled him off. Then I hit the wolf latched onto my left thigh in the face.

Smash. Smash. Smash.

I continued smashing my clenched fist into his snout. Finally, his jaw relaxed and I grabbed him by his collar and flung him off. I could see the other wolves standing around waiting for their turn. I only had a second. Half a second. I pushed myself up with a grunt. My left leg and right arm were useless. I took one step and three of the wolves came at me. One hit me on each arm. Another went for my left ankle. They dragged me down.

I let them.

The fight had drained out of me.

I took a deep breath. I'd died once. I knew the drill. As the blood drained from my body, my blood pressure would drop and my heartbeat would increase, trying to compensate for the lack of blood.

And then I saw him. The big black wolf. Cartman. He was jetting forward, about to sink his inch-long daggers into my throat and rip—tear—the life out of me. I saw his eyes. Saw him zeroed in. Never wavering, just like that first day.

I could feel Cartman's breath on the back of my neck. I could feel him run his nose on the back of my head and sniff my wet hair. My dad used to do that with his baked potato. He would lean down and sniff it. Then he would smile. Then he would devour it. I wondered if Cartman was smiling.

I felt his teeth scrape my neck. His jaw open, the joint stretched to its absolute breaking point. And when his brain sent the signal to those muscles to clamp down. Then I would be dead.

And then I heard them. Three cracks.

I peered behind me. Cartman lay directly behind my head. His mouth was still open. There was a small hole just above his left eye.

I looked up. Ethan was ten feet away, standing on the snowmobile, his gun still trained in my general direction.

I looked around. The wolves had scattered. Gone.

Erica jumped off the snowmobile and ran to me. She fell to her knees and cradled my head in her lap. She whispered, "Are you okay?"

"I've been better."

I tried to sit up. I hadn't felt much while it was happening. Now I felt everything. My entire body was on fire.

Ethan made his way over. He had the gun up and was scanning the area for any sign of the deadly predators. He stood over me and I gave him the obligatory "thanks for saving my life" nod.

He nodded back.

Then he laughed and said, "You look like shit."

"Thanks."

They helped me to my feet. There were four dead wolves scattered in a five-foot radius. One pup, the one whose throat I'd stuck the stick into, was laboring to stay alive, his chest still rising and falling.

Erica took a look at me and said, "If it wasn't for that ugly-ass snowsuit, you'd probably be dead."

She was right. Without the snowsuit, most of my flesh would have been ripped from my body. As for the damage assessment, my right shoulder was ripped to shreds and covered in a decent amount of blood. The left leg of the snowsuit was tattered. There was a large rip in my right torso. And the entire sleeve of the snowsuit's left arm had been ripped off clean.

I lifted my left forearm and inspected the bloody gash. A full set of teeth marks, top and bottom. This wound alone would need ten or twenty stitches.

All in all, I was in bad shape. But assuming I found my way to a hospital in the next couple hours, I would live.

We heard movement. The pup was trying to stand. He got his feet under him and tilted his head back. A shrill howl escaped. I think he was calling for backup.

Ethan took two steps toward the pup, raised his gun, and shot the wolf execution style between the eyes. Its body went limp.

Ethan had a wry smirk on his face. But not for long.

There was a loud crack and both Erica and I whipped our heads around. Under the cover of the wolf's cry, we'd failed to hear the approaching skis. The Professor was standing no more than twenty feet from us, *my* rifle leveled in front of him.

Erica and I followed the rifle's gaze. Ethan's body was on its way down. He fell to his knees in the deep snow. His mouth was agape, his eyes clenched shut. He was already dead.

CHAPTER 52

THE PROFESSOR WHIPPED the rifle around, pointing it somewhere between Erica and me.

Neither of us moved.

He had his white mask pulled up on his forehead. Even with the red curse, it was as if all color had drained from his face. He looked awkward with the gun, holding it with both hands against his stomach.

I waited for him to pull the trigger.

Then the gun fell from the Professor's grasp and he started trudging to Ethan's lifeless body. He passed it without a glance and fell to the ground near one of the fallen wolves. He cradled the wolf's head in his hands and began whimpering.

Erica and I watched with a mixture of awe and fright. A father would act no differently holding one of his fallen sons. The Professor made his way to each wolf, holding each one, caressing their thick coats. The only sound in all of the mountains was the sobbing of the broken man.

I took a step in the direction of Ethan and Erica grabbed my elbow. I gave her a look as if to say, "It's okay."

She relented and I took the ten trudges to Ethan's body. He lay face down, arms at his side. Blood had begun to ooze from the large crater in the right center of his back. There was a good chance the bullet severed his spinal cord and Ethan died before his brain registered a single thought.

I pried the gun from Ethan's fingertips with my left hand and shoved it in my waistband. Then I lifted his left pant leg. He had a Smith and Wesson .38 in an ankle holster. I know it's bad juju to speak badly of the dead, but under my breath I whispered, "Shithead."

I stood and made my way back to Erica. I handed her the .38. She took it, checked the chamber, and then gave me a quick nod.

I asked, "What do you want to do?"

"We have to take him in."

I knew *she* had to take him in. I didn't know what *I* had to do. One, the guy was off his fucking rocker, which didn't make what he did to Ellen and Riley okay, but it gave him a little leeway. These wolves were his family and whatever he did, he did it so his family could survive. Be together. His conscience had been replaced by animal instinct. Two, the guy had a miserable life. Probably one of the worst in existence. Had he suffered enough? I thought of Riley. Yes, she didn't deserve to die, but what if she'd been killed by a wolf? What kind of grudge could I hold toward an animal? Had her death at the hands of this deranged man been so much different? I was starting to think not.

As for the wolves, I didn't hold anything against them. I couldn't. It wasn't logical. They had only been doing the job God had bestowed on them. Having said that, I was ready to get my ass as far away from them as possible. Not to mention getting out of the snow, getting some of these wounds stitched shut so they'd stop leaking all that blood, and curling up with Erica by the fire. And maybe having a bowl of Frosted Flakes.

On a side note here, I'm not sure if it was on account of the loss of blood, but I was starting to second-guess my instincts. It'd been the look on the Professor's face when he'd shot Ethan. Something hadn't been right. Something was off.

I said, "I vote we just leave him."

Erica gave me a sideways glance. Of course, she had an entirely different outlook; her job was in jeopardy, and by bringing in the Professor she would be on the fast track to lead detective.

Erica was deep in thought, weighing the pros and cons of taking in the Professor or leaving him. I think we both knew that if we did leave him, he would never be heard from again.

And then you had Ethan. Don't think it hadn't occurred to me that the only person who had the resources to put me behind bars was right this second bartering with God for a spot in the rafters.

Erica snapped me from my reverie. She asked, "What do you think?"

I ignored her question. I was more preoccupied with the fact that the adrenaline from my little wolf attack was wearing off and the true severity of my injuries was starting to come to a head. The pain had turned into a dull throb, but I was more concerned with the light-headedness and dizziness. These were both indications I was losing blood. And lots of it. My knees were starting to shake and my vision was beginning to blur.

I licked my increasingly dry lips and said, "Not to alarm you or anything, but I'm not feeling too hot here."

At last she looked at me and said, "You don't look very good."

"Thank you for corroborating that."

Erica nodded. I could see she was still trying to reason her way through the situation. She'd glance at me, then the Professor, then Ethan, then the snowmobile. She continued this for a good twenty seconds. How was she going to transport the wackjob Professor, the quickly deteriorating Thomas Prescott, and Ethan's remains? It was sort of like that cannibals and canoe riddle, save for the cannibals. And the canoe.

She looked at me and said, "Can you drive the snowmobile?"

For the record, I was having trouble standing at this point. "I can try."

"That's a no."

I felt two shadows behind me and said quietly, "Don't move."

Two wolves had circled around the large rock and were now directly behind us. I slowly turned and looked over my shoulder. I hadn't seen these wolves before. Neither wore collars. These were *wild* wolves.

In another instant there were three wolves pacing just ten feet behind us. My vision was starting to double, and the wolves were overlapped by three white ghosts. One of them locked eyes with me and snarled, revealing his twenty ivory daggers. His ghost did the same.

I took the gun out of my waistband and held it in my left hand. It didn't feel quite right, but I was still confident I could hit a charging wolf.

Keeping my eyes on the wolves, or sets of wolves, I whispered to Erica, "Go for the snowmobile. I'll cover you."

She nodded and slowly began walking to the snowmobile. Had the wolves made even a muscle twitch in her direction, I would have blown them to pieces. But I didn't know how many bullets were left in the magazine and I'd already met my quota of wolf kills for the month.

I gave a quick glance in Erica's direction. She'd made it to the snowmobile. The engine roared to life and ten seconds later, Erica had pulled alongside me. I gingerly hopped on behind her, my left leg screaming, while keeping my gun leveled at the now five wolves.

I wrapped my good arm around Erica's waist. She drove until we were a safe distance away and ground to a halt. We both turned. The wolves had advanced to their fallen brothers and sisters and methodically began sniffing, licking, and prodding the dead.

The Professor watched the wolves, then launched into a similar system of sniffing, licking, and prodding.

One of the white wolves leaned back on his haunches and let loose a deafening howl. His counterpart added his voice and their duet rolled down the mountain. Riley had said howling was a sign of fellowship, but this howl wasn't. It was a sign of mourning.

We heard another loud noise, more barking than anything else, and it took us a moment to register the sound was coming from the Professor. He was on his hands and knees, head back.

Erica whispered, "Is he howling?"

"I think so."

"He's crazy."

"Yep."

Then I saw them out of the corner of my eye. In the trees. Three more of them. The howling hadn't been a sign of mourning after all. It'd been a battle cry.

I nudged Erica and pointed. She followed my outstretched arm and nodded.

They darted from the trees like three bullets and converged on the Professor simultaneously. This wasn't something I wanted to see. It felt like a world where humans shouldn't pry, a world where humans didn't belong. The Professor could vouch for that.

Erica started the snowmobile and we raced away. The Professor's screams could still be heard a half mile later.

CHAPTER 53

IT'S a bad sign when they're stitching you up and they have to send out for more thread. One hundred and thirty-seven stitches in all. I felt like a football.

By far, the worst of my injuries was my right shoulder. Cujo had torn nearly every ligament and every tendon in my right deltoid. And these, apparently, do not mend themselves. I underwent three surgeries in the first week, with promises of more in the months to come.

I'd asked the doctor if I would ever throw a baseball professionally again. He said I would not. In fact, he said that I should probably get used to eating with my left hand.

The new *Time* magazine came out the day after my third surgery. The cover was a picture of four dead wolves surrounding the remains of a devoured Professor Koble. The headline read, *"To Catch A Predator."*

The story detailed Ellen Gray's disappearance all the way up to the Professor's untimely demise.

Two days after the magazine came out, I was discharged from the hospital.

I was dressed in the clothes Erica had brought for me, my

trusty gray hooded sweatshirt and matching bottoms. My right arm was in a sling beneath the sweatshirt and as I lowered myself into the wheelchair, I could feel something brush against my hand. There was something in the front pouch of my sweatshirt.

I reached my left hand into the pouch and extracted the folded white pages. It was the bank statements I'd taken from Adam Gray's house. I shook my head. It seemed so long ago. Ages.

I unfolded the pages and the small picture fell out, fluttering to the ground.

The wheelchair stopped.

Erica knelt down and picked up the picture. She gazed at me with the intensity of someone who's newly in love, and said, "What's that?"

I wasn't sure if I wanted to confide in Erica about the breaking and entering. At least not until we'd consummated the relationship. Which, according to the doctor, I shouldn't partake in until the stitches were removed. I think it had something to do with the thrusting.

I went with, "Just a photograph."

She stared at the picture intently, then said with a smile, "A friendly reminder of your friends that nearly devoured you?"

She handed the picture back to me. I didn't know what she was talking about for a good minute. My eyes were drawn to the beautiful fall foliage and the snowcapped mountain on the far horizon. Not to them.

In the top right corner of the picture, nestled behind a tree, were two wolves.

CHAPTER 54

IT'D BEEN two weeks since I'd been discharged.

Sunny was once again listening to her iPod. She was biting on the eraser of a pencil, her eyes focused straight downward on another Sudoku puzzle.

Initially, I'd suspected Adam had been having an affair with her. She was beautiful in an *I bought my face* sort of way, and she was none too qualified to be the receptionist of the most sought-after defense attorney on the planet. I'd assumed Adam had been bopping her on the side and had given her the position when the spot had opened up.

But in actuality, Adam had been having an affair with her predecessor.

I'd taken a second look at the transactions on the seldom-used *Bank of Victoria* account. I had written off the twenty-something thousand dollar payment to his Alma mater, Seattle Pacific University, as a donation.

After a couple phone conversations in which I called myself Adam Gray, I found out the money was in actuality for fifteen credit hours of law school classes. After a bit of cajoling, I got a name. Julia Zadiez.

I remembered back to the first time I'd visited Adam Gray. The nameplate sitting on the desk. Julia.

I was able to wiggle an address out of the lady on the phone. I made a quick stop at her apartment complex and had a chat with her landlord. He'd last seen her in mid-November. Then she'd left.

I recalled that, according to Sunny, Julia had flown to be with her mother who had fallen ill and would be gone indefinitely. The landlord said a week after Julia left, a man came by and paid for the duration of her lease, then moved all her stuff into storage.

I inquired about the man. He had been large, with thin salt-and-pepper hair and a white goatee.

Sound familiar?

The man had told the landlord that Julia's mother had fallen terminally ill and that she had moved home on a whim to be with her until the end. The landlord said he found this curious because he'd had a conversation with Julia once, while fixing her showerhead, and she'd mentioned her mother died when she was very young. The landlord had then inquired as to her father. Julia had said that she hadn't spoken with her father in many years. He was back in Louisiana.

The father wasn't hard to find. There were only three Zadiezes in Louisiana, and I hit pay dirt on my first call. According to Greg Zadiez, he hadn't spoken to his daughter in more than three years. Last he heard, she'd moved to Seattle and was working for some hotshot attorney.

———

Five minutes later, the door to Adam's office opened and he emerged. He was wearing another of his designer suits. This one, black with thin pinstripes and a green and black striped tie. He smiled, his goatee wrinkling around the edges of his mouth, and said, "Sorry to keep you waiting."

I stood up gingerly, my thigh still quite tender, and took a couple steps forward. My right arm was still in a sling, and I was forced to shake hands with my left.

Adam said, "You look like shit."

I laughed. Ethan had said the very same words. Then he'd died twenty seconds later. Would history repeat itself? I instinctively felt the pressure of the cold steel digging into my hip. It was my father's Smith and Wesson. It was loaded this time. One bullet in the chamber.

I followed Adam into his office. He offered me a drink and I told him that I was craving a five-dollar water. He said they were six bucks and went over to the bar to retrieve me one.

I'd had two separate phone conversations with Adam since I was nearly eaten alive, the first from the hospital. We'd chatted for a good half hour. It was a conversation mostly comprised of euphemisms, the likes of *I can't believe it...But it's all over now...You never would have thought...Really makes you think...*and *We have the rest of our lives to ponder this one.*

Then I'd spoken to him again a week later to thank him for the get well present he'd bought me. Inside the card stuffed deep within the massive fruit basket he'd sent me had been tickets for a ten-day African cruise. He said it was all the rave right now. I told him it was just what I needed. And it was.

He returned with my water. He had taken the liberty of pouring himself a couple fingers of scotch. I took the water from him, took a swig, and asked, "Keeping busy?"

He nodded. "We start jury selection in the Albert Jones case next Monday."

Apparently, Albert Jones was an old Seattle Seahawk, kicked off the team for drug charges a couple years back. He'd been charged with three counts of vehicular homicide. He killed a family in his Range Rover. They'd found a crack pipe and two rocks on the passenger seat.

I said, "Sounds innocent."

"Aren't they all?"

No. No, they aren't. And today would be a proclamation to that very principle. I stared at him, but said nothing. I couldn't help but notice Adam appeared tired. Worn out. He didn't have that energy, that sparkle that he usually exuded.

I made my way over to the aquarium. I wanted to check up on my favorite weenie-fish. I spotted him hiding behind the fake scuba diver. Maybe he'd seen me come through the door. I tapped the glass with the Perrier. Several fish darted around their man-made ocean. From behind me, I could hear Adam squirm. I tapped the glass a second time. The fish frenzied, then settled. I couldn't spot my purple friend anywhere. I think he'd made for the cave.

I waited for Adam to say something. He did not. I took a deep breath and said, "You weren't on your yacht that day."

I turned around.

Adam was leaning against his desk. Shaking the ice in his scotch glass just below his lips. He didn't respond. Just continued shaking his scotch, staring off into the distance.

I wasn't sure he knew exactly what I was saying, so I simplified things for him. "You said the day your wife disappeared you were on your yacht with your client." I added, "You were not."

Gray swiveled his eyes so he was staring directly at me. It was almost the same stare as when he'd noticed my presence at his trial. He rattled the ice, knocked back the last of the scotch, then set the glass on the desk. But here's the scary part: he didn't use a coaster nor did he appear to care that he didn't use a coaster.

He smiled and said, "No, I was not."

Something had always been missing. The more I thought about the Professor, the less I was convinced he killed Ellen or Riley. It was the look on his face when he shot Ethan. He hadn't wanted to do it. Ethan had forced his hand. He had only killed him to save his wolves. Save his family. Was he a killer? Certainly. I'd witnessed it firsthand. But, I couldn't see the guy murdering in cold blood. I couldn't see the Professor putting a gun to Ellen's forehead and pulling the trigger, or using a knife to kill Riley for that matter. And so I went back to the drawing board. It had always been about the North Cascades. That had always been the connection. But there was one thing missing: Adam. How was Adam connected to the North Cascades? And then it hit me. The photo.

The photograph had started me thinking, and I did some investigating. I checked the ferry records for the day Ellen Gray went missing. I had to grease a couple palms, but four hundred dollars later, I was holding a list of the makes, models, and license plate numbers of all the cars on the ferry that day. Turns out that on the 8:00 a.m. ferry—the same ferry Ellen took before she went hiking—there was a black Jaguar with vanity plates.

NTGLTY.

I took a step forward, "In fact, you were in the North Cascades. Same as your wife."

"Yes, I was."

————

Neither of us spoke for a solid minute. I took another couple steps toward Adam. His whole demeanor had changed in the last few seconds. He was like a punctured beach ball. And for the first time, I knew I was looking at Adam Gray. Not the lawyer, but the man.

He said, "How much do you know?"

"Most of it."

He nodded. He didn't ask how I knew. I don't think he cared.

He stood up and began pacing around his desk. I watched him very carefully. He made his way over to his bookcase. He threw a quick glance over his shoulder at me, then he started. "We needed to go over that little shit Proctor's cross-examination. I do my best thinking on the *Habeus Corpus*, and Proctor and I planned on being on the yacht for most of the day. Ellen and I were both up early. It was one of the few times we'd both slept under the same roof in a long time."

I nearly said, "Because you usually slept in your condo with Julia Zadiez." But he was on a roll, and I didn't want to interrupt him.

"Proctor showed up just as Ellen was heading out the door. Proctor was always really nice to her, overly so, but the guy made her skin crawl. Shit, he made *my* skin crawl. Ellen was wearing khaki shorts, a tank top, and had a backpack on. Proctor asked where she was going. She said she was going hiking. Then she jumped in her car and sped away.

"We were on our way out to the yacht when Proctor says, 'You really think that bitch is going hiking?'"

"I told him that I didn't give a shit where she went."

"He said, 'I bet that bitch is having an affair.'"

"I told him that if he called my wife a 'bitch' again I was going to break his fucking neck. But it did get me thinking."

I said, "Because you were having an affair yourself. You knew how the game was played."

Gray's body went stiff. I watched his hands for any sudden movement. I flexed my left hand, just in case. Gray relaxed, turned, and said, "No, it got me thinking because we were going to get divorced. It was only a matter of time. One of the guys at the office was sleeping with Ellen's press secretary, and he'd let it slip that Ellen was planning on filing for divorce right after she won reelection."

Bad Kim.

Gray was just getting started. "This was like the fifth Sunday in a row that she'd said she was going hiking. I almost hoped that she was sneaking off to see some guy. It would give me a lot of leverage come the divorce settlement. Proctor says that we should follow her and that we can go over his testimony in the car. Didn't seem like too bad of an idea. Proctor tells me I should grab my camera so I have proof."

He took a breath. "We were one of the last cars to get on the outgoing ferry. I could see Ellen's car about three rows ahead of ours. We stayed in the car so we wouldn't run into her and went over his cross.

"Then we followed her. Just barely kept her car in sight. Followed her for two hours until she parks at the trailhead inside the national park. I said to Proctor, 'There. She's going hiking. Just like she said.' I remember him shrugging.

"Ellen disappeared up the trail. It didn't take long to see why she was up there. It was amazing. Shit, I hadn't been to the mountains in probably ten years. The fall colors were at their peak and there was this mountain range with white caps. It was perfect.

"I told Proctor to read over his testimony, and I grabbed my camera. I climbed up this little dirt trail for about a mile, took a couple dozen pictures, then hiked back down. Wasn't gone more than an hour and a half."

I thought about Adam snapping pictures, nestled up in the brush, trying to get the lighting just right. He's got the trees in the frame, reds, oranges, and yellows. The king's crown of white icing dripping off the top of the mountains. And then just when the picture can't get any better, two wolves emerge from behind the trees. Adam had taken the one picture that his wife so much desired. He had photographic evidence wolves had returned to the North Cascades.

Adam was still rambling, "Ellen's car was still parked there when we left. We got back to my place around four, spent a couple hours on the yacht going over his testimony, then we called it a day."

He swirled the last remaining cube of ice around in his glass.

He looked up. "I get a call the next morning from some guy on her security detail asking if I'd heard from my wife. I told him I hadn't. He said that when he'd last heard from her the day before, she was going hiking, that he hadn't spoken to her since. I didn't see it as relevant that I'd been the last one to see her. So I decided to keep my mouth shut.

"Later that day, when the cops started asking questions, I just couldn't tell them. It would look like too big of a coincidence. Her disappearing while hiking. Me following her, then snapping pictures. The husband is always the prime suspect. And when it leaked that our marriage was all but over, I would have been crucified. So I lied."

I said, "That's a pretty good story."

He furrowed his brow. "It's the truth. Honest to God. It's what happened. I swear to God, I didn't kill my wife. You have to believe me."

Before I could answer, he said, "I thought this was all over. That crazy Professor killed her. Because she wouldn't let those wolves live here or something. I mean, this is all over and done with."

No. It just started.

He looked at me. Then, almost shouting, he said, "You have to believe me, I didn't kill my wife."

"I know."

He cut his eyes at me. "You know?"

"I know you didn't kill your wife."

"Because that crazy Professor did."

"The Professor didn't kill your wife."

The Professor had just been unlucky. A final unfortunate event to add to a long list of unfortunate events that had plagued his life.

There was a rattle at the door. A second later, the doors burst open and a man entered. Daniel Proctor. He looked at Gray and said, "This better be fucking good."

I smiled and said, "He did."

CHAPTER 55

THE RIGHT SIDE of Daniel Proctor's mouth went up, the sneer running up the side of his pointy nose and into his slicked-back hair. He gave me the once-over, then said, "What the fuck are you doing here?"

I smiled and said, "I missed you too."

Adam took a step forward. "You two know each other?"

"I put him in intensive care for a couple weeks about eight years ago." I turned to Proctor and said, "They put your face back together nicely."

Proctor scoffed and I could tell he was envisioning me getting eaten by a shark or something. He moved his sneer from me to Adam and said, "All right, you want to tell me what the fuck you called me for? And what are these new charges against me?"

Adam appeared to be fighting down a smile. He said, "I didn't call you." He let that sink in then added, "Listen closely to me, you despicable piece of shit. I no longer represent you. I told you that. I hoped to go the rest of my life without having to listen to another syllable that came out of that deplorable, retched, fecal hole you call a mouth. A day hasn't gone by since your trial that I haven't felt dirty. Dirty because I let you loose. Might as well run around the city with a can of anthrax. You fucking piece of shit."

If I didn't know better, I'd have thought Adam wasn't too fond of Daniel Proctor.

Proctor ignored his rant and said, "Then who called me?"

I smiled. "I did."

"You?"

"Me."

"What the fuck do you want?"

"I wanted to apprise you of the new charges against you."

"New charges, my ass." After a second's pause, he added, "What new charges?"

"Three counts of first-degree murder. Ellen Gray, Riley Peterson, and Julia Zadiez."

I saw a thin smirk flash across Proctor's face, an instinctive flinch of pride. In that moment I was certain.

I turned to Adam. His face had gone white at the sound of Julia's name. I said, "Yeah, the secretary you were having an affair with. He killed her."

Something had always been missing. Ellen Gray, the yacht, the timeline of her death, it never did quite add up. It had always been like thunder trying to catch up to a lightning strike. That's because everyone had been looking at it all wrong. Adam Gray hadn't been framed for his wife's murder. He'd been framed for his mistress's murder.

Proctor laughed and said, "This is complete bullshit. I'm out of here." He took a couple steps in the direction of the door. "You want to talk to me, direct all questions to my lawyer. Saw two other firms in this building. In fact, I'll have them call you. This is fucking harassment."

I was standing right next to the door, leaning my shoulder against it. My left hand was hidden behind my back.

Proctor looked at me and smiled. I read the smile as, "You're a dead man, Prescott." He reached out his hand and pulled on the knob. The door didn't budge and he said, "What the fuck?"

About halfway through Adam's rant, I had taken the liberty of turning the deadbolt on the door. I raised my left arm and stuck the gun up to his temple. "Sit the fuck down. You aren't going anywhere."

———

I walked him over to the couch. It was a different couch—nearly identical, but a soft tan as opposed to the cinnamon of earlier.

Proctor didn't look quite as fearful as I would have liked. I nearly pulled the trigger. But I wanted to get a couple things straight before I sent him to the great beyond. His seat in the fiery pits wasn't going anywhere.

I'd forgotten about Adam in the excitement. He was standing at the bar pouring himself another scotch. I waved him over with the gun. "Come over here. I want you to hear this."

He made his way over. The two of us stood, towering over the defiant Daniel Proctor. He didn't appear to be going anywhere and I lowered the gun. I said, more to Gray than Proctor, "Here's what happened."

I took a cleansing breath. "I don't think he planned on killing your wife. It was spur of the moment. But when you grabbed your camera and started hiking up the mountain, he decided the opportunity was too good to pass up. He grabs the gun, the gun from your glove compartment, and runs up the trail after your wife.

"I'm not exactly sure what happens here. He approaches her. Maybe he tries to rape her. But your wife, she's a strong woman, probably puts up a pretty good fight, and he ends up shooting and killing her. He stashes the body somewhere and runs back to the car. He was probably gone half the time you were."

Gray glanced at Proctor then said, "When I got back to the car, he had shit all over him. He had blood all over his face. He said he'd gone to take a piss and had gotten whipped in the face by a tree. I didn't push it."

I nodded.

"You get back to the house and go out on the yacht. Proctor runs down to the galley, grabs a rag, and wipes the blood off his face." This was how Ellen's blood had made its way onto Adam's yacht. I doubted if the governor had ever stepped foot on her husband's prized possession, alive or dead. "You spend the next couple hours going over his testimony."

Adam amended that. "An hour at most. He said he wasn't feeling well so we called it a day."

I nodded. Made sense. He wanted to dispose of the body as soon as possible.

I said, "He hightails it back up to the mountains and locates where he stashed your wife's body, which, sadly, has already been partially devoured. Devoured by a pack of wolves the Professor had been illegally transporting to the mountains. One had even ripped off her backpack and dragged it several miles to where it was found near the glacial ravine."

This was slightly ironic, seeing as the very reason Ellen Gray was up there in the first place was that she had a suspicion the Professor was transporting wolves to the North Cascades.

I looked at Proctor. He was sitting rapt, engaged. Like when a third-party tells *your* joke. I may not get the lead-in verbatim, but you could be damn sure I knew the fucking punch line.

I continued. "There's a river only a quarter mile up the trail and Proctor tosses her body in. The better part of a month goes by. Proctor loves that the tables have been turned. Here his attorney treats him like dirt, like the piece of shit that he is, treats him like the murderer that he is, and now all of Seattle is looking at his attorney, the untouchable Adam Gray, the same way. He loves it. Can't get enough. But slowly the story dies. There is no evidence against Gray. And it turns out that people believe him when he says that he had nothing to do with his wife's disappearance."

I turned to Proctor and said, "That had to burn you up. When you tell people you're innocent, they scoff. But Gray, everyone believed him."

Proctor didn't react. I think he worried that Gray or I, or both of us, were wired. I didn't expect the guy to say another word. In fact, the only words I expected to ever hear from Daniel Proctor's mouth were "Please don't kill me."

I said, "So time is running out on Proctor. He only has a couple more weeks out on bail, and then if he is found guilty, he will be going away for a long, long time. He knows his lawyer is good, but he's pushed his luck. He killed that girl, and he's going to jail for a long time. Not even the famed Adam Gray can get him out of this one. Besides, he knows Gray hates him, so why would he go to bat for him? No, surely his luck has run out. So he frames his attorney for murder. At worst, his case will be a mistrial and he will have another six months out on bail. At best, Gray will go to jail before he does."

I looked at Adam. "The night you were attacked, you were with Julia?"

He nodded. For the first time since I'd met him, he looked distraught, sad. He might not have loved his wife, but he loved Julia.

He took a deep breath and said, "I was putting her through law school. She'd just finished her last final, so I took her out for drinks. We were usually pretty good about not going out in public, but we had a legitimate excuse so we decided to risk it." He looked down. His mind couldn't help but play the devil's advocate. What if they had stayed in that night? Or worse, what if he hadn't been sleeping with her? Would she still be alive?

I've played that game enough to know it doesn't help. It eats at you. Rips at your insides.

I asked, "Did Proctor know?"

"Know?"

"Know you would be with her that night?"

Adam thought for a moment. He looked at Proctor. "Yeah, we were supposed to go over some more of his testimony that night, but I couldn't stand another second with the guy. I didn't even want to win the case anymore. I wanted to see him rot. He'd seen the two of us around each other. I think he knew what was going on. He asked me a couple times if I was fucking her. Actually said that he wished he could fuck her. I wanted to kill the sick bastard myself for that."

Adam's face was flushed, and he'd barely choked out the last sentence.

I said, "So he follows the two of you. You leave the bar. He probably waited until you were in the underground garage. He's got a tranquilizer gun he got off the Net and shoots you in the leg. Shoots her as well."

They'd found traces of Ketamine in Julia's system.

"I'm thinking that he'd planned on taking you with him, maybe even putting you on the yacht. But you fight him off and get away. He takes your car. Drives to your house, takes out your yacht."

I skip the part about what he probably did to her on the yacht. Hans did the autopsy, and I knew she'd been brutally raped. Three bullets in the stomach.

"He drives to the most highly trafficked waterway in the Sound and dumps the body. If all goes according to plan, the body will be found within a couple days, Proctor can spill the beans on his lawyer and the secretary's romance, and Gray will be arrested for her murder."

But her body didn't surface. However, in a twist of fate, Ellen Gray's body does surface. It has been carried into the Sound by the raging river.

I pulled out a piece of paper I had folded in my back pocket. Hans had faxed it to me at the library. I handed it to Adam. He unfolded the paper and looked at it. It was a picture of Julia Zadiez's corpse. The private detective he'd hired had come up empty. But his PI hadn't been as smart as me.

I said, "I'm sorry."

I'd had Hans run the fingerprint of the Jane Doe from the yacht against all missing persons or Jane Does in the last six months. He came up with a match on a woman found about thirty miles north of Everest by a fisherman. She was found two weeks after Ellen's body was found, the very day Adam was arrested for his wife's murder.

Other than a small blurb in the Everest community paper, the story was all but lost in the shuffle of the governor's body turning up. Had anyone looked closely at the two, they wouldn't have been able to see any connection. One body had been in the water for nearly six weeks, carried into the Sound by one of the North Cascades raging rivers, a bullet in the forehead, and nearly half eaten. The other had been in the water for roughly two weeks, savagely raped, three bullets in the stomach. The only similarities were that all the bullets came from the same gun, a .32, and that both women shared a very rare blood type.

Gray's eyes had glossed over.

I said, "After Julia went missing, you hired a private detective to look for her. You couldn't go to the police; it would look too suspicious coinciding with your wife's disappearance. You didn't even call the police after you'd been attacked; you thought it would look too conspicuous. So you made up some story about Julia's mother, hired a new receptionist, and moved all her stuff into storage. You knew nobody would come looking for her or report her missing; her mom was dead, and she hadn't spoken with her father in years."

Gray looked up from the photo and stared at Proctor. His lip was quivering.

I looked at Proctor and said, "This asshole might have tipped off the police to the Julia connection, but to his great surprise his lawyer gets him off. He's a free man."

I added, "You recognized me that day in court. So come New Year's Eve, you follow me up to the mountains with the idea of either killing me or finding a way to make my life miserable."

I thought about the small flicker of light I'd seen from Riley's window. I looked at the square bulge in the front left pocket of Proctor's jeans. He'd been smoking cigarettes as he patiently awaited his next murder. I could feel the blood rushing through my temples, and I instinctively brought the gun up and pointed it at his dick. He didn't appear to like this much and squirmed on the long couch.

I gritted my teeth. "You waited for me to leave. Then you—"

I couldn't. I didn't want to think about him dragging her from her bed into the kitchen. He probably tries to rape her, but she's a tough girl. Maybe she gets away. But not for long. He grabs her, takes the blade from his pocket, the same blade he's used to kill before, and slices her throat.

But I wanted him to know I knew everything. I finished, "After you killed Riley with your knife, you plucked the knife from the dishwasher. Maybe you'd been watching through the windows with binoculars, maybe you knew I cleaned the dishes. Or maybe you just got lucky. Doesn't matter. You dip the knife in Riley's blood, then drive to my house. The door is unlocked. You stroll right in, probably walked right past me there on the couch, go into my sister's room and plant the knife."

He smiled. Can you believe that?

He fucking smiled.

I smashed the gun across his face then stuck the barrel in his mouth.

He shook his head and started crying. Tears running down his cheeks. He was trying to speak. I pulled the gun out. I wanted to hear this. I wanted to hear him beg. He whimpered,

"Please...please...come on...you don't want to kill me...I'm not worth it...let the justice system deal with me...I'll do life, man...I'll tell them everything...I'll tell them everything I've ever done...just don't kill me...come on, man, you're no killer...Don't throw your life away on a piece of shit like me."

I said, "I won't go to prison."

He wiped the tears from his eyes. Straightened himself. "Of course you will. First degree murder. This is premeditated. You'll never get off."

Gray had made his way to his desk. I don't think he wanted to get any of Proctor's blood on himself. I pointed to him with the gun and said, "See that guy over there?"

Proctor looked at Gray.

"That's my lawyer."

Proctor turned white.

I took a step forward, pointed the gun at his forehead, and said, "I should have done this eight years ago."

Proctor began to sob.

I pulled the trigger.

There was a soft click but nothing happened.

The old gun had jammed.

Proctor opened his eyes.

I was staring down at the gun, still wondering why it hadn't discharged, so I didn't notice the movement.

There was a loud *thump* and I glanced up.

Gray was standing over the top of Proctor, who was now slumped onto the couch. Blood was splattered on Gray's face and all over his suit. In his right hand, covered in blood, was the silver rhino.

Gray took a step backward.

The right side of Daniel Proctor's face was no more. Caved in. Blood ran down what was left of his ear and down his neck. A soft gurgling came from his mouth as he fought to stay alive. His eyes swiveled in his head then settled on both Adam and me. I suspect the last image Daniel Proctor processed was the two people he despised most in this world—smiling.

And then he died.

Adam and I traded glances.

I let out a deep sigh and said, "It might be time for another couch."

CHAPTER 56

PUGET SOUND WAS CHOPPY.

I spotted a wave two hundred yards out and kept my eyes trained on it as it approached. A wrinkle of white among a thousand others. The wave curled into the side of the boat and disappeared. A thin voice beside me said, "You said there would be ducks."

"I lied."

Harold was silent. Even without the ducks, I knew he was in heaven. The crisp air, the soft ocean breeze, the gentle rocking of the large ferry. A bird soared high above and I pointed upward. Harold craned his head back, the skin on his neck folding into six small ripples, almost like the waves on the water. Harold kept his head like that for a while, watching the giant eagle soar majestically overhead.

In time, the eagle disappeared into the gray horizon. Harold turned around and pushed his way to one of the small benches adorning the top of the ferry.

I sat next to him. I patted the small fanny pack the nurse had given me. It carried two syringes. If Harold had another cough attack, I was supposed to insert the syringe into his thigh. I didn't much mind needles myself, but the thought of sticking a needle in someone else made me feel queasy. But a single cough hadn't escaped old Harold since I picked him up, so I wasn't overly concerned.

The casts on Harold's wrists had been removed, but he still wore two plastic braces. He looked like he was getting ready to go rollerblading.

The two of us sat in silence for a good while. We were the only ones atop the ferry.

When the ferry docked, we sat there for twenty minutes. I pointed out a couple famous people's houses to Harold, but he didn't much seem to care. I could barely make out the tip of Adam Gray's estate. Speaking of whom, Adam had called the police and turned himself in sometime after I'd left his office. He was looking at charges for second-degree murder.

It very well could have been me facing the charges. *Should* have been me. I'll never know why the gun hadn't gone off. When I'd gotten home, I'd taken it apart. It was perfect. The bullet still resting peacefully in the chamber. But some questions aren't meant to be asked. Later that night, I tossed the gun into the Sound.

The Sound, where it'd all started.

As for Adam, he'd hired the very best, or second-best, attorney on the planet, and the last time I talked with him, he hadn't sounded too worried.

Newcomers to the ferry began to stumble up to the top deck, but other than one young couple, they disappeared as quickly as they came. The ferry started back across the waterway.

Ten minutes into the voyage, I noticed Harold hadn't taken his eyes off the couple. They were standing at the ferry's edge, by the railing—not far from where Harold and I had stood just an hour earlier—holding hands.

I watched as the edges of Harold's mouth turned up just

slightly. Then he said, "It wasn't an elaborate plan. It was just a couple of rats."

In the shed where they kept all the tools, there was a decent amount of rats. Big, brown rats. Jimmy decided three would do.

It was one of the hottest Septembers on record, and they kept the windows open for the most part. But on Wednesdays, because they were to be cleaned, they closed the windows. But they did not lock them.

Jimmy waited until the teacher sat down. Harold watched as all the girls took out pens and pads and started scribbling. Elizabeth sat on the far right, three rows back. Harold tried valiantly not to stare at her, but it was hard. Here she was just twenty feet from him. He wanted so badly just to reach out and touch her. To knock on the glass and wave to her. But he couldn't. He'd be hauled out in two blinks. And then what?

Harold watched as Jimmy slowly pushed the window open. Just an inch. A silent inch. Then one by one, he fed the rats through the opening. Harold couldn't help but notice the wicked smile on his face when he finished.

They continued down the row of windows as if nothing happened. Three windows later, there was a scream. It reminded him of his sisters on Christmas morning, but worse. The girls had scrambled onto their desks, crouched, and were emitting screams that would drown out a police siren. And then the room cleared out, the girls bolting for the exit.

Harold climbed down the ladder. He'd written the note the previous night. The first note had been five pages. It took him ten drafts to trim it down to one.

Moments later, the doors to the south building crashed open and forty girls spilled out. Some were crying. Some were shaking as if invisible bugs crawled across their skin. Harold looked for Elizabeth. He didn't' see her. Then he saw a girl leaning against a tree laughing. It was her.

The other fellows had run over to the group of girls to make sure they were okay. And to make it look less inconspicuous when Harold approached one of them and slipped her a note.

Harold took a deep breath and started through the barrage of girls.

He stopped a couple feet shy of Elizabeth, who still had her head leaned against the tree. He said, "You okay?" His voice was shaky.

She turned, wiped the tears from her eyes, and said, "Yeah, it was just a couple of rat—"

She stopped, her jaw still open.

Harold put a finger up to his lips. He leaned to the ground, then stood up and said, "You dropped this." He handed her the note, then turned and walked away.

As he moved past the small group, he gave a quick glance behind him. Elizabeth had the note clutched to her chest. Tears streamed down her cheeks, but she was no longer laughing.

I patted Harold on the leg and said, "You old dog, you."

He laughed. Then coughed.

I waited for the second cough, but it never came. After a tense moment, I asked, "What did you say in the note?"

"That I couldn't live without her."

"That's it?"

He nodded.

"That took you a whole page?"

He smiled.

"Did you ask her to meet?"

"Yep."

"Where?"

"I told her to meet me in the movie theater on Sunday night, to go with her friends. It was a movie I'd already seen. I told her to go get popcorn when the house in the movie caught fire. I figured they probably didn't like the girls going out alone. But they obviously let them go to the movies."

"They did have phones back then, didn't they?"

He shrugged.

"Well, did it work?"

"Yeah. It worked."

Harold leaned against a pillar and waited. He could hear the movie from where he stood. He could hear the whir of the fire engine on screen. He waited and waited, but she didn't come out. There were six people standing in line to get popcorn, but they were all guys.

After two minutes, Harold decided she hadn't come. His heart sank. Then he felt a light touch on his arm. It reminded him of the first time he'd felt her touch in the icy water.

Neither said a word. Their hands found each other. They ran from the theater, down a couple blocks, and turned down an alley. She said, "I knew it was you. That night at the movies, I knew it was you. I knew you'd come back for me."

They threw their arms around each other and kissed. It was everything Harold had pictured at the train station four years ago. And more. They kissed. They cried. They laughed.

At first it was once or twice a week. Then Elizabeth was sneaking out every other night.

Each Wednesday, Harold would have trouble not staring at her. Not staring at his Elizabeth. The love of his life.

At the end of October, Harold was waiting for her outside the back fence of the college near a seldom-used gate. He heard a rattle, and then she appeared. As always, they kissed for a long while before they even said a word. There was a park nearby and this was their location of choice. Rarely did they ever encounter anyone.

That night Elizabeth finally told him what had happened. Harold had never pushed it. He didn't care about the past; he only cared about the present. Elizabeth said that her father had ransacked her room and found the letters they sent each other. He forbade her from ever speaking to him again. She said she would run away. But she couldn't.

They moved to Seattle two days later, and a week after that she was in boarding school. The school was on strict instructions from her father that she was not allowed to use the phone, mail a letter, or leave the campus. It was as if she was in jail.

Harold had always figured as much. Elizabeth cried as she told the story. Harold wiped the tears from her eyes, telling her a million times that everything would be okay.

She didn't look convinced and said her father would never let them be together. It would never be okay. They were from two different worlds. Harold told her they would deal with that when they had to and not to worry.

But when they parted, it was all Harold could think about. How could her father be so ignorant? So close-minded?

Two days later, Harold once again heard the familiar rattling of the gate. Elizabeth emerged and ran to him. They embraced, holding each other under the moonlight. Then Harold heard a soft rattle and looked up. Two men stood not ten feet from them, one with a flashlight.

One of the men said, "There they are, sir. She's been sneaking off to see him for about a month now. I didn't know if I should tell you at first, but I worried about it."

The other man stepped from the shadows. It was the dean with the slicked-back hair. The mean guy that let them in the gate every Wednesday morning.

Elizabeth broke from Harold and said, "Daddy."

My eyebrows rose to the crown of my hair. I said, "You're kidding."

"Nope. The dean was Elizabeth's father."

"You didn't recognize him?"

"Well, I always felt something familiar about him, but I wrote it off as something from the army. That day when I'd first seen him, he had this huge mustache and he was skinny. Since then, he'd shaved the mustache and put on a good fifty pounds."

I nodded and said, "What happened?"

Mr. King looked at Elizabeth and said, "Who is this boy?"

Before she could answer, Harold stepped forward and said, "Harold Humphries, sir. I believe we met a few years back."

He didn't seem to remember Harold. Harold jarred his memory. "My father used to lease land from you in Missouri. I saved your daughter's life. You thanked me by slapping me in the face and throwing rocks at me."

Recognition flashed across his face. "Oh, that boy."

Harold stuck his chest out and said, "I just want you to know that I love your daughter very much. And I plan on marrying her."

Harold could see Elizabeth from the corner of his eye. She had her head buried in her hands. Her father let out a loud bellow and said, "Marry her?" He let loose another deep bellow from within his large gut and said, "Boy, you shall never see my daughter again."

He turned to his security guard and said, "Arrest this boy for trespassing."

The security guard shook his head and said, "Can't boss."

"What do you mean you can't?"

"He isn't trespassing."

Mr. King peered at the man. Harold surmised the guy wouldn't have a job come the next morning. And Harold, he was thinking about just surviving to see the morning. And he planned to have Elizabeth in his arms when it came.

Mr. King looked at his daughter. He seemed repulsed. He said, "Get over here."

She brought her hands down, gulped a half dozen times, then said, "Daddy, I love him. I want to marry him."

He took a step forward and slapped her. "Marry him? Why, he's nothing but trash. Nothing but trash. Just like his daddy. You will not marry him." He raised his voice and said, "Hear me. You will not. I won't allow it."

Harold was shaken by the blow to Elizabeth. The dean turned to him and said, "You hear me too, boy. You are nothing but trash. Now get. Get, or I'll kill you. Swear to the mighty, I'll kill you."

Harold took a step between the man and his daughter and said, "Go ahead. Kill me."

Elizabeth's father yanked the baton off the security guard's belt and hit Harold in the stomach. Harold doubled over. Dazed, he managed to

get to his feet. He stood tall. The baton cracked him over his left eye.
Then on the ear. He crumbled to the ground. The hits came in droves.
Harold could no longer feel the pain. After each blow, he thought about
Elizabeth. No pain could compare to the thought of losing her again.

After each beating, Harold rose to his feet.

Elizabeth was clawing at her father, yelling for him to stop. Mr. King
dropped the baton and spit on Harold. Then he turned to his Elizabeth
and spit on her.

He said, "You're no daughter of mine."

I was standing over Harold now.

I said, "He let her go?"

He nodded. "I woke up with her in my arms the next morning."

I was smiling so hard my lips were beginning to cramp.

I asked, "Why didn't you hit him back?"

"He wasn't worth it."

I nodded. "So, did you two get married?"

"Yep. A month later."

He was quiet for a moment then said, "She got pregnant soon after."

Two minutes went by.

I saw a single tear run behind his glasses.

He said, "She died giving birth."

The air was sucked out of me. I sat down next to him.

"Died giving birth to our little girl."

I exhaled deeply.

He looked at me and said, "Her name was Lilly."

I smiled. Lilly was my mother's name.

"Lilly Humphries. She was beautiful. I kept her for three months, but every time I looked at her, held her, I was reminded of Elizabeth. I relived the nightmare over and over. I couldn't do it. The Korean War was just getting under way. I re-enlisted and gave Lilly up for adoption."

I didn't know what to say.

"When I got back three years later, I was still devastated. I met a girl, Lynn, whom I fell in love with. Not the same love I felt for Elizabeth, but a love nonetheless. I went to work for Boeing again. We started a family. Had three beautiful kids."

"What about Lilly? Did you ever find out what happened to her?"

"After my kids had grown up and left, I paid one of the those companies to track her down. She'd taken her adoptive parents' last name. Hiller."

"Lilly *Hiller*?" My voice cracked.

He nodded.

I gulped.

"She married a man and had children. One boy and one girl."

My brain was going a million miles an hour.

I asked, "Did you ever contact any of them?"

"Not until very recently. But I did send them birthday cards each year."

I took a deep breath.

Harold hiked up his pant leg. He once again stuck his hand in his sock and pulled out a yellow piece of paper. It was a newspaper clipping. He handed it to me.

I unfolded it and read the headline. "Jet Crashes in the North Sierras."

I had the very same clipping in a box in my closet in Maine. The box also held thirty-three birthday cards from an anonymous sender.

AUTHOR'S NOTE

Thanks for reading *Gray Matter!* I know there are millions of books out there and I just want to thank you for choosing one of mine.

A decade ago, I was Googling this and that when I stumbled on a bunch of anti-wolf legislation. Three books, a DVD, and a wolf bobblehead later, and *Gray Matter* was born. The anti-wolf bill in the book is real. The real bill, House Bill SB 5740, was introduced on 2/10/03 and would prohibit the introduction of the gray wolf anywhere within the state of Washington. It died in committee on 3/26/03.

Here are some other examples of anti-wolf legislation:

- Waushara County, Wisconsin (2005) - Bill "deplores and condemns" state and federal agencies to relocate wolves into the county.
- Moffat County, Colorado (2004) - Bill opposes the reintroduction of wolves.
- Carbon County, Wyoming (2003) - Resolution uses state authority to establish predatory animal control to protect livestock.
- Wheatland County, Montana (2003) - Resolution prohibits "the presence, introduction or reintroduction of wolves" in the county.
- Sublette County, Wyoming (2002) - Bill passed

determining gray wolves "economically and socially unacceptable species in Sublette County."

- Fremont County, Wyoming (2002) - Resolution 2002-05 prohibits the presence, introduction, or reintroduction of wolves within Fremont County.
- Siskiyou County, California (2002) - Bill 01-231 opposes the introduction or reintroduction of unacceptable species that are predatory and harmful to man and to livestock into Siskiyou County.
- Grant County, New Mexico (2000) - The Grant County Commission adopts a resolution to "prohibit" the release of wolves with a history of cattle depredation into the southwestern New Mexico county.

If you enjoyed the read, please take a minute and write a review.

Thanks for reading :)

God is love.

Nick

ABOUT THE AUTHOR

Nick Pirog is the bestselling author of the Thomas Prescott series, the 3:00 a.m. series, and *The Speed of Souls*. He lives in South Lake Tahoe with his two pups, Potter and Penny.

You can learn more about him at www.nickpirog.com.

ALSO BY NICK PIROG

Printed in Great Britain
by Amazon

75182444R00215